Princess of Wands

Baen Books by JOHN RINGO

Ghost
Kildar (forthcoming)

Princess of Wands

Into the Looking Glass

A Hymn Before Battle
Gust Front
When the Devil Dances
Hell's Faire
The Hero (with Michael Z. Williamson)
Cally's War (with Julie Cochrane)
Watch on the Rhine (with Tom Kratman)

There Will Be Dragons
Emerald Sea
Against the Tide
East of the Sun, West of the Moon (forthcoming)

The Road to Damascus (with Linda Evans)

with David Weber:
March Upcountry
March to the Sea
March to the Stars
We Few

Princess of Wands

John Ringo

PRINCESS OF WANDS

This is a work of fiction. All the characters and events portrayed in this book are fictional, and any resemblance to real people or incidents is purely coincidental.

A Baen Books Original

Baen Publishing Enterprises
P.O. Box 1403
Riverdale, NY 10471
www.baen.com

ISBN-13: 978-1-4165-0923-3
ISBN-10: 1-4165-0923-2

Cover art by Stephen Hickman
Interior image used by permission. Copyright © Arts Parts/Ron and Joe, Inc.

First printing, January 2006

Distributed by Simon & Schuster
1230 Avenue of the Americas
New York, NY 10020

Printed in the United States of America

10 9 8 7 6 5 4 3 2 1

Dedication

Dedicated to the memory of K. Steinberg,
a fine Southron Jewish woman.

Raise a glass of something
pink, frosty and alcoholic.
Her voice and presence will be sorely missed.

As this book was being prepared for print, Hurricane Katrina came ashore and utterly destroyed many of the sites included in the story. It can only be hoped, at this time, that those scenes will someday return to us.

Our prayers go out to the people of Louisiana and Mississippi.

The Princess of Wands

A tarot card in the Crowley deck

"The character of the Princess is extremely individual. She is brilliant and daring. She creates her own beauty by her essential vigour and energy. The force of her character imposes the impression of beauty upon the beholder. In anger or love she is sudden, violent, and implacable. She consumes all that comes into her sphere. She is ambitious and aspiring, full of enthusiasm which is often irrational. She never forgets an injury, and the only quality of patience to be found in her is the patience with which she lies in ambush to avenge."

—*The Book of Thoth*, Aleister Crowley

Book One

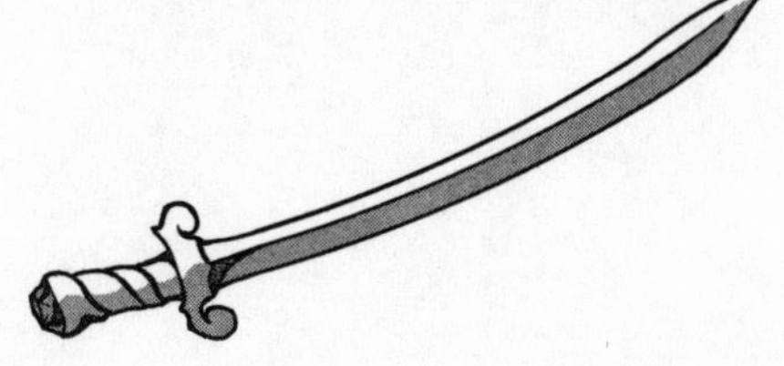

The Almadu Sanction

Chapter One

The body of the young woman had been twisted into a fetal position and strapped with duct tape. Then it had been dropped in a black plastic contractor bag and rewrapped. Which seemed like a heck of a lot of trouble if you were going to just dump the body in the woods.

Detective Sergeant Kelly Lockhart stroked his beard as the coroner's assistant stretched the body out. The corpse had been in the bag long enough for decomposition to work its way on the ligaments that stiffened the body in rigor mortis. And for the smell to change. But Kelly had seen far worse in his ten years as an investigator. And the department wanted to know, right away, if she was another victim of the Rippers.

Kelly was six two and a hundred and sixty pounds when he was watching his weight. Most people describing him used "thin" because "skeletal" was impolite. He'd started growing his hair when he got out of the army and hardly quit in the ensuing twelve years. It hung down his back in a frizzy, uncontrolled mass and was matched by a straggly beard and mustache.

Technically, since he'd worked his way out of vice and into homicide, he should have cut both back. But he still worked, occasionally, under cover and he'd managed to convince his bosses to let him hang onto the whole schmeer. Since he had a good track record for running down even tough murder cases, the powers-that-be turned a blind eye to someone that looked like a cross between the grim reaper and Cousin Itt.

As the corpse's legs were stretched out the open cavity of her torso and abdomen became evident and he squatted down to look at the incision. Something sharp, but not as sharp as a knife, had opened the young woman's body up from just above her mons veneris all the way to her throat. The edges of the cut were haggled; it was more of a rip than a cut, thus the name the papers had slapped on New Orleans's latest serial killer. And, as usual, all her internal organs were missing.

"Fuck," he muttered. "You know the problem with being me? It's always being right."

"Same MO," the coroner's assistant said, pointing at the cut. "I'd love to know what he's using."

"*They're* using," Lockhart replied, standing up as another car pulled down the dirt road. "And if I didn't know better, I'd say it's a claw, a big one like a velociraptor's."

"A veloco . . . what?" the coroner's assistant said, confused.

"What, you've never seen *Jurassic Park*?" Kelly said. "A dinosaur, you Cajun hick."

The edge of the bayou made the roads wet and treacherous but the driver of the black SUV expertly avoided the worst of the puddles and parked next to one of the parish unmarked cars. When he saw who was driving, Lockhart tried not to groan. And it looked as if the FBI agent had a boss with him.

"Detective Lockhart," Special Agent Walter Turner said, nodding to the detective. The FBI agent was black, just short of thirty, with a heavy build from football that was getting a bit flabby. "This is Mr. Germaine. He's a . . . consultant we sometimes call in on serial cases."

Germaine was a tall character, about six four, maybe two hundred thirty pounds, very little of it flab. Sixty or so, clean shaven, short black hair with gray at the temples, and a refined air. The suit he was wearing hadn't come off a rack. A very *expensive* consultant, Lockhart suspected. Then the consultant stopped looking at the body and locked eyes with the detective for a moment.

This is one dangerous bastard, Lockhart thought. As an MP he'd spent just enough time around the spec-ops boys to know one dangerous mother when he ran across one. Not the gang-bangers, although they were nobody to turn your back on. But this was somebody who would kill you as soon as look at you and whether you put up a fight or not. He kept looking around, not too obviously but obviously enough, keeping total situational awareness like a cat at a dog convention. No, a lion at a dog convention, wondering if he should just go ahead and kill the whole pack. What the fuck was the FBI doing carting around somebody like that?

"Can you tell me anything that's not in one of the earlier reports?" Germaine asked, quietly.

The "consultant" walked strangely. Kelly had seen a lot of walks in his time. The robotic walk of a tac-team member, arms cocked, fists half closed, legs pumping as if trying not to leap all the time. The street "slide," feet half shuffling, hips moving. Military guys with their stiff march. Germaine's wasn't like any he'd seen before. His hands, instead of being turned in like most people, were rotated with the palms to the rear and barely moved as he walked. Legs were slightly spread, heel strike then roll to toe, stand flat foot as the next rose up in the air and forward. The ankles hardly flexed at all. Back straight but shoulders held down.

It was almost as if he had to think about each step.

He had an accent, faint, not one that Lockhart could place. European anyway, not British. Other than that faint trace his English was perfect. As perfect as his suit and just as obviously a disguise he could take on and off. The accent might not even be genuine.

"If it's like the others, not much," Lockhart replied with a shrug. "All the previous bags were clean of prints, body had been washed. Semen in the remaining vaginal tract, multiple

DNA, none from any known sex offender. FBI's already gotten samples," he added, nodding at the special agent. "What's your specialty? Profiling?"

"I'm called in when the FBI suspects there are Special Circumstances to an investigation," Germaine said, walking over to the corpse. He squatted down and pulled out a pair of gloves, putting them on before reaching into the gutted corpse. He fingered the cut for a moment, lifting a bit of the mangled flesh along the side and then pushed the abdominal wall back to examine the underside. If he felt anything about manipulating a violently mutilated teenaged female, it wasn't evident.

"What are special about these circumstances?" Lockhart said, a touch angrily. "We've got five dead hookers and a group of rapists and murderers. Sick fuckers at that. Where are the guts, that's what I want to know. Draped on display? Eaten? Pickled in jars to await the body's resurrection?"

"Partially the group aspect," Special Agent Turner said. "Serial rape-murders are almost always individuals. And usually when there *is* a group, somebody cracks and burns it."

"The papers are saying it's a cult," the coroner's assistant replied. "Ritual killings."

"Perhaps," Germaine said, reaching up to close the girl's staring eyes. It was a gentle action that made Lockhart rethink his initial evaluation of the "consultant." "But cults can be taken down as well," the consultant continued. He stood up, stripped off the gloves and nodded at the FBI agent. "I've seen everything that's important."

"Got a bit of bad news," Special Agent Turner said, wincing. "You know that scale you recovered from the second body?"

"Yeah?" Lockhart said, uneasily. The thing had looked like a fish scale but it was about three times as large as any he'd ever seen. They'd sent it to the FBI to try to figure out what species it had come from. Probably it had been stuck to the body or hands of one of the rapists, a fisherman and God knew that there were enough in the bayous, which would probably be a dead lead. But a clue was a clue. You just kept picking away at the evidence until you got a match. Or, hopefully, somebody got scared and agreed to turn state's evidence in exchange for not being charged with capital murder.

"The crime lab lost it," Turner said, grimacing.

"Lost it!" Lockhart snarled. "It was the only thing we had that wasn't complete bullshit! How the hell could they *lose* it?"

"Things like that happen," Germaine said, placatingly. "And, eventually, we'll find the perpetrators and get a DNA match. One scale will not keep them from justice, Sergeant."

"What about the odd-ball DNA?" Lockhart asked. "Our lab said they couldn't make head or tails of it."

"Still working on it," Turner replied. "You get occasional human DNA that doesn't parse right. Your lab doesn't see as much DNA as the Crime Lab does; they've seen a couple of similar cases. We can match it fine for court, if we get the right perp."

"Which we will," Germaine added, steepling his fingers and looking at the trees that surrounded the small clearing. "On my soul, we will."

Barbara Everette stepped out of the tiled shower, patted herself dry with a towel and began blow-drying her long, strawberry blonde hair. The roots were showing again, about two shades redder than her current color with the occasional strand of gray. It didn't seem fair to have any gray at the ripe old age of thirty-three.

She dropped the blow-dryer into its drawer and brushed her hair out, examining herself critically in the mirror. She was either going to have to cut back on the carbs or find *some* time to exercise more; there was just a touch of flab developing around the waist and, yes, as she turned and checked there was a touch of cellulite around the top of the thighs. The body was, otherwise, much the same as it had been when she married Mark fifteen years before. Oh, the D-cup breasts were starting to sag a bit and showed plenty of wear from little baby mouths, but it still was a pretty good body. Pretty good.

She dropped the brush and took a cat stance, twisting through a short kata to stretch her muscles. Ball of the foot, turn, swipe, catch, roll the target *down* to the side, hammer strike. All slow, careful movements, warming up for the trials ahead.

She slipped on a tattered golden kimono, sat down at the vanity and did her make-up. Not too heavy. A bit of eye shadow, liner, very light lipstick. She still didn't have much to cover up.

Make-up done she stepped into the minimally decorated master bedroom, making another mental note among thousands to brighten it up a bit, and started getting dressed. Tights, leotard, wriggle into casual summer dress on top, brown zip-up knee boots with a slight heel. Her father had taken one look at them when she wore them last Christmas and immediately dubbed them "fuck-me" boots. Which . . . was Daddy all over.

Another brush of the hair to settle it after dressing, a pair of sunglasses holding back her hair, a slim watch buckled on her wrist, and it was time to go pick up the kids.

Barbara picked up her pocket book as she walked out the door, her heels clicking on the hardwood floor. The bag was a tad heavier than it looked: the H&K .45 with two spare magazines added significant weight to the usual load of a lady's purse. But she wouldn't think about going out the door without clothes nor would she think about going out the door without at least a pistol.

She climbed in the Expedition started it and waited for it to warm up. The SUV was a touch extravagant and simply *devoured* fuel but at least two days a week she ended up with six or more kids packed in the vehicle. It was a choice of a big SUV or one of the larger mini-vans, with not much better fuel economy. And Mark had flatly rejected the mini-van idea. If the stupid liberals back in the '70s hadn't created the CAFÉ regulations, SUVs never would have been economically viable. Serves them right. If they hadn't created the need, she could be driving a reasonably fuel efficient station wagon instead of this . . . behemoth.

When the temperature needle had started to move she drove sedately out of the neighborhood and then floored it. She knew that she already had too many points on her license and the local cops had started to watch for the green Expedition as an easy, not to mention pretty, mark. But cars were for going *fast*. If she wanted to take her time she'd have walked. And it wasn't as if she wasn't busy.

The radar detector remained quiescent all the way to the school zone by the high school and by then she'd slowed down anyway. She waved to the nice sheriff's deputy that had given her a ticket a couple of months before and got in the line of cars, trucks and SUVs that were picking up children from middle school.

Finally she got close enough to the pick-up area that Allison spotted her and walked over, her face twisted in a frown. The thirteen year-old was a carbon copy of her mother physically, with the true strawberry blonde hair that was but a memory to her mother's head, but she had yet to learn that a volcanic temper is best kept in check.

"Marcie Taylor is such a bitch," Allison said, dumping her book bag on the floor and climbing in the passenger seat.

"Watch your language, young lady," Barbara said, calmly. "You may be correct, but you need to learn a wider vocabulary."

"But she *is*," Allison complained. "She said sluts shouldn't be on the cheerleading team and she was looking *right* at me! She's just pi . . . angry because I got picked and she didn't! *And* she's trying to take Jason away from me!"

Barbara counted to five mentally and wondered if now was the time to try to explain the social dynamics of Redwater County. Up until the last decade or so, the county had been strictly rural with the vast majority of the inhabitants being from about six different families. Three of the families, including the Taylors, had been the "Names," old, monied for the area, families that owned all the major businesses.

Recently, as nearby Jackson expanded, the area had started to increase in population and the economy had become much more diverse. Chain stores had driven under the small-town businesses of the "Names" and while they retained some social distinction, it was fading. Even ten years before, Marcie Taylor would have been chosen for the cheerleading squad, despite being as graceful as an ox and with a personality of a badger, simply because of who her father was. And at a certain level she knew that. It undoubtedly added fuel to her resentment of a relative newcomer—the Everettes had only been in the county for ten years—getting such an important slot.

Barb had seen, had lived through, countless similar encounters being dragged around the world by her father. Marcie Taylor had *nothing* in arrogance compared to Fuko Ishagaki. But pointing that out wouldn't be the way to handle it, either.

"Why did she call you a slut?" Barbara asked, instead.

"Oh," Allison breathed, angrily. "There's some *stupid* rumor that I've been screwing Jason!"

"Ah, for the days when a daughter would put it more delicately," Barbara said, trying not to smile. "Have you been? Because if you are, we need to get you on birth control *right now*, young lady!"

"No, I haven't," Allison snapped. "I can't believe you'd *ask*. God, mother, I'm *thirteen*."

"Didn't stop Brandy Jacobs," Barb said, pulling into the line of traffic at the elementary school. "Not that you're that stupid. But if it's before you're eighteen, just make sure you ask me to get the pills for you *beforehand*, okay? I'd, naturally, prefer that you not have sex prior to marriage. But, given the choice, I'd much rather have a sexually active daughter who is *not* pregnant than one who *is*."

"God, mother," Allison said, laughing. "You just *say* these things!"

"Honesty is a sign of godliness," Barbara replied. "And you know what sort of a life you'll have if you get pregnant. Married to . . ." She waved around her and shook her head. "I won't say some slope-brow, buck-toothed, inbred, high-school dropout redneck simply because I'm far too nice a person. And far too young to be a grandmother." She lifted a printed sign that said "Brandon and Brook Everette" and then dropped it back in the door-holder as the lady calling in parents waved. The teacher was Doris Shoonour, third grade, and she immediately recognized Barbara. Everyone in both schools recognized Barbara. She'd been president of the PTO twice, worked every fund-raising drive and fair and could always be counted on as a chaperone on a school trip. Good old Barb. Call her Mrs. Dependable.

Finally she reached the pick-up point for Brandon and Brook and the two got in, bickering as usual.

"Hurry up, stupid," Brook said, banging at her younger brother's butt with her book bag.

"I'm going," Brandon said, irritably. "Quit pushing."

"Quiet, Brook," Barbara said. "Brandon, get in."

The seven-year-old finally negotiated the seats and collapsed with a theatric sigh as his eleven-year-old sister tossed her much heavier bag in the SUV with a thump and scrambled aboard. Both of the younger children had inherited their father's darker looks and were so nearly alike in height that they were often mistaken for twins.

When the attending teacher had shut the door, Barbara pulled out, following the line of cars.

"Mom," Allison said, "I want to go to the dance after the game Friday night."

"No," Barb replied, braking as a car pulled out right in front of her. "May the Lord bless you," she muttered at the driver.

"Why not?" Allison snapped. "I've got to go to the game *anyway*. And everybody *else* will be going to the dance! You can't make me just come home!"

"Because I said no," Barb said, calmly. "And no means no."

"You're *impossible*, mother," Allison said, folding her arms and pouting.

"Yes, I am," Barbara said.

Except for the regular argument in the back, the drive home was quiet.

"Get ready for tomorrow," Barb said as they were going in the door to the two-story house. "Brook, get your dance bag. Allison—"

"I *know*, mother," Allison spat, headed for the stairs. "Change into my work-out clothes."

"Brandon . . ."

"I'm going, I'm going . . ." the seven-year-old said. "I don't think I *want* to take karate anymore."

"We'll discuss it later," Barbara answered.

While the kids were getting ready, and keeping up a steady stream of abuse at one another, Barb got dinner prepped so all she'd have to do when they got home was pull it out of the oven. She often thought that the worst part of her current life was deciding what to cook every night. Followed closely by cleaning up after dinner and then the actual cooking.

So after much mental agony she'd simply decided on making a rut. Tonight was Thursday and that meant meat loaf. She'd made the loaf earlier in the day and now slipped it in the oven, setting the timer to start cooking while they were gone. Broccoli had been prepped as well and she slipped it in the microwave. She set out two packages of packaged noodles and cheese, filled a pot with water and olive oil and set it on the stove. When she came home all she'd have to do was pull the meat loaf out of the oven, get the water boiling, start the microwave and twenty minutes after they were back they'd be sitting down for dinner.

Technically, Mark could have done it all since he'd be home at least an hour before they were. But Mark was vaguely aware that there were pots and pans in the house and could just about make Hamburger Helper without ruining it. She'd wondered, often, if she shouldn't have at least *tried* to get him to learn how to cook. But that was water under the bridge: after fourteen years of marriage it was a bit late to change.

By the time she was done it was time to start chivvying the children out the door. Brandon couldn't find the bottom to his gi or his blue belt. Brook was missing one of her jazz shoes. Allison was dallying in the bathroom, trying to find just the right combination of make-up that would proclaim she was an independent and modern thirteen-year-old without being in any way a slut.

The gi bottom was fished out from under the bed, the belt had apparently disappeared, the shoe was found under a mound of clothes in the closet, and a couple of swipes of eyeliner, some lip gloss and a threat of punishment got Allison out of the bathroom.

All three children were dropped at their respective locations and when Allison was kicked out the door, still sulking, Barbara heaved a sigh of relief and drove to the dojo.

Algomo was a small town but unusual in that it successfully

supported two schools of martial arts. For reasons she couldn't define, except a desire to, at least one night a week, avoid her children for an hour or so, Brandon had been enrolled in Master Yi's school of karate and kung-fu whereas Barb spent Thursday evening at John Hardesty's Center for Martial Arts.

She parked the Expedition, mentally cursing its wide footprint and inordinate length, and walked in the back door of the dojo. There was a women's locker room where she slipped out of the dress and boots and donned tight leather footgear that were something like Brook's missing tap shoe. Then she entered the dojo.

The room was large with slightly worn wood flooring and currently empty. In forty minutes or so the next class would flood in and she'd help with it for another forty minutes or so and then go pick up the kids.

For now she was alone and she started her warm-up, working through a light tai-chi exercise, stretching out each slow muscle movement. After she was slightly warmed up she sped up her pace, adding in some gymnastics and yoga movements for limberness.

"You know," John Hardesty said from the doorway. "It's a good thing I'm gay or I'd be having a hard time with this."

"You're not gay," Barbara said, rolling from a split to a handstand, legs still spread. She looked at him from between her hands and chuckled at his expression. "See?"

John Hardesty was middling height and weight with sandy-brown hair. His wife, Sarah, helped out a couple of evenings a week and between them they had five children, one from his previous marriage, two from Sarah's and two together. If he was gay, it was a very closet condition.

"Why do you do this to me?" John said, going over to the lockers and pulling out pads.

"It builds character," Barb replied, flipping to her feet. She fielded the tossed pads and started getting them on.

Once they were both in pads, with helmets and mouthpieces in, they touched hands and closed.

John started the attack with a hammer strike and then bounced away lightly, staying out of reach of her grappling attack. He'd learned, through painful experience, not to even think of grappling with her.

In honesty, the reason that Brandon and Brook, and up until recently Allison, studied with Master Yi, was that Master Yi was simply *better* than John. John had Barbara, a touch, on speed. And he was definitely stronger; any reasonably in-shape male would be. But Barb had started training when she was five, when her father had been a foreign area officer assigned in Hong Kong. Over the succeeding twenty-eight years she had never once been out of training. The quality varied and the forms *definitely* varied; over the years she'd studied wah lum and dragon kung fu, karate in the U.S. and Japan, hop-ki do in Korea and the U.S. and aikido. But by the time she was Allison's age, she could have won most open tournaments if they were "all forms." And if all attacks were allowed.

John Hardesty, on the other hand, was straight out of the "tournament" school of karate. He'd won southeast regional a time or two, come in second nationally, and now owned the de rigueur local martial arts school. He was good, but he was by no means a superior fighter. And he'd come to that conclusion after sparring with Barbara only once.

Master Yi, despite using "karate" to describe his school, had been studying wah lum before Barb was born and *was*, or at least had been, a truly superior hand-to-hand warrior. If the kids were going to train with anyone local, she wanted it to be Master Yi. In fact, she often wished that she trained with Master Yi instead of with John. You didn't get better by fighting someone who was your inferior. But, occasionally, she picked up something new.

Barbara followed up with a feinted kick and then two hammer strikes that were both blocked. But the second was a feint and she locked the blocking wrist with her right hand, coming in low with two left-handed strikes to the abdomen and then leaping out of range.

"Bitch," John said around the mouthpiece.

"Had to call Allison on using that term," Barb said, backing up and then attacking in the Dance of the Swallow. It was right at the edge of her ability and she nearly bobbled the complicated cross during the second somersault, but it ended up with Hardesty on his face and her elbow planted in his neck. "Don't use it on me."

"Christ, I hate it when you pull out that kung fu shit," John said humorously, taking her hand to get back on his feet. "Bad week?"

"Yeah," she admitted.

"Well, if you need to kick my ass to get it out of your system, feel free," Hardesty said, taking a guard position. "I have to admit that fighting you is always interesting. Anything in particular?"

"No," Barbara admitted as they closed. This time two of Hardesty's rock hard blows got through her defenses, rocking her on her heels, and she was unable to grapple either one of them. She'd *take* a blow if it meant she could get a lock; once she had most opponents in lock she could turn them into sausage. But she could feel her concentration slipping and she disengaged. "I'm just *tired*," she said, stretching and rubbing at her pads where the blows had slipped through.

"Take a break," John said, lifting his helmet and pulling out his mouthpiece. "You deserve one."

"I'm going to," Barb said. "This weekend. Mark doesn't know yet."

"He's going to be *so* thrilled," John quipped, slipping his mouthpiece back in. "You ready to get thrown through a wall?"

"You and what army?"

Chapter Two

She helped with training until it was time to leave and then headed for the locker room. Technically, she helped with training the younger kids so she didn't get charged tuition. In reality, they both knew that she was training John as much as she was training the kids. Who was the master and who the student? But training *other* people's kids had never bothered her. She'd thought about becoming a teacher full-time; she was already an occasional substitute. But Mark made enough money that she didn't have to work and he preferred that she stay at home. And she believed, in a fundamental and unshakeable fashion, that Mark was the master of the house. If he wanted her to stay home and be a housewife, she'd stay home.

Barbara had been raised an Episcopalian and in her teenage years, when other kids were getting as far away from the church as they could, she'd gotten closer and closer to it. She often thought that if she'd been raised Catholic, God forbid, she'd have become a nun. But her family, her religion and her country were locked in an iron triangle that defined her life. In many ways, it was religion that kept her sane. When times were bad, when she and Mark were at each other's throats, when Allison had been struck by a car, when Mark was laid off, it was to God she turned for solace. And that solace was always there, a warm, comforting presence that said that life was immaterial and only the soul mattered. Make sure the soul was at peace and everything else would eventually fall into place.

She wasn't a fundamentalist screamer. She didn't proselytize. She simply lived her life, every day, in the most Christian manner that she could. If someone sniped at her, she turned the other cheek. If the children bickered or snapped, she smothered her anger and treated them as children of God. And when someone needed a helping hand because another supposed Christian had said no or simply not turned up, she gave that helping hand.

She knew that a good bit of her belief centered around what she called "the other Barbara." One time in the sixth grade she'd been sent home, almost expelled, for putting a boy in the hospital. He'd been teasing her and when she tried to walk away he'd grabbed her. So she'd broken his nose, arm and ankle. She had not used any training; no special little holds or martial arts moves were involved, just sheer explosive rage. It was the rage, as much as anything, that she used her religion to control. She'd learned it from her mother who had much the same problems and who explained that, besides the necessity for belief in the One God, religion's *purpose* was to control the demons in mankind.

Barb worked very hard to control her demons, because she knew what the results would be if she did not.

It didn't mean she was an idiot about it. The world was not a nice place and never would be short of the Second Coming. To her, "turn the other cheek" meant "let the small hurts pass" not "be a professional victim." So she made sure her children were as well grounded as possible, gave them all the advice she could, showed them a Christian way of life in all things and made sure they knew how and when to defend themselves.

When she was in college, shortly before meeting Mark, she had been attacked on her way home from the library late one Wednesday evening. The path was lit but the location was obscured by trees and landscaping and the man had been on her before she knew he was there. She could have screamed, she could have tried to run, he only had a knife after all. Instead she broke his wrist, struck him on the temple with an open-hand blow and walked to the nearest phone to call the police.

After the police took her statement she had gone back to her dorm, thrown up and then prayed for several hours. She had prayed for the soul of her attacker and her own. For her attacker she had prayed that he would find a way to Jesus lest the evil in his soul give him to Satan for all time. A soul lost was a soul lost. For herself she had prayed for mercy. For she had, in her anger, given his wrist an extra, unnecessary, twist, that had elicited a scream of pain. She prayed for mercy for letting her anger, which she knew to be volcanic, slip in the circumstances. And for the wash of pleasure that scream of pain had caused her. She'd been really upset by the attack.

The attacker had been picked up at the hospital while having his wrist set. DNA matched him to a string of rapes around the LSU campus so Barbara hadn't even had to press charges. She still prayed, occasionally, that while in prison he would find his way to Jesus. Every soul, even that of a rotten little rapist, was precious.

When she got home the TV was on, tuned to ESPN. Mark was settled on the recliner, a position he would assuredly occupy until time for supper. She got him a fresh beer, turned on the water to boil and got out the meat loaf. Twenty minutes later she had the kids washed and at the table.

"God, thank you for this food," Mark said, his head bowed. "Thank you for another day of good life, for all the things you have given to us . . ."

Barb tuned Mark out and sent up her own prayer of thanks. It *was* a good life. Intensely frustrating at times, but good. Everyone was healthy, no major injuries, decent grades, Mark had a good and steady job. She felt . . . under utilized, but bringing three sane and reasonably well balanced kids into the world was probably the best utilization of a life she could imagine.

When Mark was done she picked up her fork and looked at Allison.

"Other than the unpleasantness with Marcie, how was your day, Allison?"

She insisted on conversation at the table, a habit she had gotten from her mother, God rest her soul. Mother Gibson had followed her Air Force husband around the world, often ending up alone with the kids in some God forsaken wilderness like Minot, North Dakota. Often the only conversation she could have was that with her children.

The kids had learned. A simple "Good" or "Bad" would elicit parental disapproval of the most extreme kind. So Allison swallowed her bite of broccoli and frowned, trotting out the prepared speech.

"I think I did okay on my chemistry test . . ."

When dinner was done, all the kids in bed but Allison, who was doing homework, the dishes in the dishwasher and Mark back watching television, Barbara went over to the couch and sat down.

"Mark," she said, softly, "I need a break."

"Huh?" Mark said, looking away from a rerun of *Friends*, then back at the TV.

"I need a break," she repeated. "I'm going away for the weekend."

"What?" he asked, looking over at her again. The station changed to a commercial and she now had his undivided attention.

"I'd like you to pick the kids up tomorrow," she said. "And take the Expedition in the morning, I'll take the Honda. I just need a short vacation."

"Who's going to cook supper?" he asked. "And Allison asked me if she could go to the dance tomorrow. I said yes. Who's going to pick her up?"

"I said *no*," Barb sighed. "Because I knew you'd ask that question."

"We just had a vacation a couple of months ago!" Mark protested.

"*You* had a vacation," Barbara replied. "I made sure that Allison didn't wear that thong bikini, got sunscreen on everyone, treated Brandon's sunburn when he didn't get it replaced, made sure there were snacks for the beach . . ."

"Okay, okay," Mark said. "I get the picture. But that still doesn't answer who's going to cook!"

"You'll go to the game on Friday anyway . . ."

"And that's another thing," Mark said. "I thought you wanted to go to the game. You always *do*!"

"I go to the games because it's a *duty*, Mark," Barb said. "I don't *enjoy* them. You can eat at the game, everyone will anyway. I'll leave a casserole for Saturday evening. Sunday you can go out. I'll be back Monday."

"And I was planning on going to the State game on Saturday! Who's going to drive me home?"

Barbara tried not to sigh or mention that that was part of her reason for wanting to get away. If the day went to form, Mark would be far too drunk to drive before the game even started.

"Catch a ride," she snapped. "I'm sorry, Mark, but I *have* to get away." She took a deep breath and counted to ten mentally. When that didn't work she repeated it. In Japanese.

"Okay," Mark sighed as the show resumed. "Where are you going?"

"Gulfport, probably," Barb answered. "I'll get a cheap hotel room and just . . . read I think."

"Whatever," Mark said, watching Jennifer Aniston bounce across the screen to the couch.

"And you'll need to get the kids to school on Monday," she said.

"Okay," he replied, clearly not listening.

She stood up and walked to the bedroom, got undressed, cleaned off her makeup, climbed into bed and picked up her latest trashy novel. Another day down. Just one more until she had a break. She could use a nice relaxing weekend.

Augustus Germaine held the scale up with a pair of tweezers and rotated it against the light, shaking his head.

"I thought that Almadu was dispelled, what, seventy years ago?" Assistant Director Grosskopf said.

"All are not dead that sleeping lie," Germaine answered, continuing to examine the scale. "What once was can be again. And, clearly, is. The thorium traces are distinct, as is the patterning of the scale. Someone has been very naughty." He set the scale down on the laboratory bench and looked over at Dr. Mattes. "Concur?"

"Oh, yes," Vonnia Mattes, Ph.D., replied, shrugging. "And the construct DNA, of course."

"So it's a manifestation of Almadu for sure?" Grosskopf asked, pointedly. "That's a full *avatar* manifestation. I can't exactly send *my* agents in on that!"

"No, it's clearly Special Circumstances," Germaine said with a sigh. "I'll find someone to attach to your investigation. The usual covers." He frowned and bit his lip, wincing. "But for a full manifestation . . . I don't really *have* any agents, *available* agents, that are up to dispelling one of those. Not to mention their followers. This is likely to get . . . noticeable."

"Five dead hookers are already *noticeable*," Grosskopf pointed out.

"Noticeable as in explosions, weird lights, people going insane and *lots* of dead bodies," Germaine snapped. "This is not going to be an easy take-down. The last cult involved depth charges, torpedoes and a full cover-up. And even then that beastly writer got ahold of some of it!"

"Whatever," Grosskopf replied. "Just get it shut down. Fast. Before somebody *outside* the organization stumbles on it."

"Well," Germaine said, shrugging, "if they do, I don't think they'll live long enough to tell anyone about it."

Blessed peace.

Barbara enjoyed driving, especially when she was by herself. She loved her children and her husband, but it just wasn't the same. A reasonably open road and good car meant time to think, time to pray, time to dream without constant interruption. As she pulled onto the Natchez Trace she pushed a CD into the player and felt the ethereal strains of Evanescence wash over her, rinsing out her soul in music. She'd been told that Evanescence was first classified as a Christian rock band despite its Goth look. She didn't know if it was true or not but it was probable. Surely only God would have a hand in such glorious music and most of the songs could be interpreted that way. Certainly "Tourniquet" was a direct call to God although "Haunted" always made her wonder.

The radar detector remained quiet all the way to the outskirts of Jackson where the traffic started to pick up anyway and she had to slow down below eighty. She weaved expertly in and out of the traffic for as long as she could, never being aggressive, never getting angry even at the idiots that clogged up the left-hand lane. She didn't know where she got the ability to sense what other drivers were going to do, sometimes even before they seemed to know. But when a car cut into her lane suddenly she'd know it before the first move. Sudden braking rarely caught her unawares even though she was in an alpha state of road daze. She just handled it until the traffic got so heavy she couldn't maneuver, then settled in the middle lane and rode the flow into Jackson.

She was planning on picking up 49 in Jackson and taking it over to Hattiesburg then down to Gulfport but at the last minute she changed her mind, picking up I-55 instead and heading for Louisiana. She didn't know why, but for once she could just follow her feelings. She had a sudden craving for Cajun food, real Cajun food from down in the bayou and decided to go with it. Besides, she'd been to Gulfport every summer for the last five years. She wanted something *new.*

When she was growing up, all she'd wanted was to settle in one place. Just some stability and not having to wonder what country you'd woken up in. Sometimes she'd wondered if she'd fallen for Mark simply because he represented that stability. Mark was from Oxford, which wasn't all that far from Tupelo, and when she'd met him the farthest he'd ever traveled was to Daytona Beach for spring break.

Since being married, and never traveling any farther than Daytona, Barbara had started to notice how much she missed it. When the kids were young it was one thing; she was occupied full time taking care of them. But since they'd become more or less self functional for day-to-day activities, she'd started to *crave* something new. Which meant *not* going to Gulfport again.

Besides, U.S. 49 was a crawl from Jackson to Gulfport, especially on a Friday.

The traffic on I-55 was heavy with weekend travelers and she was reduced to a *relative* crawl of high seventies. She continued on 55 nonetheless, following it all the way down to I-10 and then striking out into the unknown. She followed U.S. 90 for a while and then took a side-road, heading into bayou country and trying as hard as she could to get lost. She had a GPS and checked that it was tracking, so no matter where she ended up she could find her way back.

However, the meandering on side roads with their sudden turns to avoid going into a swamp got wearying after a while. She'd had so much to do she hadn't gotten on the road until around three and it had been a long nine-hour drive to the bayou country. So as midnight approached she started looking for sign of a hotel.

The road she was on wasn't even mapped on the GPS and the very few stores and filling stations she passed were mostly closed. But, finally, she saw a Shell station with its lights still on and pulled in gratefully. She filled her tank and then went into the crumbling cinder-block building, wrinkling her nose at the smell of dead minnows and less identifiable things.

There was a slovenly looking fat woman with greasy black hair and a dirty smock behind the counter. People who were overweight didn't bother Barb, Lord alone knew she had to fight to stay in any sort of shape, but dirt did. There was no reason in this day and age that a person couldn't take at least a weekly bath and throw their clothes in the washing machine from time to time. But they were all God's children so Barbara smiled in as friendly a manner as she could muster.

"I'm looking for a hotel," she said, smiling pleasantly. "Is there one around?"

The woman looked at her for a long time without speaking, then nodded, frowning.

"Im de parsh set been Thibaw Een," the woman said, pointing in the direction Barb had been traveling. "Bein closin soon."

Barbara smiled again and nodded, blinking in incomprehension. It was the thickest Cajun accent she had ever heard in her life. Back home the locals sometimes put on a thicker than normal southern drawl to confuse visiting Yankees and people from Atlanta. If you talked like your mouth was full of marbles it made you virtually incomprehensible. She wondered if the woman was doing that to her but was too polite to ask for a translation. So she nodded again and walked back out to her car.

Apparently somewhere down the road was the "parish seat," which would be the center of the local county government. Where, hopefully, she could find something called the Thibaw Inn or similar.

Even in road daze she never really went to condition white: totally unaware of her surroundings. She had been raised by a father who was marginally insane from a paranoia perspective and he'd spent hours teaching her to keep her guard up to the point that it was old hat. But she hadn't really *examined* her surroundings and when she did she considered turning around and heading back to bright lights and the big city. The road was flanked on either side by bayou and the arching cypress overhung it, draped with gray Spanish moss, some of the longest she'd ever seen. The bromeliads were waving gently in the light night wind and combined with the croaking of the frogs in the bayou and the call of a night bird they gave the scene an eerie feel.

With the exception of the station, which was shutting down as she stood there, there was not a light in sight. There was a glow back over her shoulder, probably New Orleans, but for all that she could have been standing there in a primordial forest. A splash off in the bayou was probably from an alligator slipping into the tannic water, but it could just as well have been some prehistoric monster.

She shivered a bit and got in the car, starting it and then pausing. Turn around and head back to New Orleans or Baton Rouge? Or go on?

On the other hand, the news out of New Orleans made a

black night in the bayou seem positively friendly. And it was a long darned way around to get to Baton Rouge.

On was, presumably, closer and it had been a long day. She put the car in gear and headed west. Somewhere around here there had to be a hotel.

Kelly had started off his detective career in vice and New Orleans' French Quarter was as close as he could call anything to home. So he walked along Chartres Street with an air of ownership, dodging the occasional group of tourists and looking for familiar faces.

Familiar faces were few and far between, though; the ladies seemed to be running shy of the street. There were a few around, though, some of whom recognized him from previous busts and for once seemed glad to see him. He wandered over to Dolores as she waved to a passing car.

"Hey, Dolores," he said, grinning. "How's tricks?"

"Short, small and too slow, like usual," the hooker replied. "I am, of course, simply a young lady who enjoys dates with generous gentlemen and sex has nothing to do with it, nor does money."

Dolores Grantville, age thirty-seven, hometown somewhere in Arkansas. Five foot eight, willowy, mostly from a coke habit, dishwater blonde. Six previous convictions for prostitution, one drug arrest, nol pros when she burned her dealer. Blue eyes, face worn far beyond her years. And scared. Really scared.

"You heard about Marsha, right?" Kelly asked.

"Probably before you did, Kel," the hooker replied, smiling tiredly as a passing tourist beeped his horn. Her face twitched and she watched the street scene, avoiding the detective's eyes. "You got any leads?"

"If I did, would I be here?" Kelly asked. "What do you hear?"

"Nothing," Dolores said. "They're just up and disappearing, Kelly. I mean, Marsha was a young one, they've all been young ones. But she was streetwise, you know? She'd been turning since she was fourteen or so. If somebody can pick her, they can pick anybody. Probably some regular trick, but nobody can put a finger on one or we'd all be telling you, okay?"

"Okay," Kelly agreed. "When'd you see Marsha last?"

"Saturday," Dolores said. "She was talking with Carlane. Be in the evening, don't know what time. Earlyish. Nobody's seen her since. Well . . . not until the papers."

"She used to hang with Evie, right?" Kelly asked, considering the information. Carlane Lancereau was a pimp, a long time one. Pretty heavy-handed, but that came with the territory. And he'd been around for years; there was no reason to think he'd suddenly gone nuts and started ripping up hookers. "The one that calls herself Fantasy?"

"Evie did a runner two weeks ago," Dolores replied. "Lots of the girls have. New Orleans don't seem like a good place to be right now. I don't know where she went, maybe Baton Rouge, maybe St. Louis."

"Nobody saw Marsha after she was talking with Carlane?" Kelly asked.

"You think it's Carlane?" Dolores responded, eyes wide. "He's been around since before I got here."

"No," Kelly said. "That's not what I said. I'm just getting old and trying to cut down on the walking. Since I'm looking for the last person she was known to have talked to, which is *never* the murderer, I'm just trying to figure out who that was. If it wasn't Carlane, who was it?"

"Christy said she saw her late evening, maybe after midnight," Dolores replied, frowning in thought. "Up Dumaine Street, off her regular beat. Looked like she was heading somewhere. But last time *I* saw her was talking to Carlane and she ain't been seen since Saturday night."

"Okay," Kelly said, sighing. "You see Carlane, tell him I'm looking for him, like him to give me a call. Just a friendly conversation. Or I can go find him, or have the black and whites go find him, and it won't be so friendly."

"I'll pass it on," Dolores said. "You be careful."

"Always," Kelly replied, walking off into the crowded night.

Chapter Three

"You get anything talking to the girls?" Lieutenant Chimot asked.

They were going over the daily take on the case. The department had set up a task force with Chimot, who was one of the three lieutenants in Homicide, in charge. It was late, but nobody was getting much sleep as long as the investigation was going on. There were five other sergeant detectives working the case but Kelly sort of figured if anybody was going to find the perp it would be him. The other detectives were straight-arrow homicide dicks; in other words they could just about see lightning and hear thunder.

Most homicides were pretty straightforward investigations. There was a dead body on the floor and a person, usually a spouse, standing over it mumbling about whatever had set them off. File the paperwork, go to court, walk the jury through the chain of evidence and you were done. Then there were the gang shootings, which usually came down to somebody boasting and squeezing the name out of a singer.

Serial killers were different. They usually worked alone and they were generally smart, often very smart. They covered their tracks. Talk about profiles all you wanted, they didn't fit in happy little categories. They could be black, white, Hispanic or more mixed than Tiger Woods. They could be single or married. They might frequent hookers or avoid them like the plague. No two were ever exactly the same, whatever profilers tried to say. They were not all, or even mostly, single white males with a "loner" personality. The Green River killer had been a married white male who was referred to as "exuberant." The Atlanta killings perp was a single black male. The Los Rios killer had been a married Hispanic.

And this case was right off the charts. Very rarely did serial killings involve multiple individuals. There had been one series in California that involved two killers and a case in Charlotte that had involved six or seven. But in the latter case, one of the killers turned evidence before they'd killed more than one girl. The last case he could think of that had involved high multiples perps *and* multiple killings was the Manson case.

The one near constant was that they tended to *start* with hookers and eventually worked their way to . . . tastier game. Nobody wanted a gutted corpse, but by the same token there was a much higher interest in missing schoolgirls than in hookers. Kelly liked the streetgirls for all they could be a pain in the ass. But they chose their jobs and they knew the risks. He didn't want to be there when a black bag got slit open to show some junior high girl who had been snatched walking home from the bus. Or some oblivious college girl who had just been trying to have a good time on Bourbon Street.

"Dolores saw her talking to Carlane sometime Saturday night," Kelly said, glancing at his notes. "And she was seen later, alone, on Dumaine Street. I'm going to talk to Carlane but I'd say it's a dead-end."

"Who's Carlane?" Detective Weller asked.

"Pimp," Chimot answered. "Been around for at least twenty years. Bastard to his girls, but . . ."

"But why would he all of a sudden start offing them, right?" Kelly said. "And none of the girls were from his string; they were all independents."

"Trying to increase his take?" Chimot said. "Not really his MO, though, is it?"

"No," Kelly agreed. "But I'll talk to him. Right now, it's the only lead we've got."

The town couldn't be called a one-horse town because there wasn't enough grass for a horse to eat. It was basically a slightly wider, slightly drier spot in the swamp. There was a dilapidated courthouse, a small Piggly Wiggly, a closed gas station and an old mansion that had a sign out front that said "Thibideau House." Since there was a "Vacant" sign next to it, she had to assume it was the town's lone hotel and there was a light on that revealed a large, covered front porch.

She parked around the side and went to the front, hoping that the light meant somebody was still awake. The door was open so she pushed on it and listened to the creak with a slight sense of humor. You don't get good creaks like that every day. They need either real artistry to create or just *years* of neglect. It was more than the hinges, the whole *wall* seemed to creak as the door swung open.

She poked her head through the open door and looked inside curiously. The ornate foyer was in as bad condition as the exterior. The house had clearly once been a prime residence to someone addicted to gilt and red velvet. Time and the elements had worked their way on the foyer, however, to an even greater extent than on the door. She cat walked across the floor, just to make sure none of the flooring was going to give way. But there appeared to be no one in sight.

"Cooee?" she called, trying not to laugh. "Anybody home?"

All she needed was to be broken down by the side of the road for the bad movie impression to be complete. No, there should be a—

"You be late, missus," a husky voice said from her right. Stepping through the door Barb could see an old black woman rocking next to the empty reception desk. "You be very late."

"I'd say I was lost, but I don't know if it counts if you're trying," Barbara said, grinning and walking all the way into the dimly lit lobby.

"Only counts if you don't want to be lost, missus," the black woman said, grinning back. "Been tryin to get lost my-own-self before. Always find my way back home."

"Nice place," Barb said. "I don't suppose there's a room available?"

"We bout full up of empty rooms, missus," the woman said, getting to her feet creakily and going behind the desk. She swung an old fashioned ledger around and pointed to a line. "Need your name and address and such and your make of car and tag. If'n you don't know the tag, jest a description will do."

Barbara picked up the old pen tied to the ledger with fishing line and after trying to get it to work dug in her purse for her own. Finally she had the ledger filled out.

"Be thirty dollar a night," the woman said. "Don't take no plastic. If you ain't got the cash, you can pay me tomorrow."

"I've got cash," Barb said, trying not to smile again. It was so charmingly informal it reminded her of Malaysia. The back areas, not Kuala Lumpur which was just New York with worse humidity and drainage. She dug out two twenties, crisp from an ATM and received a crumpled five and five incredibly dirty ones in change. She hadn't felt so at home in years.

"Lights are out upstairs," the woman said, picking up a flashlight. "Not in the rooms, just the hallway."

Barbara hoisted her bag over her shoulder and followed the old woman as she ascended the grand staircase. She could practically hear the tread of the master of the house walking out to the balcony to greet his guests and retainers. There'd have been slaves, or at least servants, scurrying among the guests and a chandelier about covered in candles. Now it had a worn runner and lights that, apparently, refused to glow at all.

"Circuit's out," the old lady said, gesturing at the sconces as if reading her mind. "Called the 'lectrician. Lazy bastard ain't been by in two weeks. Got your choice of views: bayou or town square."

"Oh, I think I'll take town square," Barb said.

The room was just as fusty as she expected, smelling of mildew and neglect. But the linens were fresh and appeared clean.

"Bath is down the corridor," the woman said, pointing to the door. She suddenly looked at the flashlight in her hand with an expression of worry that made Barbara try not to laugh again.

"I've got my own flashlight," Barb said, pulling a minimag out of her purse and switching it on. It was at least twice as bright as the dim torch the woman had been using. She reached in and flipped on the room light and was relieved that that, at least, worked.

"See you in the morning, then," the woman said. "I'd not advise going out at night, sometimes the gators get up on the road."

"Wasn't planning on it," Barbara admitted. "See ya."

After the woman was gone Barbara turned off the room light and her flash and waited for her eyes to adjust. She wasn't going to go out in that hallway with her eyes blinded, that was for sure. It was only after waiting a few moments that she thought of one small detail.

Checking the door she determined that the knob was not designed for a key and there was no latch on the inside.

"Now *that* is unusual," she said to herself, straining her eyes in the darkness and running her hands over the door. Even in that flea-bitten hotel in Petra there'd been a lock for the door. Oh, well, needs must.

She examined the furniture by the faint light from the window and was unsurprised that none of it would be useful for blocking the door. It required a very specific height and design of chair to block a doorknob and the chairs in the room were heavily stuffed easy chairs, not the straight backed chair that would work.

However, not for nothing was she a reader. The pen she'd used to sign the register was heavy metal, a gift her father had given her when she went off to college and it had a matching fountain pen. She never used the latter but they were both in her purse and with a few poundings from the romance novel she'd been carrying they were both wedged in the crack between the door and the jam. It would be possible to force the door but not quietly or easily. If the old lady had any questions about the noise she could feel free to complain. In the morning.

The window led onto the roof of the porch and *that* at least had a latch. She made sure it was secured and then got out of her clothes. The soiled linen packed away in a mesh net bag, she pulled on a pair of running shorts and a T-shirt, then laid the H&K by the side of the bed along with the spare magazines and regular clothes. Finally, feeling a tad sheepish, she pulled out the holster and laid that next to the pistol. Since it was only for a running gunfight, pulling it out told her she was assuming the *need* for a running gunfight.

"Just because it's like a scene in a bad horror movie doesn't mean I'll have to fight off Jason," she muttered to herself. "But I am definitely getting out of this burg *tomorrow*."

"My lord, we have a problem," Germaine said, kneeling in the holy circle, head bowed.

The figure of light seemed to nod in response.

"Our information indicates that there has been a remanifestation of Almadu," Germaine said. "I seek heaven's aid in our holy cause."

"We are stretched, my very old friend," the voice said in his head.

"I don't have agents to handle this, my lord," Germaine said, quietly. "We, too, are stretched. And Almadu is a particularly hard case."

"Look for the Hand of God in strange places," the figure said, fading. "All who work His will are not among your host."

Street people were not morning people and neither was Kelly. But he'd been up at first light, rattling cages. He knew where they lived and the answers might be surly answers but he got them. The only problem was that Carlane seemed to have disappeared.

"It's the street," Lieutenant Chimot said, shrugging and taking a deep suck on his coffee. "People come and go."

"How long's it been since you've heard of Carlane being off the street?" Kelly asked, yawning and digging vigorously in one ear. "Nobody has seen him since he was talking to Marsha, and now Dolores is gone. I got the landlady to let me in her room. All her stuff is there so she didn't move. And I asked her to pass on to Carlane that I wanted to talk to him."

"You're starting to think it's him," the lieutenant said, leaning back in his prolapsed chair and looking at Kelly over a pile of paperwork.

"I want to talk to him," Kelly said, shrugging. "It doesn't make sense for Carlane to have suddenly gone nutter. But he was the last person seen with Marsha and now he's missing. I think we can swear a warrant as a material witness and put out a search and detain."

"You checked to see if we've got his DNA?" Chimot asked.

"Yeah, a sexual assault case where the victim refused to press charges," Kelly said. "I checked. He's not one of the rapists."

"If he's an accessory and he knows we want to talk to him, he'll have gone to ground," Chimot said, musingly. "Might be waiting for it to blow over, especially if he knows we don't have any evidence on him. Go talk to Mother Charlotte. She's been around longer than Carlane; she might know where to go a-hunting. And put out a search and detain. I'd dearly like to talk to our old friend about now."

Barb packed her bags and headed out of the room, feeling much better about the town than she had the night before. She'd taken the chance to have a shower and while the water was brown and stunk, it was better than nothing. She'd had worse. Not in a long time, admittedly, but she'd been looking for adventure, whether she'd put it that way or not, and this was certainly an adventure.

But one that she was just as glad to have past so she tossed her bag in the trunk of the Honda happily, got in, inserted the key and turned it. Only to receive a click. Turn. Click. Turn. Click.

"That is just too much," she said. She'd like to swear but she'd worked so hard to teach herself *not* to that she found her mouth locking up as she tried. Finally she simply muttered: "Sugar."

Fine. The Honda had a very comprehensive warranty. She opened up the glove compartment and pulled out the paperwork until she found the 800 number for the extended care service. They'd tow the car to a dealership, which was going to cost them a pretty penny she suspected, and get her a rentacar. She pulled her cell phone out of her bag, dialed the number and hit send.

No signal.

She looked at the indicator with a frown and a shrug. In the country there were plenty of areas where the signal was weak. Eventually it opened up when a cell got free. Fine. She'd wait.

After about thirty seconds with no flicker of the indicator she shook the phone and waved it through the air, hoping the magic electrons would somehow be caught. Still no signal.

"Sugar."

She got out of the car, noticing that it had gotten hot even in her brief sojourn, and walked back in the hotel.

The same old lady was on the rocking chair and seemed to be asleep.

"Pardon me, ma'am," Barbara said, softly. "Ma'am?"

"Uh?" the old woman said, sitting up and smacking her lips. "Sorry, was up late."

"Yes, ma'am," Barb said, smiling sweetly. "I seem to be having car problems. Is there a phone around? My cell won't work."

"Ain't none of them towers around," the lady said, peering shortsightedly at the cell phone still clutched in Barbara's hand. "Pay phone down at the Piggly Wiggly. Ain't got none here."

Barb was reasonably sure that the last meant that the hotel had *no* phone, which seemed remarkably antiquated even for south Louisiana. But she just nodded in thanks and walked out.

By day the town was somewhat more pleasant than by night. The courthouse still looked as if it could use a coat of paint, or maybe a major fire, but there were a few more houses than she'd thought and a bait and tackle shop that doubled as a liquor store. Maybe she'd go fishing. Or get stinking drunk and explain just what she thought of the place. No key on the door, no bathroom in the room, it was worse than *Egypt* for God's sake.

No, not God. Take not the name even in thought.

The Piggly Wiggly was . . . fair. No dirtier than others she'd seen and the pay phone was at least operational. She pulled out the paperwork and thirty-five cents, then called the service company.

Yes, I have a problem with my automobile, one. Yes, I need roadside assistance, one. No, I don't want to use the automated system. No, I am not at my home. Yes, I'd like to speak to an operator. I'll *wait*!

As she punched the various buttons on the Kevorkian disconnect phone-tree she stood with her back to the glass of the Piggly Wiggly, ensuring that she could keep an eye on what was going on around her. It wasn't because of the situation, it was just how she used the phone. She'd rotated to the right side of the phone despite the fact that it put her back to the glass because that way she could hold the phone in her left hand and keep her right free.

"Thank you for calling Honda Warranty Service International, my name is Melody, how may I help you?"

"My car won't start," Barbara said. *I was hoping to order* pizza, *how do you think you can help me?*

"Where is the vehicle?" Melody asked with a distinct midwest accent.

"Thibideau, Louisiana," Barb said. "At the Thibideau Inn."

"Do you have your warranty number?" the girl asked, brightly.

Barbara read off the numbers patiently.

"I'm sorry, ma'am," the girl said with a real note of distress in her voice. "There isn't a Honda dealership within service range of Thibideau, Louisiana. However, we do have an allied service representative, Thibideau Tire and Auto, who should be able to get you on the road again. Are you at the vehicle location now?"

"No," Barb said, trying not to swear even mentally. "I can get there before they can, though. But there's no phone there."

"That will be fine. According to the computer they should be no more than thirty minutes getting there."

"I need a rentacar," Barbara said.

"I'm sorry, ma'am, but, again, the location is outside of rental service area," the girl said, really distressed. "But, I'm sure that . . . Thibideau Tire and Auto will be able to get you going quickly."

Left hind leg of a camel. *Sugar*.

"Thank you for your help," Barb said, sweetly.

"Thank you, ma'am, and I hope you have a good day."

Sugar, sugar, sugar!

She pulled the coins out of the drop and inserted them again, dialing zero and then her home number at the tone.

"If you'd like to place a collect call, press one."

One.

"I'm sorry, ma'am, but that's an answering machine," the operator said after a moment.

"Can you hold a moment?" she asked.

"Yes, ma'am," the operator said.

She dug in her purse and came up with a handful of change.

"Can you change it over to a for-pay call?"

"Yes, ma'am. That will be seventy-five cents for two minutes."

She inserted the coins and then waited until the answering service picked up.

"Mark, this is Barb. I'm not in Gulfport. I went down to the bayou for some atmosphere and Cajun food. I'm fine and I should be home on time on Monday. The car's broken down but there's a local service place. I'll try to call you ag—" Beep.

Sugar.

"Come in, Sergeant Lockhart, come in," Madame Charlotte said from the deeps of her shop.

Kelly pushed aside a bead curtain and paused in the doorway, waiting for his eyes to adjust to the gloom.

"I'd ask you how you knew it was me, but I don't think I'd like the answer," Kelly said, smiling.

"I gots a video camera," Madame Charlotte said, pointing to the monitor mounted over Kelly's head. "You wouldn't believe the terrible people try to steal from an old lady."

"Must not be locals," Kelly said, sitting down across the table from the medium. "They'd be afraid of being turned into a snake or a zombie or something."

"I don't do that sort of thing, Mr. Detective," Madame Charlotte said, grinning, her teeth standing out against her jet black face. She was a slight woman with gray-shot hair peeking out from under a colorful kerchief and a face wrinkled like the lines on a map. "Not so's you'd notice."

"Glad to hear that," Kelly said, smiling back.

"But I knowed you'd be stopping in yesterday," Madame Charlotte stated. "Saw it in the cards. Terrible cards, lately, just terrible. You need to watch your step, Sergeant Lockhart, the Reaper is your sign, him who takes the souls."

"That's because I'm so thin," Kelly replied.

"Laugh if you will," the medium replied. "But you be searching for Carlane. Hisself is gone from here, gone back to whence he come."

"Where's that?" Kelly asked. "And why'd he leave?"

"He has the sign of the Wizard," Madame Charlotte said, laying out the card. "And the Hangman," she added. "He messing with powerful magic and ain't got the training. Powerful. I wouldn't mess with nothin' like this and I be a mistress of the arts." The medium laid her cards out and pointed to one. "But there's another. This be the sign of the Princess of Wands. She's a powerful force for Good. Good will be by your side, Detective Sergeant Kelly Lockhart. Just you look sharp for the sign of the Princess or . . . you won't be lookin' no more."

"Do you know where Carlane has gone?" Kelly pressed.

"Aye, back to the swamps that bore him," Madame Charlotte said. "He's from down Thibideau way. Look you there, Sergeant Lockhart, but you be watching you back. There's powerful art stirring in the swamp, powerful and every man's hand against you. Look for the sign of the Princess. She be your only hope."

Chapter Four

The first good thing that had happened since getting to this forsaken burg was that when she got to the car the tow-truck had just arrived. The driver was a short man, swarthy and with lanky black hair. He could have been the brother of the convenience store clerk. In fact, thinking back, all of the locals had had the same look, like they were all from the same extended family. Come to think of it, she wished she'd never thought of it.

"It won't turn over," she said as the man got out of the truck.

"Could be the battery," he said in a thick Cajun accent. "Could be the alternator. I'll try to give it a jump."

He uncoiled wires as she opened the hood, then hooked up and gave her a sign. Click.

"Connections are tight," he called from under the hood then shut it. "Got to take it to the shop."

"Is there a mechanic available?" she asked.

"I'm the mechanic," the man said, giving his first grin. "Mechanic, tow truck driver and owner. Claude Thibideau. I'll get you fixed, long as we got the part."

"And if you can't?" she asked.

"Order it from New Orleans," he said, drawling the name as "Nawleen." "Sometime they can't get out this far on a Saturday. Don't deliver on Sunday neither. Might be Monday before I can get it fixed. You okay with the hotel?"

"Just fine," Barbara replied, lightly, trying not to curse. It was getting *very* hard. "Very nice atmosphere."

"What you doin' down here, anyway?" the mechanic asked as he hooked the car up to tow. The truck was the old fashioned kind that actually *pulled* the car rather than putting it up on a lift-bed.

"Just . . . traveling," Barbara replied. "Seeing new sights. Do you want me to come with you?"

"Be best," the man said from under the car. "If it's a part, I'll give you a ride back to town. Ain't much to see. Send word when I can get it fixed."

"I've got a book," Barb replied. "Could I take just a minute?"

"Sure," the mechanic replied. "Gots all day."

Barbara had dressed for the anticipated drive in her boots, a pair of jeans, a cream silk blouse and a dark leather jacket. But the outfit was far too warm to go wandering around Thibideau; already the town was steaming in the morning heat. So she popped back in the hotel, tiptoeing past the sleeping attendant or owner or whatever she was and slipped into the bathroom.

A quick rummage in her bag showed that she'd failed to anticipate heat at all. All of the blouses were long sleeve. The jeans she could survive and the boots were fine but she *really* needed something lighter. Right at the bottom of the bag her hand closed on what felt like a T-shirt. Pulling it out she frowned and shook her head. The shirt had been given to her as a joke by her sister. Once upon a time, Barb had been madly smitten with Middle Earth. When she was fourteen she had sworn that she was going to name her first female daughter Galadriel and she'd wanted, badly, to be an elven princess.

So her sister Kate, who still read fantasy and even went to those convention things, had sent her the T-shirt. Sighing, she pulled it out and changed, quickly, making sure that the color of her bra didn't show through. It was the coolest thing she had to wear so for once fashion was going to have to take a back seat to comfort. It wasn't like she was planning on making this place a regular stop or had anyone to impress. And if Thibideau, Louisiana couldn't handle a . . . well-stuffed T-shirt with the caption "Aloof Elven Princess" on it, they could . . . well, that was just too bad.

"Carlane Lancereau was born in Nitotar, which is in Thibideau Parish," Kelly said, tossing a file on Lieutenant Chimot's desk. "Madame Charlotte says he's 'gone back to the swamps from whence he come.' "

"That's gotta be a quote," Chimot said, opening the file and glancing in it. "You've never said whence in your life. Isn't much of *anything* comes from Thibideau Parish."

"Except hookers, drug dealers and pimps," Kelly replied. "I want to go down there."

"Way out of our jurisdiction, Sergeant," Chimot said, raising an eyebrow. "Why? It's not like you don't have enough work here."

"Gut?" Kelly replied. "I want to see if I can find him. He's still only a material witness, not even a suspect. Not much we can do but ask questions. And Thibideau's got almost nothing in the way of police; we can't just drop the detain order on them and hope they track him down."

"We got a make on one of the johns Claudette was seeing the evening of her disappearance," the lieutenant said, rubbing his chin. "Previous arrest for battery and a kidnapping that got downgraded to a misdemeanor solicitation charge. Judge decided he was telling the truth that he'd just picked up a prostitute and had a misunderstanding about the price."

"Fine," Kelly said. "Let somebody else run it down, I want to go looking for Carlane. I'll be back on Monday, latest."

"Go," the lieutenant said, shrugging. "But you draw a weapon and you'd better have an iron-clad reason. One that will survive *Thibideau* justice."

"You mean they've *got* a judge down there?" Kelly said, grinning, as he picked up the file and walked out the door.

"Ma'am," the mechanic said, walking into the dirty waiting room and wiping his hands on a towel that was so grungy it was adding to the mess, "can't hardly tell you how sorry I am. It's the alternator, all right, and the local warehouse is flat out. Be Monday before they can get one to me. I'll get you going quick when it comes in, though."

"Fine," Barbara said, closing her book and setting it back in her purse. "That will be fine."

"I can give you a ride back to the hotel . . ."

"Is there a *restaurant* around?" Barb asked, her stomach rumbling. There was a concession machine in the waiting room but one look at the contents had convinced her not to try it. She'd rarely seen fly-specks *inside* of one before.

"The bait shop's got a bar that serves food," Mr. Thibideau said, shrugging. "They do a fine jambalaya. You can get bacon and eggs and such as well, but I do recommend their jambalaya."

She'd had pork fried rice any number of times for breakfast in Thailand, but jambalaya for breakfast would be a first.

"Could you drop me off?" she asked, sweetly.

It was a two hour ride from New Orleans to Thibideau, even in what was clearly an unmarked police car. The roads for the last hour were all two lane and twisted in and out among the bayous. There was very little in the way of signs of habitation and what there was tended to be rattle-down tar-paper shacks. It was hard to believe that no more than sixty miles away as the crow flies there was a major metropolis.

Thibideau was in keeping with the rest of the area, not much more than a wide spot in the eternal swamps. He parked by the courthouse in a spot marked for police vehicles and walked inside, passing an untended reception area and looking for any signs of life. He finally found it in the county clerk's office where a harassed looking woman in her forties was sorting through paper.

"Detective Sergeant Lockhart, New Orleans PD," he said,

holding out his badge and ID. "Was wondering if you knew where I could find the local sheriff?"

"Died," the clerk said, shrugging. "Last month. Heart attack. Deputy Mondaine's doing his job."

"Sorry about that," Kelly said, unconvincingly. "Where can I find Deputy Mondaine?"

"Around now?" the clerk said, shrugging. "Maybe down at the bait store getting lunch."

"You wouldn't happen to know a Carlane Lancereau by any chance?" Lockhart said, smiling.

"Never heard of him," the clerk replied. "Some Lancereau up Nitotar way, but they live out in the bayou. Gotta take a boat and asking them questions won't get you nowhere. Maybe the deputy can help."

"Could you, perhaps, call him on the radio?" Kelly asked, smiling again.

"Broke," the clerk said. "I got to find this damned title, if you don't mind."

"Not at all," Lockhart replied. "Thank you for all your help."

The jambalaya *was* good but it was also fiery with spice and the restaurant didn't serve unsweetened tea. So she was drinking Diet Coke, which was the best of a bad lot, to wash down the fiery jambalaya, then having another spoon of the jambalaya to wash out the taste of the Coke.

It reminded her of the dinner she'd gone to with her parents. The people were friends of her father, Abyssinian exiles, and they'd hosted an authentic Abyssinian dinner. She couldn't remember what any of the food was called, but it was good. However, it was also very hot. And the only thing to drink was small glasses of some high proof liqueur. Since she was being on her best manners, she ate everything that was put in front of her. And because she couldn't handle the spice, she'd washed it down with glass after glass of liqueur. Before she knew it, she was tight as a tick and telling the hostess the woes of her life, often in quite graphic terms.

It was then she'd decided that she really needed to be careful with liquor. Fortunately, Mom had been doing much the same thing and hardly noticed.

To get to the small eating area of the restaurant required going through the bait shop, which was an experience she'd rather never have had. The live bait tanks appeared to never have been cleaned out and she suspected the dead shiners roiling in yellow foam had probably perished immediately upon entry to the tanks. The whole place was filthy with dead cockroaches in the corners and a layer of grime that would require a thousand gallons of bleach to fix. At least the cup was Styrofoam, and appeared mostly clean and she'd taken it without ice.

The woes she had laid upon the hostess were the woes of being a good Christian girl. Besides the usual, no sex until marriage, there was the whole "being a Witness" thing. If you were a good Christian, you couldn't tell a person when they were being brain-dead. You had to subtly hint that an idea was as stupid as a slug at a salt convention. You couldn't say things like "here's a dime, buy a clue." Or "why don't you clean this place up, it's filthy. And take a bath once in a while!" Or "what do you mean you can't get the part? I want to talk to a district manager right now!" Or "learn to cook! It's not that hard!" You just had to smile and hope that things would work out for the best.

It was a pain in the . . . it was frustrating.

She was contemplating the negative aspects to being a good Christian woman when the cop sat down.

He had the same look as most of the locals, large eyes set a bit close together, rounded chin, wide cheekbones that didn't look classically Cajun. But his hair was shorter than the norm and he was at least clean. But there was something about his eyes. She really didn't like the look in them. One look from him and her "creep-meter," as Allison would say, went into overdrive.

"What's a pretty lady like you doing in a place like this?" the cop asked, waving at the slatternly waitress. "Gimme a plate of jambalaya an' a Coke, Noffie." He was spending about half his time making eye contact and the other half examining her T-shirt. Or, more likely, what it covered.

"I was just passing through and my car broke down," Barbara

answered, taking a sip of Diet Coke and giving up on the jambalaya.

"You call your folks and tell them you're all right?" he asked as the jambalaya was served. Barb noticed that he got quick service; she'd waited nearly ten minutes until the waitress had gotten done talking to one of the regulars.

"Yes, left a message for my husband," she replied. "Told him where I was."

"That's good," the officer said. "Oh, I'm Etienne Mondaine. I was the chief deputy 'til old Claude keeled over from a heart attack last month. You got any problems, you just give me a holler."

"Thank you," Barbara said, taking another sip of the rapidly warming Coke. "I usually can avoid problems, though."

"Where you from?" the deputy asked, not looking up from his plate. He was rarely drinking and seemed immune to the spice.

"Algomo," she said. "Little town outside of Tupelo. Wanted to take the weekend off, go see the sights."

"Not many sights around here," the deputy said with a wheezing laugh. "Ain't much to do, neither. Can rent a boat and go fishing or frog gigging. Or . . . other distractions?" he said, raising an eyebrow.

"I brought books," Barb said, closing off that line of investigation. It was one of the less subtle come-ons she'd heard and she'd heard a lot of them. "I think I'll just find a comfortable spot and read."

She'd taken a seat where she could watch the door of the restaurant and wrinkled her brow as a newcomer walked in the place. He was tall and almost skeletally thin with long, frizzy, blond hair going a tad gray and a matching beard and mustache. He was wearing jeans, T-shirt and a jacket but there was a distinct bulge on his right hip. And he certainly didn't look like a local. Nonetheless, he walked immediately over to their table.

"Deputy Mondaine?" the newcomer said, fishing out a badge and ID. "Detective Sergeant Kelly Lockhart, New Orleans PD."

The bait and tackle store overhung the water and there only appeared to be one entrance. Inside, Kelly saw just about the nastiest live bait wells it had ever been his joy to examine; the forensics guys could spend a lifetime just cataloging the material in the tanks. There was a door to the left, though, that apparently led to a small restaurant and bar. When he walked through, it took a moment for his eyes to adjust, then he saw the deputy sitting on the far side of the room talking to a rather good looking blonde.

As he approached the table he noticed that the . . . seriously stacked blonde was wearing a T-shirt with an inscription on the front but it wasn't until he got over to the table that he could read it in the relative gloom.

"Aloof Elven Princess."

His first reaction was to try not to laugh; he recognized the logo. It was from a website that lampooned the *Lord of the Rings* in quite humorous terms. His second reaction, which he hoped was unnoticeable, was total shock.

Don't weird-out on me, he thought. *Plenty of shirts around with princess on them.*

"Deputy Mondaine?" he asked, showing the deputy his badge and ID. "Detective Sergeant Kelly Lockhart, New Orleans PD."

Mondaine could lose some weight; he more than filled his black uniform, and he wasn't wearing a vest. Of course, in a town like this they probably weren't the utter necessity they were in New Orleans, either.

"Is that like, 'I'm from New Orleans PD and I'm here to help you'?" Mondaine said, dryly. "The check's in the mail?"

"I won't c—" Kelly started to say then stopped at the expression on the blonde's face. "Yeah, like that. I'm looking for a guy named Carlane Lancereau. Know him?"

"Lancereau?" Mondaine said, wrinkling his brow. "There's some Lancereaus live up in the back bayou over Nitotar way. Carlane don't ring a bell. Why?"

"He's wanted for questioning in the Ripper murders," Kelly said, pulling out one of the flyspecked chairs and sitting down. "Not a suspect, just a material witness. Last-seen person with one of the victims. An informant told me he's come down this way. He may be staying with his family."

"I'll ask around," the deputy said, taking a last bite of his jambalaya. "I'd say 'you want to come along' but people are probably going to tell me more if you're not."

"I understand," Kelly replied. "You don't mind if I ask around town, do you?"

"Not at all. I'll be back in about an hour," Mondaine said, standing up and ambling from the room.

"Hello," Kelly said, looking at the blonde and wrinkling his forehead. "I suspect you're not from around here, either."

"No, I'm not," she said, trying not to grin. "I was just passing through town last night. Stopped at the hotel and this morning my car wouldn't start. Alternator. They can't get the part until Monday."

"*Wonderful* place to spend a weekend," Kelly said, dryly. "So much . . ."

"Atmosphere," the blonde finished, waving away a fly that was trying to settle on her straw. "I've decided to use the word 'atmosphere.' And if you end up staying over, don't go out at night."

"Oh?" Kelly said. "Why?"

"Alligators," she replied, smiling slightly with no smile at all in her eyes. "They tell me they come right up in the town. Very bad idea to walk around at night."

Kelly opened his mouth up to reply, then looked down at her chest again and closed his mouth.

"My eyes are up here," the lady said, dryly, after the examination had taken up a few seconds.

"I know, I've made my decision," Kelly replied distractedly, looking up a few moments later. "I was reading. Slowly." He looked around and then frowned again, his entire face crinkling, then clearing. "Let's take a walk," he said, standing up and offering an arm.

"I have to pay my bill," the blonde pointed out.

"Why?" Kelly said, grinning. "The deputy didn't. Clearly the food is free."

"I have to pay my bill," she said, again trying not to grin.

Kelly waited while the lady paid her bill and even left a small tip, which he felt was excessive considering the quality of food and service he had seen. When she was done he accompanied her outside. It was slightly cooler outside under the trees than in the sweltering bait-shop.

"What's your name, lady wearing the Secret Diaries T-shirt?" Kelly said as they walked to the edge of the parking area and stopped under a tree.

"Barbara Everette," Barb replied. "57 Wildwood Lane, Algomo, Mississippi."

"Barbara," Kelly musingly. "Barbara . . . can I call you Barb?"

"Yes?" Barbara answered.

"Barb, I'm going to tell you a story," Kelly said. "I am going to tell you this story, despite the fact that I find it fantastical, because I want you to know I'm talking to you because of the *story* and not because of your . . . remarkable endowments and pretty face. Although those certainly help."

"Okay, tell me the story," Barbara said, dryly. "And avoiding reference to my endowments will help your case."

"Well then, once upon a time, this must have been, oh, yesterday?" Kelly said, looking up at the sky and nodding. "Yeah, yesterday. Once upon a time I went to visit a medium, bordering on small. Now, before you get hooked up on the 'police using a psychic' crap, let me explain that this medium, Madame Charlotte, is very good. But not, in my opinion, because she taps into mystic understanding that mortal ken should not wot of, no, but because she's been tapped into the street for literally decades. She knows everyone, understands people and can make some pretty astute guesses. You with me so far?"

"Oh, yes," Barb said. "You can even use words of more than one syllable."

"Beauty *and* brains, how wonderful. Anyway, I went to visit Madame Charlotte to try to figure out where my old friend Carlane had run off to. Carlane is a pimp, a rather nasty one but there's no reason to suspect he's become a serial killer. However, I'm starting to get a real desire to speak to Mr. Lancereau, because people are hiding him."

"What do you mean?" Barbara asked, wrinkling her brow.

"When you ask people about someone, and you're working on a public case like the Ripper, they tend to be either very helpful or very uncommunicative," Kelly said, trying to explain something it had taken him years to figure out. "If they're being helpful but don't know the person, they say things like 'have you checked the phone book?' And they're helpful in random ways. Some of them are more common: 'I don't know him but I'll call my sister she knows everybody' and the phone book question. They don't all say: 'well, there's some Lancereaus up Nitotar way but that's out in the swamps and you'll need a boat.'"

"That's what the deputy said," Barb pointed out.

"That's *three* times I've gotten that identical response," Kelly replied, holding up three fingers. "Which means that three out of three people in this town have been *instructed* on what to say in the event of questions. And that makes me *very* interested in Mr. Lancereau."

"I didn't go to New Orleans because of the Ripper killings," Barbara said, her face working. "Are you telling me that he might be *here*?"

Kelly paused and looked around the town, frowning.

"There are at least six people involved in the killings . . ." he said, cautiously.

"How do you know that?"

"Semen traces," Kelly responded, coldly.

"Thanks so much for the blunt answer," Barb replied, wincing. "Go on."

"Carlane Lancereau is not one of the rapists," Kelly continued. "But I'm beginning to suspect he knows who they are."

"And the chief deputy is . . . what? Hindering your investigation?" Barbara asked.

"Certainly not giving full support," Kelly replied. "I'm going to be fascinated if he turns up with Carlane in an hour."

"Why?" Barb asked. "Then you take him back to New Orleans?"

"Perhaps," Kelly said, frowning. "But I don't actually have anything to hold him on. All I can do is ask questions. If he gives me the runaround, there's not much I can do."

"So . . . why did you tell me about the medium?" Barbara asked.

"Ah, Madame Charlotte," Kelly said, regaining the thread. "Madame Charlotte told me that Carlane had come down here, back to his swamp. But she *also* told me that that Carlane was playing with powerful ju-ju. More powerful than she was willing to play with. And that I was in grave danger, which is no surprise since we're talking about at least six people who are willing to involve themselves in rape and murder. Last, but not least and most important to you personally, she told me that I should look for help from the sign of the princess," he finished, looking at her chest again.

Barb quirked an unnoticed eyebrow and lifted her shirt outward.

"Bingo," Kelly said, grimacing. "I wasn't seriously looking for the sign of the princess, but lo and behold, there it was. Talking with a rather unhelpful deputy shortly after the death of the local sheriff." He looked back up and stared in her eyes. "So, Mrs. Everette, what do *you* know about Carlane Lancereau?"

"Oh, come *on*," Barbara snapped. "I'm on vacation and my car broke down. It's in the shop; want to go look at it? All I want to do is get the heck *out* of this place!"

"But that doesn't explain why Madame Charlotte would tell me to look for the sign of the princess," he said, gesturing at her chest. "I'm trying to figure out why she told me that, well, a *soccer mom* was my only hope of survival."

"Lots of girls wear shirts that say princess," Barb pointed out with a shrug. "Maybe I'm not the right sign of the princess."

"There's that," Kelly replied. "But I was wondering . . . would you care to assist me in my investigations?"

"Can I at least leave my bag in your car?" she said, shrugging with her left shoulder to indicate her clothes bag.

"Of course," Kelly said. "Want me to carry it?"

"I can carry it as far as your car," Barbara said, smiling.

Chapter Five

When he popped the trunk on the unmarked police car, Barb let out a whistle and bent down into the trunk. Although he tried not to notice, Kelly was forced to admit that all her assets were not up front.

"What the heck are you doing carrying around an AR-10?" she asked, dropping her bag into the back. "Is it the carbine or the full auto version? Never mind. It's the full auto, I can see the markings on the reverse. And a pump twelve gauge?"

"Deer hunting," Kelly said, shrugging as she straightened back up.

The AR-10 was a .308 version of the venerable M-16 rifle. It was actually designed to mimic the M-16A2 but used a much heavier round. The M-16 used a high-velocity 5.56 millimeter bullet whereas the AR-10 fired a high-velocity 7.62 millimeter bullet. An M-16 round tended to wound a man rather than kill him. An AR-10 round tended to put him in the morgue.

"Yeah, right," Barbara scoffed. "You know those things tend to jam about every tenth round?"

"I noticed," Kelly admitted.

"Not enough gas blowback," Barb said, shrugging. "And the

tubes get fouled. It gets really bad over a hundred rounds. There's a type of powder that cuts down on it but not many .308 rounds are made with it. They need a lighter buffer spring, too."

"You do say?" Kelly said. "If I have to fire more than fifty rounds, I'm in the wrong fire-fight. I'm a detective, not a tac-team member. And I don't think even *they* fire more than fifty rounds in *any* situation. Where did you learn about AR-10s?"

"All that is gold does not glitter," she said, grinning. Then she tossed him her purse.

Kelly caught it, noticing the additional weight immediately, and frowned.

"That is highly illegal in the state of Louisiana," he said, tossing the bag back. "Don't get caught with it by, say, a local cop. Or you might end up in the local slammer and I really don't think that would be a good idea."

"I've got a concealed carry permit for Mississippi," Barbara said, frowning. "Louisiana has a reciprocal agreement, so I'm covered. But, while I'm not into resisting arrest, I think I would if it meant dealing with local justice. The term 'prison movie' comes to mind. I . . . did not like that deputy."

"As a professional police officer, I do of course feel that resisting arrest would be the wrong thing to do," Kelly said. "As a thinking being, however, I suggest that if it comes to it you use every bit of force, short of lethal, necessary to avoid being arrested by Deputy Mondaine. The other question that comes to mind is, can you use that thing? Because if you can't, you shouldn't be packing, Mrs. Everette."

"I've probably put ten times as many rounds through it as you have your service pistol," Barb said, shrugging. "Including on tactical ranges. Not that I've had much chance lately. But what I aim at, I hit. And it's a court of last resort, anyway. I have . . . other skills. Which I will use on you if you make any 'packed and stacked' cracks."

"What . . . are you, Barbara Everette?" Kelly said, carefully.

"I'm just what you called me," Barb said with a frown. "A soccer mom. I had to have *one* da . . . danged weekend where I wasn't taking care of somebody else. Just one. And I ended up . . . here," she said, waving her hands around. "In . . . this! Fortunately I had a father who thought his girls should be able to defend themselves."

"Okay," Kelly said, nodding. "I'll play it as it lays, then. I don't suppose your cell phone works?"

"Nope," she said. "No towers around here. I asked."

"In that case, we need to find a pay phone."

"Down by the Piggly Wiggly."

At the Piggly Wiggly he bought a phone card and went out to the pay phone to call in. While he was doing that she went to the drugstore next door and bought her own phone card, a small black backpack, a six-pack of bottled water, some cold Pepsi in twenty-ounce bottles, a bag of ice and some energy bars. If worse came to worst she could survive on those for the weekend. As she was walking back to the front she stopped by the drugs section and picked up some Tylenol and Claritin-D.

When she'd paid for her items she passed Kelly, still talking on the phone, and went in the Piggly Wiggly to use their bathroom. It was only marginally dirty as such places went. She emptied half the ice in the sink and put the half-filled bag in the backpack, then stuffed the drinks in the ice. Once that was done she put the energy bars and drugs in the side pockets and carefully disposed of her trash in the overflowing trashcan.

When she came back out, Kelly was finally off the phone and she called home. Still no answer so she left an updated message and called Mark's cell phone. No answer there, either. He'd probably turned it off.

What she wanted to do was ask him to come down and pick her up. A creepy town was bad enough. A creepy town with a tough cop who was looking to *her* for a chance for survival was worse. She was trained to stay alive and get *out* of danger situations. The first position in every self-defense class is the running position. And everything in her was telling her to *run*.

But Mark was going to be in no condition to come pick her up and even if he was the drive would be hell on both of them and she'd be paying back for years.

No, she was just going to have to wait for the car to get

done or figure out an alternate plan. She could call Daddy and wail. In which case he'd be on a plane for New Orleans in no more than an hour and here in about . . . ten. The thought was immensely reassuring but she couldn't do *that* any more than she could call Mark. She was a big girl and she was the one who had just up and left for the weekend. It was up to her to get out of the town.

Preferably alive. If she *knew* she was in danger she'd pick up the phone. Then again, if Detective Lockhart was sure she was in danger, he'd carry her out of the town in an instant.

"You talk to your boss?" she asked when she was done with the phone.

"Yeah, Lieutenant Chimot," Kelly said, frowning. "I told him what seemed to be going on and he agreed it was suspicious. I also told him I was going stay on overnight and come back in the morning. I don't think the good deputy is going to show."

"Neither do I," Barbara said, grimacing. "What are you going to do now?"

"Ask around," Kelly said. "See if I can find anybody who *doesn't* give me the run around."

"Lieutenant Chimot, my name is Augustus Germaine."

Chimot had received a call from the director of the FBI explaining that one of their consultants was coming over to see him and that he should listen to what he said and believe it. "*No matter how strange it seems,* believe *it*."

The FBI and local police had a so-so relationship. In certain cases, and kidnappings were one of them, the FBI had override authority. That meant that some snot-nosed punk straight out of the academy could order around anyone on the case, up to and including the chief of police. Generally they were polite about it but enough had been right pains in the ass that local police rarely looked forward to the FBI poking its nose in. They had excellent support and the manpower was often useful, but truth be told most of the cases the FBI ended up "supervising" were solved by some local detective who actually knew the area and the players involved.

The FBI hadn't taken over the Ripper case, but Chimot knew it was close. He suspected that the "consultant" was going to tell him that. Just what he needed to hear from some closet academic.

Germaine, though, was something different.

"Mr. Germaine," Chimot said, standing up and offering a hand. "It's a pleasure to meet you."

"I doubt that," Germaine said, bluntly, giving the hand a quick but firm shake. "Your department has had more than a few run-ins with the FBI and the Justice Department and there's not much love in either direction. But that's not important in this case, what is important are the Special Circumstances."

"What . . . circumstances?" Chimot asked, sitting down. He cocked his head in interest at the tone; the capital letters had been noticeable.

"There are certain investigations that take on odd hues," Germaine replied, taking his own seat. "And I'm going to explain to you what is really going on in this one. At the end of the conversation, you'll realize that you can't pass it on to anyone because they would assume you'd cracked under pressure. And if you decide to chance it, don't. Because we don't let this information get out. Period. Understand me?"

Chimot looked at those piercing black eyes and nodded, a cold chill running down his back.

"That's a little blunt," Chimot said. "And aren't people usually *asked* if they want to know stuff like this?"

"No," Germaine replied. "Because if they *have* to know, they're told. And they generally keep their mouths shut for reasons that will become obvious. Is that clear enough to start?"

"Yes," Chimot said.

"You're a smoker, Lieutenant," Germaine said, quirking one cheek in a grin. "Please, light up. Cigarette smoke does not offend me."

"This is a no-smoking building," Chimot said.

"You have a smokeless ashtray in your bottom left-hand drawer," Germaine replied. "And you usually open the window to make it less obvious. Please feel free to light up. But you probably want to save a hit from the bottle of Jim Beam next to the ashtray until after the conversation."

Chimot glared at him but fished out the ashtray and lit a Marlboro.

"Go," he said when the cigarette was lit.

"The FBI gets involved in most serial killing investigations since they almost always involve kidnappings. And ones that do not rarely matter to them, but they do to *us*. Most serial killers are simply evil humans that enjoy the power rush involved in the killing and control of their victims. But a few do it due to Special Circumstances. Special Circumstances is the FBI's cautious euphemism for the supernatural. Shall I continue?"

"Go ahead," Chimot said. "If you were nuts, the director wouldn't have called me."

"I am the European and American head of a group that supports the investigation of Special Circumstances. We have an arrangement to share information and assist in investigations with the FBI. There is a similar arrangement with Interpol, Scotland Yard, what have you. We also have worked with local authorities from time to time. In this case, we were uninterested until the FBI crime lab identified one of the semen samples as construct DNA. That is, the DNA of a supernatural being that had manifested on earth. The scale, which was not lost by the way, we have it, is from the avatar of an entity named Almadu. Are you familiar with the name?"

"No," Chimot said, his head reeling from more than nicotine. "You're serious."

"Very," Germaine said. "Almadu is a god who was first identified by the Babylonians, one of the eleven monsters summoned by the dragon goddess Tiamat in her battle with Marduk. There are indications that he was listed as a daevas in the Zoroastrian religious tracts that were destroyed by Alexander in Persepolis. Possibly associated with Lilith who may, in fact, be Tiamat/Kali. A water god, usually depicted as looking like a cross between a fish and a dragon. He requires human sacrifice and often engages in sex with the sacrifices. Occasionally he will reproduce with a human female and create an amphibian cross species. They don't look very human but can pass for it in a bad light. The last manifestation of Almadu was in the 1920s in Massachusetts and involved a colony of such crosses. It was, we believed, wiped out and Almadu was dispelled. He apparently has been brought back from the nether realms. It is *he* who has been gutting your victims."

"You're telling me there's some fish god going around screwing hookers and then murdering them?" Chimot asked, shaking his head. "You're right, I can't tell anybody this. They'll think I'm nuts. I'm not too sure about you."

"Lieutenant, in the . . . very long time that I have been in this organization, I have seen things that would drive you mad," Germaine replied, calmly. "Almadu isn't even close to the worst. Almadu is, however, very bad. A full physical manifestation requires enormous power, more than I'd have thought he could gather. Either he has a large group of worshipers, numbering at least in the tens of thousands, or there have been far more murders, sacrifices, than you suspect. I've run a match on the criminal database and I think that some *sixty* street ladies have disappeared in one place or another in the Louisiana and Mississippi area. It's hard to tell, obviously—people just disappear from the street, change their names, what have you—but that would explain the full manifestation far better than five. However, with the full manifestation, he can begin using powers that he would not have without it. And I would anticipate his numbers of worshippers would grow. I suspect that he's soon going to leave these parts for somewhere he can gather sacrifices without so much oversight. And we dearly want to prevent that, for obvious reasons."

"So why are you telling me this?" Chimot asked.

"Two reasons. The first is that if you close on his place of worship, you are liable to encounter resistance beyond what you're used to dealing with. Think of it as attacking a group of ardent terrorists, for that is in many ways what they are. And there are no police tac teams on earth that are prepared to handle Almadu. Very few earthly weapons will harm him. He is vulnerable to fire and electricity, but shooting him will only make him angry. He also can charm people, make them believe he is a good god, control their actions and so forth. He prefers sacrifices that die in terror, but he is not averse to charming attackers and then eating them, stealing their souls to do his service in the Dark Realms."

"That's what he's been doing to the victims?" Chimot said, swallowing.

"Yes," Germaine answered. "The other problem is that anyone who gets close to him is in danger. I don't have *any* agents available who are trained and capable of assisting right now. To defend oneself against the power that Almadu can use requires ardent belief in *another* god. A Catholic priest or a Protestant minister or a Wiccan high priest or priestess who really *believed* might be sheltered from his power, might be able to channel a shield against it. Might. One of my agents *would* be, if I had an agent of the caliber to take him on. But your average Joe Cop would be as undefended as if he was in a firefight with no vest. It's important that you understand that. Do you?"

"I hear what you're saying," Chimot admitted. "But I'm having a hard time believing it."

"That, of course, is the problem," Germaine said, smiling sadly. "It requires that the agent not only believe, fundamentally, in evil as a separate power but that the agent believe, again fundamentally, that there is an equivalent power of good and that it can defeat evil. Without that belief, an agent, or the noted Joe Cop, is unshielded."

"Crap," Chimot said, shaking his head. "We've got a problem."

"Which is?" Germaine asked.

"We have a possible lead in the case," the lieutenant said, swallowing and putting out his cigarette. "One of the people that was talking with one of the victims has disappeared. And, come to think of it, one of our informants mentioned that he was dabbling in 'old time religion.' We have reason to suspect he went back to his hometown, which is right down in the bayou . . ." He paused and looked at Germaine, raising an eyebrow.

"With access to water and eventually the oceans," Germaine

said, nodding. "Anywhere in Louisiana practically fits that description, but it's logical that it may be the center. Go on."

"Anyway, Detective Lockhart went down there to see if he could find the suspect, Carlane, and he says the people there are giving him the runaround."

Germaine sighed and looked at the ceiling, frowning.

"The reality is that when there is a full manifestation, people tend to believe, strongly," the agent said after a moment's thought. "What may start with a few followers spreads. If it doesn't spread naturally, people will be brought into Almadu's presence and he will . . . assist them in their belief and worship of his power. If the center is this place that your suspect returned to . . . What is that, by the way?"

"Thibideau," Chimot said. "A little speck down in the southwest bayou."

"Yes, a small town," Germaine said, nodding. "Everyone knows everyone else. Very little movement in, some out. And manifestations can manipulate things. Minds. Actions. They can give their earthly followers earthly support, economic and social. A person removed. A business deal completed on very favorable terms. Even treasures lost in the deeps of the sea. It is likely that you're facing a whole town of believers. Those who were strong, who resisted his power, would have been removed. Some of them to feed his power, others through 'accidents' or 'natural causes' if they were too high profile to disappear."

"The sheriff down there died of a heart attack about a month ago," Chimot said.

"Likely he was resistant to the power," Germaine replied. "Which means that Almadu is still weak. Or the sheriff unusually strong. I wish, how I wish, I had just *one* fifth level agent to assign to this case."

"What about you?" Chimot asked.

"This is not the only case that is currently occupying my attention," Germaine said, dryly. "I did mention covering both the U.S. and Europe, yes? You have no idea what some of the Muslims who think they're fundamentalists are summoning. And you don't want to know. Then there's the fact that I'm not a believer."

"What?" Chimot asked, suddenly realizing that he'd bought into the story and wondering if *he* was insane.

"It is not necessary to be a believer to run things," Germaine said, quirking one cheek again. "In fact, it can be a bit of a problem. You see, all the members of the organization are not believers in the *same* god. Few are Christians, for example, many are pagans, a few are Hindu, although they count as pagan as well. Being able to say, honestly, I am not a believer in *any* credo helps when the, inevitable, quarrels break out. And my . . . cynicism is as deeply ingrained as the belief of my agents. But I do my job, none better or so I'm told. However, if *I* were to engage Almadu I would probably succumb to his glamour. Perhaps not, I have my own methods of defense. But I would not choose to challenge him. And then there's the other problem of assigning an agent."

"Which is?" Chimot asked. "As if all those aren't enough?"

"Such an agent, such a strong believer, has . . . a fine taste to the soul is perhaps the best way I can put it," Germaine replied. "They, in and of themselves, are targets for the Dark Powers. They are . . . tasty, strong, marinated in belief. And if Almadu *does* rip such a victim's soul from body, eat the victim's guts, that is, they will serve him in the Dark Realm whether they care to or not."

Barb quickly discovered that "street-work" was hot, miserable and frustrating. They had walked around the town for two hours, talking to everyone who would stop at the sight of Kelly's badge. She had gone through two bottles of water and a Pepsi, and given three more bottles of water to the detective. And they had found not one person who admitted to any knowledge of Carlane Lancereau. And in almost every case they had been told that the Lancereaus "lived up Nitotar way" and "back in the bayou, you'll need a boat." A few added that the Lancereaus probably wouldn't be helpful anyway.

Late in the day they ran upon the single exception, being ejected from the bait shop.

"All I want is a taste!" the old man shouted at the closed door. He was unkempt and looked as if he'd recently been sleeping in the bayou, his clothes covered in mud and vegetation. He was short and might once have been strong and broad but age and, presumably, alcohol had left him thin and wasted looking. He also had a slightly different cast to his features, more traditionally Cajun than the locals.

As Kelly approached him the man spun around in fear and then relaxed when he saw the two newcomers.

"Hello," Kelly said, extending his badge. "My name is Detective Kelly Lockhart from the New Orleans Police Department. I'd like to ask you a few questions."

"No," the man said, shuffling off. "I don't have answers. You go away. Get out of town while you still can."

"Excuse me," Kelly said, hurrying to catch up. "What do you mean, while we still can?"

"Just *go*," the man said, fiercely. "I ain't talkin' to you. Ain't nobody gonna say they seen me talkin' to you. Get out of here. Go!"

"Would a drink help?" Kelly asked.

The man paused but didn't turn around. Then he shrugged.

"Down the end of town there's an old boathouse," the man said, quietly. "You bring me a bottle. Hard stuff. I gotta have my bottle so the voices won't get me, too. Don't let nobody see you come. Right before dark. You need to be back in your room by dark or you'll never leave."

Then he hurried off.

"I'd dearly like to talk to him," Kelly said, musingly, as he turned away from the figure. "But the only place to get a bottle is in the bar, and they'd know why."

"I've got a bottle," Barbara said. "In my bag."

"What's a nice Christian lady like you doing with a bottle of whiskey in her bag?" Kelly said, amused.

"I'm Episcopalian," Barb replied, lightly. "We don't have prohibitions against drinking. And it's a habit I picked up from my mother. I haven't drunk any of it, but it's sitting there in case I need it. Jim Beam."

"What would you need it for?" Kelly asked as they walked back towards the courthouse.

"I dunno? Brushing my teeth?"

"With whiskey?" Kelly said, aghast.

"Better than water in some of the places I've been," Barbara said, shrugging. "Don't mix it with toothpaste, though, that's really horrible. Mixed with water it kills almost anything that can ail you, though. And it tastes better than iodine."

"What an . . . interesting point," Kelly said. "Where'd you learn that?"

"Borneo," Barb replied.

"Borneo?" Kelly said. "I thought you were from Mississippi?"

"My *husband* is from Mississippi," Barbara said, smiling slightly. "I'm not from anywhere. My father was an Air Force officer, a bomber pilot. When they demobbed—"

"Demobbed?" Kelly asked.

"Demobilized, sorry. When they demobilized most of the B-52 fleet he was given the choice of being riffed, sort of like laid off . . ."

"Riffing I know. . . ."

"Or retraining. He took retraining and managed to get a foreign area officer slot. So for the first ten years of his career we wandered around from airbase to airbase and for the last fourteen years, which are the ones I remember the best, we moved around east Asia from embassy to embassy. Hong Kong, before the hand-over, Japan, Malaysia and Borneo to be specific. And travel to other countries while we were there."

"And that's where you learned to brush your teeth with Jim Beam?" Kelly asked.

"My mom learned it from some colonel's wife when she was a JO . . . a junior officer's wife. The colonel's wife had picked it up from some civilian lady she'd known way back in Iran before the fall of the Shah. And that's why I've got a bottle of Jim Beam in my bag. It's just a pint flask, but it should do. So, what are you going to do with it?"

"I'm thinking that I'd *like* to talk to him but what I really should do is go back to New Orleans," Kelly mused. "If he's right, and there's going to be a problem tonight, getting out of town is the right thing to do."

"You are *not* leaving me here," Barb said.

"No, of course not," Kelly replied.

"And that ignores the question of if your car is going to work or not," Barbara said, suddenly feeling a chill. "We haven't been in sight of it most of the day."

"You are just the most *optimistic* person," Kelly said. "Let's go check the car and then get your bottle."

"You're going to meet with him, then?" Barb asked.

"Yeah. I'm tired of working in the dark."

Chapter Six

"The cop was talking to Chauvet," Deputy Mondaine said.

The meeting was in the back of the old church where the sacristy had once been. The room had been fixed up to minimal standards and now served as the office of the cult. On the back wall, by the window, was a black flag with a shape like a weird green dragon. In one corner was a sculpture of the same creature, twisted and horribly deformed. Carlane Lancereau was standing behind the desk, looking out over the bayou with his hands folded behind his back.

"I told you we should have had him killed," Mondaine said when there was no response. "Sacrifice him to the Master."

"Such a soul would be of little use, worn and devoured as it is by time and life," Carlane said. "And what is he going to say? That devils live in the swamps? That the whole town has succumbed to evil? That there are voices in his head? That should go over well. And after tonight, it won't matter. The master will have fed and fed well. After tonight he shall be fully manifest upon the Earth. And then, we move. Be prepared."

"I will, Your Unholiness," Mondaine said, bowing.

"But bring Officer Lockhart and the woman to me," Carlane

said, turning to face the deputy, his eyes glowing a sickly green. "Lockhart's soul is steeped in the evils of the street and worth little. But the woman glows with power. She will be fine food for the Master."

"Wait," Lockhart said as they approached the car. It was parked by the courthouse in one of the reserved parking spaces. He pulled his keys out and thumbed a control. There was no apparent response.

"Shit," he muttered, thumbing the control again.

"What's supposed to be happening?" Barbara said, lifting an eyebrow.

"It's supposed to start," Lockhart replied. "We had a rash of attacks on police during the drug wars. Now all the unmarked cars can be started remotely since starting was one way that was used to bomb them. It's not starting."

"Maybe the battery is out on your little controller thingy," Barb said, quirking one cheek in a slight grin.

"Maybe," Lockhart said. "Stay here."

He walked over to the car and opened the door with the key, then attempted to start it.

"And, then again, maybe your car has broken down," Barbara said, walking over.

"This is really annoying," Lockhart replied. He slid out of the car and underneath, soiling his clothes on the dirty parking lot. After a certain amount of fumbling from under the car he slid back out.

"The ignition wiring harness has been cut," he said, frowning. "And a section is missing. Since it goes to the computer as well as the solenoid, just hooking up another wire won't work."

"No car," Barb said, frowning slightly

"No car," Lockhart agreed, nodding. "Which is stupid since I can just call New Orleans PD and have someone come out and pick me up. *Us* up."

"So what now?" Barbara asked.

"You get your bag," Lockhart said, going around to the back of the car. "We'll go to the hotel and get a couple of rooms.

Then I'll get the bottle and head down to the Piggly Wiggly and give Lieutenant Chimot a call. You stay in the hotel."

"Nuh, uh," Barb said. "Horror movie time. What you just said is 'let's split up.'"

"Good point," Lockhart said, grinning. "Okay, plan b. We both go to the phone. I call the PD. Then we get your bag, go back to the hotel and do the transfer. I'm *not* taking you with me to talk to the drunk. You stay at the hotel."

"Let's go," Barb said, waving in the direction of the store. "But let's get my bag first."

She hoisted the backpack on her shoulder and followed the detective the two blocks to the store.

She watched his back as he pulled out his phone card and punched the number.

"What?" Lockhart said after a moment.

"What what?" Barbara asked.

"Listen," Lockhart said, lifting the receiver.

"The number you have called is no longer in service, please check the number and dial again. Two-three-two. The number you have called is no longer . . ."

"What number did you dial?" Barb asked.

"The *eight hundred* number," Kelly snapped, slamming the phone down and digging in his pocket for change.

"Don't mind me, I'm just a scared old lady," Barbara said. "But let me point out that it's getting dark."

"I know," Kelly said, thumbing quarters in the phone. He dialed a number rapidly and then cursed. "Son of a *bitch*!"

Barbara could hear the same recording.

"Let me try," she said. "Got any more change?"

Her home number wouldn't work and neither would her father's number in Denver. Neither did the operator pick up when she dialed zero.

"Okay," Kelly said, shaking his head. "Somehow *they*, whoever they are, are fucking with the phone."

"Watch your language," Barbara snapped automatically. "Okay, I would say we are officially in Indian Country and cut off from reinforcements, wouldn't you?"

"Yes," Kelly said, trying not to smile.

"In that case, our job is to survive and either wait for supports or get out if we can," Barb said, nodding to herself. "The hotel isn't great, but it's the best we're going to get. We go there, hunker down, and hope like hell when you don't check in the lieutenant sends somebody out for you. Will he?"

"Probably," Lockhart said. "I told him enough to have him worried. But I want to talk to the old man. Stick with plan b. You go get a room, I'll pick up your bottle. I'll get a room also, but we'll hunker down in yours."

"I assume I can trust you to be gentlemanly," Barbara said, smiling, as they started to walk back to the hotel.

"Of course!" Kelly said. "I am nothing if not a gentleman."

When Barbara got back to the hotel she considered her options. The fact was that she was scared. More scared than when she'd been attacked in college. Nearly as scared as when Allison had been struck by a car. She had come to the conclusion that something was very wrong in Thibideau, Louisiana, and that the wrongness was probably going to reach out for her. All day long she'd felt a strange uneasiness like being just a little sick. She knew she wasn't; it was something else. Something weird.

"Dear Lord," she said, sinking to her knees and clasping her hands, "I ask you to hear my prayer. I believe I am in the midst of evil and I ask only that your divine power comfort me in my trial. I will act on my own behalf if evil men come for me but, Lord, I sense a greater power of evil at work. Shelter me from that, I ask in Jesus' name, and I'll take care of the rest. For though I walk through the valley, thy rod and thy staff they comfort me. Watch over me as the shepherd watches his sheep and I will do my Christian best to stay alive. Amen."

She felt comforted after that but she'd made a promise to the Lord and it was time to see what she could do to ensure she kept the promise.

"First things first," she muttered, unzipping her boots. "The f . . . the boots have *got* to go." If she had to run, better that it be in running shoes. If she fell and twisted her ankle, she'd never live it down. Hell, she probably wouldn't *live* much longer.

The jeans . . . were too tight. She had a looser pair. They were darker as well. The tennis shoes were white, but mud would fix that if she had to. Dark blouse, the dark leather jacket. Among other things it would mildly deflect a blow from a knife. If she had to sneak, her face and hair would give her away. She pulled out a black silk blouse and, wincing, began slitting the seams. A few quick stitches with her sewing kit and she had a perfectly adequate hood. She cut eyeholes with the locking-blade knife from her purse, finishing with the dying rays of the sun.

She dumped the drinks out of the backpack, dumping out the remnant water in the bottom on the floor, and slid her purse into it. She pulled out her holster and put that on, slipping in the spare magazines and then, after a moment's thought, racked a round into the chamber of the H&K and used the decock lever to drop the hammer safely. She put the pillows on the bed under the covers, making a lump. What the heck, it worked in movies. Then she grabbed her makeup case and sat down cross-legged in the corner. She had one shade of very deep blue eye shadow that would probably work for camouflage. She rubbed some around her eyes and then all over her hands. It was slightly shiny, but better than skin.

She rummaged through her bag looking for useful items. Makeup . . . all the use it was going to be. Nail polish . . . nothing came to mind. Lighter. That went in a pocket. Locking knife, that clipped to her right pocket. Nail polish remover. Potentially useful but where to carry it? She slid it in the backpack and added the remaining bottles of water, wishing she'd picked more up at the store. Sodas as well. Hair-spray . . . oh, yeah. Take.

She put everything useful in the backpack and then dumped the bag off to the side, wishing she had a roll of duct tape. No particular reason, but duct tape had a thousand and one uses. One of them came to mind and she crept quietly over to the dumped out empty water bottles and collected them. If she *found* a roll of duct tape . . .

She realized what she was contemplating and froze.

"First degree murder," she muttered, frowning as she sat back down in a lotus position. Well, if it came to premeditated murder or dying, she was just going to do the deed.

Yes, "thou shalt not kill" correctly translated as "thou shalt not murder." But that was what she was contemplating. If she had to *fight* her way out of town, she wasn't going to do it like a cowboy in the westerns. She was going to do it the way daddy taught her: Survival, Evasion, Resistance and Escape. Never come at a frontal position. Use concealment as long as possible. Never give an enemy an even break.

Murder them before they knew you were there.

Murder. The bottles could be used as field expedient silencers. Using a silencer was, de facto and de jure, proof of prior intent. First degree murder.

She was getting angry, too. The deep, cold-hot anger that she worked every day to control but this came with a righteous strain that somehow made it stronger and more potent. She could feel the demon straining at its leash and she knew that soon it would be let loose. Murder, she knew, wasn't the true stain on the soul, it was the tarnish that came with the feelings surrounding it, the anger and the sick feeling of power to give or take life. That was the center of the sin against oneself, against God.

But there were times, and this seemed like one of them, when letting the demon out of the jar was acceptable and appropriate. She wondered how hard it would be to get the lid back on.

She was contemplating that moral and legal dilemma when she suddenly realized it was full dark.

And Kelly hadn't returned.

Kelly stepped to the rotten door on the side of the boathouse, hand on his service Glock, and ducked inside, looking around.

The room was gloomy and covered in spider webs, half the roof gone. The old man was in a corner, shaking and moaning. But he was the only one there.

Kelly walked across the concrete floor, searching the shadows for threats and then shook the man on the shoulder at which he screamed.

"Shut up!" Kelly said, quietly.

"Oh, God," the man said, rolling over and grasping at the detective. "Please tell me you brung a bottle! Please! I gotta have a taste!"

"Here," Kelly said, drawing the flask out of his waistband and then holding onto it as the alcoholic clawed at it. "Just a taste," he said, opening it and letting the old man have a swallow.

"God, that's good," the man said, trying to hold on as the detective wrestled it away. "Please, let me keep it! I need it to make the voices go away!"

"Not until you tell me what is going on," Kelly said, squatting down. He let the man have another drink then pulled the bottle back and capped it. "What's your name?"

"Claude Chauvet," the man said, hugging his arms to his body. "I'm from up Houma way. Used to do construction, fishing, whatever I could do for money. Had a wife and kids once, then the bottle started to get to me. Been wandering for a while. Fetched up here about a year ago. Old sheriff dropped me in the tank til I was dried out. Fed me up, got me a job on one of the boats. Couldn't keep me off the sauce but I worked, you know? Wasn't a great place, but it was as good as any to die and I knew I was gonna go soon. Too much booze, liver's going."

"So what's this with voices?" Kelly asked. "And do you know where Carlane Lancereau is?"

"Sure," the old man grunted in laughter. "But gimme another taste. I need some help to tell it."

Kelly let him have another swig and took the bottle back.

"Tell," Kelly said.

"'Bout six months ago, things started happening. People got stranger than they'd been, really angry sometimes. Were a couple of murders, which hadn't happened in a while. People started to talk about strange lights over by the old church and that fella Carlane started turning up real regular. Drove a fancy car, had fancy clothes. Sheriff couldn't stand him, said all the Lancereaus were plumb bad. Then some kids went missing. Some people thought they were runaways, sheriff thought different. Got really angry with Deputy Mondaine about it. Couldn't find nothing, kids had disappeared like they never was. Parents moved away, said they'd been getting threats about making a stink. Then the voices started . . ." He trailed off and looked longingly at the bottle and Kelly let him have another taste.

"Ain't really voices," the old man said in a strained voice. "More like visions." He looked up at the cop sharply and coldly. "Everybody's got demons, mister cop. You know that. Things they think about that ain't exactly . . . right. You do, too."

"Everybody," Lockhart agreed.

"Well, imagine you're pulling in a basket of crawfish and your boss is yelling at you to hurry it up and you can *see* yourself cutting the bastard's throat. Just like it's real. Feel the blood running down your hands, just like you'd already done it. Feel a rush, like a drug, at killing him. Then all of a sudden you're back pulling in line, like nothing happened."

"I'd say you were having DTs," the cop replied.

"Ain't like them," the drunk said, shaking his head. "Sometimes you see things can't be real. Big shapes you just know if they see you nothing's gonna save you. See yourself doing . . . bad things. Got to where it was like it was all the time. But when I was drunk . . ."

"The visions went away," Kelly said.

"Yeah," Claude said, shaking. "That's why I got to have a bottle. Yeah, I'm a drunk, but I need the bottle so the voices will go away. Sometimes they're voices, speaking a weird language, calling me. Then the old sheriff died. Strong as an ox he was. A right bastard if you crossed him but he was a *good* man and *healthy*. And he just up and died. After that it got bad. Started hearing . . . screams from the church of a night. Bad screams. And chanting, weird chanting, like humans trying to say the words in my head, but we can't say those words right."

"Okay," Kelly said, standing up. "Here's your bottle—"

"He won't get a chance to drink it," Deputy Mondaine said from across the room.

Kelly turned around slowly and lifted his hands at the sight of the twelve gauge pointed at his midsection. And Mondaine wasn't alone. Kelly recognized the owner of the bait and tackle store and one of the clerks from the Piggly Wiggly. At least five men, all with guns pointed at him.

"You can die right now," Mondaine said. "Or you can pull your gun out real slowly and drop it on the floor."

Kelly slowly pulled the automatic out with two fingers and dropped it on the ground, then turned around with his hands over his head.

I should have stayed with the Princess, he thought as something crashed into the back of his head. All he saw was white.

Barbara sat in the corner in a lotus position, praying, until she heard the creak of the door downstairs. Then she stood up, quietly, and catwalked to the window. She'd tested the floor and found all the spots that creaked and she carefully avoided them. She also stood back out of the slight light from the window to survey the top of the porch. Sure enough, there were several figures, at least four, clambering up onto the roof via a ladder.

"Lord, I ask that you infuse me with the warrior soul of David this night," she said, quietly. "And forgive me my actions, speech and thoughts. Because, Lord, I am seriously going to kick some unrighteous ass in Your Name, Amen."

That last prayer done she reached down inside, set "Good Barb" off to one side and opened up the jar. It was time for Bad Barb to come home.

All the fear seemed to wash away, leaving something hard and cold and ancient in its place. Her breathing slowed, details seemed to jump out at her, a vase on a shelf, the smell of the bayou, the scuffling of feet outside her door.

She catwalked back over to the shadow in the corner and waited, hand going to the sidearm and then withdrawing. Use that only if necessary.

With a crash a chunk of cinder block came through the window and at the same time someone tried to open the door. There was a thudding sound from there as three men piled through the broken window, one of them yelping as he apparently cut himself on glass. Just as the first man was throwing himself on the pillows on the bed and shouting in surprise, three more came through the door and piled into him.

Funny as the resulting scramble was, Barb was in no mood for entertainment. So she quickly walked across the room and kicked one of the bystanders in the balls from behind. Hard.

All six of them were howling and cursing so loud that they never noticed him go down. She gave him a hard kick in the temple as she went by, nonetheless. Then she got seriously to work.

She slammed a closed fist, a hammerblow, down on the neck of one of the figures at the back of the group, right at the top of the neck where the spine inserts to the skull. Concussion on the first through third vertebra almost always induces instantaneous unconsciousness and it did in this case. It could also cause death if the blow was hard enough and Barb was not pulling her strikes. Mrs. Nice Lady was no longer in residence.

One of the group seemed to sense that something was going on behind him and turned. Barb caught his left wrist with her right hand and twisted it up and back while holding the elbow, dislocating it on the fulcrum of her left hand. He howled like a banshee as she gave the elbow an additional twist, then was cut off in mid howl as her open palm struck him on the temple.

The group was finally aware that the person they were wrestling with on the bed was one of them and was trying to come to terms with being under attack, but she wasn't going to give them much time.

A man was reaching for her from the right and he got a dislocated thumb for thanks then another kick to the balls followed by an elbow in the chin that drove him into unconsciousness. This left Barb balanced to the right and she used it to high kick to the left, catching one of the group in the throat and undoubtedly breaking his hyoid bone. That was a kill for sure and certain if somebody didn't do a tracheotomy. But she didn't let it slow her down.

The last two attackers were the one on the bed, who was getting off as fast as he could, and the guy who had been grappling him. She feinted a kick at the balls at the standing man and then followed the motion forward with an open hand blow to the nose. As the man's hands came up to his shattered nose she punched him in the solar plexus and drove a hand up under his descending chin. Then she wrapped his head in one arm and stepped forward, over and back, rotating his neck through three dimensions and snapping it like a twig.

The last attacker was scrambling for the window but she was in no mood to deal with him later. She stepped forward and kicked him in the small of the back, throwing him into the wall, then punched at a pressure point in the upper back, temporarily immobilizing him with pain. Then she dislocated his shoulder, kneed him in the groin as she twisted him around, broke his instep and drove a hammer blow into his upper neck as he bent over from the blow.

She looked around the room and nodded. There was some groaning but most of the figures weren't so much as twitching. At least two were dead, probably more. The thought suddenly made her queasy so she put it out of her mind, she had *no* time to throw up, and took one more look around.

"Time to leave," she muttered, looking at the dark hallway and then the slight light from the window. "No real choice there," she said, quietly, picking up her backpack and moving to the door as silently as she could. She looked at the broken glass and then leapt up and forward over it, legs stretched like a hurdler, body bent to avoid the upper sill. But while she was still in midair she saw the figure by the ladder rising up, holding a rifle or shotgun in his hands.

She landed carefully and drew her sidearm with a practiced and automatic motion, cocking the lever and firing twice at center of mass. She was rewarded by seeing the target fall off the roof with a quiet grunt of surprise and a small cry. He couldn't know it was she who had come through the window and he'd hesitated so he wouldn't shoot one of his friends. That wouldn't happen every time. Especially now that the relative silence of the night had been ruptured by pistol fire.

She decocked the pistol and holstered it, buckling it in place, then ran to the edge of the roof, jumping down and landing in a roll. She came up on one knee, drew her pistol and scanned for targets all around. The previous target was on the ground, groaning, so she ran to him and looked for the weapon he'd been holding.

"A pistol in a gunfight is only good for getting a shotgun," she muttered, scanning the ground. "A shotgun is only good for getting a long gun."

She found the long gun a few feet from his body and picked it up, examining it and trying not to curse.

It was an AR-10, the identical model that Kelly had in the trunk of his car. What were the odds of that?

She went to the groaning figure and quickly rifled his body, looking for ammunition for the rifle. He was wearing a camouflage blouse that was just about covered in blood, so she wasn't going to be borrowing it. There were two spare magazines, one in each blouse pocket. Those went in the back pockets of her jeans.

She straightened up and pulled back the charging handle of the AR-10, ensuring that there was a round in the chamber, then headed around the back of the hotel as voices and flashlights closed in on the front.

There was an overgrown garden in the back that terminated in the bayou. She moved through it as silently as she could until she was on the far side, away from the voices, and then suddenly bent over, pulled up her mask and was sick as quietly as she could manage.

When she was done throwing up she pulled the backpack off her back and took out one of the bottles of Pepsi. She carefully opened the top to quiet the hiss and let the shaken bottle relieve some pressure, then quickly opened it and used it to swill out her mouth, spitting to get the taste out. Then she capped it, put it back in the bag and listened to the night.

There was shouting from inside the hotel and she could see flashlights up on the second floor. None of the words were coherent but she thought she recognized the voice of Deputy Mondaine.

Big surprise there.

It was definitely time to get out of town. The problem was *wheels.*

She walked quickly to the edge of the swamp and rubbed mud on her running shoes, wiping her hands off on the grass. Then she picked up a twig by feel and slid it into the barrel of the gun to check that it was clear. It was.

That done she hoisted the rifle into a tactical position, butt by her shoulder, barrel down, and headed west, away from the voices. She wasn't sure what was to the west, but it had to be better than this place.

Chapter Seven

Kelly awoke to screaming.

He had the worst headache of his life, like a pounding hammer in his head, and the screams were making it worse. But he couldn't blame Dolores; he'd be screaming too.

He was in the nave of the old church, handcuffed and, from the feel of it, somehow shackled to the floor. The floor of the back of the nave had been removed, revealing an empty hole and, from the sounds of it, water. Apparently at one point the church had been built out over the swamp and for some reason the current group of madmen had opened it up.

There was a low wooden altar in front of him with Carlane standing in front of it, wearing black robes with green symbols on them, his hands raised above his head and chanting in some strange language. On the far side an old-fashioned whipping post had been erected and the hooker from New Orleans was chained to it, hands overhead, and two men wearing robes were working her over, in turn, with a set of cat-o-nine-tails. Each time the hard-swung leather thongs touched her flesh she let out a scream. There was blood running down her back and over her legs.

There were three other men in robes flanking Carlane, their heads bowed, chanting a low, monotonic response, and a group of worshippers, about twenty, down in the main area of the church, were waving their hands overhead and repeating the response.

"*Agathalu Almadu!*" Carlane chanted. "*Asertu Almadu! Thagomod Tthu!*"

"*Asertu Almadu!*" the robed figures chanted with the worshippers repeating.

"Souls for you, Almadu!" Carlane said. "Come to us, Almadu! Bring us to power!"

"*Asertu Almadu!*"

The nave was lit with candles and Kelly shook his head, trying to believe he was imagining the scene. But the screams were real, and the crack of the whips in flesh.

"Feel the pain, Lord Almadu!" Carlane shouted. "Calling to you, Lord Almadu! Pain for you, Lord Almadu! Give to us the *power*!"

"*Asertu, Almadu!*"

"He comes!" Carlane shouted, throwing his arms wide and his head up as if struck by something invisible. "Bring her!" he said in a deeper tone.

Dolores was unshackled quickly, falling to her knees in weakness, but the two men with whips expertly hoisted her up and dragged her to the altar. Then, as the other three joined them, four of them grasped her arms and legs, the fifth pulled up his robes and roughly mounted her. Dolores barely let out a whimper until her body began to rock against the hard wood, rubbing her lacerated back against it and eliciting a weak shriek of pain.

"We prepare her, Lord Almadu!" Carlane shouted. "Come to us, Lord Almadu! *Asertu,* Lord Almadu!"

"*Asertu, Almadu!*"

One by one the men mounted the hooker, changing off to hold one of her wrists or ankles. Kelly, his mind professionally analyzing the scene while simultaneously being horrified by it, noted that that was five of the six rapists. He was fully aware that he'd found the answer to the Ripper case. All he had to do was wait to find out who the actual killer was and who the sixth rapist was. Not that it really mattered, every single person in the building was an accessory in fact and all five of the rapists would be tried as if they were the murderer with all the rest probably getting life sentences. And Carlane, of course, was going to the chair.

Assuming that anybody found out about this and lived. Since he was pretty sure he was a dead man. He really didn't want to be raped, though.

"*Fthagna!*" Carlane shouted. "He comes for his sacrifice! The master comes!"

The fifth acolyte quickly pumped to a finish and got off the moaning woman as the water in the opening began to boil. Kelly lifted himself up to get a better look and then wished that he hadn't.

He told himself that he was not going insane but he really wanted to. The thing rising up out of the water was nightmare. His mind kept trying to put a definitive stamp on it, to compare it to something that it found familiar, but it was too strange. A fish face, with glittering, glowing green eyes that were alive with malicious intelligence. Gill fringe, a line of raised dorsal spines, connected by webbing. Tentacles around the mouth. Huge, humanlike, arms with broad hands and webbed, taloned fingers. It was monstrous, the humanoid torso at least six feet across. More tentacles sprouted from the shoulders and down the back or maybe it was long, moving, hair. None of that described the blasphemous unreality of the monster.

At last it had emerged from the opening, which was just about wide enough for it, and stood on two frog feet, rearing thirty feet in the air. Then it bent down and its member engorged and Kelly suddenly understood who or what the last rapist was.

Dolores let out a shriek of pain and fear as the massive member penetrated her and began thrusting, hard. The beast's bellows overrode her screams, though, drowning them out as it thrust and thrust and finally came with a last bellow.

Kelly cracked his eyes open and then closed them again as the the thing inserted one talon in the woman's belly and ripped upward, crunching through the sternum with a sound like popping plastic wrap. Dolores let out one final shriek of agony and then the thing inserted its hands in her chest and ripped it wide open, reaching in and tearing out her heart to stuff the beating organ in its mouth.

Kelly tried not to retch at the wet smacking sounds as the thing fed on the entrails of the hooker. Finally he couldn't control it and threw up all over the rotting wood in front of his face.

"Lord," Carlane said, as if that had signaled him. "We bring you another soul. Not as good as that one, but a soul nonetheless. Bring him," he added to the acolytes.

Barb had followed the edge of the bayou, skirting behind houses and even into it once around a boathouse, headed west. But there were no vehicles, or signs of life, in that part of town. Finally, she slipped along the side of a house, blessing the apparent absence of dogs in the town, and peeked out into the road.

There were men in the square, about seventy yards away, and others were moving from house to house, obviously searching for her. Some were too close for comfort and they were clearly moving faster than she was. She could try to hide, but she suspected they would find her; there just wasn't much good concealment around.

But she was well away from the men and in a much darker area than they were. And they were using flashlights which would blind them. Even the men in the square were in light, some of them standing by trucks with the lights on. One of the trucks was pointed, vaguely, in her direction. But it had only one good light, the other pointing up and to the side. And the good light was casting a pool of light about half way between her position and theirs. Her best bet was to cross to the other side and head east along the bayou. Try to double back on them. Maybe find one of the cars or trucks with keys in it.

She held the AR-10 down by her right side, away from the searchers, and put her head down, then stepped out away from the house, slowly.

Keep your head down. Move slow. Not stealthily, just slow. Bend over. Change your silhouette. People see what they expect to see. Use shadow, there's one, a tree casting a faint shadow of reflected city light. Don't hurry. Be the night. I'm invisible. You can't see me.

It worked. It took her nearly five minutes to cross the open area but there were no shouts of discovery, no fire from the searchers. Whatever their prior plans, after the chaos she'd left in her room they had to be planning on killing her on sight.

She moved quickly past a house and then down to the bayou, turning left and hefting her weapon. She figured that she'd come back up by the old church where she'd be behind them.

She had made it to the area behind the courthouse when she heard the first scream. There was a faint crack of a whip along with it. And it seemed to be coming from the church.

"Oh, no," she muttered. "You are *not* going to play paladin. Get the hell out. Bring reinforcements."

She moved forward cautiously, skirting the group by the square with extreme care, then moved up away from the bayou as her skin started to prickle. Suddenly she saw herself chained, Mark on top of her thrusting into her like she was being raped. She forced the image out of her mind and gave a brief prayer asking forgiveness. She knew her demons and she'd fought them her whole life. Suddenly there was another flash, the pleasure she'd felt twisting that one bastard's arm completely out of socket. It hadn't been, strictly, necessary. She'd let her anger take charge.

She kept moving, fighting vision after vision. Herself submitting in a way the Bible never envisioned. Killing the stupid bitches like Marcie Taylor's mother that thought they were so holier than thou. Sex with Kelly, him taking her, hard, holding her hands down and using foul language, her own voice joining in.

She couldn't stop the visions, but with each one she said a prayer for forgiveness, asking that the Lord exorcise the demons that worked on her soul and help her fight the evil that lurked in every human. The Lord would forgive her her occasional bad thought, she knew that. Jesus had died for mankind's sins and he had promised forgiveness to his chosen people. She had lived her life as a Christian, a good Christian lady and wife. She had brought her children up as good Christians, and good people, which sometimes wasn't the same thing.

"Lord, give me strength," she prayed, quietly. "Come into me and give me the strength of Samson, the wisdom of Solomon, the power of Jesus to forgive my tormentors even as they nail me to the cross. Help me, Lord, please, in this hour of my need. Be my staff of strength."

She was at the wall of the church without even realizing that she'd been walking there, her mind half in reality and half in the land of vision. But as she stepped up to the church she felt a shock, hot and cold running over her body as if cold fire had been poured into her veins. For just a moment she wondered if she'd gone insane, as bestial bellows echoed in the church and through the night swamp. But then the visions were gone, replaced by a sense of peace. But not an inactive peace. She felt a presence urging her to something, something vital, and she slipped to the side looking for what she knew must be there.

She didn't know much about cars or swamps or monsters taking over holy ground. But she knew churches. And they all had a side door.

Kelly struggled as hard as he could but with four men holding him there wasn't anything he could do. He was thrown down on the blood-spattered altar and looked up into the face of the beast that had just slaughtered Dolores. What was that thing about spitting to show you weren't afraid? He couldn't have spit for the life of him. His mouth was dry and he realized that he'd pissed himself. He didn't care, he was about to die and there wasn't a damned thing he could do about it.

"PD is going to chop you up and feed you to the gators," Kelly said, looking at Carlane.

"By the time they come here, we will be gone," Carlane said, laughing and holding up a hand to forestall the beast. "My Master is complete, fully manifest. No power on earth can stop him. But we will go. We will hide and bide our time. Build our strength. And then . . . the day of the Dragon will come again."

He waved to the beast and stood back, avoiding the blood that was about to be shed.

She had seen a steel gas tank outside the building when they had been asking futile questions. All she had to do was get inside. What she was planning was going to make her a felon at the very least. It would probably be a capital charge. Again, she wondered if she was going insane, but she knew, with rock hard certainty, that this was the Lord's work. And if the Lord wanted her to do it, she would.

The side door, unfortunately, was locked. But that presented no real problem. She took one of the empty pop bottles out of her bag and held it against the opening on the barrel of her .45. Then she waited for another of those bestial bellows and fired a round into the lock. The sound was not as quiet as it should have been. The bottle caught most of the exiting gas that created the distinctive "crack" of a pistol shot, but some of it worked out around the edges with a sound about like a squib. This was when she needed duct tape and she chastised herself for neglecting it. However, the lock crumpled, the rotted wood shattering around it, and she dropped the bottle on the ground.

The room beyond was dark and the bellows from within the church were unnerving. But she found what she was looking for down one of the hallways. The kitchen was rank with the smell of rotting food but it had been in recent use. She turned on one of the burners and ensured that the gas was hooked up then set the AR-10 down and waited for another bellow.

What she got instead was a shriek of mortal agony but that would do. As the sound echoed she tore at the oven with hysterical strength, dragging it out and away from the wall. Then she clambered over it until she found the copper gas line, using her knife, which had a serrated portion, to saw at the line until she smelled gas leaking out. She sawed some more, pushing the line apart and hearing a hiss.

That left only one thing to do. She picked up the AR-10, stepping into the hallway as the smell of gas became overwhelming, and flipped it off safe and onto semi-auto. Then she walked to the door that should lead to the nave, under which faint light was trailing, and shook her head.

"Yea, though I walk through the valley of the shadow of death, I will fear no evil," she whispered. "For I am the baddest bitch in the valley."

With that she kicked the door in.

Well, at least it's not going to rape me, Kelly thought as one giant talon reached down for him. Then there was a shot. And another. And the thing straightened up, turning its fish head to the side.

He craned his head around as one of the acolytes fell across him, his face pulped from a round through the back of his head, and saw the strangest thing he'd ever seen, including the giant monster that had been about to gut him.

It was a ninja, holding what looked very much like his AR-10, with a white shining all around him like a giant halo.

Make that "her." The tits were distinctly noticeable.

Barb leapt through the door and took a kneeling position, scanning for targets. It was what her father would call a target rich environment. The nave was crowded with worshippers and there were several men up in the nave. There was also a giant fish thing which seemed to be preparing to rip Detective Lockhart wide open. But, for some reason, her barrel tracked onto the back of the head of the man standing at the altar and her finger stroked the trigger.

The head burst like a melon, pitching the man forward, and the giant thing straightened up as she shot two of the robed figures. Then it reached down and casually raked its talons across Detective Lockhart' stomach, following that with picking up one of the robed figures and biting his head off.

By then the worshippers had started to react and she turned left, firing five rounds into five bodies and clearing some space. That done she darted towards the altar, dodging a grab by the giant fish thing, to reach Detective Lockhart.

He was badly torn on the stomach and the thing was standing

right over him. So Barb flicked the lever to full auto and emptied the rest of the magazine into its belly.

The thing let out a bellow of pain, but the wounds closed as fast as the rounds struck, just making little pock marks like rocks dropped in a pond. The thing reached for her again and she dove to the side, rolling to her feet and slipping another magazine into the well.

As she dove to the side, the thing appeared to forget about her, stepping down off the chancel and picking up another worshipper. It gutted the man with a move like a fisherman gutting his catch and then ripped the man's chest open and started feasting.

Barb trotted to the wounded sergeant and pulled him off the bloodstained altar, dragging him away from the kitchen side of the building.

"Can you stand up?" she asked, pulling as hard as she could. But he was a big guy and she was running on pure adrenaline.

"No," Kelly said, blood foaming at his mouth. "Go. Get out."

"Fuck that," she spat, lifting him into a fireman's carry and heading for the other side of the church. There was a door there that led directly into the nave. It was padlocked, but she was more than willing to blow the hinges off if that was what it took. The worshippers had headed for the back of the church, fleeing their "god," so they weren't going to be a problem.

But her move had brought her to the attention of the fish monster and it shambled towards her before she could even make it to the stairs down from the chancel.

"Begone!" she shouted, rolling Kelly down to the floor and holding up her left hand, the right holding the AR-10 like a pistol, tucked into her body. "Begone in the name of Our Lord Jesus Christ! Go back to the Hell you belong in!"

The thing seemed to shudder at her shout but raised a giant hand to strike her down.

So she pulled the trigger.

What came out was nothing she'd ever seen before, a line of white fire, as if each of the rounds were white tracers and every one ran true. At the touch of the fire the thing shrieked and backed up. So when that magazine was done she slapped in the last and gave that to him, semi-auto this time, every round aimed. By the time she was done, he had backed up halfway down the nave and was on his knees, black smoke pouring from his chest, abdomen and head. But even as she watched, the damage was healing.

She hefted Kelly again and shambled for the door as fast as she could. Finally she got to it and smashed the lock with the buttstock of the gun, shattering it and making the weapon useless. So she tossed it to the side and stumbled out into the night.

Kelly was a dead weight, unconscious or dead she wasn't sure. But there were cars and trucks parked under the trees and she kept heading for them on weaker and weaker legs, reaching down to draw her .45. There was a bellow behind her and she looked over her shoulder, with difficulty, to see the monster tearing at the door she had exited through. It seemed a little pissed.

There had been candles in the chancel. A couple of them had fallen over but gone out in the blood. The rest . . . propane was heavier than air. But even though most of it would pool along the ground, some was bound to raise up. When, when?

As she was thinking that the world went white and she was thrown off her feet.

She could only have been unconscious for a moment because when she got to her knees pieces of the church were still raining down around her. The fish thing had disappeared but from the screams from within the burning building, she guessed that he was having a fine old fish-fry.

"All that catfish and so little time," she muttered.

She looked at Kelly and shook her head at all the damage. Besides what was obviously a flailed chest he'd caught some splinters from the exploding church. Feeling for a pulse at the neck she got nothing. It didn't seem fair to have carried him this far and have him die on her.

"Fuck," she muttered. "Fuck, fuck, fucking fuck . . ."

Some of the former worshippers were still on the ground from the explosion; others were getting to their feet. She walked over to the nearest one and put the barrel of her gun to his forehead.

"Give me your fucking keys," she ground out.

When the dazed man had handed them over she picked him up by the front of his shirt.

"Which one?" she asked.

"Red truck," he muttered, pointing. "What happened?"

"I killed your fucking god," Barb said, throwing him to the ground and trotting to the truck. She realized as she did so that it was the mechanic. "AND MY CAR HAD BETTER BE READY ON MONDAY!" Well, at least the truck should work.

Mondaine turned at the shots from the church and swore. "The bitch got behind us!"

"Who the fuck *is* she?" Henri Lancereau cursed.

"I don't know," Mondaine said, trotting for his police car. "But she is going to die tonight. If we can't give her soul to the Master, then we'll just have to send it to hell."

He hurried to his car and drove to the church, pulling up out front in a squeal of tires. But even as he started for the front door a wave of people came rushing out. Suddenly, with the sound of a hail of bullets, his head exploded in pain.

He sank to the ground, moaning, at the white fire that filled his head. He was usually one of the acolytes and his link to the Master was strong. Now it filled him with pain as the Master was filled with pain. But it stopped and he stumbled to his feet, shaking his head to clear it.

"What's happening?" he yelled as people streamed by. "What's *happening*?"

He pulled his shotgun out of the car, heading for the front and then angling to the side. It sounded like the Master was at the back left for some reason. He was trotting around the side when the building erupted.

When he came to, he felt a horrible wash of dread. The link he'd felt to his Master this last six months was gone. It felt as if the *Master* was gone. He suddenly remembered, unshielded by the power that had filled him, all the things he'd done, all the women he had raped and killed *before* the Master's first manifestation and raped and helped to kill since. The pleasure that he'd gotten from it, and still did. He had gone to the Master freely.

But with the Master gone, retribution was sure to fall on all of them. Unless . . . it would be hard to cover up. But nobody in the town would talk; they were all implicated. A fire in the old church. People dead. They could clean up the remains of the hooker. He wasn't sure what would be left of the Master.

If . . .

That bitch. There was *one* fucking witness. What she would say would seem insane, but she could point fingers, talk about things best left buried.

Where the fuck was she? Dead in the church?

But then he saw a figure, striding across the parking lot. A look, a move.

Her.

He stumbled to his feet, looking around. Many of the Cult of Almadu had not come freely to the worship and apparently, bereft of their cozy link to the Master, many of them had gone insane. Others were sitting with their heads in their hands or stumbling around drunkenly.

He had to stop her. He saw the bitch getting in Claude Thibideau's red pickup and hurried back to his squad car.

It was a long way to the next town.

One of the things Barbara had been careful to carry along was the hand-held GPS she used for navigation. She started the truck, put on her seatbelt, pulled the GPS out of her backpack, unfolded the little suction cup thingy and slapped it on the windshield. Then she put the truck in gear and floored it, spinning gravel and squealing tires as she hit the blacktop.

The GPS was taking a while to find satellites, but that was okay. The first possible turn wasn't for a few miles. She put the headlights on bright, pressed the accelerator down and settled down to put miles between herself and Thibideau. She wasn't sure what she was going to tell the authorities. Tell them it was attempted rape by the deputy? Anything to get them into the town, asking questions. Or, maybe, just walk away? No, that was the wrong thing in the eyes of the Lord.

Oh . . . heck. The things she'd said. And done.

"Dear Lord, please forgive me for some of my words, thoughts and actions this night. I really was . . . Well, I'm sorry. . . ."

She was a half mile out of town, approaching the first curve, when she saw lights behind her, closing fast.

The parish car was an unmodified Ford Crown Victoria, but there was no way that a pickup truck could outrun it on the bayou roads. It was lower to the ground and could take the turns faster, not to mention being faster in the straightaway. Slowly, he gained ground. And there was nothing around, nowhere for her to go but straight on. He'd push her off the road, put a bullet in her head if she was still alive and then feed her body to the gators. He wasn't getting anywhere close to the bitch after what she'd done to Claude and Marceau and the rest. What was she, a fucking ninja? Soccer mom, my ass. The truck could get pulled out and dumped. Or fixed up. Whatever. No witnesses meant no witnesses. Probably some of the people in town would have to be . . . cleaned up as well. More gator food. Save that for later.

He'd closed from better than a mile to less than a hundred yards. All he had to do was run her off the road.

"You'd think a mechanic would soup up his own truck," Barbara muttered as the police car started to drift to the left. He was going to try to hit her on the rear end and spin her out. At the speed she was going, she was likely to go into a roll. And that would be that.

"Fine," she muttered. "You wanna dance. Let's fu . . . let's dance."

She slammed on her brakes and pulled to the left, fighting the truck as it tried to get away from her.

The truck suddenly braked, swerving to the left and caught his right front quarter panel. He was going nearly a hundred miles an hour and the slight change in vector pulled the car into an out-of-control spin. The last thing Deputy Sheriff Mondaine saw was the tree-trunk headed for his windshield.

The impact had jarred the truck and Barbara fought it for as long as she could. She'd gotten it down under forty, skidding all over the road and headed for a curve, when the right front tire hit the grass on the shoulder and sent the truck into a spin. It made it halfway through and then started to roll. Barbara saw grass and trees and then the water reaching up for her.

Epilogue

Barbara lay in the hospital bed, looking up at the ceiling and occasionally rattling the handcuff on her left wrist. For the past three days she had tried to explain to people that she was not crazy. For which act she had been chained to her bed and visited by a stream of psychiatrists.

"Mrs. Everette," the doctor said, gently. "I know you think you saw what you're saying you saw. But under extreme stress, hallucinations can occur. You've been under a lot of stress, lately. We've spoken to your husband and he tells us that you were already acting . . . erratically . . ."

"I am not crazy," Barbara said, trying not to cry. But who was she to judge? The first thing a crazy person was sure of was that they weren't crazy. Who was she to think that the Lord and Savior would give her the power to dispel a demon? She knew that she tried to live her life in a Christian manner, but she was no warrior of God. She knew that.

"No, you're not crazy, Barbara," the doctor said, shaking his head. "Apparently there was a group of rapists and murderers that were keeping the town under their thumb. But the only person who saw this god-monster was *you*. Now, the police are aware that you may have committed some acts that you could be charged with. But they're willing to overlook that, given that you stopped the Ripper killings. However, with your continued delusionary state . . ."

Barb tuned him out. They were going to let her go, only if she promised not to talk about what she'd seen. Realistically, there wasn't anyone she could tell. Who would believe her?

"Barbara, I'm going to come back in a while," the psychiatrist said, standing up. "If you'd like, I could prescribe a sedative . . ."

"No, thank you," she said. "My body is a temple of God. I'll take a pain killer if I need it, but no mind-altering drugs."

"I'm sorry, but it may come to that," the doctor said, shaking his head. "We'll talk later."

She lay back, closing her eyes against tears, her abdomen shuddering with the need to cry. Kelly was dead, his chest flailed by the monster. She'd failed him. That was the thing that kept coming back to her, not the victory, if there had been one, but the sight of his pain-ravaged face telling her to "go, go."

She opened her eyes and glared at the door as there was a light knock.

"Come in," she ground out. She was done with being Mrs. Nice to these people. Maybe God would forgive her that as well.

The man who entered was not, apparently, a doctor. And older guy, very well preserved, though, with distinguished gray at his temples and black hair. Nice suit.

"Who are you?" she asked.

"Augustus Germaine. I'm here to congratulate you."

"On what? Being crazy?"

"You're not by any means crazy, Mrs. Everette. And I'm sorry it's taken me this long to pull the strings to get you out of here. A warrior of the Lord who dispels an avatar of Almadu deserves far better. However, up until yesterday I was in Serbia tracking a werewolf that was causing a spot of trouble. Would you consider having dinner with me? I have a job offer I think you might entertain."

Book Two

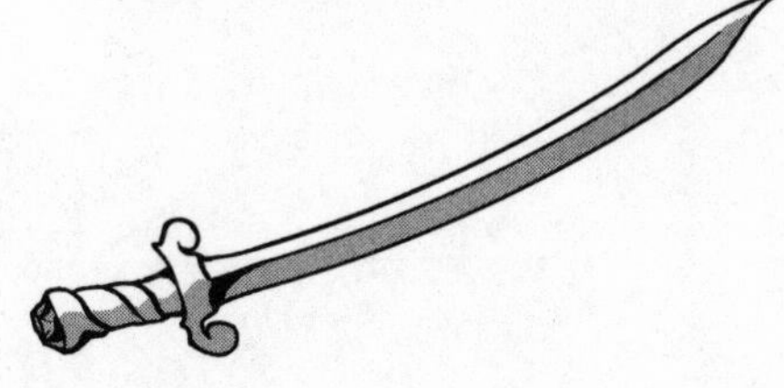

The Necromancy Option

Chapter One

The picture on the flat-screen projection was of a pretty young woman, slightly overweight, with black, obviously dyed, hair, lying on her back with her throat cut from ear to ear. Her lips and eyelids had been painted in black and there was a symbol painted on her right cheek in what appeared to be permanent marker.

"Victim Number Nine, Sharon Carter," Special Agent in Charge Jim Halliwell said. "Age, sixteen. Home, Newberry, South Carolina. MO standard for case R-143-8. Found in a remote, wooded, area. Anal, vaginal and oral sexual assault. Markings drawn on the body with magic marker. Marks of stakes in the ground and remnants of military parachute cord ties. Ligation marks on hands and ankles. Biological tracings of a white male with brown hair. Footprints indicate somewhere between five foot seven and six feet in height. Stake marks are of a military type stake. Perpetrator may be current military or of military background."

"So, basically, we're where we were with victims four through eight?" Agent Donahue said. "All the clues in the world and no idea who the perp is?" Greg Donahue's six foot four, heavy-set, frame was leaning back in his chair, frankly sprawled, in contrast to the other six agents watching the briefing, all of whom were sitting erect with every sign of attentiveness. They put Halliwell in mind of a group of well-trained Dobermans with one sprawled St. Bernard in the middle.

"Not quite," Halliwell replied with a note of satisfaction. "Agent Griffith might have an idea," he added, gesturing at the young man at his side.

Griffith was twenty-six, medium height and overweight with brown hair that was already receding. Unlike everyone else in the room his clothing was rumpled and his tie pulled down and askew. The FBI liked clean-cut agents with an almost military bearing. But over the years they had learned that certain types of personalities did not grow on trees. So for the Griffiths of the world, an exception was made.

"I've been comparing known similarities in all the cases," Griffith said, throwing up a complicated chart. "All of the victims have been in their teens, female, all the rest. However, what got me was that most of them had a 'Goth' look to them."

"Victims four and seven didn't," Donahue pointed out.

"Goth?" Agent Laidlaw asked.

"Black eye make-up," Donahue answered. "White face powder, black clothes and hair. Sort of a vampire look. Really common with disaffected middle class suburban kids of a certain type. Generally they're a bit more intelligent than the norm in their school, don't fit in very well, tend to *not* be druggies but try to set themselves off. If they read much, it's vampire stuff like Anne Rice."

"Anne who?" Laidlaw asked. "I'm getting lost here."

"Rice," Donahue sighed. "*Interview with the Vampire*? Ring any bells?"

"No," Laidlaw admitted.

"So a lot of them were Goths," Donahue said, giving up. "What's the point?"

"Well, it was a point of similarity," Griffith said. "So I ran it down. It turns out that all of them had attended a con within two months of their deaths."

"Con?" Laidlaw asked.

"A science fiction, fantasy or gaming convention," Griffith answered. "Actually, in seven of the nine cases, it was a science fiction literary convention. One media convention and one gaming. Each of them, though, has had a horror track and LARPing."

"Goth LARPers?" Donahue asked, frowning. "Horror fans?"

"Maybe," Griffith answered. "Since we just got the connection, we haven't run down all the leads. I don't know what they were engaging in at the cons. Might be LARPing, might have been gamers, might have been general con-goers."

"What in the hell is a *LARPer*?" Laidlaw asked. "Now I'm getting totally lost."

"LARP," Donahue said, sighing again. "Live Action Role Play. Basically a role playing game where people wander around the con playing it. Goes on all night and all day, damned LARPers sitting outside your room at four in the morning talking about how to ambush the werewolves or whatever. It's a pain in the ass."

"You've been to cons?" Griffith asked, surprised.

"A couple," Donahue admitted, shrugging. "Mostly to get signatures from authors I like. And, hell, there are people there that you don't have to explain who Anne Rice is," he added with a chuckle. "Or Robert Heinlein or Poul Anderson."

"We're trying to build a suspect list based on this connection," SAIC Halliwell said. "The profilers think we're looking at a person between the ages of eighteen and thirty. With the other items, hair color, skin color and height, we can begin building a suspects list. If we can find out who has been attending the cons. Besides the victims, obviously."

"Depending on the con, you could be looking at anywhere from six hundred to forty *thousand* attendees. That doesn't narrow it down much. Even if you just look at the 'white males with brown hair.' "

"It's more than we had," the SAIC said.

"No traces of makeup left by the perp," Donahue pointed out. "So our perp might be mildly intelligent and not dressing the part. Or he might not be a Goth. Goths generally hang out with Goths."

"Which is why I'm thinking LARPer," Griffith argued. "Goths interact with non-Goths more in LARPing than anywhere else. And there *are* non-Goth look people that hang with the Goths."

"Hell, all of the conventions will have lists of who attended," Donahue said, shrugging. "Get those and you can narrow it down quite a bit."

"We tried that," Halliwell admitted. "The first problem is the people that run the conventions were pretty unwilling to cough up the lists. . . ."

"I can imagine," Donahue said, grimacing. "Con-goers and organizers tend to be . . . well, I guess it could best be put as either libertarian or liberal. Giving the FBI lists of their attendees has to really go against their grain."

"The other problem is that most of them don't have good records of people that just show up," Halliwell said. "They don't require ID for example. And although we had matches on people at several of the cons, no matches on *all* of them that met the description and profile of the perp. Also no across-the-board matches on hotel reservations."

"So now what?" Donahue asked.

"We're going to insert agents at cons," Halliwell said, shrugging. "Undercover, obviously. Their task will be to try to ID suspects that meet the description and profile. Pictures and names when possible."

"We'll be looking for people that are 'day-trippers,'" Griffith pointed out. "Most of the cons have a different badge for that. But it's not guaranteed; they might be rotating names some way. Someone who is interacting with the Goths but may not be dressed as one."

"Each of you will be assigned a con," Halliwell said. "And we'll keep sending agents to others, trying to build a list, until we close the case or the con angle proves to be a bust." He paused and frowned then shook his head. "Donahue, Griffith, you got any suggestions on how to go undercover to a con?"

"Yeah," Laidlaw said, grinning. "Where do we get our Klingon outfits?"

"What you wear doesn't really matter," Donahue said, frowning. "But you have to have a reason to *be* there, other than to laugh at the geeks. Or you're going to stand out like a God damned sore thumb and blow the investigation. Just the FBI *look* is going to make you stand out. The clean-cut, short-hair, erect bearing is going to peg you as a military guy, maybe cop, right away. You'd be amazed how many of both go to the cons—about half the guys who wear Storm Trooper armor are local cops for example—but they generally try to keep a low profile in that area. And if you're going to be going around asking questions, you're going to have to have a reason for it. Depending upon the con, and who is going, I'd suggest an intensive reading course in one of the author guests. Or if it's a media con, get familiar with one of the TV shows or movies that one of the guests was in. Get a book or a picture signed. Go to a couple of the panels. If you're gothing, get to know some of the bands and *understand* the attitude, even if you don't have it. If it's a gaming con, you're going to have to be able to *game* and that's a skill I don't know if any of you have. *Don't* laugh at the geeks. *Don't* go around with the 'get a life' attitude or, again, you're going to blow the investigation. Laidlaw, you golf, right?"

"Sure," the agent said, frowning.

"Can you explain why you go out to chase a little white ball around a course?" Donahue asked. "You get paid money to do that? No. You do it for fun. Your friends do it. When you're done you get to hang out at the nineteenth hole and drink beer and lie about your game. That's all that cons are. It's where people with similar interests come together. They're not *your* kind of people, they're *their* kind of people. And they're just as . . . disparaging of golfers as you are of them. And since most of them have a better vocabulary than you do, they can be disparaging *better*, trust me. Get that in your head, get some background, and you'll be fine. Dress casual, *really* casual, and take good walking shoes."

"There's one other potential link," Halliwell said. "An author called K. Goldberg has been a guest at seven of the nine conventions. You read any of his stuff, Donahue?"

"Her," the agent said, shrugging. "No, but I've heard of her."

"The next convention *she's* at is in Greensboro in a month," Halliwell said, correcting himself. "Read some of her books, bill them to the Bureau. That's your con."

"Great," Donahue said, grumpily. "I'm supposed to infiltrate Goths. Why did it have to be *Goths*?"

Barbara Everette dropped Allison off at dance class with a sigh of relief and headed towards the Wal-Mart shopping center on the edge of town. She pulled onto Mississippi 15 and began weaving through traffic, pushing the Expedition up to well over the posted speed limit.

As she approached the Wal-Mart she looked at her watch and frowned, then glanced at the gas gauge. The Expedition had plenty of gas but it was time to check in.

She pulled out of the left-hand lane, inserting the vehicle into a small space between two pick-up trucks, and then whipped into a turn lane, pulling into a battered Quik-Mart. She topped off the tank with a couple of gallons of gas, then went into the store, picked up a Starbucks vanilla Frappuccino and headed to the counter.

"Hello, Mrs. Everette," the dark-skinned owner of the store said, smiling. He took the twenty she gave him and made change for the Frappuccino and the small amount of gas. Part of the change was a gold coin that appeared at first glance to be a Sacagawea dollar.

"Thank you, Mr. Patek," Barbara said, nodding. "Go with your god."

"And you with yours, Mrs. Everette," the man said, bowing slightly.

Barbara pulled back into traffic then drove to the Wal-Mart shopping center. Instead of getting out right away, she opened up the coin, wrestling with it slightly to get it to pop, and unfolded the note inside.

"Religious Retreat. Foundation for Love and Universal Faith,

Women of Faith Division. Invitation and tickets by mail, Tuesday or Wednesday. Mission of one week plus duration to follow."

She rolled up the note and tossed it in her mouth. The sugar-impregnated rice paper dissolved pleasantly on her tongue. When it was gone she walked into the Wal-Mart to pick up sundries, sipping on her Frappuccino to get the taste of ink out of her mouth.

"Agent Donahue," Halliwell said as Greg entered his office. "Sit down, please."

Donahue glanced at the visitor in the office as he sat down, then looked over at his boss.

"You wanted to see me, sir?"

"This is Mr. Germaine," Halliwell said, gesturing at the newcomer with a frown. "He's a . . . consultant on the R-143 investigation."

"I wasn't aware that we'd called in a consultant," Greg said, frowning. The visitor was well dressed in a tailored suit. The FBI used a variety of consultants and Donahue mentally pegged him as a specialist in some forensic field.

"Greg, you've been with the Bureau . . . twelve years, right?" Halliwell said, with a hint of nervousness. "But most of that time in Robbery, right?"

"Yes, sir," Donahue said.

"This is your first kidnapping investigation," Halliwell added. "I've been in kidnapping and serial for over twenty years now. And . . . well, I've seen some things that, let's just say they don't make the news, okay?"

"I'm not following you, sir," Donahue said, frowning. "What *sort* of things?"

"The term is 'Special Circumstances,' Agent Donahue," the visitor said. He had a light accent, maybe British overlaid with something else.

"What does Special Circumstances mean?" Greg said, feeling like he was interviewing a suspect rather than having a meeting with his boss.

"It means the supernatural, Greg." Halliwell sighed. "And

before you decide I'm nuts, don't. About the sixth investigation I was on turned out to be a vampire. A real, honest-to-God, bloodsucking, charming, stronger-than-human vampire. I am *not* shitting you, okay?"

Greg's face bunched up, his eyes closed and he actually felt his blood run cold.

"You're not joking, are you, sir?"

"No, he's not," Germaine replied. "When there is an investigation that has Special Circumstances, the FBI calls us in. They, in fact, keep us informed on all investigations that *might* have such circumstances. We'd been tracking R-143, mostly because the cabalistic symbols on the bodies are, in fact, the correct symbols for a particular form of necromantic rite. But we had hoped that it involved, let's just say a normal psychopath. Unfortunately, we've recently been informed that such was not the case. We have reason to believe that the girls are being sacrificed to a particular lesser deity, call it a demon. Such sacrifices create power which can be used by the sacrificer. Furthermore, sufficient power can permit the deity to manifest on earth. We would prefer to prevent that from happening. Things get . . . remarkably ugly when that occurs."

"What does this have to do with me?" Greg asked.

"We have far fewer agents available than the FBI," Germaine said, smiling faintly. "On the other hand, we also have some techniques the FBI does not to narrow down the field of suspects. We believe that, of all the potential conventions, the one that you are going to attend has the highest likelihood of attracting your perpetrator. Therefore there will be a Special Circumstances consultant attending that con. They will probably accompany you to it. In the event that you find the perpetrator, I would recommend that you inform the consultant. It is possible that the person may have abilities that you will be unable to combat. By the same token, the consultant may need . . . back-up. Depending upon who is sent they may have an attitude of nonviolence towards all but the necromancer or entity. Therefore, if your perpetrator is not using ritual, or does not summon a manifestation, you and the local police may have to handle the capture." Germaine paused and thought for a moment. "However, if there *is* manifestation, it is probably better if you let the 'consultant' handle it."

"If it hadn't been for the SC operative in that vampire investigation, I wouldn't be here," Halliwell said. "I've dealt with them several times over the years. Sometimes it turns out to be nothing, just your usual murdering madman. But when you need an SC operative, you *really* need an SC operative. Understand?"

"No, sir," Greg admitted.

"Well, let's put it this way," Halliwell said, grimacing. "If the SC operative tells you to jump, don't even ask how high. Just jump. Period. Or you're liable to end up as a corpse."

"And, I might add," Mr. Germaine said. "A corpse whose soul now resides in hell as the plaything of the demon you were opposing."

"Yes, sir," Greg said, swallowing.

"One more thing," Halliwell said. "Nobody finds out about SC unless they have to and they're considered trustworthy. The very *existence* of Special Circumstances is top secret. You don't tell anyone about it, you don't admit to its existence outside of the circle who know about it. There is no 'Special Circumstances' department in the Bureau. It doesn't exist, period. You cannot talk about the special aspects of this investigation with *anyone* except myself or the director. And, obviously, the SC operatives you may encounter in your career. You're now on an inside track in the Bureau. It won't get you promoted faster but . . . you'll see things and know things that very few do."

"Assuming you survive," Germaine said, with another faint, secret smile. "Special Circumstances investigations are notoriously hard on regular agents."

Chapter Two

As Barbara fixed dinner she considered how to broach the subject of her trip to Mark. She loved her husband and, as a good Christian woman, considered him to be the head of the household. And Mark was not going to want her to go. However, she also knew that the group she was involved with was, without question, doing God's work. This was to be her first formal training session, not to mention first official mission, and she intended to be there when called.

She finished fixing dinner, fried chicken, mashed potatoes and broccoli, then set it out on the table, calling the family to feed. It took a while.

Allison was on the phone with a friend. Getting her to hang up involved threats to lose the privilege for a week. The first games of March Madness were on so dragging Brandon away from the TV practically involved oxen. Mark had already decided that he was just going to eat off a tray, so Brandon wanted to know why he couldn't as well. Since Mark was ignoring the argument, Barb got no support from that direction. By the time she got Brandon over to the table and a TV tray on Mark's lap, the phone had rung again and Allison was back on. Even Brook was hiding in her room so it took nearly fifteen minutes from the moment the broccoli was ready before they sat down.

They had just said grace, Barbara saying the prayer since Mark was glued to the Georgia Tech game, and settled down to their food when Allison made a face.

"This broccoli is *cold*!"

Barb counted to ten, slowly, then did it again in Fusian. If she didn't she might say something . . . unChristian to her daughter. Demons were going to be a *vacation*!

Barbara waited until the break between the third and fourth quarter to spring her surprise.

"Mark?" she said, sitting down on the couch.

"Yeah?" he asked, distractedly, as the announcer ran over the highlights of the previous quarter along with what was going on in other games.

"I've been invited to a religious retreat with the Women of Faith Foundation," Barb said. "I'll be gone for about a week. And I may be going somewhere afterwards, I don't know how long that will be."

"Uh, huh," Mark said. "I can't believe they didn't score that as a foul, would you look at that?"

"Mark," Barbara said, with just a hint of impatience. "Did you hear me?"

"Uh . . ." Mark said, finally turning to look at her. "No?"

"I'm going to a religious retreat," Barb repeated. "For a week. Then maybe somewhere after that, I don't know how long."

"A *week*?" Mark snapped. "Who's paying for it?"

"The Foundation," Barbara sighed. "And my plane fare."

"Why?" he asked.

"It's through the church," Barbara replied, only half lying.

"Who's going to . . . ?" Mark said, pausing.

"Cook? Clean? Do the laundry? Pick up the kids from school?" Barb asked. "Shop?"

"Yeah," Mark replied. "I've *got* a job!"

"Brandon and Brook can stay in the after-school program. I'll get someone to cart Allison to cheerleading. For the evening things, like karate and dance, you'll have to do it. I'll leave a list of chores for the kids and premade food for some of the nights. Then there's take out and delivery. You'll survive, I'm sure."

"You don't have to be sarcastic," Mark said, sighing. "Why do you have to go I guess is what I mean."

"A foundation is paying for me to meet with other women of faith in a dialogue on the nature of faith," Barbara replied, admitting that it was only half of the truth. "It's important, to me, to our church and to God. I'd hoped to get your blessings on it, not resistance."

"Whatever," Mark said as the game started up again. "Like you said, we'll survive."

"Thank you," Barb said, but she knew darned well he hadn't heard it.

The "religious retreat" was at a small facility in western North Carolina. Barbara could have driven, but the foundation had provided plane tickets to the Asheville airport so she found herself negotiating her carry-on through the small crowd and wondering who was going to be meeting her.

As she exited the restricted area she saw a short, plump, older woman with a face full of wrinkles and wearing a paisley dress who was holding up a sign that said: "Barbara Everette." The woman's silver hair was pinned up on her head with silver pins and she wore what, to Barb's eyes, was an enormous number of necklaces, most of them silver and bearing both cabalistic symbols and other "fantasy" motifs. The centerpiece was a massive dragon's head cast in silver that seemed to be roaring defiance. Her makeup was also . . . outré in Barbara's opinion, heavily applied and very extreme, the eyeliner working up almost to the edge of her hair and making her look somewhat elfish.

Barb, who had dressed in a cream silk shirt, light maroon washed silk jacket, a matching skirt and heels and was wearing only a pearl necklace and her wedding ring felt that she was either over dressed or underdressed but that, certainly, they were going to make an odd pair. However, she approached the woman, holding out her hand.

"I'm Barbara," she said, smiling. "Please call me Barb."

"Sharice Rickels," the woman said, lowering the sign and taking her hand. "Glad you could make it. I'm looking forward to talking."

"It . . . should be interesting," Barbara said, uneasily. "I have to pick up some checked baggage."

"Not a problem," Sharice said, depositing the card in the nearest trash and leading her over to the baggage claim area. "I heard, many of us have heard, how you were chosen to attend the Foundation meetings. We were, to say the least, impressed. Also impressed that a Christian would both be able to do what you did and not find the Foundation odd or impossible."

"You're not a Christian?" Barb asked, curiously.

"Oh, Lady, no," the woman said, laughing merrily. "You'll find few among our ranks. There are some Catholics, a few, but you're the first Protestant I've met. Most of us are what you would term pagans. I'm a Wiccan, reformist—mind you, I don't have the body for sky clad. Well, not anymore," she added with a grin. "I had my days, lovey. But most of us are pagan. Wiccan, Hindu, Asatru, got a lot of Asatru . . ."

"I don't even know what any of those are," Barbara said, curiously. "And they're all . . . members of the Foundation?"

"Yes," Sharice said, shrugging. "There are . . . oh, I suppose you could use the term 'politics' even in the foundation. More like . . . theatrics, if you don't mind the pun," she added, grinning. "Power is a function of followers and interest on the part of the deity. Asatru is gaining in strength, not only in the foundation but in the world. They're worshippers of the Norse Gods, by the way. Thus they're increasing in power and that's good. Of course, there's the sub-branch that follows the chaotic tenets of the Jester and that's a pain in the butt, as you can imagine. Hindus, of course, have great power, but it's dispersed what with one thing or another. You think we have problems here, you have no idea how bad it is in India or other regions where Hindus are prevalent. We've been hoping for more Christians.

America is an essentially Christian country and the power levels available to ardent Christians are just amazing. But the faith is so . . ." She paused and looked embarrassed. "I'm sorry, I was on a hobby horse."

"I think you were about to say something like 'closed minded,'" Barb said, shrugging. "I suppose it is."

"But we do what we can with the power available to us," Sharice said, brightly. "Really, the . . . other side is as crippled as we are. They have many worshippers in secret, but they can't coordinate like we can."

"There's my bags," Barbara said. "Could you maybe get a skycap? I've . . . got a few."

"A few" turned out to be five, including her carry-on, which she added to the stack.

"I *think* we can get all of these in my car," Sharice said, nervously. "I hadn't realized you'd be bringing so many."

"I suppose I shouldn't have," Barb admitted. "But I didn't know what the meetings would be like, what to wear, and the last time I traveled I traveled so light I didn't have the right clothes at all. So I sort of brought . . . everything I might need."

"I'll go get the car."

Sharice's car was a three-year-old Malibu, light green and . . . cluttered. The back seat was covered with books, bags and implements, some of which, like the skull-headed mace, made Barbara question if she was meeting the right person. The front seat held a large bag with a black knife handle and some candles peeking out, while the floor was filled with magazines, most of them with demons, dragons or fairies on the cover.

"I suppose I should have cleaned it out," Sharice said, embarrassedly. "But I like to have clutter around me. It's what's called comfort clutter," she added, hoisting her obviously heavy bag into the back. "And . . . I've learned to have my tools with me at all times."

Between packing the trunk and the back seat they got all the bags in the car. Barb tipped the skycap, then got in the car, kicking the magazines aside to get some floor space for her feet.

"I understand you pack," Sharice said as they pulled out of the front entrance.

"Yes," Barbara said, unhappily. She'd left her .45 in the Honda at Birmingham Airport and had felt half naked ever since.

"Glove compartment," was all Sharice said.

Barb opened it and smiled, pulling out the holstered H&K USP .45. It was even the SOCOM model, much more accurate than the standard model she usually carried. She drew it from the holster, dropped the magazine and ensured it was clear then slid the mag back in and tucked it in her waistband. There were two more mags in the glove compartment and she put those in her purse.

"I'm not much into guns, myself," Sharice said with a sniff. "I prefer to use my powers to change the surroundings for the greater good. Also, guns are rarely useful against the primary enemies." She paused and shrugged. "But they are useful for dispensing with their agents here on earth."

"I grew up with guns," Barb said, returning shrug for shrug. "My father taught me to use them and made me start packing when I was a teenager. I suspect that a couple of times I probably would have been date raped if the guy I was with didn't know I was armed, and more than capable of using it."

"I see," Sharice said, frowning. "I won't contest your position. As long as each comes to good, that is all that matters."

Barbara contemplated the scenery as Sharice drove the car up I-40 and into the Appalachian Mountains. She had lived in quite a few places, and visited others, but the Appalachians were one area she'd never seen. Most of the mountains in her experience were much higher and arid but the Appalachians were covered in trees and there were flashes of green and a few buds to relieve the brown-gray of the forests. It was a clear day and as the car turned off onto a side road she could see for miles. Many of the mountains had houses tucked into their sides in such a way that when the trees were full of leaves they must have been invisible. It was a place of quiet beauty and she hoped she would be coming back again.

She hadn't paid attention to the route but she did when they turned onto a side road and up the side of a mountain. The road was poorly maintained and very twisty. They passed a couple of houses, vacation or retirement homes she was sure from the look, then cut up over a ridge and back down to a gated fence with a manned guard shack. On the left side of the gate was an embossed metal sign, about two feet square, that said: "The Foundation for Love and Universal Faith. Est. 1907." The unarmed security guard waved at Sharice and apparently pressed a control because the gate started to open.

"We mostly depend upon working in the shadows," Sharice said, as she drove through a section of tended white pines. They were tall but there was an understory of smaller cedars that cloaked whatever was beyond them from sight. "But everyone has to have one place they can go where they are fully secure. The Foundation is guarded by far more than a rent-a-cop, I can assure you."

"I . . ." Barbara said, then stopped. "I can feel it." And she could, a tingling like after a shower. It felt . . . fresh and clean as if the miasma of the world had dropped away.

When they cleared the pines she smiled, looking at the buildings of the "Foundation." There were several of them, most resembling chalets but with a few using other architectures. She recognized some of it as Oriental and a small building that could be a mosque, but the rest was so eclectic as to defy even her knowledge. A small stream ran through the hollow that they clustered in and the buildings seemed to fit its pattern naturally. Scattered among them were a wealth of gardens, most of them brown at this time of year. But she could see that in the spring and fall they would be a riot of color.

"This is the hard time," Sharice said, as if reading her thoughts. "The bad time, when the spirits of the winter, the spirits of darkness and cold, hold sway. Some of them are simply neutral, but many side with evil. From Samhaine to Beltane is when we are at our lowest ebb, when the spirits of the dark come forth to do battle and we must challenge them despite our relative lack of strength." She paused and then grinned. "Or, maybe, it's simply Seasonal Affective Disorder."

She pulled the car around the back into a small parking lot that was mostly grass and trees with an occasional parking pad.

"You're in the Gletsch Chalet," she said, pointing at the building which was a more or less traditional Alpine chalet on the other side of the stream. There was a small bridge and the walk was not far.

"I guess I'd better start unloading," Barb said. "What's the dress code?"

"There isn't one, sweetie," Sharice said, smiling. "You can be as dressy as you'd like or just wear jeans and a flannel shirt. Nobody will comment." She paused and frowned. "Some of the attendees at training . . . costume as their avatars. Especially on First Night. And you'll probably find some of them . . . odd."

"I can imagine," Barbara said, shrugging. "I'll manage."

"I want you to try to understand, though, Barb," Sharice said, firmly. "Most of those who are drawn into Special Circumstances are fringe people. People who are actually a little psychic as you would call it. They've mostly been outcasts in their lives. They've taken up the fringe lifestyle of groups that accepted them as they *are*, rather than trying to make them . . ." She paused and then gestured at Barbara.

"So, what you're saying is, I'm the outcast?" Barb asked, lightly. "You'd be surprised how out of place I've felt most of my life."

"But *you* adjusted to that mask," Sharice said. "You put it on and you wear it well. These are people who, by and large, never could. You are what we call a 'mundane.' A person who can't enter into the fringe or, at least, doesn't enjoy doing so. And mundanes have made most of these peoples' lives hell. They laugh at them for their oddity. By the way you act, dress, speak, you are . . . well, yes, you're on our side. But you're the enemy they have dealt with their entire social lives. You asked me how you should dress? Forget the pretty make-up, forget the nice heels, forget the washed silk. Put on a T-shirt and jeans and some running shoes and just . . . be yourself. As 'yourself' as you can manage. Or don't. If yourself is dressed to the nines every single moment, dress to the nines. But understand that your fellow warriors aren't the church lady teller at the bank."

"Okay," Barbara said.

"Dress however you want, look around and then make your decision," Sharice said, sighing.

"Can I ask a question?" Barbara said.

"You just did," Sharice answered, smiling. "But go ahead."

"Have you ever been . . . ?"

"On assignment," Sharice filled in for her. "Yes, but I'm retired." She paused again and shrugged. "You get old. You get to the point where you just can't run with the big boys. The knees are shot and sometimes the wisest simply—flee. You've seen too much and . . ." She shrugged again. "You just want to rest your weary bones and not hear the screams anymore."

"You were . . . powerful," Barb said, cocking her head to the side and really examining the woman for the first time.

"Still am, dearie," Sharice chuckled. "Still am. And old and maybe I've gained some wisdom. Which was why I was asked to pick you up."

Chapter Three

It took Barb fifteen minutes to haul her bags into her room and they just about filled it. She pulled out the dresses and hung them up, then unpacked the bags as she contemplated the schedule booklet that had been in her room. Registration opened at 5:30, then there was a "Get Together" in the Philosophy Center. There were two seminars in the evening: Advanced Demonic Identification and Cabalistic Symbols: They're Not Just For The Bad Guys.

Her schedule had helpfully been marked up by someone, with certain seminars highlighted. She had a full schedule for tomorrow, starting with "Introductory Demonology" and running through "Introduction to Pan-Theology." But other than registration and the get-together, which apparently was when dinner would be served, she didn't have anything marked for today.

She considered Sharice's suggestions on dress but simply couldn't appear in public with these people for the first time in jeans and a T-shirt. So she chose a simple dress, cotton-polyester and patterned, and a pair of low pumps. She intended to bring along a down duster against the chill that hung in the air and that would get worse after dark. She contemplated her makeup and touched it up, stuck the pistol in her purse and went forth to find registration.

As she entered the Administrative Center, which was designed like a temple of some sort, she got her first real look at her fellow attendees. There were two Buddhist monks in saffron robes, a man with "punked" hair and a number of piercings on his face, two women in what she could only describe as "ceremonial" robes covered in what she supposed were "cabalistic" symbols and a number of other people that she categorized, aware that it was uncharitable, as "geeks." Two of them were obviously a pair, possibly husband and wife, the man tall with dark hair and heavyset and the wife short and . . . okay, she could lose a few pounds.

She stood in line behind them, patiently waiting and, okay, eavesdropping.

"I'm worried that they're going to assign us to the Lycaean case," the woman was saying. "I hate New York."

"Dartho said there's a case going on at the cons," the man said. "Maybe we'll get that."

"I could do cons," the woman said, grinning. "At least we'd be able to fit in. I hate working directly with the Bureau. The damned agents are always looking down their collective nose."

"I know," the man said, frowning. "And it's not like they can outshoot us or outthink us."

"I'm sorry," Barbara said, touching his shoulder. "I couldn't help but overhear that you shoot."

"Is there a problem with that?" the woman said, somewhat nastily.

"None at all," Barb said, smiling at her. "It's just the person that picked me up from the airport seemed very . . . down on violence. And I enjoy shooting. So I was surprised."

"Oh," the man said, trying not to look at her chest and failing miserably. "Well, there's a range here. But, yeah, a lot of the operators are really down on guns. They seem to think that that's what the cops we work with are for."

"Part of it is a misunderstanding of the three-fold path," the woman said, shaking her head. "Evil given returns three fold, you know? But using violence in the service of good *is* good.

It's not violence itself that stains the soul but the nature of the feelings when violence is used."

"I see," Barbara said. "What if . . . what if when you use violence for good you know that the . . . side of you that is doing that is not, essentially, good?"

"That can be a problem," the woman said, earnestly, talking a bit fast so that the words ran together. "That is a crack that the Enemy can use to strike through to your soul. The best way to use violence is to be so steeped in the muscle memory that when you enter combat you simply respond, emotionlessly. Or so it seems."

"Have you . . . ?" Barb asked.

"No, actually," the woman admitted. "So far we've never had to draw our weapons. But we're fairly new to all of this. My name's Julie Lamm, by the way," she added, smiling and holding out her hand. "And this is James, my husband. And you are . . . ?"

"Barbara Everette," Barb said, holding out her own as she tried to keep up with the rapid patter of the woman's voice. She had never realized it was possible to both have a southern accent *and* talk like a New Yorker.

"Crap!" James said, his eyes widening. "*You're* Barbara Everette?"

"I'm very pleased to meet you," Julie said, her own eyes wide. "And I take back any suggestions that I made."

"I don't see why," Barb said, shaking her hand and James'. "I'm here to learn."

"Learn what?" James asked. "You took down a sixth level avatar! There are only about three agents in the U.S. that *might* have been able to do that!"

"James, stop that," Julie said, wise understanding in her eyes and her speech slowing. "Barbara, you have to understand that what you did is considered . . . amazing. I hadn't known who you were or I wouldn't have been so . . . definite. To simply hold your soul against such an adversary shows that your soul is very tough, very strong. Yes, using anger in combat might open up a channel to the Enemy. But it would take a strong avatar to use it, especially if Almadu was unable to do it. Almadu is one of the Children of Tiamat. A very ancient and powerful godling. If you were able to withstand his glamour, then it's likely that your soul is . . . very pure."

"I was protected by the hand of the Lord," Barbara said, simply. "I . . . felt the . . . what did you call it?"

"Glamour," Julie said. "It's one way of saying a mental projection. They come in various . . . guises. But each tries to use the evil that you feel in your soul against you. If he was unable to . . ."

"Oh, but he did," Barbara said, relieved that she could actually talk about her experience with people that didn't think she was insane. "I . . . walked through . . . horrible visions. But then the Lord entered me and they . . . stopped. I could feel His light in my soul, shielding me."

"I heard you had a full manifestation," James said, interestedly. "Actual physical projection."

"I'm not sure about that," Barb said, humbly. "But I could not have done what I did without the shielding hand of the Lord over me."

"Christian?" the man with piercings asked, somewhat hostilely. He had died black hair and blue eyes that were almost black. He was wearing a tattered pair of black jeans and a plain black T-shirt. Barbara realized that if you ignored the piercings he was actually good looking in a thin and hollowed out way. He had gotten his badge and it read simply "Dragon-Kin."

"Yes," Barb said, simply. "I'm an Episcopalian."

"This is Barbara Everette, Dartho," James interjected.

"Oh," Dartho said, nodding. "Pleased to meet you. Good job in Louisiana. For a beginner." He didn't really sound as if he was pleased to meet her.

"Thank you," Barbara said, dryly, cocking her head to the side. "I take it you're not a beginner?"

"No," Dartho said, turning and walking away.

"Wooo," James said, shaking his head. "I hadn't expected that."

"Dartho's a powerful adept," Julie said, shaking her head. "And highly trained. Not one of the ones that think violence is only for the police, either. But probably not powerful enough to have done what you did. That has to grate on him. Especially since you're . . ." Julie gestured at her and shrugged.

"Good looking?" Barb said, hotly. "Well dressed? Normal looking? A . . . what's the term, a 'mundane'?"

"Yep," Julie said, grinning. "That would be it. Between who you obviously are, what you represent, and how much more powerful you are, as a newbie, he has to be sort of hot under the collar."

"That is so . . ." Barbara said and stopped.

"Human?" Julie asked. They'd reached the head of the line and she nodded at the person handing out badges. "Julie and James Lamm."

"Right here, Julie," the woman said. She was heavyset with teased out red hair wearing a T-shirt captioned in Latin. "Good to see you again."

"Glad to be here," Julie said, sighing. "But there's a lot of tension."

"Barbara Everette is attending," the woman said, nervously. "We're all on pins and needles. I hear she's a real . . ."

"Mundane?" Barb finished for her. "Barbara Everette," she added, smiling.

"Actually," the woman said, shaking her head ruefully. "I was going to say 'Bible-thumper.' " She handed Barbara her badge and shrugged with a grin. "I think you're the only Christian attending this time. We'd heard that you get your power from the White God and you don't get powers like those without being steeped in faith."

"You also don't get them by simply going to church on Sunday and looking down your nose at everyone else the rest of the week," Barb said, hanging the badge around her neck on a provided lanyard. "Or, for that matter, by looking down your nose at all."

"That's . . . true," the woman said, rapidly reevaluating her.

"So I won't be Bible thumping this week," Barbara said. "Or standing in the hallways screaming at everyone that they're going to hell."

"Oh," the woman said, chuckling. "Good."

"Although I may point out that there is but one path to Heaven," Barbara added, grinning. "Through the Saving Grace of Our Lord. But only if anyone asks."

She turned to see that Julie and James had been waiting through the by-play and joined them.

"I can see that this is going to be an interesting week." Barb sighed.

"You're not what anyone expected you to be," Julie said. "Some of the high-level adepts, like Dartho, tend to be sort of . . . stuck on themselves. That doesn't interfere with their work, but I sort of expected you to be . . ."

"Pride is a sin," Barb said, shrugging. "Sin destroys the soul and closes it to God. And I'm here to learn. I *am* a . . . newbie. What my dad would call an FNG. And . . . yes, I feel like a fish out of water. I hadn't expected . . . this," she finished, gesturing to the people in line. There were more weird outfits than she'd ever seen in her life. At least Julie and James were dressed normally. "But I *have* to learn if I'm to do this job to the best of my ability. And doing less would also be a sin against God."

"Not to mention getting killed," James said, frowning. "And getting your soul ripped out and tossed into eternal torment."

"That too," Barbara admitted. "There are things . . ." She stopped and shook her head at the visions. "My husband has been complaining about the nightmares I've been having. I can't exactly tell him that I'm reliving watching a demon feeding on its worshippers. Not to mention trying to feed on me. Nor is there an analyst I can approach about it."

"There are some here," Julie said, leading them off. "And you might want to talk to them. What you're suffering from is straight-forward post-traumatic stress. There are aspects of it that learning about help. There are probably things that you think about your experience that bother you. And those are, quite often, very normal and have a logical basis. Dr. Braun can probably help you quite a bit."

"That would be nice," Barbara admitted. "But I'm not sure I'll have time this week."

"Don't worry, you will," James said. "There's only so much

you can absorb at once. They'll probably suggest that you take a heavy load at first, then trail off towards the end of the week. Besides, a lot of the learning in this field is what's called institutional memory. You'll pick up the theory in the seminars but you can only really learn by doing and then talking it over with more experienced operators."

"Are you operational?" Julie asked as they left the building.

"I'm not sure what you mean by that," Barb admitted. "But I was told I was going to be given a mission of something like a week's duration at the completion of this week."

"That's operational," Julie said, with a note of curiosity. "They generally pair a new operator with an older one. Do you know who you're going to be with?"

"No," Barbara said. "I very much hope it's not Dartho, though."

"He's not that bad once you get to know him," James said.

"Yes, he is," Julie contradicted. "Stuck on himself doesn't begin to cover it. His guardian is . . . weird. A Chinese dragon-god with odd tastes. If it weren't for his actions I'd say that he was on the side of the Enemy. But he has done too much good to believe that."

"I'm sort of following you," Barb admitted as they crossed one of the many bridges, this one made of twisted bamboo.

"We're heading for the First Night get-together," Julie said. "They're serving a buffet for dinner. It's . . . traditional. We gather for the first meal and new people, like yourself, get introduced. You won't have to make a speech or anything, just stand up and wave so everybody knows who you are."

"Ah," Barbara said. "I feel like I'm in a fishbowl already. This should be great."

The Philosophy Center was the largest building in the facility. Barb didn't recognize the architecture immediately, but she suspected it was northern European. Heavy logs made up most of the structure and they had been elaborately carved with looping abstract figures and staring faces.

"It's based upon a long house," Julie said, following her gaze. "An Asatru worship center. They call it the Philosophy House because it's where people tend to gather to talk. And debate. Lots of debate."

"What is there to debate?" Barbara asked as they entered the high entrance.

"Well, take what I said about anger," Julie said, frowning. "The Asatru have a philosophy that is far away from Christianity or, to an extent, even Wicca. Their highest calling is to become berserker, angry beyond the level of control. To destroy their enemies as servants in Valhalla and, most important, to die courageously in battle. To die in bed sends you to the Cold Lands, Hel, rather than Valhalla. And the Cold Lands are rather boring. So anger is, to them, a manifestation of their gods rather than a weakness for the demons to exploit."

"I see," Barb said, looking around at the crowd in the room. "Oh, my."

"Yeah," James said, grinning. "People have a tendency to dress up on First Night."

In one corner of the room where what she had to assume were the Asatru, a group dressed up in medieval clothing, some of them in partial armor and all of them armed with swords, axes and hammers. One of them definitely went for the "fantasy" version: a tall, statuesque redhead who could have been, might be, a super-model, in a chain-mail bikini with a sword slung over her shoulder. There were any number of what she had pegged as "druid" types, Wiccan probably, in hooded ceremonial robes. The two Buddhist monks were seated with a dark-skinned group she figured for Hindu in elaborate costumes, the women in saris, their hair pinned up with gilded combs, and the men in embroidered pajamas.

She saw Sharice near the front of the room, talking with a group of older women, some of them in outfits that she could only call "witchy." And Dartho was surrounded by a group of even younger men and women, all of them pierced, spiked and tattooed.

There were more people in "mundane" outfits in the room than in "costume" but it was hard to realize. The costumers just stood out from the crowd. Probably one of the reasons they costumed.

"I underdressed," she said to Julie, chuckling. "If I was going to dress as 'myself' for this, it would have been the little black dress, heels and the pearl necklace. My version of costume."

"I could have worn my ceremonial robes," Julie said, shrugging. "But they're not particularly comfortable unless you're sky clad underneath."

"I take it you're *not* Christian, either," Barbara said as they made their way into the room. She still hadn't asked what sky clad meant, but that description gave her a very good idea.

"No, we're Wiccan," Julie replied. "We were originally handfasted but we did the whole official marriage thing with a justice of the peace when we were buying a house. I'm a priestess. We're both computer consultants in our 'mundane' life, which gives us time for the work of the Foundation."

"I see," Barb said, shaking her head. "I thought Sharice was a bit of a shock," she continued, nodding in the direction of the woman.

"Sharice is a doll," Julie replied, grinning. "She used to be a fifth level adept, a very high high priestess, one of the few that made it out alive, I guess you would say. And sane. Enormous power, you can feel it when you're near her, and very wise in its use, wiser than I am. When the time came she just . . . walked away. Now she's more or less permanently resident here. She's . . . offended a lot of the major powers that we battle, so being in a stronghold is a good idea."

Sharice had gotten up from where she was sitting and now strode through the crowd to the trio.

"I see you've found some friends," Sharice said, hugging Barbara. Barb wasn't a huggy person, too many people, even females, that wanted to hug her just gave off the wrong "vibes." But she gratefully accepted one from Sharice, feeling the power that she emitted in this, to her, comfortable setting and basking in it for a moment. "That's good. Julie and James are good people."

"So I've noticed," Barbara said. "I guess I really am a mundane, though. This is all a bit . . ."

"Weird," Sharice finished for her, smiling broadly.

"I was going to say strange," Barb admitted.

"Come meet some of my friends," Sharice insisted, pulling her towards the table she had been occupying. "Of course, most of the people in the room are my friends, but we have to start somewhere."

Sharice introduced her to a bewildering array of people with names like "Klandar" and "Persemon" and "Vashto" and she came to realize that all of these people cloaked themselves in alter egos. The names were almost like code names for spies and she suspected they had the same reason; a cloak to hide behind. Persemon, a woman in her forties with graying blonde hair, turned out to be a consultant in business administration. Barbara just knew that when she was working she was as "mundane" as it got, probably a bit of a ball-buster in a businesslike skirt-suit. But here she could be . . . her other face. The face that she assuredly didn't show to CFOs and CEOs. Which was more true might be the real question.

She was dragged over to meet the Asatru delegation. They ranged from factory workers to more computer consultants. The girl in mail turned out to be, yes, a model and "exotic" dancer named Janea. That threw Barbara for a moment, although she hoped that she hadn't revealed her shock. She was beginning to be able to accept that her fellow . . . warriors of the Light, she supposed, were not all, or even *at all*, Christian. But one that was an exotic dancer was a bit hard to take. She had always pegged such women as, being frank, dumb, low-class sluts. But Janea turned out to be not only friendly and funny but wise and intelligent. She'd have liked to talk to her more, but she was dragged away to meet another group.

The buffet was opened without ceremony, the men and women who had been putting out the covered dishes joining into the crowd imperceptibly. Nobody rushed it; groups just got up from their talking to wander over and serve themselves. There was a keg set up in the corner, close to the Asatru delegation and probably why they'd chosen their seats there. In addition there were bottles of wine and at one point someone thrust a glass into her hand. It was a nice, light white, probably a pinot grigio, and she sipped it as she followed Sharice around, being introduced.

The reception at each group was interesting. Some were apparently friendly, but she could feel a strong defensive reaction from them. However, after a few words, when she didn't immediately start telling them they were going to hell for being pagans, the defensiveness seemed to melt. Some were overtly hostile and that was harder to overcome. She could tell that Sharice had been right, these people were, by and large, outcasts from "normal" society and they didn't like the intrusion she represented. But most got over it quickly and by the time she'd made the rounds of most of the room the word seemed to have gotten around that she was "okay, for a mundane."

She also faced something that she had never dealt with before: hero worship. She was used to being automatically accepted and even admired for her looks. But this group mainly was interested in her battle with Almadu and the reactions to her brief synopsis ranged from awe to understanding but respectful nods. The Asatru delegation was especially enthusiastic, roaring in joy when she explained how she'd shot her way into the corrupted church and killed the high priest and his acolytes then blown it up, destroying the avatar. The Hindus touched their heads in honor while the monks, one of whom turned out to be among the top prelates of Buddhism, bowed to her.

She could feel it going to her head and brutally suppressed it. Pride, even in a difficult job well done, was a sin. She knew that her main strength in this group was her constant struggle with sin. And in that struggle, pride could come in on sneaky cat feet.

Julie and James had wandered off at one point but she and Sharice linked back up with them when they went to the buffet. Sharice led the way, talking as she ladled her plate.

"You are a very interesting person, Barb," Sharice said, taking a spoonful of what looked, and smelled like, Szechwan vegetables. "Very wise for your years and very open at the same time. I can see why your White God has gifted you and called you to the field of battle."

"It was an accident," Barbara said, looking over the offerings. Most of the dishes were vegetarian and she had to admit that she still was a carnivore. And many of them were heavily spiced and she'd gotten a strong aversion to spice overseas. "Yes, The Lord worked through me, but my being there was accidental. I thank Him every day, though, for His blessings upon me. Not only the power to do His work, but the life He has given me."

"You truly believe it was an accident?" Sharice said, chuckling. "Why didn't you go to Gulfport, which was what you'd been planning for so long? How did you end up in a small town in the middle of nowhere, as far from what you'd been looking for as it was possible to be? How did you, a warrior of the Light, come to be in the one place you *needed* to be for the battle against darkness? And you believe it was an *accident*?"

Barb opened her mouth to reply and stopped. Put that way, it didn't look like an accident.

"Some of us are recruited to this work," Sharice continued. "I saw Janea at a Renn Faire and could feel the untrained, untapped power in her. I recruited her on the spot. It took a bit for her to realize that the situation was *real.* And if you think you have problems, imagine hers. She thought she'd gotten dragged into a very bizarre cult. That was, until her first mission. Then there are those among the fringe who have wrapped themselves so into the supernatural that they believed without proof. But those are, by and large, useless to our work. Anyone who really believes in vampires without having met someone who fought them is . . . essentially broken in a way that is useless. But the ones who are prepared to accept it, are powerful, are balanced—those are precious to us."

"I wasn't prepared to accept it," Barbara said. "I was *forced* to accept it. It was that or ignore what all my senses were telling me."

"And then there are those," Sharice said, nodding. "Most, however, don't survive. And a sixth order avatar! Good Mother of All! In my *prime* I would have hesitated at that. Understand, I know you are having a hard time accepting the adulation you are getting. But I am the only person in this room who would stand a *chance* against such a being. And your weapons skill, much as it pains me to admit it, was crucial. There is no way to have shielded a tac-team against the glamour. Only a high order adept who was *also* capable of fighting the acolytes and believers could have done what you did."

"Xiao?" James said, curiously.

"He would have been Augustus' choice," Sharice said, nodding definitely. "However, at the time, he was in the hospital. Otillia was in New Mexico, tracking down a manifestation of the Coyote that was spreading bubonic plague. Hertha was in Los Angeles, dealing with a pack of windigo. He might have pulled her off of the latter and set someone like, oh, Dartho or Virdigar on it. Probably would have if Barb hadn't taken care of it for us. But those are the only three that I can imagine would have succeeded. And now, four," she finished, looking at Barbara, calmly.

"But you must learn where your power truly lies. Often, the gods will give great power to the believer who is facing their enemies. But it is a capricious thing and it is likely you would not be given as much again, in the same situation. You are going to have to learn to hold it, to use it and to know its breadth and depth. This is something that is rare in Christians, this working with the Power of God. Finding just how much your White God will Gift you, and how. There is more than just the power to do harm. The gods can send understanding of the situation, healing, protection and even a touch of foresight. You need to learn your powers, all of your powers, their extent and form, then blend them into a whole."

"I wish I had had healing," Barbara said, sadly. "Kelly literally died in my arms. I wish that I could have . . ."

"In time, perhaps," Sharice said, nodding. "There is that in you, I can feel it. You are a very nurturing person, which is the first step to being a Healer. You are a violent one as well. It is a dichotomy that is hard to manage. You do so by revealing the nurturer and hiding the killer. Turning a face of love to the world while the bloody hands rend at your heart. I would say you need to be careful of the bloody hands, but, truly, you must be careful of both. Sometimes our adversaries are tricky to a fault and they will seduce you through your nurturing side if you let them."

Everyone seemed to have gotten a plate and was eating or already done when a man stood up from one of the tables and walked to the front of the room. He was unassuming, a bit tall, with brown hair and regular features, wearing a long purple ceremonial robe covered in golden stars. Barbara had been briefly introduced but could not for the life of her remember his name.

When he reached the front of the room conversation slowly drifted off and he raised his hands above his head ceremoniously.

"Let the Light shine upon this gathering," the man said. "Let the Powers of Good guard us and our counsels. Let us feel joy for our triumphs and grieve for our fallen, knowing that the battle goes on and will go on as long as the stars shine and the sun burns. And let us come to know our fellows as warriors of the Light." He paused and looked around the room, apparently picking out faces.

"We only have three new persons to introduce this time," he said. "Hsu Hsiu and Jiao Hicheng come to us from Nepal." He gestured to the two monks and they rose, bowing deeply. "Jiao Hicheng is the Kotan Lama and Hsiu his apprentice. They have traveled here to brief us on some of the more esoteric deities which are being seen in modern China and which we can anticipate will eventually start cropping up in the immigrant areas. I would like to thank them for coming all this way." He bowed in return and there was a brief spattering of applause as the monks sat down.

"And then we have our newest warrior," the man continued. "Barb? Could you stand up? This is Barbara Everette, everyone. Most of you know the story and if you don't I'm sure someone will relate it. Suffice to say that Barb manifested powers of an order that flatly floored everyone in the leadership of the Foundation. She has agreed to join with us in our battle for the Light and against Darkness. She, unusually, is a Christian, but as firm a believer as anyone in this room and a kind and gentle lady. A wise and loving addition to our group. However, anyone who can blast their way through a room full of Maenad worshippers, kill a high priest and acolytes and then destroy and dispel an avatar of Almadu, is far more than a pretty face and a nice smile. Do *not* get on her bad side."

Barbara blushed and waved to the scattered chuckles and applause and then gratefully sat down. As she did she caught what could only be called a baleful look from Dartho.

"Well, that's all I have," the man said. "You've got your schedules. The highlighted panels are only suggestions, feel free to sit in on any that you prefer. There's a previously unscheduled worship service for the Wicca contingent on Friday, that being the night of the gibbous moon. Sky clad is optional."

With that he simply walked back over to his seat and the conversations started again.

Barbara touched Sharice on the arm and frowned when the woman turned to her.

"Would it be . . . unwelcome if I went over to talk to Janea?" she asked, diffidently.

"Mother of All, child," the woman said, smiling. "That's what this evening is for. Go! I could see that you two bonded."

She covered the move by putting her plate with the other dirty dishes and getting another glass of wine. She usually only had one but she figured she could handle two if she nursed the second one. Then she wandered towards the Asatru delegation.

Two of the men were clearly drunk, roaring out an off-key song that had something to do with making people die. Several of the others, slightly less inebriated, had joined in. Janea was talking with a bear of a man, big, blond, bearded and hairy to the point that his back hairs were sticking through the weave of his light tunic. Barb came over and sat down, not interrupting.

" . . . wondered if we'd ever find it," the man said. "The manifestation wasn't a shape-shifter, but it was very good at make-up and it was stalking the costuming parties so it just looked like . . . a made-up human being."

"What about the feet?" Janea said, frowning. "Its feet were reversed."

"It had a prosthetic on that made it look as if it had clubbed its 'normal' feet and the others were for show," the man said, shrugging and taking a drink of beer. "Of course, when the tac-team blew in the door, they were in big trouble. I'd warned the Special Agent that bullets weren't going to hurt it."

"Iron," Janea said, frowning again in thought. "Fire. Cold steel?"

"Cold steel," the man said, half drawing his sword. "One thrust, a jolt of power and it dispelled. Badly injured one of the tac-team members. Fortunately, it was HRT and they more or less expected it. They hadn't been briefed on its resistance and they really tore the special agent a new one."

"I *still* haven't had a live one." Janea sighed theatrically, then brightened, putting on the face of a little girl. "But the year is young!" she added with a giggle.

"You will," the man said, turning to Barbara and grinning. "Just like the woman of the hour."

"Nothing of the sort," Barb said, firmly. "I'm here to learn. I'm learning just listening. What was it you were fighting?"

"A Tikoloshe," the man said, shrugging. "South African. Preys on women, but most of the various demons do. It had been haunting rave clubs in the Baltimore area, probably summoned or brought by one of the immigrant witch doctors. We finally found its lair and, well . . ."

"You haven't been introduced," Janea said. "Hjalmar Johanneson, this of course is Barbara Everette."

"Pleased to meet you," Barb said, taking his hamlike hand.

"Likewise," Hjalmar replied. "My mundane name is Quenton Barber. I used to work in a plywood mill. These days I do construction when the Foundation doesn't have need of my services."

"I take it . . . well, actually I don't know," Barb said, uncertainly. "Do you get paid?"

"Quite well," Janea said, laughing. "The Foundation draws on various sources of funding. Quite a bit from churches that are aware of our mission for example. About a third from the Catholic church alone. But, of course, when we're called in as 'consultants,' the Foundation is paid and then we get paid." She paused again and bounced up and down in her chair so that her breasts jiggled like gelatin. "I'm saving up for a boobie job!"

"The one thing you *don't* need is a boobie job," Hjalmar said, shaking his head.

"I'd sort of been wondering," Barbara admitted, still unsure if *she* got paid and if she did how she would explain that to Mark. "But to get back to the point. You knew it was susceptible to . . . what? Iron and fire?"

"Part of training," Janea said, shrugging. "There's a bunch of books you'll be getting. Some of the information is . . ." She shrugged again.

"The thing about demonology," Hjalmar said, scratching deeply at his beard, "is that most of the source books are . . . semi-fictional. Very few serious researchers realize that demons and such are real. And witnesses tend to be . . . well, any eyewitness is a poor witness. They generally can't get their heads around the reality of demons, especially, and they see things that aren't there even if there's not a glamour. Or they miss things that are there. And as to dispelling methods and the like, normally demons are only engaged in battle. There have been very few captured and studied and those only by the Foundation and a few other groups. Then there's the fact that they're so . . . incredibly abundant in history. So you study these books, most of them more alchemical than scientific in nature, and hope like Hel the source book is right and your identification is right. Take the Tikoloshe, for example. The primary source book *doesn't* list it as having reversed feet. But all of our case studies have recorded it as having reversed feet. Nor does The Book have it as susceptible to iron and fire. But it is. Cold steel, as well, if you add power to the equation."

"So if HRT had used, say, bayonets?" Barb asked.

"Wouldn't have worked," Hjalmar said. "Unless they were meteoric iron. Well, pure elemental iron would probably work. I had to have Frey work through me to dispel the demon. Even then it was touch and go. I could feel its power working against the god's and it had built up a lot of power in its killings. But we, together, were able to overcome it."

"HRT has first class shooters," Janea said. "But they don't have anyone that channels. There's some talk of rearming them, but they generally *don't* do Special Circumstances and trying to explain why they're taking courses in special entry techniques using, oh, swords and crossbows . . ." Pause. " 'Why, yes, Congressman," she said in very businesslike tones, " 'we're quite serious about that line item . . . ' I can just see it now."

"Generally if we *know* that we're going to need heavy help, we can call on the experts," the man said, grinning faintly. "Such as Opus Dei."

"Opus Dei?" Barbara said, aghast. "That's a Catholic religious group."

"Yeah, sure," Janea said, laughing. "That's all. 'Hallo,' " she said in a thick and bad Italian accent, " 'My name is Cardinal Enrico Sarducci. You killed my father. Prepare to die!' "

"Sure," Hjalmar agreed, laughing. "That's all they are. But when you see a bunch of guys in cassocks and collars carrying ballistic nylon bags show up, you know the shit has well and truly hit the fan. I think they might have called in Opus for Almadu, if they'd known how powerful he had become. But even Opus doesn't have a channeler as strong as you are. They are, though, very well shielded by their faith and their sacraments. They could have, oh, cleared the way for a more powerful channeler. There are a few in the Church," he admitted, grudgingly.

"The Wiccans seem to produce the strongest channelers," Janea said, seriously. "But their strongest channelers are, as far as I know, exclusively nonviolent. Full up vegan, sky clad, the works. And really nonviolent. The top operators are all from fairly minor sects who have a strong connection to a fairly weak god. Take Dartho; his god is virtually unknown and not particularly powerful."

"And very chaotic," Hjalmar added, rubbing his beard thoughtfully.

"And chaotic," Janea admitted. "He might even be a face of the Jester or Pan. But Dartho has such a strong connection to him that he can get more power from less source than some who have stronger deities as backing." She paused and sighed, putting on a little girl face, mooning like at a rock star. "Ahhh,

Darthoooo . . . he's so . . . sick," she finished, changing back to her "normal" personality. "His god, well, he's really into pain. Voluntary, mind you, but so was Aztec sacrifice, certainly the greater sacrifices. You know what BDSM is?"

"Yes," Barbara admitted. "Sort of."

"Well, can you imagine a *good* sect based around BDSM?" Janea asked.

"No," Barb said, definitely.

"I actually can," Janea said. "But it's a stretch. And that's the . . . nature of Dartho's sect, of his god. They feed the god with pain, voluntarily derived, and the god feeds them with power."

"That's sick," Barbara agreed, glancing over at the table Dartho had occupied and finding all of "his" group gone.

"You do what you have to for power," Janea said, shrugging. "And sometimes *more*," she added in a husky contralto, wriggling sexily.

"Our gods have, for millennia, been weak," the man said, frowning at Barb, then shrugging. "They were displaced by the White God."

"Well, *I* didn't do it," Barbara said, wincing.

"No, of course not," Janea interjected. "But it's one of the reasons Christianity is a sore point. Especially Protestantism, which doesn't recognize saints."

"What does that have to do with it?" Barb asked, totally confused.

Janea and Hjalmar looked at each other for a moment as if trying to decide which one had to tell the little girl that Santa wasn't real.

"Well," Hjalmar said, blowing out. "You see, most saints are old gods that got . . . assimilated by the religion of the White God. Michael, for example, is probably an avatar of Mars and Frey, who are almost certainly the same god. There are others. But when the Protestants took away even those souls, those prayers, it truly bit the old gods in the butt. So they sort of tolerate Catholics and Eastern Orthodox, but they've got a bug up their butt about Protestants. And . . . some people tend to bring that annoyance along with them. I mean, most of us went in the direction that we took because we didn't find normal society . . . normal. For us. Add to that, in this group, actual communication with their gods, and the gods having a case of the ass with Christianity and, well . . ."

"I'm not the most popular girl in town," Barbara said.

"You're not the most popular girl in town," Janea agreed. "But . . . you're clearly a woman of great inner strength and beauty. That simply shows through in everything you do and say. And you have a strong channel to one of the most potent sources of power on earth. From our perspective," she added, gesturing around, "you are also a fell warrior. So we Asatru accept you as if you were our own, despite being a representative of the White God. For your warrior skills if nothing else. Dress her in a chain-mail bikini and she'd be the talk of the town!" she added, giggling like a schoolgirl. "Ooh, we could go around as a pair of twins! Twins always make more . . ."

"Not on your life," Barbara said, laughing at the woman's constant change of character. "I most certainly *would* be the talk of Jackson, if I ever wore something like that. Even in private," she added, somewhat bitterly.

"But we are all one in this struggle," the man interjected. "Don't take the occasional odd reactions to heart. We know that you are a fellow warrior and accept you as such. It's simply hard for some of us to grok your presence here."

"Grok?" Barb said. "I feel as if half the time you're speaking an alien language!"

"Well," Janea said, laughing. "In this case, he was. It's from a science fiction novel called *Stranger in a Strange Land* . . ."

"That's from the Bible," Barbara said, frowning.

"Many of Heinlein's titles were," Hjalmar said.

"I won't get into the story," Janea continued. "But, to grok means to understand something so completely that it is part of you. Reading *Stranger* was one of the things that made it easy for me to become a dancer."

"I was wondering about that," Barb said.

"I could sense your shock when Sharice told you," Janea said, nodding. "You hid it well but part of my power is understanding and reading emotions that aren't visible. But . . . well . . ." She paused and tried to figure out how to explain to this nice "church lady" why she did what she did. "There are several reasons that I'm a dancer. I've never even decided which is the most important. One reason, and the easiest to explain, is that it's supplementary income to the Foundation. We get paid when we're on assignment, but only then. So everyone has to have a 'day job' except the real pros like Otillia and Hertha, who are so busy it's not funny. And it needs to be a day job you can take time off or simply walk away from. I'm a top dancer at several major clubs. When I tell the club owners 'I'm going away for a couple of weeks on another assignment' they don't blink. And they don't give me any hassle when I turn back up. And the money's *very* good. I pull in a grand pretty much every night I'm working and more, sometimes quite a bit more, on some nights."

"That's a lot of money, but . . ." Barbara said.

"You're worried about my soul," Janea said, smiling. "Asatru does not hold the same things as sin that the White God holds as sin. My patron, Freya, can be seen as another face of Ishtar/Hathor, the God Mother, Aphrodite/Venus if you will, the All-Woman and Mother of Fertility. She is my patron and through my use of my body to bring pleasure, I worship her."

"Okay," Barb said, cocking her head and frowning. "Now, *that* I have a hard time with."

"But can you accept it?" Janea asked.

"For you, perhaps," Barbara said thoughtfully, after a long pause. "Not for me."

"Of course not," Janea said, nodding seriously. "Your White God would be most angry with you if you chose my path. But my path worships my goddess. I not only dance, I am a *very* expensive call-girl; a priestess of Freya should be paid through the nose as a form of worship. Men come into my hands, angry, upset, mad at their wives, having difficulty at work. I soothe them, I placate them, I bring them joy and teach them to bring themselves joy, and I don't mean with their hand but with their spirit. When men come away from me, they take a mystical memory, but no sense of bonding. This, too, my goddess gives to me. And they return to their lives, to their mates, with a better sense of balance in the world."

"Wait," Barb said, closing her eyes and raising one hand. "You have sex with *married* men?"

"Very few *unmarried* men can afford me," Janea said, laughing. "I'm neither cheap nor easy, honey," she added in a credible Mae West imitation. "I adore the kindness of strangers. But I assure you I have saved far more marriages than I have broken," she continued, seriously. "And those that I broke, needed to be broken. Parasitical marriages with one partner sucking the life from the other like a leech or an ugly succubus. I remember one partner I had, an older gentleman and quite sweet. His wife had died and he married a much younger woman. She was sucking him dry, emotionally, and giving him nothing, not even her body, in return. He came to me, suggested by a friend who knew me. And when he went away he divorced the little tramp and sent her packing."

"Okay," Barbara said. "Now that I can . . . grok."

"Men who come to me are either very rich and in marriages where neither partner is truly bonded to the other," Janea said, "or simply well-to-do and in dire straits. They pay through the nose for my time and in turn I give them . . . healing and understanding of where their hurts center. It is my gift. It was a gift I first practiced because of the dictates in *Stranger,* and other Heinlein novels, trying to be a 'Heinlein Girl.' But later I came to an understanding of my place in the world, and of my goddess. This gave it a spiritual dimension that had been . . . limited if not entirely lacking. And, in turn, it led me to this place, at this time, to explain this to you, who would make a *wonderful* hetaera. But I hope you never do, for your White God would surely turn his face from you."

"Perhaps, perhaps not," Barbara said, shrugging. "He is merciful beyond reason or understanding. However, my own . . . upbringing would never allow me to be so . . . open . . ."

"Wanton?" Janea said, pouting theatrically, arching her back and stretching. "Sens-you-ous?" she added, raising an eyebrow and writhing in the chair.

"I'll stick with . . . open," Barb replied, grinning. "I can arch with the best of them, sweetheart! But, within me, if *I* felt it to be a sin, that would damage my relationship with God. I have enough demons to contend with; I don't need more."

"We none of us do," Hjalmar said, nodding. "But, remember, they are different for the different creeds. Wicca is not so much different from Christianity as they would like. It is a constructed religion. Well, all neopagan religions are constructed religions. But Wicca is *very* much a constructed religion and they know it. And it was constructed in a very Christian environment and many of the 'evils' in Wicca are Christian evils, evils that never would have mattered to, say, the druids that they harken back to. Their demons are much like yours, the fear of anger and so on and so forth. But for the Asatru," he said, standing up and flexing, "power is our highest calling. We are not a slave religion. Fear is our demon. Death in battle, our eyes red and staring, in anger so great it is transcendent, this is our *calling*," he boomed, his face hard. He closed his eyes, suddenly, and breathed deep and long, his jaw flexing, until finally he relaxed, sighing.

"Thus easily does a god take one once you become fully open to your channel," he said, sitting down, shakily. "I simply opened a channel to my inner aggression, to show you the true nature of Asatru, and Frey took me. I think, to take a look at you. But his warrior anger was filling me, calling me to battle even in this place of peace. Someday," he said, wistfully, quietly. "Someday I will be called to a hopeless battle and my god will fill me and I will berserk into mine enemies and be slain. Then shall I be taken up upon the arms of the Valkyrie and ride with them to Valhalla for all eternity. . . ."

"I think I finally understand why I came here," Barbara said after a long pause.

"To hear the word of Asatru?" Janea said, grinning.

"Perhaps," Barb replied, seriously. "I hold a great deal of anger in my soul. I'm very careful to not let it out, to Witness as a Christian should, every day of my life. And the anger at petty people, daily frustrations, I still feel that those are sins. Turn the other cheek is the right way to deal with those. But . . . I wonder if . . . if righteous anger, the anger of Samson in the temple and the anger of David, if this is not a facet of . . . God."

"The White God has been a very angry and vengeful god on occasion," Hjalmar said. "Sodom and Gomorrah come to mind."

"But not since the Coming of Jesus," Barbara pointed out. "Jesus was a man of peace and he brought peace wherever he went. Well . . . except to the moneychangers in the temple," Barb admitted. "Even with the Devil he simply ignored his temptations."

"True," Janea said. "But what if the Devil had attacked the children who were listening to His sermon?" she asked, cocking one shapely eyebrow. "Those that he called forward to sit at his very feet. Would he have been so forgiving?"

"Probably not," Barbara had to admit. "I'm surprised that you know the Bible that well," she added.

"Well, it used to be a case of know thine enemy," Janea admitted. "I mean, I generally work in the Southeast. I especially did when I was just getting started. And, well, the Bible-thumpers . . ."

"But you'll also find that learning *a lot* of comparative religion is a good idea in this job," the man said. "There's no religion or myth you want to overlook. The foundation has an extensive library and I wish I could read absolutely everything in it but I don't have the time."

"I've read the Bible, the Talmud and the Koran," Janea said, ticking off the list on her manicured nails. "Each in multiple translations. And the Apocrypha. And the Dead Sea Scrolls translations. As well as all the Vedas and shamanistic Buddhism tracts. And I still feel like I only scratched the surface."

"America is a country of immigrants," Hjalmar pointed out. "In, oh say Borneo, you'll only find the spirits of Borneo."

"Interesting choice," Barbara said with a laugh. "I lived there once."

"Yes, but Westerners are few," Hjalmar corrected. "They don't bring . . . northern European werewolves or vampires with them. Very few people are acolytes of the dark powers and they tend to stay in the U.S. if they're from the U.S. Ditto Europe. But the immigrants that come to these shores . . . many of them are from the far places where evil still waits on quiet feet for the unwary. It is not only the workers and the farmers and the hunters that come to these shores, but the various shamans and priests that they support. And the acolytes of the dark powers that hide in their midst. Then there are all the idiots who buy a grimoire in Barnes and Noble and think they're playing when they try to summon. Little do they know."

"You can find *summoning* spells in Barnes and Noble?" Barb said, aghast.

"In at least one book that was published there is an accurate method for summoning a Persian daevas. It was a minor daevas, but nonetheless we were busy for a while and Ahriman was reinforced strongly by the souls of many . . . well, call them innocents. It was called the Green River Slayings."

"I thought they caught the guy who did those?" Barbara asked.

"Well, he was one of the ones who read the spell, wasn't he?" Janea said. "There have been several mass murders and serial killings driven by that particular daevas."

"Fortunately," the Asatru said, "we were able to get the second printing modified so the spell was wrong. And, of course, the summoner had to do certain rites that *guaranteed* their soul was tarnished. They also had to have at least a trace of power. But between the acolytes that come from other shores, where they had been in balance with shamans combating them, and the penchant for study that some Americans have—"

"We're getting overrun," Janea said, shrugging. "There simply aren't enough operatives, especially high level ones. Expect to be busy."

"Well, that should go over well with my husband," Barb said, dryly.

Chapter Four

Barbara contemplated the previous evening as she made her way to her first seminar: Introduction to Demonology. The evening had turned into one long free-form discussion. History, mythology, legend, archaeology, particle physics and cooking had all entered in at one time or another. She had talked with the lamas for a time and been mightily impressed. They weren't just yellow-robed mystics from the back of beyond. The lama had a Ph.D. in physics from Reading University and his apprentice was working on his masters in comparative religion. The lama admitted that he had obtained his degree *before* it was discovered he was the umpteenth reincarnation of the Kotan Lama. But both of them were well traveled; indeed it was the first time Barb had been able to discuss the Far East with anyone in a long time, let alone with someone remarkably intelligent and, yes, wise.

She had spoken with some of the Wiccans, who ranged from very down to earth to very . . . out there. Barbara knew now, beyond belief, that demons roamed the earth in many guises. But she was still pretty sure that crystals couldn't cure warts, much less fend off demons. She did listen, however, to some of the more . . . functional members of the group, who gave her a series of small charm tips that could be used for minor household protections. When she wasn't sure if the use of magic violated her faith, it set off a long discussion of same by people who had, she suspected, far more knowledge of the Christian Faith than the Reverend Dr. Jasper Winton Mulgrew, her minister.

She had gotten to bed very late, for her, her head reeling. The people had ranged from very strange to fascinating. All had been far more intelligent than the friends she and Mark had made in Jackson. And, generally, wiser. She had found herself having to rev her brain up in a way she hadn't known since her university days, or before, simply to keep up with the flow of conversation. And she also found herself bewildered by a series of in-jokes that seemed endless. Of course, with a group like the Foundation, with everyone being "in" on the secret, in-jokes were only to be expected. But what in he . . . heck were space goats and why did they baaa every time Hjalmar opened his mouth?

There was a small group in the room when she arrived, some of whom she recognized from the night before. She took a spot near the front, nodding to a few of the people she recognized, and opened up the portfolio that had been provided. It was embossed with the "People of Faith" symbol and had a pen in the slot already. There were large boxes stacked in one corner of the room and from the labels on them she suspected they were boxes of books. If so, and if they were for them, she was going to need a book bag. There was also a covered easel with a flip chart of some sort. There were quite a few pages to the flip chart.

The teacher turned out to be Sharice, wearing another brightly colored dress. She bustled to the front of the room, dropped her load of books on the table and turned to the group with a smile.

"Good morning," she said. "I don't usually teach intro demonology so I hope you'll bear with me while I get up to speed. Generally there's a joke about now," she added, smiling, "but I don't know any jokes about demonology. Except one. How do you know the difference between a demon and an angel? We battle the one and we work for the others." She looked around at the snorts and nodded.

"That is essential to keep in mind. Evil is *defined* by the environment, by the culture. The Mongols slew hundreds of thousands of people and considered that to be a *good* thing. Might makes right was their way of life. Modern Islamic fundamentalists consider the killing of innocents to be religiously justified in their Holy War. Are the manifestations that they create evil? The Aztecs ritually sacrificed thousands of human beings at a time, many of them *volunteers* for torture and ritual murder. Was that evil?" She looked around at the group and shrugged.

"By our modern lights, by *our* Faith, the answer is: yes. These actions are evil and the entities that support, encourage and revel in them are evil. Our patrons use us to battle those entities upon this plane. They use us to save souls from the clutches of their enemies and our souls are offered to them in return. However, that is what you have to grasp. The essential battle is for souls, for power. Our enemies have a desire to seize souls, through whatever means is available to them. Our patrons also desire to bring souls into their area of control and wish to prevent their enemies from securing them.

"It is without doubt that at one time many modern demons were gods who were worshipped and sacrificed to within a positive societal context. However, over the years most of them have been displaced by more positive gods, including most especially Yaweh and the White God, and the sacrifices once given to them have dwindled. From the perspective of anyone in this room, this can only be regarded in a positive light; the religions of Baal, of Kali, of Tzetzacoatl were abominations and their surviving acolytes are monsters. But demons and the bloody gods still continue to struggle to capture the souls of the innocent and they come to us in a variety of guises. And using physical sensory cues to identify them is what this class is about. Later, the use of secondary senses, related to your god-bond, will be covered."

They were issued four books that, as Sharice put it, were simply primers on the subject, and then Sharice ran through a list of the more common entities they might encounter. Vampires and werewolves Barbara had heard of but some of the most common entities derived from *faiths* she had never heard of. Many of the demons and devils of Christianity were traced, as individuals or classes, back to Zoroastrianism and even to Babylon.

Most of the class seemed to consider the information extremely elementary but Barbara was entirely out of her depth. She had never really been interested in the occult and suddenly finding it central to her life was beyond odd. But she persevered, taking copious notes and flipping through pages in *The Golden Bough* and *The Masks of God,* trying to keep up.

By the end of the class she was sure she'd never be able to identify even the simplest manifestation and her head was swimming with names like "selkie" and "bunyip" and "daevas," of which there seemed to be legions.

When the class was over she looked at her schedule and sighed. Next was "The Touch of God: Introductory Channeling." She'd faced what she now recognized as "an intermediate godling" and channeled heavily to fight it. But right now all she wished was that she was back home, getting lunch ready for the kids.

She stood up, clutching her books, and stepped to the front to talk to Sharice.

The instructor finished talking to a mousey woman who nodded at Barb as she walked out and Barbara confronted the witch.

"You seemed to have left out Allah," she said, quizzically.

Sharice paused and then shrugged.

"Allah is as much on the side of light as The White God," Sharice said, frowning. "However, the current cultural expression by the majority of the active members of Islam is highly negative and in many cases involves interaction with negative intermediaries. Those who are using the name of Allah for their activities range from dupes to those who know very well the entities are enemies of their God. However . . . just as there are very few Protestant Christians among our ranks, there are very few members of Islam. Some day, perhaps, Islamics will adjust their culture and quit making pacts with the daevas and djinn.

But, until then, I can't in good conscience put the religion of Islam fully on the side of Light."

"Are you sure that Allah is . . . I guess 'on our side' would be the way to put it?" Barb asked, diffidently.

"Oh, no question," Sharice said, cautiously. "The fact is . . . it's very hard to separate Yaweh, the White God and Allah as entities." She looked at the expression on the woman's face and nearly laughed. "Yep, all this horror is, in fact, being done in the name of the White God, whether they realize it or not. Trust me on this one. You'll find out for sure some day. There is, as far as anyone can tell, not a shred of difference between the three entities. All the Children of the Book worship the same God. The One God if you will. And that One God is *mightily* pissed at the 'fundamentalists' from what we've been able to glean."

"I see," Barbara said, unhappily.

"If it makes you feel any better," Sharice said, "from what we've got from history, there are various periods in each of the three major religions of the One God where the adherents, in fact, fell out of favor. The religious wars in Europe, the period in Israel when Jesus appeared, the crusades. All of them had the One God pissed. But . . ." She paused and frowned. "For some reason direct action on His part has become . . . almost impossible. The *why* of that has been a bone of contention in the Foundation for some time. Now all that He can do is work through his earthly supporters," she finished, waving at Barb. "But when He does, he has a mass of power like none other."

"I guess I can accept that," Barbara said. "It doesn't change my approach to Him. He is still the God that sent His only begotten Son to die for our sins."

"Hold that thought," Sharice said, seriously. "Faith is our armor. You'll learn much here and some of it may shake that faith. Don't let it. You have *felt* the power of God. That is beyond faith, beyond reason. Know that what you believe, how you act, is what your God is looking for in a believer. Dedicate your soul fully to Him and you will be armored against any evil. But know, too, that we all follow our own paths to Him. Each person's path is unique to that person."

"That takes some getting used to," Barbara admitted. "My faith tells me that the only path to heaven is through the saving grace of Our Lord Jesus. That where two or more are gathered in His name, that there he resides."

"How many names are there for God?" Sharice said, smiling. "When we Wiccans gather in our circle, we call upon the One. Is that some separate entity? Or is it, in fact, another face of the One God? Are *four* or more gathered in His name?" She nodded at the thoughtful expression on Barb's face and then gestured at the door. "You have more classes to tax your mind and soul. Go to them. Learn. So that the next time you are called to God's work you will be better prepared in knowledge. Let the spirit be your own."

She had arrived on Monday and through the week she attended class after class on every conceivable subject. Some of them, like "Sexual Magic," made her squirm. Others were so esoteric that she wasn't sure what connection they might have to her Calling. But, as the week stretched out, the schedule lightened up. She read the various tracts that had been given to her and then dove into the Foundation's library for more advanced reading. She found that researching the occult was fun in and of itself. And she began to see what Janea had meant by it being a lifetime study.

She also found out how much she was being paid in a short class called "Administrative Introduction." If she worked full time, she'd be making more than four times as much as Mark. That took some adjustment. Even the training was being paid for, at her current rate as a "Class Three Adept." She also found out that the highest rating was Class Five, of which there were only three in the entire group. From a side comment from Sharice she got the impression that if she had been graded purely on the basis of her performance with Almadu, she'd have been immediately promoted to Class Five. And Class Fives made more than twice as much as she was currently earning.

On Sunday afternoon, after attending divine services at a small Methodist church in the valley, she was sitting in her room, curled up with Joseph Campbell's *The Masks of God: Oriental Mythology,* when there was a tap on her door.

"This is your welcome wagon," Julie said, when she opened the door. The woman was, surprisingly, accompanied by Janea, who was dressed simply in jeans and a jacket. "All work and no play and all that. Time to go have some fun."

"I *am* having fun," Barbara said, holding up the book.

"Different fun, then," Janea said, shaking her head. "Shoes you can get dirty. Jeans. Warm shirt and jacket."

"That the uniform of the day?" Barb asked, but waved the two in. She had been dressed in sweats, but she changed quickly, shrugging on a jacket.

"Bring your piece," Julie said. "We're leaving the compound."

They met James at the parking area, then drove out of the facility and down to the main road. There they turned right and up into the hills.

"Okay, where are we going?" Barbara asked.

"There's a pretty good range up here," Julie said. "It's owned by the local NRA club, but the Foundation helps with the maintenance."

The crack of firearms was clear from the parking area when they arrived and there were several vehicles she remembered seeing at the Foundation. The parking area was well away from the range and it was a bit of hike up the hill. Barb helped Julie carry the large ballistic nylon bag she was toting while Janea easily hefted a large rucksack. James had another nylon bag.

"We don't have a range at the Foundation because of the wimpies," Julie said, panting, as they reached the top of the slope. There was a gated fence and though the fence Barbara could see a half dozen people she recognized standing at a firing line. Others were to the rear, waiting to fire. There were a variety of targets, paper and metal, set up downrange and a large and solid berm.

"Good to see you, Barb," Hjalmar said, walking over to the group. He was wearing a shoulder holster with a Beretta semiautomatic in it. "I understand you can shoot, but how briefed are you on range safety?"

Barbara hesitated then shrugged. "Well, I'm enough of a range safety nut that seeing a person walking around with a weapon in a shoulder holster, which points the barrel at anyone behind them, is making me nervous."

"Oooo-kay," Hjalmar said, chuckling. "I'll give you a pass on the range safety briefing, then."

Barbara drew her sidearm and cleared it, then set it on the table to the rear. There were boxes of ammunition stacked and she ensured that there was plenty of .45. After that she snagged a pair of earplugs and put them in.

In the meantime, Julie and James had opened up their bags and were setting out the contents. They clearly were more "into" weapons than she was. They had brought everything from a small caliber automatic that Barb tagged as an Astra .25 up to three assault rifles, an AK variant, a CAR-15 variant and one she didn't recognize.

Most of the shooters she vaguely recognized, after she adjusted for "mundane" clothes, as Asatru. But there were a couple of women she thought were Wiccan and at least one guy who she was pretty sure had been part of Dartho's group. He was shooting a Colt Python when they arrived and while he was there with everyone else he seemed subtly outcast by the group.

When the current group of shooters had completed their series, James and Julie waved her forward with Hjalmar following. Barbara noticed that the other stations had shooters, but they seemed to be waiting for her.

"We're interested in your shooting," Hjalmar admitted. "We'd heard about the shooting in Louisiana and . . ."

"You want to see if it was exaggerated?" Barb asked, smiling in a friendly and disarming manner.

"I guess," Hjalmar said.

"Well, I got handed this piece on the drive to the Foundation," Barbara said, setting the unloaded .45 on the shooting table. "And it hasn't been zeroed. I'd been looking forward to an opportunity."

"Go ahead," Hjalmar said, setting up a five point target on a trolley and running it out to ten meters.

The target had one large central bull's-eye and four more at the corners. In addition, there were "dots" running out from the bull's-eyes in an X pattern. Barb carefully loaded and armed the .45. Then took up a modified Weaver stance, feet spread, one slightly forward of the other, two hands on the weapon with one arm nearly straight and the other cocked slightly. It was her most comfortable shooting stance. She'd tried various others over the years but always come back to the Weaver.

She carefully targeted one of the dots, rather than the bull's-eye. The first round hit the outer left corner of the paper. Which looked like really lousy shooting, except she'd been aiming at a dot in the upper left corner.

"Flyer?" Hjalmar asked.

"Out of zero," she replied, pulling a small screwdriver out of her purse and adjusting the rear sight to the left and down. She lifted the pistol again and targeted a different bull's-eye, again targeting one of the dots. This time the round nicked it, low and to the right. She repeated the zeroing action and then shrugged.

"It's in," she said.

"You're all over the target," Hjalmar protested.

"You're assuming I was aiming at the bull's-eye," she said, quietly. Then she lifted the pistol and fired five rounds, fast. Re-aiming she fired five more, then the last two in the clip, spaced. She dropped the clip, inserted another and slid the slide forward in one rapid blur. "Reel in."

As the target approached it was apparent that there was a perfect four-leafed clover centered around the main bull's-eye and the lower left one. The upper left and the upper right had rounds squarely through the X ring.

"Reel another one out," Barb ordered.

This time she fired five rounds, fast, at the center bull's-eye, then switched to her right hand only and fired another five at the upper right, then left-handed to the upper left, then switched to her third, and last, clip and fired the bottom two, one, handed. Last she fired five rounds, spaced, one-handed, switching from right to left in deft "gun-fighter" tosses.

When it was reeled in, the target had five almost perfect cloverleafs and a round through the cardinal points of the paper, outside the center bull's-eye, with one additional on top. A couple of the outer bull's-eyes were slightly out of position but given they were fast, one-handed shots, they were still phenomenal.

"Crap," Hjalmar said, quietly. "I guess it *wasn't* blowing smoke."

"I've been shooting since I was eight," Barbara said, calmly. "I've put more rounds though a USP than most SEALs I've met."

"Why cloverleafs?" the guy with the piercings asked. "I mean, why not through the bull's-eye if you're that accurate?"

"I trained for combat shooting," Barb said with a shrug. "If you train to put rounds through the same hole over and over again, you tend to hit the same spot on a target. You want to choose your spot, aiming for major arteries or nervous points. And if you're taking more than one round to put your target down, putting the rounds in different spots." She picked up the gun again, refilled a magazine and armed then targeted the metal post targets, each six-inch circles, putting all five down in about five seconds.

"The problem with going for really targeted shooting in combat, of course, is that your target is moving," she added, placing the gun down on the table again. "And it's harder to hit the point targets you'd prefer."

"And you can high-level channel," James said, breathing out in surprise.

"I've been gifted by God," Barb said. "Training helps. I'm only starting to learn to control my channels. That has been interesting training. I'm also going to be interested in finding out the vulnerabilities of the enemies of God. I wish I'd had some idea where on Almadu there was a vulnerable point. As it was, I had to just fill him with lead and hope for the best."

"Most constructs don't have the vulnerabilities of natural beings," Hjalmar said. "So it probably didn't matter where you placed your rounds. But I have to admit that you're the first time I've heard of channeling into your actual rounds. That, right there, is an amazing gift."

"The gods never give gifts without reason," Janea said, thoughtfully. "I wonder what your purpose is?"

"I'm sure that will be plain someday," Barbara said, picking up a magazine and starting to refill it. "In the meantime, though, let's have fun!"

Chapter Five

They spent about three hours out on the range, switching guns and seeing who was "range boss", the best shooter on the range. After a while, though, it became pretty clear that Barbara was a hard match to beat.

"I think you could probably go to Camp Perry," Hjalmar admitted after watching her put five rounds in the black at fifty meters.

"I wanted to go for the shooting team in college," Barb admitted. "But then I met Mark. He . . . allows me to go shooting from time to time. But he doesn't support it, strongly. Not strongly enough for me to consider something like that. And he is my husband, the master of the household. It is enough that God has granted me these gifts to use in His name."

"Now *that* I have a hard time handling," Janea said, disgustedly. "How you can just let him dictate—"

"We all come to God in our own way," Barbara said, smiling at her.

"Uh . . ." Janea said, her mouth open. And then she shut it and grinned. "Hoist on my own petard."

"By," Barb corrected. "By your own petard. It was a name for a grenade. It means blown up by your own bomb. And . . . yes," she added, grinning back.

She noticed that the "Dartho" type was having a hard time with one of James' automatic rifles, the CAR-15, and slid over to his position.

"How are you doing?" Barbara asked.

"Not as well as you," the young man said, shamefaced.

"Have you been shooting long?" Barb asked. "And I don't think we've been introduced, I'm Barb Everette."

"Ghomo," the young man said, nodding at her. "And, no, this is the first time I've been shooting. I always wanted to but my parents were death on guns."

"There's more to it than just picking up a gun and shooting," Barbara said, gently. "I got taught by my father as a girl and I've been doing it for years. There's a lot to learn."

"I know," Ghomo said, sighing and plinking another round downrange. "But . . ." He looked around at the others and shrugged, setting the gun down. "I guess I really don't fit in here."

"Of course you do," Barb said, angrily. "You are one of the Foundation. That is enough." She looked over her own shoulder and sighed. "Okay, you're probably right that people don't immediately cotton to you. Dartho, I think, doesn't have many friends outside his circle and you're carrying that load with these people. But you don't carry it with me. So why don't we work on your shooting for a while. But let's start with pistols."

She ran him through stance and breathing control, then trigger control and sight alignment. After that she had him fire a series, talking about what had happened with each of his "flyers." He had a tendency to jerk the trigger, among other things.

"You're anticipating the recoil," Barbara said, gently. "When you fire like this, you should try for a sort of Zen state of awareness. Do not anticipate, simply do."

"You're pretty strange for a church lady," Ghomo said, reeling out another target.

"Not so strange," Barb replied. "There are church ladies and church ladies. I have always refused to be Sister Bertha Better-Than-You."

"Who?" Ghomo asked, setting the pistol down. "I'm sorry, my arms are getting tired."

"Shooting is exercise," Barbara said, nodding. "You should work out with barbells, working the muscles so that you can maintain accurate fire even after a long series. And one of the most important aspects of learning to shoot well is, well, shooting. Learning to fire properly and then drawing and firing over and over until what is called 'muscle memory' is developed. So that if you have to use your weapon, you do it in full alpha state, automatic actions like driving a car."

"You know," Ghomo said, smiling, "if there had been more ladies like you in my home town, I might have stayed a Christian."

"I'm sorry that your experience of the faith was negative," Barb said, honestly. "It happens. Especially to those who don't quite fit in. Small town?"

"Yeah," Ghomo said. "I grew up in Alexandria, Alabama. It was getting bigger when I left, but it was still pretty small-town. I was always the weird kid in school, all twelve years and kindergarten. I'd ask the wrong questions, you know? And my parents were real Bible-thumpers. One time they took me to one of those camps where the demons get cast out. All it did was make me angrier. And sadder, too. I just wanted to . . . fit in. But I never could."

"Believe it or not," Barbara said, smiling, "I understand. But for me it was moving all the time. I never quite fit any mold people wanted to put around me. I . . . learned to wear a mask. To be the mask, in a way. But even now, people consider me strange in my own town. I've learned not to ask the wrong questions at the wrong time, who I can trust to show . . ." she waved around at the range. "This. My stranger side, to them. Even though I live in a very conservative area, where the men all go hunting in deer season, nice ladies aren't supposed to pack. Or shoot, for that matter, unless it's something ladylike like a twenty gauge for bird hunting.

"And I've had my problems with churches. Not with my Faith, understand, but with the social expression of it. Sister Bertha Better-Than-You is a character in a song by Ray Stevens. But he was a good judge of character and knew the characters to be found in small towns. Every town has the Sister Berthas, the ladies who sit in the front pew and look down on those who sit in the back, who bite and scratch in their ladylike way to get the best social position. And the reverends that support them in that, for the funding they bring in and the weak power that being mean gives them. Small towns are small towns. They want everyone to fit in a nice neat little mold. And if you don't fit in the mold, they try to break you. Because you challenge their image of what is fit and right. I'm sorry that it drove you away from the Faith, though."

"You are really strange," Ghomo said, sighing. "And you really get your power from . . . Jesus?"

"From God," Barb said, nodding. "The power, I suppose, of the Holy Spirit working through my faith in the saving power of the Lord Jesus."

"I can channel," Ghomo said. "A little. I get my power from Qua-Lin. I give of my essence and he returns it at need. But . . ." He paused and shrugged, looking a bit ashamed. "It always feels . . . a little sick, you know? It doesn't feel right. We of the faith of Qua-Lin work for good, don't get me wrong. But . . ."

"Each of us comes to our Faith in our own way," Barbara said. "Just remember, whatever sacrifice you give to your god returns to you manifold. He is your armor and your sword, as you are his. Hold hard to faith, whatever that faith may be, and you will be a warrior of the Light."

"Okay," Ghomo said, nodding. "But . . . I think I might explore some other faiths. It happens. I'm just not . . . comfortable with Qua-Lin."

"Do as you must," Barb said. "But if your forearms are rested, perhaps we should continue with your shooting lesson."

They shot through another series and then Hjalmar called a break.

"James," Hjalmar said, causing an outburst of "baaaa"s. "Cut that out. James, I was wondering, anything new in the demon killing line?"

"Oh, not that," Julie said, hiding her face in her hands. "James, tell me that's not what's in the other bag."

"Well, as it happens," James said, grinning, "I just happen to have brought along . . ."

"You always do this to me," Julie said, throwing up her hands in mock horror as James dipped into the still unopened rucksack.

What came out was the most bastard weapon Barbara had ever seen. An airtank backpack hooked up to . . . well, it had three magazines and a big barrel . . . She finally admitted she couldn't make head or tails of it.

"James is our resident Q," Janea said, grinning. "Let's see what he's got this time."

"Well," James said, laying out the weapon and extracting one of the obviously homemade magazines. "Barb doesn't have much of the background here . . ."

"Ever since James joined us," Hjalmar said, picking up the magazine and looking in it, "he's been hoping for what we call a Hellmouth incident."

"See, generally what we deal with is one minor entity, or a necromancer gathering power to summon one, at a time," Janea interjected. "But sometimes . . . when was the last real outbreak?"

"1954," James said, promptly. "It was dealt with by Steve Reeves, who used to play roles like Hercules and Tarzan. He had, quietly, converted to Zoroastrianism and had been drawn into the Foundation. There was a full outbreak in the Hollywood Hills and he and another actor . . ." He paused and frowned.

"Tyrone Power?" Janea asked.

"Somebody like that," James said. "Anyway, there was a manifestation of Tiamat who began spawning her brood, as she is wont to do. And they had to fight the brood and her."

"Fortunately," Hjalmar said, "Tiamat's got more enemies than Satan, if that's possible. Reeves is supposed to have channeled an avatar of Gilgamesh, or maybe Enkidu, nobody was certain which it was. Real derring-do time. Lots of half-formed monsters, vampires and werewolves by the score, Hercules so filled with the power of multiple gods he was hyped up like, well, Hercules . . ."

"Not the score," James said. "There weren't more than three or four of each. And they attacked in daylight, during the dark time of the moon, so both weren't at their best."

"They went in with a group of stuntmen and such, fought their way through the brood, killed Tiamat by cutting off her heads, one by one, and burning them with fire, then killed her earthly body," Hjalmar continued. "Lost a goodly number of the red shirts in the process, started a fire in the scrub that covered up the battle and got out. But ever since James joined us . . ." he said, waving at the weapon.

"Well, just in case," James said, grinning. "I've been working on the ultimate Hellmouth weapon. This is the Mark Six . . ."

"Wait," Janea said. "You showed us the Mark Three last time. What happened to Four and Five . . . ?"

"Don't ask," Julie snapped. "The dog's never been the same since . . ."

"As I was saying," James interjected, loudly. "This is the Mark Six. Based around a paintball system, it is a much superior weapon to the Mark Three . . ."

"Not to mention Four and Five," Julie muttered. "Goddess, that was a lot of trouble to clean up . . ."

"In magazine one," James continued, ignoring the commentary and inserting the magazine in Hjalmar's hand, "you have your basic wooden stake." He aimed at a human silhouette target and let fly. The stake managed to hit the target, at ten meters, in the right shoulder, just about out of the silhouette. But it was there for all to see, a wooden stake, stuck in a thin cardboard target.

"Not much penetration," Hjalmar said, laughing.

"I'm working on that," James shot back. "And then in magazine two, you have your general purpose stake." He adjusted a series of controls and let fly again, hitting the target closer to the center. This time, however, whatever had flown through the air went right through the target.

"Not bad," Hjalmar said. "But what was it?"

"This," James said, stooping to the rucksack and pulling out what looked like a thick crossbow bolt with a wicked barbed head. "The bolt is ash wood, which is reported to be effective against most Northern European vampires. The head is steel plated with silver. Good against general targets *or* werewolves and other entities that are affected by silver. And last but not least," he said, pushing back on the head and exposing an ampoule. "Holy water ampoule with silver nitrate suspended in it."

"Wow," Hjalmar said, grinning. "That'll do a number on quite a few beasties. Fluffy bunny huggers strike again!" he shouted, raising a laugh.

"Okay," Barbara said, holding up her hand. "That sounds like *another* in-joke."

"Do the acronym," Julie said. "Foundation for Love and Universal Faith. FLUF. A few years back, one of the FBI agents who was being supported called the Wiccan operative a 'fluffy bunny hugger.' Which she *was*, but very good at what she did. The rest of us, though, find it hilarious."

Barbara looked over at Hjalmar admiring the bastardized paintball gun and had to admit he was anything *but* a "fluffy bunny hugger."

"What's in magazine three?" Ghomo asked, diffidently.

"Paintball rounds," James said, adjusting more controls and firing a burst of blue rounds that splattered all over the target. "I like paintballing. And I'm trying to figure out how to manufacture them with holy water instead of paint."

"I'll take one with just the all purpose stake," Hjalmar said.

"That will be the Mark Seven," James admitted.

"Nine," Julie said, shaking her head. "And what you did to the poor cat should be illegal. . . ."

After a weapons cleaning party at the spacious longhouse most of the Asatru used, Barb took a shower and put on a "dressy dress" for dinner. It was the end of the conference and most of the members were going to be either going back to their regular lives or on to assignments. Barbara was in a bit of a limbo;

nobody had assigned her to the mentioned mission but on the other hand nobody had suggested she go home.

She put on her duster and made her way across the compound towards the Philosophy House. However, as she crossed the bridge to it, making a mental note that running water was anathema to various malignant entities, she saw Dartho striding towards her with an angry set to his shoulders.

"Do *not* woo my acolytes," he shouted at her as he approached. He pointed a finger in her face and continued in a near scream. "Do *not* shove your Christian mythology down the throat of my people, do you understand me?"

"I understand that you have three seconds to get that finger out of my face or I'm going to break it off and feed it to you," Barbara replied, calmly. "As to wooing your acolytes, you probably should do that yourself. I take it you're discussing Ghomo?"

"I don't have enough male subs as it is!" Dartho shouted angrily, but withdrew the offending digit. "I can't afford to lose one to your damned God!"

"Perhaps you should have considered that before he came to *me* for counseling," Barb said, feeling a righteous anger building in her. "He is a fine young man who is questioning his faith. Do *you* support him in his faith, Dartho? Were *you* on the range teaching him? Where *were* you Dartho? What were *you* doing when he needed someone to talk to? Is this about *him,* Dartho or about *you*? He spoke of giving of his essence and, in return, getting a smidgeon of power. Where is the power going, Dartho? Are those acolytes you call *yours*, not your *god's,* I notice, about worship of your god or worship of *you*, Dartho?"

"I am a high priest of Qua-Lin," Dartho screamed. "Do not *begin* to try to understand the mysteries of my god, Christian! It would blast your tiny mind!"

"I don't care about your mysteries, Dartho," Barb snapped. "But if the worshippers are losing faith, perhaps their *priest* should do something about that! Not come screaming at someone who gave a person a moment's thought, a moment's help, a moment's comfort! Perhaps you should have considered tending to your flock, *priest*, instead of whatever earthly pursuits you were practicing, *priest*! Christian I am and Christian I shall be. *MY* faith is not tested here, Dartho!"

"Whoa," Sharice said, hurrying from the longhouse. "No religious battles in the compound. I could feel both of you from inside the Philosophy House."

"Tell her to leave my worshippers alone," Dartho snarled.

"I can *talk* to whomever I want," Barb snapped. "I do not proselytize. I do not condemn. I simply *Witness*. And if *Witnessing* is causing your worshippers to reconsider their very faith, then maybe you should consider what that means, Dartho."

"Both of you back *off*," Sharice said, raising her hands and then parting them, her eyes closed.

Barb felt herself physically pushed back, away from the priest and onto the bridge, and a feeling of peace descended over her. Not in anger but in searing determination, she reached into her core and summoned her own channel, driving out the externally imposed peace and summoning her own patience and understanding to replace it.

Sharice's eyes snapped open at that and she opened her mouth, closing it when she saw Barb's expression of Zen-like stillness.

"I do not permit the power of another god within my soul, Sharice," Barbara said, calmly. "My faith derives from the Lord Jesus Christ and I shall *have* no other before Him. But thank you for intervening."

"Barb, you were going to supper," Sharice said, just as calmly. "Dartho, were you?"

"No, I was looking for *her*," he spat.

"In that case, please go away from the Philosophy House and let Barbara get her dinner," Sharice said. "You're leaving on assignment tomorrow. Until you do, you two stay away from each other."

"I want you to tell her to stay away from my acolytes," Dartho insisted. "I won't have her wooing them over to her damned slave religion."

"If you are speaking of Ghomo," Sharice said, "he has not only talked to Barb. He spoke to me as well, and to Guinevere. He is questioning his faith. That, alone, will probably sever his link to

Qua-Lin. He has potential and will either return to Qua-Lin or find another god. You cannot *force* a person to believe in your god, Dartho. Nor will you *try*. Is that clear?"

Dartho ground his jaw for a moment and then turned his back on the two women, striding away.

"That was . . . unpleasant," Barbara said, stepping off the bridge.

"It happens." Sharice sighed. "And when it does, those of the losing faith always blame others." She paused and frowned, smiling faintly. "I think you scared him, as well. And he reacts to that with anger."

"I can understand being upset," Barbara said. "So am I. But why scared?"

"You're aware that your eyes were glowing, right?" Sharice said, carefully. "They changed color, from blue to something like black, and they *appeared* to glow. Not as if you were channeling an avatar; it seemed to be something entirely in you."

"Dartho takes the power that they give, doesn't he?" Barb asked, ignoring the comment as they both walked towards the Philosophy House. She had been told that in times of extreme anger her eyes appeared to glow; it had nearly caused Mark to be shoved through a wall once. She hadn't realized she was that angry at the priest and said a small prayer asking forgiveness. "The power that his acolytes sacrifice to their god. He takes it and uses it for his own purposes."

"Yes," Sharice said, simply. "But so do we all. Your power comes not from you, but from your God, from the Holy Spirit, if you will. And that power is supplied by thousands, perhaps millions, of True Believers such as yourself. So don't castigate Dartho for drawing upon the power given to his god by his small handful of followers. He uses that power in the service of Good."

"I'm not sure I completely agree," Barbara said, frowning. "The power of God is . . ."

"The power of belief," Sharice said, firmly. "The power given to God by the willing sacrifice of souls, dedicated to His purposes. That *is* the Power of God. Trust me."

"God created the heaven and the earth," Barb argued.

"Why?" Sharice asked, smiling. "Or, perhaps I shouldn't ask the question. Hold to your Belief, Barbara Everette and I shall hold to mine. Each in her own way to the work of Good, yes?"

"Okay," Barb said, troubled. She liked and respected Sharice and her words had been so . . . definite. But that was Sharice's belief, not her own. She mentally nodded to herself and put the words aside to pull out some other time and examine.

"You're being assigned as well," Sharice said, sighing. "I was going to go over that this evening. You'll only be here two more days. Wednesday evening you'll fly to Virginia to meet your FBI contact and go out on assignment."

"I was told that a more senior person normally travels with a junior," Barbara said, diffidently.

"Yes," Sharice replied, smiling, as they reached the doors of the longhouse. "You're getting along very well with Janea. Would you accept her as your initial trainer? She's not as experienced as I would like but . . . Dartho for example would not be a good match."

"Janea is acceptable," Barb said, holding up both hands in mock surrender. "But maybe . . . Hjalmar?"

"He's taking an independent assignment to New York," Sharice said, pausing in the entry area. "Julie and James are on the same assignment as you, but taking a different investigation area. There is a necromancer at work who is visiting science fiction and gaming conventions, or so the FBI believes. You are taking a convention in Roanoke. They are going to Georgia. There are other teams as well. This necromancer has killed seven girls, at least, and sent their souls to the nether hells. Someone needs to find him and put him in his place. Preferably six feet under. His demon can have that soul for all I care."

Chapter Six

"You ready to go?" Barbara asked, banging on the bathroom door.

She hadn't shared a room with a female her own age in years and she had a hard time not coming on the Mom with Janea. When she'd examined the assignment, she'd managed to get down to two Pullmans and a carry-on. But Sharice had *still* needed a borrowed van from the center to get them to the airport. Janea had *seven* bags, which were now stacked around the room in the Holiday Inn Express in Dumfries.

She had gotten up early this morning, knowing that it was going to take some time for her to shower, shave her legs and armpits and do her hair and makeup. Janea, who "didn't do mornings" had woken up much later and had been in the bathroom ever since. Barb had gone out to breakfast and returned, bringing coffee and some rolls, and as far as she could tell, Janea had been in the bathroom the whole time.

"Ready!" Janea said, throwing open the door. "What do you think?" she asked, posing.

Barbara had dressed in a conservative suit she had previously only used during her brief stint selling real estate. Pinstripe jacket and skirt, skirt falling to just below the knee, cream button-down shirt, fairly comfortable pumps in anticipation of a fair amount of walking. If more walking was required, she had a bag with cross-trainers in it.

Janea's idea of "conservative" dress for a meeting at the FBI training facility in Quantico Virginia was: five-inch black spike heels, a black, pleated miniskirt, quite short while not being entirely scandalous, that gave the vague impression of being from a very naughty schoolgirl's wardrobe and a white shirt so sheer it was impossible to miss the underwire, push-up bra. Especially since she'd unbuttoned the shirt far enough to show an enormous amount of cleavage and a hint of lace. Her hair and makeup were, however, superb.

"We're going to be late unless we hurry," Barb said, pushing up her sleeve to look at her watch.

"You don't like it," Janea said, crestfallen. "Is the shirt unbuttoned too much?"

"It's lovely," Barb replied, heading for the door of the room.

"I can change," Janea said, following her. "I've got other outfits. Some of them might be a little skimpy for the FBI, but . . ."

"It's not a problem," Barbara said, "but I'm driving."

"Oh, great," Janea sighed, handing over the keys. She had driven them from Dulles to Dumfries in the rented Grand Am, the trunk and back of the car packed with luggage. She wasn't looking forward to having the "church lady" drive, probably slowly in the left hand lane, as they tried to find their destination.

Barbara didn't comment except to take the keys and get in the car. But the reason she was driving was that Janea couldn't keep her mind on the road. She was usually all over the lane, if for no other reason than checking her makeup, couldn't maintain speed and had a tendency to miss turns. They'd had to turn around three times to make it to the Holiday Inn, which was right off of U.S.-1 and not particularly hard to find.

When Janea was settled, definitely not wearing a seatbelt, they'd had that conversation yesterday, Barb pulled out of the parking spot and headed for the entrance, slowing only for the speedbumps. When she reached U.S.-1 she pulled out into a narrow slot in traffic, tires screaming and smoke rising from the asphalt.

"Freya preserve us," Janea said, her eyes wide, grabbing at anything solid to hold herself in place as Barbara slid dexterously into the left-hand lane then back to the right, weaving through traffic. Despite rush hour traffic, she managed at times to get up to seventy in the forty-five mile per hour zone.

"We're a tad late," Barb said, calmly.

"Do you *always* drive like this?" Janea said as Barbara swerved into the turn lane to evade a car going the posted speed in the left-hand lane.

"Yes," Barb replied. "More or less. Less when I'm on time. More when I'm in a hurry. I haven't gotten into the oncoming lanes. Yet."

She managed to avoid that fate, spotting the sign for Quantico's main entrance and screaming through a narrow spot in oncoming traffic to make the left turn. She slid to a stop a few feet from the bumper of the car at the rear of the line waiting to enter the base and the Grand Am rocked for a moment on its springs. At the shriek of tires, the three Marines checking people into the base turned to look, their heads almost simultaneously tracking like turrets to identify the sound, note the Grand Am, then back to what they were doing.

"Thank you, Freya," Janea said, breathing out finally. "We have arrived alive."

"I've never had an accident," Barbara said, calmly, a faint smile on her face.

"That's incredible," Janea replied, looking at her. "I've had, like, five."

"Really?" Barb asked, moving the car forward as the line crept up to the gates. "Call it another gift. I am but a Servant of God."

"Yeah, right," Janea scoffed. "God tells you to drive like a maniac? There's a real little devil hidden under that church lady exterior, ain't there? Did your daddy teach you to drive, too?"

"No," Barbara said. "A boyfriend. He was a stockcar racer."

Janea collapsed into her seat theatrically and threw up her hands.

"I'd hate to be in the car if you were in a *real* hurry," she said, digging into her purse for ID.

"It is interesting," Barb admitted, rolling down the window as she reached the Marine guard. "Hi, Barbara Everette and . . ."

"Doris Grisham," Janea said, leaning way over so the Marine could look down her shirt. She held out her driver's license but it was a moment before the transfixed guard could remember to take it.

"We're here to see Special Agent Halliwell at the FBI Academy," Barb continued, handing over her own driver's license.

The guard shook himself and consulted a clipboard then shook his head.

"If you ladies could pull over into the lane on the left," he said, pointing to the appropriate spot. "Somebody will be with you shortly."

Barbara pulled forward to the spot and parked the car, waiting as patiently as she could, her fingers drumming on the steering wheel. Janea dug in her purse, pulled out an emery board and began touching up her nails.

"He's probably wondering when the FBI started calling in escorts," Janea said after a moment.

"I certainly *hope* I don't look like an 'escort,'" Barb said, primly.

"When you're with me you do," Janea replied, grinning. "Or maybe my manager."

Barbara just rolled her eyes and glanced in the rearview mirror. Two of the guards were heading their way.

"Heads up," she said.

"I'm sure they are," Janea answered, arching.

"Sorry about that, ma'am," the sergeant said, nodding at both of them but looking down Janea's shirt. "We had to call the FBI Academy to get verification on you. Could I see your ID again?"

Barbara handed over the IDs and ignored the fact that the other guard was looking past her as well. She wasn't used to being ignored by men and she found it . . . annoying.

"There's a thirty-five mile per hour speed limit on base," the sergeant said, handing back the licenses as the private with him filled out a parking slip. "It's strictly enforced."

"I understand," Barb replied, smiling at him winningly. It wasn't worth the effort; his eyes were glued to cleavage. "How do I find building F-134?"

The sergeant went through a bewildering explanation for a moment and then shrugged at her expression.

"Just follow the signs to the FBI Academy," he said, still having a hard time making eye contact. "You can find it from there."

As they pulled out, Janea leaned back and put her license away, then looked at Barbara.

"I'm annoying you, aren't I?" Janea asked.

"No, dear," Barb answered, reaching over to squeeze the other woman's hand. "I'm simply finding it a challenge in many ways I hadn't expected. You are a very good friend and the challenges are good for my soul."

"That's another way of saying yes," Janea said, leaning back in the seat. "I just get this way around men. It's broken up so many relationships for me you wouldn't believe. But I enjoy attention."

"That is, I suppose, a goodly thing to your goddess," Barbara said, ignoring the posted speed limit and cutting through the turns to the FBI Academy. "I, on the other hand, am realizing I'm not as perfect as others thought. Or even as sinless as *I* had thought. I hadn't realized I was as vain as I am. It's something I need to work on. So for that, if nothing else, I thank you."

"You're weird," Janea said.

"You keep saying that," Barb replied as she finally spotted building F-134. It was a brick building like most of the others on that part of the base, single story and long with several doors, most of them marked with blue signs. She hunted around until she found the door marked "Federal Bureau of Investigation Research and Analysis Lab" and then found a parking place.

When they reached the door she found it locked and pressed

the button next to it, presumably a buzzer. After a moment the door clicked to the buzz of a solenoid and they went inside.

The entry room was hard tile floor, acoustic tile ceiling and bright fluorescent lights. There was a desk with a woman sitting behind it, a rather pleasant faced younger woman who looked like a receptionist.

"Barbara Everette and Doris . . ." She locked up on Janea's last name for a moment, "Grisham. International Society for the Study of the Paranormal."

"You're expected, ladies," the woman said, smiling. "Through the door."

"Mrs. Everette?" the man on the far side said, taking Barb's hand as she came through the door. "And Miz Grisham?"

"The same," Janea said, smiling and bowing faintly as if to a courtier. "I prefer to be called Janea."

"Janea, then," the FBI agent said, virtually ignoring the way she was dressed. "I'm Special Agent in Charge Jim Halliwell. Let me take you back to the lab so we can get started."

"I take it we're not going to be working directly with you?" Barbara asked as they went down the long corridor. To the left were offices while to the right was a cube farm. As they passed one of the side corridors in the cube farm, an agent with his arms full of documents ducked back from Halliwell, then did a double take at the sight of Barbara and a triple take at Janea. By the time they'd reached the end of the corridor, there was a general buzzing from the cube farm and Barb looked over her shoulder to see various people, male and female, "prairie dogging" over the tops of the cubes.

"No, the agent assigned to your portion of the investigation is Special Agent Greg Donahue. He has the asset of having attended conventions previously."

"And is he aware that there are . . . Special Circumstances to this investigation?" Barbara asked, carefully.

"Yes, he is," Halliwell answered, opening the door to the lab.

The room had microscopes and various instruments with readouts on the front. Also a large number of computer monitors. And that was about all that Barb could determine from it.

"The FBI crime lab in D.C. does most of the direct crime investigation," Halliwell said, leading them across the room. "This lab does research into oddball aspects of forensics. Trying to determine if the DNA from pollen on a victim can be traced to a particular area or plant, that sort of thing. It also handles most of the Special Circumstances . . . oddball aspects. Fortunately, the techs are rather closemouthed about what they do." He pushed open a conference room door and waved the ladies in ahead of him.

There was a tall, thin man in a white lab coat and a larger man, both taller and much more heavyset, in the room. The lab tech, or doctor or whatever, was sitting very straight and still while the other had sprawled in his chair, hands behind his head. He sat bolt upright, though, as first Barbara and then Janea entered the room.

"Dr. Hannelore, Agent Donahue, Barbara Everette and Doris Grisham," Halliwell said. "Miz Grisham prefers to be called Janea."

"Mrs. Everette," Donahue said, standing up and taking their hands. "Janea . . ." he continued, looking her up and down for a moment and then shaking his head. "I'm going to be working with . . . you two?"

"Better assignment than you expected?" Janea said, archly, sitting down and crossing her legs so they were in clear view of everyone on her side of the table.

"Uh . . ." Donahue said, his mouth open for a moment. "Yes, as a matter of fact," he continued as he regained the capability for speech. "I was expecting . . . I dunno. A couple of little old lady psychics."

"Guess again," Barb said, placing her purse on the floor and then rolling her chair up to the table. "What do you have for us, Special Agent?"

"Dr. Hannelore?" Halliwell said, passing the ball.

"Seven victims," Hannelore replied, dimming the lights and bringing up a picture of a young woman on the projection monitor. "Each of them killed by having her throat cut. Indications of sexual assault and ligations from binding. Each with these symbols," he continued, showing a close-up of a stomach covered in a strange script, "marked on various portions of the body. We sent the symbols to an expert in these things and he identified them as . . ."

"A prayer to a Hebraic shedim," Janea interjected. "Originally a Persian daevas called Remolus. Might be related to the brood of Tiamat but seems to be a lower ranking daevas than that. The writing appears to be early Fars but it's not quite right. Hints of Sanskrit or maybe latter Sumerian. We hadn't seen this particular script before but it's interpretable according to our sources. I'm no expert in it myself. And clearly a summoning; he's trying to summon Remolus and is probably channeling from him at the very least."

"Remolus," Halliwell said, stepping over to one of the workstations and typing. "It says here that he's got no priors during our period of control of this area. 'The Soul Eater'?"

"All demons are soul eaters," Janea said, shrugging. "And the translation's a bit off. Remolus' major secondary name comes from an Aramaic inscription that translates as Soul Drawer or possibly Soul Sucker. As far as we know, there is no way that purely through necromancy he could possibly gather enough power to summon Tiamat. That takes enormous power. Although, if he did, that would be bad."

"How bad?" Halliwell asked.

"Tiamat is a gate and the key to the gate between the worlds," Janea said, frowning. "Effectively, if she stays in place for any significant time at all, and she is very difficult to kill, then you have a fully opened gate to . . . call it Hell. Demons can come through in swarms. Of course," she added, looking over at Barbara, "the heavenly host is supposed to be manifest to battle them directly upon earth. However, the power levels would be so high . . ." She paused and shrugged. "It might be better to have a nuclear war."

"Heaven forbid," Barb said, softly.

"As you say," Hannelore replied, looking at the dancer in interest. "The bodies had not been killed at the location. There is significant exsanguination. We're not sure what was done with the blood, whether it was kept for necromantic purposes or dumped."

"Probably burned as an offering," Janea said, musingly. "That's a common method with daevas. Properly there should be an effigy of the god or godling with a fire in the belly section and an open mouth. When the fire is hot, the blood is poured into the mouth, raising a fragrant offering to the god." She paused and shrugged at the looks that got. "It's a common motif. Any parts missing?"

"No," Hannelore said. "The bodies were intact."

"Odd," Janea said. "Generally organs are added to the offering. It might be an indication of squeamishness on the part of the necromancer."

"We have two of the bodies here in our morgue," Hannelore said. "We'd appreciate it if you could . . . use your abilities to see if there's anything you can tell us."

"Of course," Janea said, standing up.

"Can I get something straight?" Donahue asked. "Which one of you is in charge? I'd assumed it was Mrs. Everette, but . . ."

"I'm the more experienced," Janea said, looking over at Barbara. "And I've had more training. But Barb is . . . the more powerful."

"I think we're both wondering that," Barbara admitted, grabbing her purse and standing up as well. "Maybe by the end of the mission we'll know."

"That's . . . a problem," Halliwell said, seriously. "In a crisis, you have to know who is in charge. In the event of power manifestation, control of the situation automatically shifts to you two. Who does Donahue look to for decision-making?"

"If it's informational, Janea," Barb said.

"And if it's . . ." Janea paused, not sure how to go on.

"Tactical," Barbara interjected. "I guess that would be me."

"Great," Janea grumped. "And I'm the Asatru in the room. But, yeah, if it's tactical, I'm going to just back Barb up. Not that she'll need much help."

"By tactical you're referring to direct power fighting?" Hannelore asked, interestedly.

"And any other," Janea said, shrugging.

"I'm sorry, I have a problem with that," Halliwell said. "I don't think a civilian should be engaging in any sort of direct combat. Among other things, it's *illegal*."

"Sir," Hannelore said. "Case A-1674, the Bayou Ripper?'

"Oh, damn," Halliwell said, closing his eyes. "Sorry about the language, Mrs. Everette. And sorry for not making the connection."

"You're . . . aware of that?" Barbara asked.

"Who do you think cleared you to get out of the hospital?" Halliwell said. "And sent Germaine to you. Yes, we're aware of that. I just hadn't made the connection. I concur. In a Special Circumstances tactical situation, control devolves to you, unreservedly."

"Excuse me," Donahue said. "What does . . . ?"

"You're not cleared for that compartment," Halliwell answered the unspoken question. "I'll probably kick it open and see if I can clear you for the mission report. Let's just say that if Mrs. Everette says: 'Mine,' back off and let her handle it."

"Agent Donahue," Hannelore interjected. "Mrs. Everette was previously involved with a Special Circumstances investigation in Louisiana. The analysis, for obvious reasons, had to be done carefully. HRT handled the combat analysis. Let me just say that one portion of the analysis stated that HRT was, quote, impressed by the combat training, armed, unarmed and of special nature, of the subject and would, unreservedly, accept subject for entry to HRT based upon analysis of combat actions. End quote. I don't think I've broken any regulations by telling you that much."

"Oh," Donahue said, looking at her again.

"I'd like to make a point," Janea said. "What we are dealing with, almost assuredly, is a person, a human, who is gathering power to *create* a manifestation. The person may have power, may be able to channel, but should not be truly 'supernatural' in nature. He may, however, be able to use powers to control an unshielded person, such as Agent Donahue. That is what we have to be cautious of."

"Understood," Halliwell said. "Did you get that, Greg?"

"I'm trying to," Donahue admitted. "But what are you talking about, exactly?"

"Oh, something like this, perhaps," Janea said, closing her eyes and smiling.

Donahue felt himself overwhelmed by an unstoppable wave of lust. What was bothering him the most was that it wasn't even directed at Janea, but at Mrs. Everette. He closed his eyes and tried *not* to fantasize about what she would look like with her hair spread on a pillow, quite unsuccessfully. After a moment the feeling faded with only a lingering trace. He opened his eyes again and shook his head.

"That wasn't exactly going to *stop* me from doing anything," he said after he regained the power of speech.

"It was an aspect of my goddess," Janea said, smiling. "Her control methods are more . . . subtle than some."

"That was *anything* but subtle," Greg said, glancing at Barb and blushing.

"The point I'm trying to make is that if the person uses power on you, you may not have any control," Janea said. "You could be held against your will, at the very least, unable to take action to defend others. Or, possibly, depending upon the person's level of power and control, forced to use your weapon against others or even yourself. Self preservation is a very deeply held instinct, though. It is hard to overcome through direct means. However, you are unshielded. If you feel control slipping over you, simply work your will as hard as you can to prevent your own death and let Barbara and me handle the rest. Agreed?"

"Agreed," Donahue said, glancing at Barb again. "Are you still doing it to me?"

"No," Janea said, sighing. "But, unfortunately, the effects can have some lingering effect."

"Thanks *so* very much, Janea," Barbara said, acerbically.

"For the effects to last there has to have been some prior emotion," Janea said, coyly. "Now, I think we were going to view a body?"

Chapter Seven

It was the same young woman that had been in the pictures. Despite those, Barb, who had until recently never seen a dead body before other than at a viewing, was surprised by the waxen pallor. The young woman looked more like a yellow doll than a corpse. She held onto that thought as the sheet covering her was drawn back. It seemed grotesque to be viewing the poor girl's naked body like this, especially with the two men standing there, just looking at her as if she was a slab of meat or something.

"Okay, Barb," Janea said, gently. "I know this is rough for you. But I want you to put your hands over her and open your channel. Search for feelings that aren't yours."

Barbara watched Janea place her hands over the girl's midsection and close her eyes, then followed suit, holding them about six inches over the girl's flattened chest.

"Can you feel it?" Janea asked, quietly. "I can, faintly. Like a trace of rot."

"Like the smell of vomit," Barb said, softly. "God be with us, it's so strong!" She opened her eyes and drew back her hands, wiping them on her skirt to remove the ephemeral foulness.

"You felt it that strongly?" Janea asked, opening her eyes. "I could barely sense it."

"I can feel it from here," Barbara said, backing up. "It's horrible."

"Unfortunately you have to face it," Janea said. "I'm sorry it's so strong for you. But you have to feel it, sense it, taste it. If you felt it again, would you be able to recognize it? As distinct from other odors of foulness?"

"I've never felt anything like it before," Barb said, shaking her head. "No, I have. From Almadu. But . . . that was stronger, filling me until the Lord came to my aid. Like this but . . . maybe not the same . . . scent." She stepped forward again, holding her hands over the girl's chest for a moment, her eyes closed and face twisted in a grimace. "I can't do that for long," she said, stepping back and rubbing her hands on her clothes again, unthinkingly. "But . . . I think I'd know it again."

"We were wondering if you could perhaps go to where the bodies were found," Halliwell said. "We know that wasn't where the girls were killed. But if you can . . . feel anything that might help . . ."

"She was killed in a room," Barbara said, her eyes unfocusing. "An unfinished basement, I think. There is a smell of mold. And . . . a gas flame?" She paused and shook her head. "I'm sorry, this is all very new to me. God has given me these gifts, but they are new and untried. I don't know if I'm truly sensing something or if it is my imagination playing tricks on me."

"You'll learn," Janea said, reaching across the body to touch her shoulder. "Let's get out of this environment."

"Wait," Barb replied, looking around. The morgue had drawers for bodies on both sides of the room and she walked to the other, her hand out to the drawers until she stopped at one. "There is another who was killed by the same methods in here."

"Yes, that is the other body we're holding," Hannelore said.

"But . . ." Barbara continued, walking down the row. "There is another . . ." She paused at one and gestured. "Here. Similar. Not . . . exactly the same. But . . . very similar."

"Really?" Hannelore asked, confused. He went to the drawer

to get a number and then brought the case up on a computer. "Hmmm . . . Case J-17389. Ohio. A male. No signs of sexual assault although there are ligations. And no symbols on the body. There *was* removal of organs, but that was assumed to be sexually predatory even without signs of sexual assault. And the throat was cut. But the MO wasn't linked. It was brought here because we're doing an analysis of the ligation marks and trying to get any minor DNA contamination that might have been on the body. You're sure it's the same?"

"The feel is the same, similar anyway," Barb said, opening up the drawer and pulling it out. She paused when she saw the young man's face. He could have been an image, slightly older, of her own son. "I am sorry for this, my son," she muttered, holding her hands over the body. "Very similar," she concluded after a moment, stepping back. "Not as strong, but very similar."

Janea walked over to the drawer and held her hands over the body, shrugging after a moment.

"There's a trace of necromantic residue," she said. "That's all I can tell. It is definitely a Special Circumstances killing, but more I can't say."

"The body was found a month before the first killing in Case R-143," Hannelore said, musingly. "An early kill?"

"I think the killer hadn't settled his devotional method," Janea said. "Of course, the trace has faded over time. But I would guess that he didn't find his true ceremony until recently. But I'd be surprised if it wasn't the same killer, based on what Barb feels."

"We'll put it as possibly linked," Halliwell said, nodding. "Based on MO and secondary, unspecified, evidence."

"J-17389 was killed by a serrated edge," Hannelore said, distantly. "Sawn down. The R-143 cases are all a long bladed, non-serrated edge, inserted on the left side of the neck and then cutting out with drawing strokes. Our killer has refined his killing technique, if they're linked. Right-handed, by the way."

Barbara suddenly felt it, being raped and the point of the knife entering the side of her neck to kill her. She reached up to touch it—the feeling was so intense she expected her hand to come away bloody—and shook her head.

"I need to get out of here," she muttered, stumbling to the door.

Janea found her outside in the corridor to the lab, head bowed and hands clasped so hard her knuckles were white. She waited for the obvious prayer to finish and Barb to raise her head.

"I was calling for strength from the Lord," Barbara said, lowering her hands. "I knew I shouldn't have. This is something for which you have to find the strength within you. I don't know if I have it. If this is what the minor touch of necromancy does to me . . ." She stopped and shuddered, shaking her head.

"Well, yes, in there," Janea said. "You were opening yourself to the feelings. When you get into battle with the Enemy, your . . . sensitivity level goes down almost automatically. Or that's what I've been told," she added, shrugging. "I mean, I've never had to really face an enemy before."

"Well, I need to get further away from the morgue," Barb said, striding down the corridor. "I need to get out of this building. To take a shower. Slimy doesn't begin to describe it."

She exited the double doors to the morgue and then sat in a chair in the laboratory as the activity continued around her, willing herself to either ignore or suppress the continued miasma of evil. It was easier here but still seemed to be present and she wondered if she'd picked something up. She wanted to throw up, as if from sympathetic vomit.

"First time you ever saw a dead body?" one of the techs asked, grinning.

"That is not my problem," Barbara snarled, then caught herself as anger welled up in her soul. "I'm sorry," she added, trying to be calm. "But that is not my problem."

"Are you all right?" Halliwell asked, coming through the door and closely followed by Hannelore. At the sight of the Special Agent in Charge and the director of the lab the grin slid off the tech's face and he hurried away.

"I need to get out of this building," Barb said as calmly as she could. "For a while at least. I'm sorry but . . . that was much more unpleasant than I could possibly have imagined. Or explain."

"We were pretty much done here," Halliwell replied. "Agent Donahue can take you to the sites that are near here." He looked at Janea for a moment and shrugged. "You might want to change your shoes."

"Whatever for?" Janea asked, batting her lashes. "They help keep me on my toes. Is Agent Donahue driving?" she asked, batting her lashes again.

"No," Barbara replied. "I am. You can sit in the back. This time, wear your seatbelt."

"There," Donahue gasped, pointing to a narrow dirt road. "On the left." He grabbed his seat with his left hand and the handle of the door with his right, anticipating the slew turn.

Instead, Barbara slowed and then turned in carefully. The road was heavily potholed and might once have been a logging road but now was used for illegal dumping and, she suspected, as a parking and partying area for local kids. The trees were mixed pine and oak with an understory of what she thought might be beech. Without the garbage dumped in corners it would be a pretty area. And without the reason they were visiting it.

Donahue directed her through a couple of turns and then she stopped when she saw the police tape. The area marked out, with tape around the trees, was about thirty yards across. It had, apparently, been turned over by animals.

"When we investigate something like this we tend to tear the place up looking for evidence," Donahue admitted. Most of the pine and oak leaves from the area were gone, leaving empty loam.

"That also tends to make it harder for us," Janea said, getting out of the car and looking around. "Where was the body?"

"Wait," Barb said, following her out. She looked around the area, then ducked under the police tape, moving to a spot behind one of the larger oaks. "Here," she said, pointing to the ground. "Right here."

"You can still sense it?" Janea asked.

"Maybe I got sensitized," Barbara replied, looking at the ground unseeingly. "She wasn't covered, was she? She was on her back."

"That's right," Donahue said. "But that was in the pictures."

"There's not much else," Barbara replied, swallowing. "It's like a strong . . . I hate to use the word but 'psychic' imprint. Not only of the necromancy but of the dead body. I hope I don't start doing this for everyone who dies."

"Anything about the killer?" Donahue asked. "We don't even have a good tire track. We've got his DNA but . . ."

"No," Barbara said, closing her eyes. "Just the . . . sad feeling of death with that ugly hint of necromancy. That's weaker than the feel of death itself."

"We can probably reach one more site today," Donahue said. "But it's older."

"We'll go there," Barbara said. "See if there is anything."

"Can I drive?" Janea asked.

"No."

Even with a stop for lunch it didn't take as long as Donahue expected to reach the next site. This one was right by a minor back road. Apparently the killer had stopped, dragged the body into the weeds just beyond the right-of-way and then driven away. The area was thick with high grass and blackberries and Janea hadn't even bothered to try to crawl into the brush. However, it didn't make much difference since Barb couldn't even pick up the residue of the body.

"All the others are older," Donahue said.

"I don't think this is going to do any good," Barbara said, pushing aside some high grass. "There's hardly anything . . ." She paused and then stepped further into the grass. "You picked this area over?" She asked, turning her head from side to side, her eyes closed.

"Yes," Donahue replied. "Should have, anyway."

Barbara stopped and bent down, digging into a section of briars with a set expression on her face.

"Do you have a set of tweezers or a bag or something?" Barbara asked.

"Here," Donahue said, handing over a long set of tweezers and a plastic bag. "Don't touch whatever it is with your fingers."

"I wasn't planning on it," Barbara replied in a strained voice. She reached into the brambles and carefully extracted something, dropping it in the bag. "I don't want to be doing this, much less touching it."

"Interesting," Donahue said, taking the bag by the corner. "A gem?"

"Moonstone, I think," Barbara said, wiping her hands on her skirt again. "And it's steeped in that necromantic . . . stench."

"Let me see, please," Janea called, stepping up to the edge of the brush.

Donahue first put a small yellow marker in the briars, then gave Barbara a hand getting out of the scrub. Barbara didn't complain; the aura from the moonstone was nearly as intense as from the dead girl. Certainly more concentrated. The hand wasn't entirely unnecessary; she was shaken by being as close to the gem as she had been.

"That's a moonstone, all right," Janea said, taking the bag carefully. "And Barb's right; the aura level is massive. I'd say that it was used as part of the rite. Perhaps a decoration on the althane or on ceremonial dress. I'd strongly suggest turning this over to Special Circumstances forensics. They have some ceremonials that might give us a better handle on what it was used for. I . . ." She paused, then shrugged and handed the bag back.

"This feels as if it has been used for a power repository. But I don't know a ritual that does that, not at the levels I'm feeling from this. The writing was from an unknown source and this might be an unknown ritual. In which case, we really need to know about it; we've got a library of most of the true rituals out there."

"I'll leave that up to the SAIC," Donahue said, pocketing the gem.

"Well, leave it in the trunk at the very least," Barbara said, shuddering. "You have no idea what horror you just dropped in your pocket. Think of it as every concentrated scream, every concentrated plea, every drop of blood, every soul, in micro, there in your pocket."

Donahue slowly drew it back out, then walked to the car and put it in a case in the back.

"Wait," Janea said, digging in the small bag she'd brought along to hold her "necessary" cosmetics. She pulled out a scarf and handed it to the agent.

"Wrap it in that," Janea said, backing away from the trunk.

Barbara, even without being able to see what he was doing, could tell when the thing had been wrapped. The aura of evil was abruptly cut off.

"What was that?" Barb asked as they got in the car.

"Silk," Janea said. "I was so overwhelmed by the stench from that thing I forgot. But silk will stop most power emanations dead in their tracks."

"I'm going to make some silk bags for investigations, then," Barbara said, feeling much better with that . . . thing wrapped up. "And we need to suggest to the FBI that they invest in silk covers for bodies. I don't think that being around that sort of necromantic power is good for anyone in the building, sensitive or not."

They drove back to the Academy, dropped off the gem along with a description of where it had been found, then caught dinner at a steak house.

"I'd always heard of psychic consultants," Donahue said, as the waitress left after getting their drink order. "And I'd always discounted them. I guess I shouldn't have."

"Well, the Bureau sometimes uses what we call 'real' psychics," Janea said, chuckling. "At least, so I'm told. People who think they have the ability to feel psychic emanations. We don't do that. We have a sort of connection to a god. The god, in turn, gives us certain gifts."

"I hadn't really realized I could do that until just today," Barb said. "And now I wish I couldn't. I can still feel the residue from that thing in the trunk and we haven't really helped."

"Oh, yes you have," Donahue said. "Just that moonstone could be a major key. In this case, we have a solid case against *some* unknown perpetrator. The DNA is solid, there are various other pieces that are solid and, guaranteed, as soon as we know the perp there will be witnesses that put him and the victims, some or all, together. Just the DNA, these days, is good enough for a conviction. We just have to find him. And that moonstone could very well be the key."

"Unlikely," Janea said. "Moonstones are common in fandom and we're thinking this guy is a fan, right?"

"Yeah," Donahue admitted.

"Moonstone is relatively cheap and looks cool," Janea continued. "You see it all over. I'd been thinking about the properties of moonstone. One of them is, yeah, the enhancement of power and power storage. But not at *that* level. If there's a lost ritual that actually permits the stones to *store* power for a greater rite, then . . ."

"The stone was being used like a battery?" Donahue asked.

"Maybe," Janea said. "That's what some people do. But not *that* powerful a battery."

"I want to know how it was attached," Barbara commented. "Was it on a ring? In a setting? On a costume? What? I think if the . . . perp has whatever it was attached to at the con I'll feel it. He . . . heck, I think I'd feel it if I was in the same *county*."

"Unless it's wrapped in silk," Janea pointed out.

"The lab will be able to find that out by tomorrow," Donahue said. "The con starts Friday evening in Roanoke. It's small. In one way that will act in our favor; we won't have as many people to try to sort through. In another, it will be a problem since we'll tend to stand out if we don't be careful."

"Careful is my middle name," Janea said. "Of course, it's from my *real* name and I never use that."

"I just don't see you as a Doris," Barb admitted, smiling.

"Hush your mouth," Janea replied, waving a finger at her. "I hate that name."

"Do we go together or separate?" Donahue asked and then looked at Barbara's expression. "We're *staying* separate, obviously."

"Pity," Janea said. "Hey, if I go with Greg, there'll be more room for the luggage!"

"How much luggage do you have?" Greg asked, worriedly.

"A lot," Barb said, frowning.

"You've got a rentacar, right?" the agent asked. "Why don't I see if I can check out a Bureau unmarked Expedition. More room for luggage, more room for us."

"And you can drive?" Barbara asked, grinning.

"That, too," Donahue admitted.

"We can do that," Barb said. "I'm not sure how we get back."

"We can fly out of Roanoke," Janea replied. "You can fly home direct. We'll drop the rentacar off before we go down."

"Let's do that," Donahue insisted. "Among other things, it will give you a chance to catch up on your reading."

"More reading?" Barbara said, smiling.

"You're going to have to be able to discuss the collected works of K. Goldberg," Donahue said.

"Who?"

"She's a horror and mystery writer," Donahue said, handing over a book with a dripping knife on the cover. "You'll want to read at least one book of hers before the con. You can keep that one; get it signed if you wish."

"Great," Barb said. "*More* homework."

Chapter Eight

"I'm not too sure about this," Barbara said as they pulled into the parking lot. Donahue had managed to wangle an unmarked Expedition after he saw how much luggage was "a lot" and the drive down had been uneventful. But as they pulled into the registration area of the hotel and Barb saw the con-goers unloading, she got a little nervous. "I haven't read science fiction in years. The only fantasy I've read is *Lord of the Rings*. And I'm only half way through Goldberg's book and it's the first horror I've *ever* read. I usually read *romance* novels for heaven's sake."

"You'll be fine," Greg said. "We've got two rooms, a double and a king. I couldn't get them adjacent but they're on the same floor and wing. Obviously, you two get the double."

"And you'll be with me," Janea said. "Other than . . . you know, how much trouble can you get into?" She had chosen to wear a pair of hip-hugger jeans, stilettos and a halter top for the drive down. As she put it: "Comfortable clothing." Barbara looked at her for a moment and shook her head.

"A lot?" Barb said, chuckling.

"Not at this con." Janea sighed. "This is a lit-geek con. Now, you go with me to DragonCon or Arisia and we'll burn the hotel down. I've got some costumes that would probably fit you . . ."

"No way," Barbara said. "I'm *not* wearing a chain-mail bikini."

"Okay, okay," Janea sighed. "Jeeze. But . . . how about a corset?"

The hotel for the con was an old resort north of Roanoke off of U.S. 221. Time and highways had passed it by and it had fallen into disrepair before being purchased by an enterprising Hindu family. They had slowly fixed it up and then offered it as a getaway for corporate functions. Together with the occasional small gathering like the convention, and some solid work, it had begun to be regain its former glory. It was set well back from the highway up a steep and winding road through leafless trees. The check-in was smooth and with the help of a luggage cart they got all their bags up to the rooms. Donahue, in contrast to the girls, had only brought two small carry-on type bags.

Once in the room Janea started pulling out outfits.

"What do you think of this one?" she asked, holding up a midriff top and a miniskirt.

"Well, it's definitely you," Barb said, shaking her head. "But we could, you know, wear the same clothes to go register."

"What's the fun in that?" Janea asked, opening up another bag. "Or this?" she added, holding up a corset and a long, matching skirt with a wide slit up both sides.

"What are you going to wear over the corset?" Barbara asked.

"Nothing, of course," Janea said, frowning. "What *should* I wear?"

"Janea," Barb said, gently. "It's *freezing*."

"You've got a point," Janea admitted, digging in the clothes. "I've got the perfect outfit."

The "perfect outfit" turned out to be another pair of hiphuggers, these with laces down the side that left large, triangular gaps, a bra and a see-through shirt. She threw a leather coat over the ensemble and then posed.

"What do you think?" she asked.

"I still think you're going to freeze to death," Barbara replied.

She'd gotten into the spirit to the extent of changing from the skirt and blouse ensemble she'd worn down into a pair of relatively tight jeans, a blouse that showed a small amount of cleavage and one of her heavier "dressy" jackets.

"We're gonna slay 'em," Janea said, grinning. "But, really, I could loan you a corset. With that jacket over my green one, it would be really outstanding. All the guys would drool. They're probably going to think we're lesbians, anyway, and some guys really get off on—"

"Janea," Barb said, tightly. "I'm *not* an acolyte of Freya. Try to remember that."

"Oh," Janea said, slightly abashed. "Sorry. Uhm . . . Greg's probably wondering what took you so long, so let's get going . . ."

When they got to Donahue's room it took him a moment to answer the door.

"Sorry," the agent said, waving them in. "I was checking my e-mail."

"You get that much?" Barbara asked, stepping into the room cautiously. She had a vague feeling of uneasiness entering the room of a person, a male person, she wasn't married to. Donahue hadn't changed and except for opening up one bag to get out his laptop his bags were undisturbed. She mentally sighed at the amount of room he had compared to them; his room wasn't crowded with luggage.

"I had a few," Donahue admitted. "But I was replying to some and I called the lab. The moonstone was apparently part of a piece of silver jewelry. There were striations on the surface indicating that it had been set and traces of silver. It's been sent on to the Special Circumstances forensics group to see what they can get off of it."

"They'll take it slow," Janea foretold. "That's a damned evil piece of rock. They'll have to set up precautions to ensure the evil won't spread or contaminate anything or anyone."

"Well, it's all we have so far," Donahue said, shrugging. "That and the generic description of the perp. Have you two . . . felt anything?" he asked, uneasily.

"No," Barbara replied, shaking her head. "Nothing."

"Generally you won't feel a necromancer," Janea said. "Or so I've been told. Not unless he . . . It's hard to explain. He doesn't have to perform a rite but if he uses power you might sense it, Barb. And if he . . . sort of thinks about necromancy . . . if he starts to slip into the mental state where he'd be . . . stalking or hunting, he might give off a trace. But if he's just . . . wandering around or gaming or something, we could walk right past him and not even notice."

"I'd think that if he was carrying whatever had that gem on it, I'd feel it," Barbara pointed out.

"I don't know whether to hope he does any of those things at the con or hope he doesn't," Donahue said, seriously. "This assumes he's even *at* this convention. But let's go register and sort of look around."

"Welcome to KaliCon." They had been in the registration line for about half an hour and Janea had already collected a legion of followers; the male con-goers kept running into walls as they passed. It wasn't a very long line but there was only one person giving out badges and "Black Kitty," or so her badge read, seemed prepared to chat with each person or group. Black Kitty was a short, wide woman in her fifties with thin reddish hair and a broad smile that gave her face prettiness that was belied by her overall looks.

"Donahue, Janea and Barbara F," Greg said. "We only registered last week."

"Well, let's hope we got them done in time," Kitty said, digging into the box that held the badges. "Sure enough," she continued, pulling out badges and slipping them into holders. "Have you been to the con before?"

"Not this one," Greg said. "I've been to a couple and Janea has been to several. Barb is a con virgin, though."

"I'm sure you'll have a good time," Kitty said, handing over the badges, which had pins to stick them on a shirt. "We're a very laid back con. There will be some room parties you might enjoy, though." She looked at Janea and a frown momentarily crossed her face. "There's a DragonCon party on Saturday I hear."

"We're mostly here to see Miss Goldberg," Barbara said, smiling. "I'd really like to meet her."

"Well, stop by the Wharf Rats suite," Kitty said, smiling again. "She spends a good bit of time around them and if she's not there you might find out where she is hanging out. She's very good about visiting with the fen. For the rest," she continued, handing over a pile of schedules, "she has a couple of panels and a signing."

"Is there a LARP going on?" Janea asked, smiling disarmingly. "I like to LARP."

"It's in the schedule," Kitty said, nodding. "Underworld, I think."

"Oh, good," Janea said, bouncing in happiness. "I love being a Hunter! It's like I live it!"

"Goldberg doesn't have a panel until tomorrow morning," Donahue said as they walked down the hallway. "And the Dealers' Room doesn't open until six. I think it's time for dinner."

"When's the LARPing start?" Janea asked, seriously. "I'd like to take that side of the investigation and Barb might enjoy it."

"There's a meeting tonight at nine after opening ceremonies," Donahue replied. "So do we eat in or out?"

"Well, I'm always up for eating in," Janea said in a sultry voice, waggling one eyebrow. "But let's eat out," she added, more normally. "We're probably going to be immersed in fandom for the rest of the weekend; one last normal meal would be prudent."

"Okay," the FBI agent said, looking at Barbara. "You okay for that?"

"For the time being, I'm just along for the ride," Barb pointed out.

"Out it is," Donahue said, heading for the parking lot.

There was a nearby Outback Steakhouse which wasn't completely overflowing. However, they did have to wait. The interior was crowded so they wandered outside, despite the falling temperatures, ending up sitting between a group of obvious fen and a group of much more obvious mundanes, a pair of couples, the men in slacks and golf shirts and the women in informal dresses. The fen were chatting loudly about something that had happened at another con. Barbara couldn't make heads or tails of it and she more or less tuned it out until the group got up to go to their table.

As the last of the group entered the restaurant one of the women next to Barb's group shook her head.

"I wonder where the Klingon costumes are," she said, cattily. "I don't think they could fit in them anyway."

"You gotta wonder what they do when they're not here," one of the men said, laughing. "I think I saw one of them working in a Seven Eleven yesterday."

"Well, the balding guy in the leather jacket is a *New York Times* bestselling author and scriptwriter," Greg replied, turning to look at the foursome. "One of the women owns a software development company that's just short of Fortune five hundred. And one of them is an out-of-work graphic artist. I didn't know the other three."

"I wasn't talking to you," the man said, sharply.

"No, but you were talking loudly enough to be heard by everyone out here," Greg responded, coldly. "Ergo, you were trying to denigrate them generally instead of specifically within your group. What I've never understood is why."

"Tribal instinct," Janea answered, ignoring the group but speaking loudly enough that they couldn't ignore it. "Also fear of social status. Maintenance of social status for a high status person is a full-time job. People like these four have status to maintain and these days they have to live in fear of the oddballs that control things like computers and information technology. Since suits can rarely figure out how to turn on their computers, much less do anything more complicated than a simple spreadsheet, they increasingly fear geeks."

"You don't know what the hell you're talking about," one of the women snapped. "I can figure out a computer just fine."

"Yes, but use the word 'router' around you and you think it's something used in a woodworking class," Janea said, turning to her and smiling thinly. "But primarily it's a throwback to primitive society where the higher status got to eat the better parts of the mastodon. And they'd eventually get kicked out of status and end up eating the knees. Keeping people in their place was important for them. Now, they go through high school and college in a comfortable in-group and then, upon exiting into the real world, find that they're dependent upon the people they denigrated in both areas. It has to be terrible for you," she added with mock caring.

"I hadn't realized you were with them," the man who had made the Seven Eleven comment said, tightly. "Sorry."

"We're not with them," Greg said, turning away. "But we are of them."

"And what do *you* do?" one of the women asked Janea, smiling but with a very bitchy tone.

"Greg is an FBI agent, Barbara is a nice little homemaker from Mississippi who has somehow fallen in with evil companions," Janea answered, smiling pleasantly. "Me, I'm a *very* expensive call girl. Don't worry about me stealing your men, though. I'm *far* too expensive for anyone who dresses up to go to Outback. And I only do men like your husbands for free if they're likeable," she added, smiling happily and bouncing enough to cause a nice jiggle.

Barb half hid her face and shook her head as silence descended upon the area. Fortunately, the group of mundanes were soon called to their table.

"I hadn't expected you guys to go picking fights," Barbara said as the group left.

"I shouldn't have," Greg admitted. "But that sort of catting really pisses me off."

"I've done it myself," Barb admitted. "Trying to fit in to an in-group in a new school. Geek bashing isn't really a full-time job for groups like that, they're much more focused on cutting each other down."

"Maintenance of status in any group is a full-time job," Janea said. "You can't believe the sort of status games you get in stripping."

"I don't work on it full time," Barbara argued.

"Hah," Janea said, grinning. "Look at the way you do your

clothes and makeup. I bet you're first in line for all the school bake sales and PTO chores, too."

"Well . . ." Barb said, frowning. "I guess so."

"Everybody does it," Janea said, shrugging. "It's normal and human. The question is the way that you do it. You can choose to cut people down or you can choose to raise them up. By raising them up, or treating them like equals, you don't really reduce your status. Their admiration for how you treat them automatically raises your status."

"Well, you cut *them* down," Greg said, frowning. "I mean *really* sniped them bad."

"I'm Asatru," Janea said, smiling. "It's my job to do battle, even verbal battle, for my tribe. And fen *are* my tribe. I just got God points. Especially by using sex as a weapon. Freya should be really happy. Most of her devotees come from tribes that find *that* tribe to be the enemy. I did battle and I kicked their ass."

"I'm not sure," Barbara said. "Call girls are automatically of such low status to people like that they can ignore you."

"The men weren't," Janea said, archly. "And the women will know that, especially later tonight. Trust me, I kicked their asses."

"You didn't use power, did you?" Barb said, frowning.

"Nope," Janea said, shaking her head. "Didn't have to, I have these," she added, in a little girl voice, bouncing and giggling again.

The rest of dinner was uneventful and afterwards they made their way back to the con.

"Opening ceremonies are at eight but I'd rather skip," Greg said when they were back in the con area. "Most of the time it's boring as hell to everyone but the con in-crowd. Most of the guests won't even show up."

"I'm headed over to the Dealers' Room," Janea said, grabbing Barbara by the arm. "We'll catch up with you later. Where are you going to be?"

"I'll probably stop by the Wharf Rat party," Greg said, clearing his throat uncertainly.

"What's wrong with that?" Barb asked, curiously.

"Well, it's like being fen," Greg said, shrugging. "When you're in something like the military or FBI, you generally don't want people to realize you're into some of this stuff. I'm sort of a Wharf Rat, a lurker anyway."

"Okay, what's a 'Wharf Rat'?" Janea asked. "I've heard of them but I've never paid attention."

"Well, there's this publisher, Pier Books," Greg answered, shrugging. "They've got a webboard where people talk about their books and . . . all sorts of other things. The people that hang out on the board are Wharf Rats. It's sort of an in-in group in fandom, those that go to cons. The outcast of the outcasts."

"Why?" Barbara asked, chuckling. "*Completely* lacking in social skills?"

"Some," Greg said, nodding his head in admission. "But mostly . . . fandom tends to be pretty liberal. The Wharf Rats . . . have some liberals but they tend to be into more old-fashioned SF and conservative. I hope you can handle cigarette smoke. And, I dunno, military types. They're not very PC."

"I think I might finally feel at home," Barb replied.

The Dealers' Room turned out to be a moderately large ballroom filled with folding tables. The offerings were eclectic. At the first table through the door was a comic book seller and next to him were a man and a woman selling silver jewelry and other knickknacks.

"Keep an eye out for moonstone jewelry," Barbara pointed out. "I'm going to circulate counterclockwise."

"You never seemed like the widdershins type," Janea said, grinning. "But . . . okay."

Barbara wandered down the east wall, checking out the selections. There were two booksellers, one specializing in signed and out-of-print books and the other with a vast assortment of newer titles. Barb stopped at the out-of-print seller's booth and perused the titles as the dealer, a short, heavily endowed brunette, was completing a sale. Barbara hadn't heard of most of the titles on display: being an SF con they were mostly science fiction and fantasy.

"Looking for anything in particular?" the dealer asked from over her shoulder.

"I'm just getting back into reading," Barb admitted, turning to look at the woman. She was older than Barbara had thought at first glance, with fine lines by sharp green eyes. "I'm more into romance."

"I've got a signed copy of *A Civil Campaign,*" the dealer said, pulling a book out. "It's SF, but it's really a Regency romance novel. Lois is an excellent writer."

Barbara glanced at the price and blanched. With all the "homework" she had, she wasn't sure when she could get to the book.

"A bit much," she murmured. "Do you have anything about necromancy?"

"Hmmm," the woman said, lifting an eyebrow. "Fiction or nonfiction?"

"I'd think that anything about necromancy would be fiction," Barb said, smiling faintly.

"Well, there are books on the occult," the woman replied, squatting to pull out a thin volume. "Mark Tommon's *Necromancy in the Western World* for example."

"Got that one," Barbara admitted. "I think I'll just look around."

"Feel free," the woman said, smiling. "I hope you find something interesting."

"Oh, it's all interesting," Barb said. "It's simply a matter of time. I'm taking a course at the moment and I don't have a lot of time for pleasure reading."

"A course in necromancy?" the woman asked.

"The occult," Barbara said, generally. "It's part of a . . . church program."

"Ah," the dealer said, her expression closing. "Christian?"

"Not . . . exactly," Barb admitted. "More ecumenical, I suppose. Thank you for your time."

"Not at all," the dealer replied. "Enjoy yourself. First con?"

"Does it show?" Barbara asked.

"A bit," the woman said, smiling. "But you'll find you fit in pretty quick."

A couple of booths down from the bookseller a dealer had a large selection of silver jewelry in glass cases, quite a bit of it with moonstone. The dealer handling the jewelry was a "pleasingly plump" brunette with long, dark-brown hair, but on the side of the booth was a massage chair where a short, heavily muscled man was painting henna on the arm of a teenage girl.

"If you see anything you like, just ask," the woman behind the counter said.

"Thank you," Barb said, closing her eyes for a moment and running her hand over the display. She stopped and opened her eyes, looking at a silver dragon brooch with a large moonstone in the breast. She had felt a definite twinge of power from the brooch, but not necromantic. It felt . . . sad but not evil. "That's very nice."

"Yes," the dealer replied, her eyes wary and a touch sad. "I had a friend who died of AIDS. His avatar was the dragon so I made that in his memory."

"I see," Barbara said, carefully, unsure how to ask the question. "When you were making it . . ."

"I imbued it with my sadness, yes," the woman replied. "You noticed."

"It's a gift of God," Barb said. "It is very beautiful and very sad."

"It was designed to draw sadness out," the woman said. "But I think, instead, it brings the sadness with it. Not what I'd intended."

"You're a witch?" Barbara asked, interestedly.

"A bit," the woman said, frowning. "I don't think you are, though."

"No, but I'm not a Bible thumper, either," Barb replied, smiling. "I'm finding that there are many ways to God. Each chooses his or her own. And you make beautiful jewelry. Do you make custom pieces?"

"Of course," the woman said. "Do you want one?"

"Thinking about it," Barbara admitted. "But I'll have to think about what."

"When you've got a design in mind, call me," the woman said, handing her a card. "My husband does the design work and I make the jewelry."

"Thank you," Barb replied, taking the card and inserting it in her purse. "Go with God."

"Thank you," the woman said, smiling. "I will."

Towards the back of the room was a large freestanding booth just about covered in weapons, armor and leather accoutrements, some of which Barbara half turned her eyes from. The racks hid the center of the booth so she peeked in, letting out a startled squeak of surprise at the sight of the dealer. He was about seven feet high and skeletally thin, with long graying hair pulled back in a ponytail. His arms were covered in tattoos so old and faded they were hard to make out. But what was especially startling were his eyes, which had red irises and a vertical pupil.

"Contacts," the man said in a deep baritone. "They're contacts."

"Oh," Barb replied, embarrassed at her reaction. "Sorry."

"I get it all the time," the man said, grinning. When he smiled his formidable looks faded into the background. "Looking for anything in particular?"

"No," Barbara said, taking a glance around the interior, carefully skipping over some of the studded pieces she suspected she knew the purpose of, and then stopping at a sword that was on display as a centerpiece. It was a katana, but something told her it wasn't just a cheap knockoff. "Oh, my," she continued, sliding past the dealer to look more closely at the sword. The price tag dangling from it told her all she needed to know about its authenticity. ". . . Murasaki?"

"Yes," the man said, sliding past her in turn and lifting the sword down carefully. "For anyone who can identify it that quick, I'll take it down."

Barb took the sword in a perfect two-handed grip and examined the wavery light reflected from the dark steel. "Beautiful," she said, turning it from side to side to look down the blade. It was perfectly balanced for her.

"I found it in a pawnshop," the man said, shaking his head. "It was just about covered with rust. The guy thought it was one of the World War Two souvenir swords. I spent three years rebuilding it, working the blade inch by inch when I had time and the right energies."

Barbara closed her eyes and opened her link, feeling for the sword. Then her eyes flew open.

"This sword has a soul," she said, softly.

"The maker put his energies into it," the man replied, just as softly. "That was why I only worked on it when I had the right energy."

"You can't give a soul," Barb said, looking up at him.

"You can give of yourself," the man contradicted. "The soul is ever refilling and the more you give of it, the more you gain."

"Did you put your soul into it?" Barbara asked, comparing the feel of the man, which was deep and a tad dark, to the feel of the sword. The sword was . . . remarkably neutral.

"Not really," the man replied, shaking his head. "I simply showed it that it was once again cherished and loved. It is not for me, though. Its soul and mine are not in full harmony. It is for someone else."

"Not me," Barb said, handing it back regretfully. "Not at sixty grand." As the man placed his hand on it, Barb's spasmed shut and she grabbed at her head as a wave of evil seemed to wash over the room.

"Are you okay?" the man said as Barb finally relinquished the sword.

"Fine," Barb gasped as the wave passed. "Headache. I have to go now."

She stumbled out of the booth and settled in a convenient chair. The wave of evil had passed but it left a numbing miasma behind it.

"Barb, are you okay?" Janea asked after a moment.

"Did you feel that?" Barb asked.

"No," Janea replied. "What?"

"Our friend is *definitely* at this con."

Chapter Nine

"It was really strong," Barb said. Janea had called Greg and helped her up to their room where they were met by the FBI agent. "It had a feel to it, like a predator. Like you look up and there are the eyes of a beast staring at you from a cliff. Not a clean beast, either, a horrible one. I think, maybe, he'd seen his quarry."

"Then we need to find him, fast," Greg said. "Before he leaves with her."

"The girls haven't been killed during the cons, have they?" Janea asked.

"No," Greg admitted.

"Then he's probably going to stalk her for a while," Janea pointed out. "Hopefully, he'll stay here for the full con. We've got time."

"Any direction to this feeling?" Greg asked.

"Not really," Barbara said, shaking her head and taking a drink of water. What she really wanted was a good, stiff drink of bourbon. "It was just . . . all around. He might even have been in the Dealers' Room."

"A dealer?" Greg asked. "That would narrow it down some."

"There were lots of people in there shopping," Janea pointed out. "I wish Barb had been a bit more fit; we could have looked around."

"I didn't get any feel from any of the dealers," Barbara said. "Or any of the pieces, not a necromantic feel. One of the dealers was . . . a tad strange. But . . . he didn't have the right feel, either. He was dark, but not evil."

Greg considered her for a moment and opened and shut his mouth. Then he shrugged.

"The only thing I can figure out is to have you circulate," Greg said, frowning. "Maybe if you meet him you'll get a feel or whatever."

"I'm not sure I'm going to be willing to be open enough to get a . . . feel the rest of the con," Barb said, sighing. "But you're right."

"I'm going to the Wharf Rat party," Greg said. "Janea?"

"I'm going to go LARP," Janea said, definitely. "I'd give odds it's a LARPer."

"I'll just wander around," Barbara said. "People talk to me. I'll see what I can dig up."

"Everybody's got cell phones," Greg noted. "Janea, if you get a twinge, call Barb and me. We'll gather and study. I'll do the same. Barb, if *you* get a twinge, call me. Right away. I know you ladies are . . . experts with this. But the idea here is to make an arrest. Before we go I'm going to call in and let them know that we have a good probability of having the suspect on site. FBI Headquarters will get some back-up up here. Hopefully Hostage Rescue Team."

"If it comes down to a duel of power," Janea noted, "HRT will only be in the way. And they'd *better* not come on with 'we're the experts here' because they're not."

"There are HRT members who are briefed for Special Circumstance," Greg pointed out.

"I know," Janea snapped. "But they've also been damned brain-dead about it from time to time. And then you've got soul-sucked and dead HRT guys on your hands and there are questions and problems and . . ."

"I take your point," Greg said, swallowing.

"The same goes for you, Greg," Barbara pointed out, quietly. "If whoever this is has built up serious power, or has a serious channel, you could be the liability here. If I tell you to leave, you *leave*, got it?"

"Got it," the FBI agent said, unhappily.

"I'm sorry I got bitchy," Janea said, putting a hand on his arm. "But finally getting a real target nearly in the sights gets me horny and I get a backache. Sorry."

"Uh, that's all right," Greg said, swallowing.

"Freya can be a bitch that way," Janea said, sighing sadly. "She gets more attached the hornier I get. What I really need about now is a good screw. But we've got work to do."

"Yes we do," Barb said, trying not to smile at the agent's wide eyes. "But I'm going to change first. If I have to move, I don't want to be doing it in heels. You can't run in them worth a damn."

"Oh, it's just a matter of learning how," Janea argued. "You get up on your toes and sort of dance like a ballerina. It's not hard. Hell, I dance in higher heels than those all the time. And run. You just have to have the calves for it. And you look so good in heels."

"Well, I *don't* have the calves," Barbara said. "So I'm going to change into running shoes. You can wear whatever you want."

"Yes, Mother," Janea said, grinning.

"I'm going to head out," Greg said. "Especially if you're going to be getting naked."

"But guys look at *me* naked all the time," Janea pointed out, reaching for the tie at her neck. "Don't you want to?"

"Maybe later!" Greg said, backing out of the room.

"Damn," Janea said as the door closed. "I was hoping for a quickie."

"Not with *me* in the room," Barb said, shaking her head.

"You only had to watch," Janea pouted. "Besides, you'd be getting dressed and stuff."

"What did I do to deserve this?" Barbara asked, pulling out her jeans.

"You needed somebody more experienced than you on the case," Janea pointed out. "And boy did you get it!"

Barbara wasn't sure what to do when she got downstairs. There were a few tables of gamers in the hallway outside the Dealers' Room, which had closed for the evening. Janea had pointed out that it was unlikely the killer was a gamer. Most gamers just stayed gaming through the con and didn't interact much. If the killer was stalking the cons for targets, the gamers were not the place to look.

Most of the rest of the people seemed to be gathered in small groups talking in corners. She passed out the double doors to the outdoor atrium that the hotel was wrapped around and found the smoking area. There were a couple of groups gathered on the steps down to the pool area and a larger group around a table on the north end.

It was cold outside but Barb had sensibly added a heavy jacket to the jeans and long-sleeved shirt. She stood outside uncertainly, just looking around, and tried to listen to the conversations around her while opening up her channel carefully. When she didn't get any feel of evil immediately she closed her eyes and tried to mentally reach out.

"That's impolite you know," a girl's voice said by her ear.

Barbara's eyes flew open and she looked down into a round face by her shoulder. The person had sounded like a girl but was clearly a full grown woman, about five five with dark hair and . . . stout. She was wearing a heavy jacket and had a cigarette in one hand and a beer in the other.

"You shouldn't just go throwing power around," the woman said, shaking her head. "Among other things there are people that would want to eat it. It's very dangerous to let anyone know you're powerful."

"Perhaps I'm powerful enough I'm not worried by it," Barb said, blinking in surprise.

"Nobody's that powerful," the woman said. "And just probing people is terribly rude."

"I'm doing it for a reason," Barbara replied, defensively.

"I didn't figure you were just hunting for a good guy to get laid by tonight," the woman said, grinning. "I used to do that at Sabbats. It's a good way to figure out which guy's likely to be worth it. Oh, you steer wrong sometimes, I know I sure did. I picked up one guy who was a real loser that way. I mean, he had power but he was such a slacker he never used it and when he did it was for all the wrong reasons. But I wish I'd known about it before I met my ex. I mean, I learned about power and auras while I was with him and when I really read his aura I was like: 'What in the hell did I do?' It wasn't bad enough he wanted to have sex every fifteen minutes, and he wasn't good at it I'll tell you, but he just was so closed up. I mean, he had power, too, but he was so selfish it was like he held it in like a miser. It was the same as everything with him, he just used it for his own fun. He never cared if I had fun or not, I'll tell you that, but it was all the time or he got really angry. Oh, my name's Mandy. What's yours?"

"Barb," Barbara said, her eyes wide.

"I like the jacket, Barb. You don't seem like a pagan, are you? You look like a mundane, I was really surprised when I read your aura. You're right, you're powerful and it's god power. Who's your god?"

"The Lord," Barbara replied, calmly. "But I don't go around Bible thumping and I get along just fine with pagans."

"Wow! You're a Christian? I've met some Christians who said they were powerful but it was all so much bullshit. They were so closed up it was incredible. I thought Christianity must suck power right out of you. I'd like to meet the pope just so I could see if *he's* powerful because if he's not nobody will be, right? But you're powerful, I can see that. You have the most amazing aura, it's very bright and light blue mostly. Light blue is really unusual, I guess it's because you're a Christian. There's tinges of red, that's usually a sign of somebody who's not sure what they are but I don't think that's related to your religion, you seem really grounded in that. What do you do?"

"I'm a homemaker," Barb said after a moment to catch up. The woman not only spoke nonstop she jumped all over the place and talked a mile a minute. And she didn't seem to care much about *what* she talked about.

"What's a mundane homemaker doing at a con?" Mandy asked. "I mean, we get all kinds but you don't seem like the con type. Are you enjoying yourself? Not much happens on Friday night, Saturday is when it starts to pick up. Of course this is a small con, the big ones like Dragon and WorldCon start on Thursday usually and go until Monday. But even then it's pretty slow on Thursday. Have you thought about going to DragonCon? You could really costume with those legs and tits; you'd look great in a chain-mail bikini or a corset. Yeah, a corset would really set off your looks. You should get a good corset. There's a guy I know makes corsets, he'd love to fit you. Great hands, I wish I could afford his stuff, but it's really expensive. He can make a corset for anybody, though. He made a corset for my friend Tracy and she's, like, an M cup. And she's got this condition called mastitis so her tits are, like, solid and they stand straight out. All the other guys that made corsets had tried and given up but Kevin made one for her. He's down in the Dealers' Room, you should see him tomorrow. Medium height, great head of blond hair, you should see the Eomer costume he made, he looks just like him. Norm would look great in an Eomer costume but we could never afford it. I mean I'm barely making anything dealing tarot and Norm can't get a job. He's a trained diesel mechanic but nobody will hire him cause his dyslexia is so bad. What's funny is that he can read just fine if it's right to left, you know, but regular writing just is like impossible for him. He's really been helping me with my studies though. He used to be LeMay but he's with the Goddess now but when he was LeMay he really got into some very hard readings and he learned a lot that he's been able to help me with. He's really smart but he reads so bad that he can never pass the tests they give him for reading so nobody will hire him. Which is really stupid since he's a really good mechanic and he's built all sorts of stuff for us at the house. We've got the best altar you'll ever see and the whole circle thinks it's great. So what are you doing at the con?"

"I'm here to see K. Goldberg," Barbara said, her wide and staring eyes starting to glaze over. "I'm a big fan. Well, a fan. I heard she was going to be at this con and I decided to come get a couple of books signed."

"Really?" Mandy said, turning around. "Hey, Kay? Fan here."

"Excuse me?" Barb said, looking past Mandy's shoulder. At the base of the stairs was a group consisting of two women and a man. The man was heavyset and had the look of a laborer. His clothing was worn and not particularly expensive to start with and he was wearing an old field jacket. One of the women was about Barbara's height and age, slightly plump with a pleasant face and brown hair. The other was short, slender to the point of emaciation and much older, maybe in her sixties, with bright red-brown hair. All three were smoking, the man and taller woman holding beer bottles and the older woman what looked very much like a Mimosa.

All three looked over at Mandy at the interruption but the older woman was facing Barb as she looked up. She gave Barbara the fastest appraisal she'd ever experienced, starting at the shoes and working up to Barb's face and hair. And her face was . . . hard and closed as she did it. Then it cleared, so fast that Barbara wondered if she'd really seen what she thought she saw.

"This is Barb," Mandy said, going over to the group. "Kay, she's a fan of your books," the woman continued, gesturing at the older woman.

"Always a pleasure to meet a reader," the older woman said in a soft Southern accent. Her face now had an expression of real pleasure as she held out a soft hand.

"Barb's a homemaker," Mandy continued. "And this is my old man, Norm, and this is Ruby, she's the co-chair," she said, introducing the other two.

As Barb expected, Norm's hand was rough from work. Ruby gave her a smile that was wary and Barbara couldn't figure out why.

"What is a . . . co-chair?" Barb asked.

"Con co-chairman," Ruby said, regarding her levelly. "One of the two people running the con. I take care of dealing with guests and con-goer problems and my partner, Bill, handles operations and the con staff."

"Oh," Barbara said, blushing. "I understand. I've had to run some things, not this big. I can *imagine* the headaches. You've done an outstanding job; it's a very well run con from what I've seen. It must have taken a lot to time on your part to do all the planning."

"Thank you," Ruby said, her brow furrowing. She seemed to be looking for something in the words besides graciousness and not finding it. Possibly to her chagrin.

"Somehow I hadn't expected . . . uh, a big author to be just standing around talking out in the cold, Ms. Goldberg," Barb said, looking at Goldberg.

"Call me Kay," Goldberg replied, smiling and ducking her head shyly. "Everyone does."

"Do you write full time?" Barbara asked, not sure what you asked a writer.

"Yes, but not mysteries," Kay answered in a soft voice, ducking her head again. "I also write for the newspaper in Charlotte and I do some radio work."

"Well, you certainly have a lovely voice," Barb said, smiling.

"Tell her what else you do, come on," Mandy said, grinning.

"Oh, Mandy," Kay said, shaking her head.

"She writes football columns for the paper," Ruby interjected, smiling at the slight woman. "And she does color commentary for Clemson."

"Really?" Barbara asked, her eyes widening. "What an . . . That's just delightful. I wish my husband could meet you. You'd probably have a lot to talk about; he's a tremendous Ole Miss fan."

"I'd rather talk mysteries," Kay replied, shrugging. "At least here. I enjoy football but it's good to get away sometimes. You're not originally from Mississippi, are you Barb?"

"No, I traveled around as a girl," Barbara said, her forehead furrowing slightly. "My father was what's called a Foreign Area Officer. They go to embassies."

"What branch?" Ruby asked.

"Air Force," Barb said, looking at her in puzzlement. It was a lamentable fact that very few people she knew had much knowledge of the military.

"I was Air Force," Ruby said, nodding. "An SP. So was my ex, in the Force that is. He was a bomber pilot."

"So was my dad before he was an FAO," Barbara replied, smiling. For a former military brat, finding even one veteran in a group like this was a relief. In a way, the military was a very extended family and she warmed to Ruby immediately.

"I was in the Marines," Norm interjected.

"So was I," Mandy added. "That's where I met my ex. I met Norm later, thank the Goddess. He was a sending, I think I would have died if I hadn't met him." She grinned at the man who shrugged and smiled sheepishly. It was apparent who the big talker was in the twosome.

"I think this is as many military people as I've met since the last time I was at my dad's house," Barb said, grinning. "What about you Miz Goldberg?"

"I know a lot about the military," Kay answered. "And please call me Kay. Mandy said you are a homemaker? Children?"

"Three," Barbara said, sighing. "One of them, fortunately, old enough that she can do for her father. Mark's never learned to so much as cook. Except grilling, of course."

"All men can grill," Mandy said. "It's like something genetic. Get them around fire and they just have to cook something on it. But if you ever go to a Sabbat gathering you'll find out how much you really can do on a fire. Norm's great at cooking over a fire but I was at one where a lady held a full formal high tea, all of it cooked on fires. And it was perfect. She even had scones if you can believe it. I almost took Cheryl and I suppose I should have she would have, learned something from it. Actually, what with everyone who was sky clad probably taking a fourteen-year-old who already has a C cup chest wouldn't have been a good idea. What did I ever do to deserve a daughter that has a C cup chest at fourteen? It's not like *I* was a C cup when I was fourteen. She thinks it's funny and so are boys and the way you can twist them around your finger. She keeps saying that she's going to suck all their brains out with flying squids and make them her minions. I don't know why it's flying squids but she's fixated on that. And taking over the world. She thinks girls should think big. I told her minions aren't going to do you any good if all they can do is stare at your chest but she wouldn't listen. But my ex has custody and I wasn't about to try to explain it to him, he thinks Wicca is of the devil. Apparently wife beating is just fine by Jesus Christ— Oh, sorry!" she cut off, looking at Barbara.

"Christ is often used as an excuse for evil," Barb said, waggling her head from side to side. "I personally believe in the rule that a man is the master of the house and the woman's place is to obey. Up to a point and that point is when the actions are outside of Christian duty. The Old Testament has very little to suggest that a woman *shouldn't* allow herself to be beaten. But the foundation of Christianity is *not* the Old Testament, it is the New, the words of Our Lord and Savior Jesus Christ. And Christ was a man of peace who raised up even the fallen women. He was, assuredly, never a wife beater. And any man who raises his hand to a woman in anger is no Christian."

"We get all sorts of trouble from Bible thumpers," Mandy said, shaking her head. "I mean, so I read tarot, what's wrong with that? It's like they think we're the Devil incarnate and they don't even know what the Devil really is. I mean, the Christian symbology for the Devil is the Horned God who wasn't evil at all, he was just a fertility spirit. Sometimes human sacrifices would be made to him but that was the ritual and it's no different than transubstantiation if you think about it. Both of them involve human sacrifice and at least the worshippers of the Horned One didn't eat their victims. Well, not usually and not in the later worship. By the time Christianity ran into the worship of the Horned One most human sacrifice had been eliminated which, let me tell you, really pissed the old guy off. But the Devil didn't have anything to do with the Horned One. He's just a modification of the shedim Shaitan. And Wicca doesn't derive its powers from either the shedim or the Horned One though some call on the Horned One but I think that's all about fertility, not that Norm and I have any problems in that regard but thank the Goddess he's not like my ex. I wish *he'd* get sacrificed to the Old Gods. But they'd probably spit his soul back out."

"Yet, the God of the Old Testament and the New Testament are the same God," Ruby said, smiling and ignoring Mandy's digression. "How do you justify obeying only one set of rules, especially when they're at odds?"

"It's corny," Barbara said, shrugging. "But I really do ask myself 'What would Jesus do?' Not 'What would Solomon do?' I may sometimes feel the rage of David, but I only let it loose against persons who truly do evil, who live in it. Being rageful when . . . oh, somebody cuts you off in traffic or some woman is being snippy about whose daughter is smarter than whose, that's not being a Christian. Nor is beating your wife."

"And would that be being a Jew?" Kay asked, dryly. Barb noticed that her accent flattened out slightly. "Since that's the Old Testament God?"

"I don't know as much about Judaism as I would like," Barbara admitted, carefully. "But the Talmud encompasses far more than the books that are found in the Old Testament. And the study of it is thousands of years old, with a great deal of interpretation, as I understand it. I've never heard that wife beating is common amongst those of the Faith of Abraham. Is it?"

"Not noticeably," Kay replied, smiling. "Is this what you usually do, stand around and debate religion?"

"Oh, no," Barb admitted. "Normally I have to stand around and make nice little comments about how gracefully a friend's daughter fell on her face during cheerleading practice or trade casserole recipes. I much prefer this. The talk is much more . . . broadening."

"You'd better watch that," Mandy said with a laugh. "You'll end up questioning all sorts of assumptions."

"Not fundamental ones," Barbara said, smiling. "Those are far beyond belief for me. For one thing, I clearly separate the social overlay of humanity from the Truth of the Risen God. I won't preach, but the power of the Lord Jesus Christ is very real. As you should know, Mandy," she added with an arched eyebrow.

"This is your first con?" Ruby asked.

"Oh, yes," Barb said, laughing. "I . . . well, my husband thinks I'm at a religious retreat. And I was, but one of the ladies at the retreat was coming to the con and she knew I was a . . . reader of Miz Goldberg's books, so she suggested I come along. I find it very interesting."

"You're also here with a gentleman," Kay said.

"Really?" Mandy squealed. "Something *else* the hubbie doesn't know?"

"He's a friend of Janea's," Barbara said, primly. "I'm staying with Janea, I'll point out."

"It's not a problem," Kay said. "I was just wondering. Where did you study martial arts?"

"How did you know . . . ?" Barb said then paused. "My dad got me into it when we were in Hong Kong before the turn-over. I've been studying it ever since."

"The religious conference," Kay said. "Would that be the Foundation for Love and Universal Faith?"

"Yes," Barbara said carefully. "You know about it?"

"A bit," Goldberg replied. "What did you think of your fellow attendees?"

"They were a very . . . eclectic bunch," Barb said, looking at Goldberg with more interest. She noticed that the accent had faded again, just a bit.

"And you came from there to here?" Goldberg asked. "To observe the con?"

"Yes," Barbara said.

"Interesting," the woman replied. "Well, it's getting late and these old bones can't handle the chill as well as they used to. I'll bid you all good night."

After a round of good nights she headed for the far side of the atrium and Barb bit her lip.

"I forgot to ask her something," Barbara said. "If you'll excuse me for a minute?"

She strode after Goldberg and caught her as she was waiting for the elevator. There were three young people in black waiting for the elevator and when Barb caught the word "vampires" she perked up. But a moment later she realized they were talking about a game.

"Miz Goldberg?" she said as the elevator arrived. "I was wondering . . ."

"How I know of the Foundation?" Kay asked as they got on the elevator.

"Uhm . . ." Barbara said then paused again since they were in the elevator with the teenagers. "Actually, I was wondering about you. It's . . . something that Daddy taught me."

"I'm just a writer, miss," the woman said. "A very old one who is going to bed."

The three got off the elevator at the second floor and as the door closed so did Barb's face.

"You're a hell of a lot more than a writer, Miz 'Goldberg,'" Barbara said. "The way that you deflect questions is straight out of the manual on avoiding being pumped."

"And you're a hell of a lot more than a homemaker, Mrs. Everette," Kay replied, just as hard. "What's going on at the con?"

Barbara paused for a moment more then shrugged.

"There's a serial killer," she said as the doors opened again.

"Go ahead," Goldberg said as they stepped out of the doors. "You'd be surprised what you can say at a con. I'll just tell anyone who hears it that you were trying to sell me on writing an idea you had for a novel." She stopped and sighed. "You'd be surprised how often that happens."

"Well, this would make a good one," Barb said as they reached the woman's room.

Barbara explained the nature of their mission to the woman as the writer took off her shoes and rubbed her feet. When she was done, for the first time the woman really looked *old*.

"And Special Circumstances thinks the killer is one of my fans?" Kay asked, still rubbing her feet.

"You even know about that?" Barb asked, her eyes narrowing.

"You'd be surprised what I know, kiddo," Kay replied, her accent entirely gone. If anything it sounded a bit New York. "Yeah, I know about SC. Is that old stick Germaine still in charge?"

"Yes," Barbara said. "He recruited me."

"You should have run screaming," Goldberg replied with a sigh. She got up and went to the room's refrigerator and pulled out a split of champagne and a bottle of orange juice. After pouring equal measures into a plastic cup she drank about half of the mixture before sitting back down and lighting another Virginia Slims. She took another sip, a long drag on the cigarette and then looked Barb square in the eye. "Special Circumstances eats people and spits them out as mangled husks. I hate them in a way. Oh, I know that they do the Lord God's work. But they use their people like donkeys. No, even donkeys get some rest. I know most of the people that talk to me at cons by name. Young male?"

"Male anyway," Barb said, shrugging. "Brown hair. He might wear silver moonstone jewelry."

"I'll come up with a list," Kay said, thoughtfully. "You're circulating looking for suspects?"

"I'm . . . I have some feeling for these things," Barbara said. "It's not very well trained, but . . ."

"If he's halfway good, he'll be cloaking," Kay said, sliding up on the bed and plumping the pillows behind her. "You could walk right past him in the hall, you could talk to him and get nothing. If he's cloaking and you're not, he can see you, so to speak, and know you're either a hunter or a target. He can get more power from someone like you than from just any old child. And if he's gathering power in moonstones he can shield that from you with silk, so you won't be able to feel his power source either. You know all that?"

"I . . . sort of," Barb said. "I've picked up . . . a few of those things. But I'm new to this."

"So why are you on such an important case?" Kay asked, her eyes narrowing.

"I'm strong," Barbara said, firmly. "I am strong in my faith and the Lord's hand shelters me."

"You know that?" Kay asked. "He's a flighty God, our God. And he is *our* God. Slightly different approaches but the same God. And He has quite a few items on His plate. You can't depend on Him to always pull your chestnuts out of the fire. And you'd better be *sure* you are powerful if you go up against a necromancer."

"I have . . . battled before," Barb said. "Something more powerful than a necromancer. And the Lord sheltered me."

"You're lucky," Goldberg said, mirthlessly. "I lost a tad of my belief when . . . well, that's neither here nor there. You keep firm to yours, it is your shield and sword if you know how to wield it."

"You were in Special Circumstances?" Barbara asked, curiously.

"Not me," Kay said, shaking her head. "A . . . friend was involved in one of their investigations. He died."

"I'm sorry," Barb said, sincerely.

"So was I," Kay admitted, looking at the far wall and into the past. "But a lot of friends died and, honestly, some of them for less reason. He was . . . a bit more special to me than the others. There is a reason I'm *Miss* Goldberg in other words. And all his faith did not shield him. Or, perhaps, it wasn't as strong as he thought, as I thought for that matter. Hold hard to your faith in the Lord, young one. And I hope that His hand is over you always. Good night, Mrs. Everette."

Chapter Ten

With nowhere else to go, Barbara went back down to the atrium. Mandy and the others had disappeared so she walked over towards the group by the table. Somebody was singing and she vaguely recognized the song. Her father had sung it sometimes when he was really drunk.

"As the wind shook the barley . . ." the man said, picking up his glass and taking a slug. It was dark with something and from the bottle of Glenlivet on the table Barb could guess what it was. He was probably in his fifties, good looking in a lean-boned way with dark hair shot with gray. The group around the table was clearly enjoying the song and most of them were smoking. She noticed that one of them was the bookseller she'd spoken to earlier in the day. She wasn't smoking but she looked right at home.

Behind the group was a man sitting on a blanket, writing in a notebook and ignoring the goings on around him. He was tall from what Barbara could tell, distinguished looking with a long face and short gray-brown hair, clean shaven and dressed heavily against the cold. A woman with long silver hair was seated in a chair between him and the group, subtly blocking anyone from approaching.

"So now I'll play the patriot game," the man sang as a couple of others tried to chime in. "And I think I've forgotten the rest."

"You're just not drunk enough, Don," one of the men at the table said, laughing. "You'll remember after another bottle."

"That I may," the man said, picking up his glass and draining it. "And what is this lovely apparition I do see before me?"

"Back off," the man who had said something about being drunk said. "I get the blondes, you get the dark ones. That's the deal."

"A base canard, laddy," Don said, grinning at Barb as he refilled his glass. "For certain blondes I will make an exception."

"I'm married," Barbara said, sitting down at one of the open tables. "But you sing very well. You remind me of my father. He used to sing that to me."

"A shot to the heart!" Don said, grinning nonetheless. "Once a girl says you remind her of her father you're either shot down or into a very strange relationship indeed. However, your chastity is safe around me, lovely apparition without a name, for I do not bestow myself upon other men's wives. And I had noted the ring."

"Just anything else with a skirt," the bookseller said, smiling.

"Nothing of the sort," Don protested, taking another drink. "They must be of reasonable age and willing. And unmarried and unengaged. Other than that, yes, I am willing to grace their bed and they need not even pay me. Can any woman ask for more? What *is* your name, lovely apparition? And avoid the laddy across the table. He is a wolf in sheep's clothing and far less moral than I. He prefers his own cooking but other men's wives."

"Barbara," Barbara said, holding out her hand. "Barb Everette. And yours?"

"Donald Draxon," Don said, shaking her hand and then bending over to kiss it. "Various appellations and honorifics on that, depending upon circumstances."

"Like colonel," the "laddy" across the table said. He was at least in his forties, slightly heavy but not fat by any stretch, with a look that said he'd once been in shape. He was smoking cigars instead of the inevitable cigarettes and Barbara found the smell refreshing. "And Esquire and up-and-coming writer if I have anything to do with it."

"Ah, laddy, we'll get there," Don said. "Never fear, we will shake the publishing industry to its very foundations. What brings you to the con, Barb the Lovely?"

"I read Miz Goldberg's books," Barbara said.

"Goldberg?" Don asked, puzzled.

"Mystery writer," the still unintroduced "laddy" said. "Lives in Charlotte. Short, Jewish, a bit zaftig if a tad on the old side. All else bears not repeating in nonsecure circumstances."

"Forsooth, laddy, do tell," Don said, filling his empty glass again. "We are among friends."

"Seriously, Colonel, *not* in nonsecure circumstances," the man said, firmly.

"Bloody security," the colonel said, taking a deep drink from his glass. "I hates it, I hates it my precious, I does."

"You're really a colonel?" Barb asked, smiling and changing the subject. Although she also made a note to pick "laddy's" brain.

"An instructor at the War College," "laddy" said, smiling lightly.

"For my sins," Don sighed, sadly. "All these bright young colonels and Navy captains being indoctrinated in PC rhetoric and me the only one trying to stem the tide. You know, Barb, it is perfectly legal to take hostages and hold them against the good behavior of the inhabitants of an area? And then kill them if the inhabitants aren't good? I mean, if you do it right. Iron-clad legal."

"He's the instructor in the law of land warfare," "laddy" said. "Which is a bit like giving Satan the keys to the Pearly Gates. Especially since he's the most bloody minded, legalistically sneaky bastard the Army's ever spit out."

"I'm sorry, we haven't been introduced," Barbara said, looking at the other man. The rest of the group was just watching the by-play between the two.

"Folsom Duncan," the man said, bowing slightly. He was wearing a long black leather coat that had to be lined against the cold unless he was superhuman.

"And you're a writer as well, sir?" Barb asked, curiously. She knew she had made a mistake when about half the group laughed.

"You see!" Duncan said, mock angrily. "What is it with this genre? I've got to start writing mysteries or that unicorn story or something!"

"He's one of the biggest writers in science fiction," the bookseller said, grimacing at Barbara's faux pas. "At least based on sales. And he's always lamenting that there aren't enough good looking females reading SF."

"Don't worry about it," Duncan said, waving his hand and wafting cigar smoke around. "It's totally normal. I'm not by any stretch a household name. And the publishing industry is so diverse that readers of one genre rarely know another. Which is why I should write romances or teeny-bopper thrillers or Goth or something. That's the way to get the chicks for free. And getting the chicks for free is the only true pursuit for a grown-up male. Before puberty, of course, it's avoiding them like the plague."

"You're married," Barb pointed out, noting the wedding ring.

"It doesn't mean I can't *flirt*," Duncan said, smiling. When he smiled his face came alive and Barbara admitted that she *did* find him attractive. "I'm not quite as aggressive about it as Donald here, but I certainly enjoy the dance. It *helps*, however, to have the cachet of being a 'published author.' It sort of breaks the ice. Among other things, it skips right over the lousy pick-up lines. Women come up to *me* and say 'So what's your next book, Mr. Duncan?' Very refreshing."

"Well, not much," the brunette said, laughing. "Mostly they say, 'Who the hell are you?'"

"Thanks for reminding me," Duncan said, sorrowfully. "I'm going to write a book about unicorns. Get surrounded by young lovelies that *have* to know what's going to happen to 'whatsername.' 'Well, young lovely nubile lady,' I'll say, 'it just so happens that I have my latest work in progress up in my room. I'll squeeze you in between nine and nine-thirty. I hope you can handle multiple orgasms.' "

"I have some problems with that," Barb said, her eyes wide.

"Oh, so would I," Duncan admitted, hastily. "Among other things, my wife would kill me and there's all these laws and things about underage females. But it's a lovely thought."

"Women don't like anything that's got a scrap of science to it," one of the men at the table said. He was a heavyset older guy with a thick gray-brown beard. "They only want to read horsey stories about dragons and unicorns."

"Hey!" the brunette snapped.

"Most women," the man corrected.

"Well, there's a bit of a reality to that," Duncan said. "I mean, market-wise it's indisputable. But the question is, why?"

"Do tell us, laddy!" Don said, taking another heavy drink. "You're the thinker in this lot."

"Not the only one by a stretch," Duncan said. "But there are a few known facts about the differences, physiologically, between male and female brains. One of them is that in fetal development, males get more separation between the two lobes of the brain. It's actually a function of testosterone. That means they can separate logic from emotion more effectively than females. That gives them the ability to look at things with clearer logic, in general."

"I think I'm pretty logical," the brunette said. She didn't seem as upset about his statements as she had been about the "scrap of science" comment.

"Ah, but you're a bit *odd*, as a female," Duncan pointed out. "You yourself have commented that you act more like one of the boys. And I, who find virtually any woman from fifteen to fifty to be worthy of a passing thought about afternoon delight, am not physically attracted to you at all. Because you *do* come across as 'one of the guys' and I am irresolubly het. I suspect you've got a bit less connections than most women, ergo you can deal with a situation with less emotional input. Now, me, I probably have a few *more* connections than your average bear, thus my gift of gab and a bit of ability to write.

"It's not a hard and fast thing; human beings are individuals not groups. It's more of a bell curve with males trending more to the 'logic' side and women more to the 'emotion' side. Now, the point to that is that each has strengths and weaknesses. I *suspect* that it's why females gravitate, in general, to more emotional or nurturing professions. In business they tend more towards marketing rather than operations. In medicine they tend towards nursing and softer arts rather than, oh, surgery. And they bring strengths to those areas. It's not a matter of better or worse. A coldly analytical SOB makes a great accountant and a fair operations manager but a lousy marketing guru. But it would also explain why they tend more towards fantasy rather than SF. And especially tend away from military fiction which is much more cold and brutal than most of the rest of the genre."

"I've read a fair amount of military fiction," Barbara said. "And I certainly don't come across as one of the guys."

"Not in the slightest," Duncan said, waggling his eyebrows. "However, have you any military background?"

"My dad was in the Air Force," Barbara said.

"Culture modifies nature," Duncan said, shrugging. "You were inculcated in the military culture. It might be why you gravitated over here; it seems to happen. Military people just seem to turn up around us. I think it's something in the tone of the laughter that says: 'Really bad no-shit story being told over here.' I suspect, however, that you're not much of a science fiction reader."

"No, not really," Barb admitted. "I got forced to read some in high school, but I never really liked it."

"Bleck," Duncan said, sticking out his tongue. "Probably Bradbury or Ellison. Bradbury shouldn't happen to a goat."

"Hey, *I* like Bradbury," the brunette said.

"I know, and I forgive you," Duncan said. "You also like Ellison, which is a far greater sin against man and God. However, as the Lord said, let he who is without sin cast the first stone and I do admit to occasionally reading Asimov and enjoying it. Albeit, his very early work before he got full of himself. 'Christmas on Ganymede' was really the height of his writing oeuvre."

"You're a Christian?" Barbara asked, surprised.

"Catholic," Duncan said, shrugging. "Sort of. I know the tune and can dance to it. I really think of myself as a fallen pagan of Christ."

"What's that?" Don said, screwing up his face. "That's one I hadn't heard before."

"All the old gods got wrapped into the Christian pantheon as saints and angels and such like," Duncan said taking a sip of his own drink. Barb had assumed from the color that it was whiskey as well, but she suddenly suspected that it was iced tea. Which seemed an awfully cold drink for such a freezing night. "My namesake, for example, is naught more than various war-gods absorbed by the early Christian church. And as a Catholic, I don't have to pray straight to the Big Guy. I can use the chain of command, which works just fine for my brain. So in the very few cases where I think prayer is in order, and occasionally when it's not but I think he might like a word or two, I pray to Michael. Certainly worked for me in Division."

"How?" one of the men asked.

"When I was jumping I'd just pray over and over again: 'St. Michael, Patron of Paratroopers, Protect Us,'" Duncan said, shrugging. "Over forty jumps and nary an injury. Only guy I know who had more than twenty and never broke anything. These days I just talk to him from time to time when I need somebody to talk to who doesn't talk back."

"You were military?" Barbara asked.

"Just a grunt," Duncan said, shrugging. "Not a very good one. Now I'm a decent writer some people like."

"This is his way of fishing for compliments," the brunette said, smiling. "He's actually quite good. If you like military stuff you'd probably enjoy his books."

"Unfortunately, most beautiful, gorgeous, curvaceous, long-legged, fine-boned, well-dressed blondes do not," Duncan said, winking at her. "Especially those between the ages of sixteen and nineteen and a half. Alas, my primary market is males between the ages of fifteen and fifty. And I'm so irredeemably het. It's a shame, it really is."

"So, basically, you're screwed," the man with the beard said, laughing.

"Or not," Folsom said, sighing. "But I will triumph. Unicorns. That's the ticket."

"I-I've been th-thinking about a s-story," one of the men at the table said, suddenly. He wasn't smoking, Barbara noticed, and she wasn't sure why he was out there. He was in his twenties, at a guess, with lanky dark brown hair that had been cut in bangs that just didn't look right on him. "I-it's s-sort of unicorns in outer s-space. Well, n-not really, th-they're not really u-unicorns, th-th-th-they just look s-sort of like th-them, but not horse looking more like s-seals because th-they can fly in s-space and th-they make a s-sort of bubble of air around th-them. Well, th-they don't usually but th-they can if th-they have to and th-these kids find s-some and . . . Well, not kids, probably teenagers, th-they find th-them, I haven't figured out just why th-they're th-there but I'm working on th-that and th-these kids, th-their parents are probably s-scientists because I don't th-think th-that it would work with th-them being asteroid miners. I th-think th-that asteroid miners would probably be a bit red-neck, and th-these kids are pretty s-smart. Of course, th-they could have not really s-smart parents. Or th-the parents could be pretty s-smart because you'd probably have to be s-smarter th-than most people th-think to be an asteroid miner. Anyway, th-these kids find th-these s-sort of unicorn th-things and th-there's a group of pirates. Well, maybe not pirates, th-they might be aliens th-that are trying to take over th-the s-system. And th-the kids use th-the unicorns to s-sort of foil th-them and th-that s-sort of th-thing. What do you th-think?"

"Lovely idea, Baron," Duncan said, nodding. If he'd noticed the digressions and the fact that the entire thing had been delivered in a monotone, not to mention that the story idea was weak and the plot nonexistent, he didn't show it. Nobody seemed to and Barb decided that since they all knew the person, they must be used to it. Which was more acceptance than she'd have expected from a group of clearly military oriented people. Most air force officers would have impolitely told him to shove off long ago. "And if it sold, young lovelies would be all over you like flies on honey."

"They won't be all over me," one of the guys at the table said, grumpily. "But I really think my book has a chance."

"So do I, Sean," Duncan said, nodding. "Good story line, good characters. I think you're a little long on the info dumps but what do I know? David certainly does well enough with them."

"Still the wrong genre to fix my lack-a-nookie," Sean replied. He was solidly built, probably in his twenties, with short hair and the look that said former military.

"Finally break up with Annette?" the bookseller asked.

"Ripped my heart out and stomped that sucker flat," Sean said, bitterly. "Then she took out a restraining order. Now all my coworkers think I'm some kind of abuser."

"Well, you do have a bit of temper," Duncan pointed out.

"I never raised a hand to her," Sean said, flatly. "I barely raised my voice. And that was only after I found her in *my* bed with her new boyfriend."

"Sounds like you need to go back and reread the *Iliad,* laddy," Don said, hiccupping. "Women are the root of all evil."

"And men are the whole rest of the tree," the brunette quipped.

"Well, *I* wouldn't have fooled around on you," a muffled figure said. The person was bundled up beyond belief in the cold. She had on a University of Tennessee jacket with the hood up, a scarf wrapped around her face and mitten-clad hands thrust into her armpits. Barbara could only guess she was a female from the voice and a tuft of blond hair sticking out of one side of the hood. Even her eyes were too shadowed to be seen.

"Thanks, Sadie," Sean said, grinning. "But you're taken."

"We're just friends," the man next to her said, gruffly. He was probably in his fifties with a round face and body. With the beard and demeanor he looked like nothing so much as a rotund bear. He was the one who had made the comment about women not liking science. "And after two wives fooling around on me, I wouldn't expect anything else," he added.

"Men are naturally polygamous," Duncan said, grinning.

"Women, on the other hand, are simply designed to be unfaithful."

"Now *that's* an outrageous statement," the brunette said, smiling. "Which means you have some backing for it, knowing you."

"I'll skip the men being naturally polygamous; it's too long," Duncan said, nodding. "But the 'naturally unfaithful' is easier. Study was done a few years ago. One group of women graded men on the basis of 'hard' or 'soft' looking. Then another group graded the men on their attractiveness, but it was calculated against their menstrual cycle. The closer they got to their menstrual cycle, when they were less fertile in other words, the more attractive the 'soft' looking men got. The closer they were to fertile, the more attractive the 'hard' looking men got. When asked to choose which they would prefer as a husband, for the long term, to raise children with, most chose the 'soft' looking males. The reason generally given was that the 'nicer' looking guys would probably make better fathers. More nurturing than those hard looking bastards."

"Hah!" the round bear laughed. "I wonder how many 'urban males' are raising bastards?"

"Well, divorce proceedings are a bad random population," Sean said. "But over thirty percent of the children that are tested in disputed custody cases turn out to not be the children of their supposed fathers."

"Women are naturally unfaithful," Duncan said, shrugging. "Once you've got that through your head everything else follows logically."

"So are you one of the guests?" Barb asked, her eyes narrowing. Among other things, although he was somewhat older, the writer fit the parameters. He certainly didn't seem to care much for women. She considered trying to read him, but wasn't sure if anyone would notice. The shock she got when Mandy noticed still had her unsure.

"For my sins," Duncan said. "Every year I turn and twist on the hook, and every year I seem to return."

"And do you go to a lot of conventions?" Barbara asked, curiously.

"About four or five a year," Duncan said, shrugging. "I enjoy them but they cut into writing time. But I need them, too. They let me get out in the mix of society and recharge the writing pool. I do a good bit of traveling for research as well. I've spent a fair amount of time in Virginia lately, researching another book. Again it gets me out in society; writing is a very lonely job. Helps with characters, too."

"You might find yourself in a book someday," the brunette said. "So watch out."

"I call it soul stealing," Duncan said, grinning.

Barbara got a cold shiver at that and decided that she just *had* to open up and see what she felt from the man. But there was nothing there. She reached out and felt the sort of mixed . . . grayness she'd come to feel from some people. But Duncan had . . . nothing. Not a feel of necromancy and not what her instructors had talked about with "shielding" or "cloaking." This was more like some sort of anti-power shield or even total soullessness. He seemed powerful, and that shield certainly seemed to indicate that he was. But the power seemed oddly . . . familiar. She couldn't be sure but she didn't think he was evil. She wondered just how much he *really* talked to the saints.

"Well," Barb said, standing up and smiling. "This has been a fun conversation, but it's getting late for me so I'm heading in. If I end up in a book, I'd like to at least be informed."

"I don't know how to contact you," Duncan said, widening his eyes and batting his lashes. "And I'm not about to ask for your number, it would probably be to a suicide hotline. But I shall give you a card. If you wish to contact me you may and I will tell you if you're going to be used as a character. I make no promises about what the character goes through, however."

"He turned me into a slave girl," the brunette said, laughing.

"I've *told* you there was a perfectly reasonable explanation," Duncan said, plaintively.

"Sure there was," the woman replied, grinning. "I believe you!"

"If you didn't trust me, why are we sharing a room?" Duncan protested.

"I didn't say I didn't trust you," she replied. "I just said we had to have separate beds."

"Conditions, conditions," Duncan sighed, pulling out a card. "I hope to hear from you, Barb. Meeting you has made my evening."

"It has been . . . enlightening for me as well," Barbara said, nodding as she walked away. As she walked up the steps to the door she felt wetness fall on her face. Looking back she could see the snowflakes hanging in the lights of the atrium. She hadn't seen snow like this in years but as she looked at the beauty she shivered. The snow could hide so much.

Chapter Eleven

As she was on the way upstairs she almost collided with Janea as she ran out the stairway door.

"Where is he?" Janea said, breathlessly.

"What?" Barb asked, looking around for threats. The dancer was clearly chasing someone with bloody intent.

"Skinny kid, wearing black!" Janea said. "Dark hair, pimples!"

"I didn't see him," Barbara said, still looking around. "Well, actually, that describes half the kids at the con . . . You're sure it's *him*?"

"Damn straight," Janea said. "He manifested right in front of me, bold as brass. As soon as I . . . Ah *hah*," she snapped, hurrying down the corridor at the sound of a door closing.

Barb followed as Janea ran to the far end of the corridor and turned into another stairwell.

"Listen," Janea said, holding the door open. There was a sound of a door shutting but Barbara couldn't be sure from which direction, up or down.

"Should we call Greg?" Barb asked, nervously. Wait, why was she nervous? She'd dealt with a demon, what was a necromancer to that?

"I think he went down," Janea said. "But you go up. Call me if he's up there."

"I will," Barbara said, darting up the stairs. She checked her piece on the landing and then darted up the final steps, throwing open the door at the top. There were three boys just outside the landing, one of them bent over gasping for air.

"She's been chasing me like a hound," the boy gasped, breathing in and out heavily. "How the hell can she run that fast in *heels*?"

"Well, between the three of us, we can take her," one of the others said. He was taller and a tad older than the youngster who was hyperventilating. All three were dressed in black but the duster the man was wearing had several cabalistic signs on it. "She's only a second level Hunter."

"The hell you will," Barb said, her hand still on her piece. "She's not who you should be worrying about. Janea! Up here."

"Gotcha!" Janea yelled from downstairs.

"Just stay still and don't make any sudden moves," Barbara said, pulling out her cell phone with her left hand.

"What the hell are you talking about?" the older boy said, looking at her askance.

"Gotcha," Janea said as she skidded through the door. "Oh, holy shit!"

"Welcome to vampire central, Hunter," the older boy said, maliciously.

"I'm outta here!" Janea said, turning around.

"Not so fast, Hunter," the boy said, pulling out a card. "Let's see your powers."

"Damn," Janea said, pulling out her own card. "I've built up sixteen defense points."

"We're unified in a circle," the boy said. "That's a total of twenty-five attack points." He held up a fist and counted. "One, two, three."

"Hah!" Janea said, holding two fingers up. "Scissors to your paper!"

"Damn!" snapped the boy who had been gasping. He'd managed to recover and now he looked like he wanted to spit.

"You can escape, Hunter," the older boy said, putting away his card. "But you'd better keep your face out of sight by night. We know you now, Hunter, and we'll be looking for you. All of our circle will be hunting *you*, Hunter."

"Right, Barb, we're leaving," Janea said, taking her arm.

"You were playing a *game*?" Barbara nearly shouted as the door closed. "I was ready to *draw* on them!"

"Oh, hell," Janea said, stopping and looking at her wide-eyed. Then she began to laugh so hard she ended up gasping like the kid who'd been run to ground. Finally she stopped and wiped her eyes, smearing her mascara. "Oh! Oh! God that's funny."

"It's *not* funny," Barb said, trying not to grin. "I was all set to call Greg and put the cuffs on him! And if one of them had made a move, they'd have been looking down the barrel of a .45!"

"Okay, so it's not so funny," Janea said, still chuckling. "Yeah, we were playing a game. Come on, let's get over to the Hunter room and I'll introduce you around."

The Hunter room was a double just about filled with kids dressed in black.

"I had him dead to rights," one of them was bemoaning. "I had the cross and the stake and everything. And he won the damned toss! So there I was, dead as a doornail."

"Tough luck," the girl he was talking to said. She was about fifteen if she was a day, pretty, overweight, and wearing at least another ten pounds of mascara and fifteen in silver jewelry. She looked like she probably had naturally light brown hair but it was dyed black and her eyes looked like a raccoon's from all the black makeup. "But you can resurrect tomorrow."

"I know," the boy grumped. "But what am I going to do the rest of the night . . . ?"

"Barb, this is Timson," Janea said, drawing Barbara over to a young man who was lounging on a chair at the back of the room. "He's the Hunter leader. Timson, this is my friend Barb."

"Nice to meet you, Barb," Timson said, waving. He was tall and very fair, with light blue eyes and hair and a nice smile. If

Allison brought him home as a date Barbara would be happy to let him go out with her. When she was a little older. He was dressed in what was apparently the required black, but it was limited to a black button-down shirt that looked vaguely clerical and black jeans. He had a black leather jacket slung over his shoulder. "Are you going to play? We've got two more Hunter slots open."

"I'm not sure what I'm being asked," she admitted.

There were three other teenagers hanging out with Timson and all three, and Janea, started to explain. It didn't make heads or tails to Barb.

Apparently the game involved a three-way war between werewolves, vampires and Hunters who were humans with special powers. Everyone in the game had special tags so people knew they were playing around the con, but nobody was supposed to know which you were until you "encountered." Then they would "battle" by flipping coins or playing, as Janea had, rock-paper-scissors and, based on some points that went right over Barbara's head, you might be killed, or win, or be able to escape.

"It sounds interesting," Barb said after the five minute explanation had wound to a close. "But I'm not sure it's my sort of thing."

"Well, why don't you hang around and listen," Timson said, grinning. "It's really the most fun to be had."

Someone had handed Barbara a Coke and one of the girls slid over so Barb could sit down. The kids were friendly at least.

"What do you do, Barb?" Timson asked.

"I'm a homemaker," Barbara said, automatically. She just realized that what she *really* was was a Hunter. But in real life.

"I bet you've got kids our age," one of the boys said, shyly.

"A bit younger," Barb said, trying not to flinch.

"I wish my mom was cool enough to come to cons," the girl next to her said with a sigh. She was skinnier than the girl who'd been commiserating with the "killed" Hunter but was dressed about the same. "But she's so uncool it's, like, crazy making! I had to *beg* to get the car tonight and she wanted me home by *ten*. I mean, nothing even *starts* until midnight. And she wouldn't let me use the Beamer, I had to bring the *Volvo*! But with it snowing like it is, she told me I could stay over night."

"We all have our problems in life," Timson said, grinning.

"Are you all . . . teenagers?" Barbara asked.

"You mean living at home?" Timson asked, raising an eyebrow. "Most of the kids at the con are. I'm out of the house, though. I do survey work for a cable company."

"I go to Virginia Tech," one of the other boys said. "I'm taking computer engineering."

"I'm going to college next year," the girl next to her said. "I can't wait to get out of the house."

"Wait until you have to work for a living," Timson said, grinning. "School sucks so you're prepared for real life."

"You don't like your job?" Barb asked.

"I like it enough," Timson said, shrugging. "It pays the bills. But if I had my druthers I'd con all the time."

"This *is* real life," one of the boys said, sighing. "We can be ourselves, here."

"We don't have to deal with stuck up sorority bitches," the college boy said. "Or professors."

"Try dealing with cheerleaders," the girl said. "I'm sorry, black really *does* go with anything, *thank* you."

"That was a . . . weird group," Barbara said after they'd left the room and the group behind. "You really enjoy playing . . . that game?"

"I think of it as training," Janea said. "And I *was* one of those kids when I was in school. I was the geek in the library with the glasses; I didn't really start to bloom until much later. But I'd never heard of cons or LARPing or the rest of it." She frowned and shrugged and Barb realized that she knew a lot about the people she'd met at the con, their lives and backgrounds. But she really didn't know much about Janea.

"I suppose you could think of it as training," Barbara replied. "But should your hobby be this close to your job?"

"I enjoy it," Janea said. "And some of the kids are really bright. I've had good discussions about the occult with them.

You should probably hang out with them more. Of course, some of them are better than others. Timson's brilliant. I don't know what he's doing stuck in that job of his. He never finished college, though. He was working on a degree in anthropology but he said it just got too boring so he quit. He's one of the ones that can talk about the occult all day and night. I mean, he knows the sixty-seven names of the known daevas and each of their special powers. He can even read ancient Persian as well as Aramaic, Greek and Latin. And he's *conversational* in ancient Egyptian. I saw him translate Emily Dickinson's 'I've Known A Heaven' on the fly into Egyptian *and* sing it to 'Yellow Rose of Texas.' Now *that* was bizarre."

Barbara blinked at the image and then started at the very real sight before her. A man was walking down the hallway carrying, over his shoulder, a very large brown timber. Behind him was another man carrying an identical timber then a woman carrying a smaller . . . frame perhaps. Then more men and women dragging, rolling and carrying a variety of large boxes and bags.

"God, the snow's bad!" the man in the lead said, maneuvering past the two women. "'Scuse me."

"Where are you setting up?" Janea asked, eyeing the second man in the line who was rather handsome and well muscled.

"Rooms three seventeen through twenty-eight," the man said. "But you're not my type, sorry."

"Pity," Janea said, arching an eyebrow.

Barb waited until the whole group was past and then looked at her "mentor."

"What in that heck was that all about? And what were those big timbers for? They looked like parts of a cross!"

"They were," Janea said, clearing her throat and for the first time in Barbara's experience actually *blushing*. "They were for St. Andrews crosses."

"And those are?" Barb asked, suspiciously.

"They're . . . big crosses," Janea said. "And that's all I'm gonna say. But it's pretty apparent the Black Rose has turned up in force. I know where I'm going to be hanging out."

"I think I've had about all the bizarre I can take for one

night," Barbara admitted, shaking her head and trying to resist throttling her "mentor." "I'm going to go see if there are any *normal* people around."

"Wait 'til I drag you to DragonCon," Janea said. "You'll look great in a corset . . ."

"So what did you think of the Wharf Rats?" a woman asked as Barb walked down a second floor corridor.

"They were . . . interesting," Barbara replied, stopping and looking the woman over. She was about normal height and only slightly plump with a pleasant face and blonde hair. The fuzzy reindeer horns were the only sign she was on the outside edge of normality. Compared to most of the people Barb had been dealing with all night she seemed positively normal.

"Try annoying," the woman said, grinning. "Might makes right and all that."

"Oh, I wouldn't say that they think might makes right . . ." Barbara argued as a tall man walked up to the woman. He had long, mid-back length, slightly curly brown hair and was wearing a leather jacket heavy on the studs and buckles.

"You must be talking about the Wharf Rats," the man said, grimacing. "If it wasn't for Pier Books, none of those writers would get published at all. They're fifth rate if that."

"I'm sorry," Barb said, smiling at him quizzically. "We haven't been introduced."

"I'm Larry Winston," the man said, sticking out his hand. "I publish *Zero Option, Dark Desires* and *A Bit of Mind*."

"Oh," Barbara said, smiling and nodding. "I like your jacket."

"Thanks," the man said, frowning.

"I'm Angie," the woman said, shaking Barb's hand as well. "I'm sort of a gopher for the magazines."

"Ah," Barbara said, nodding. "I'm sorry I haven't actually read any of them."

"That's okay," the man said. "What are you at the con for?"

"I'm a reader of K. Goldberg," Barb said.

"Oh, we've published Kay," Angie said, happily. "She does wonderful dark fantasy."

"That I can believe," Barbara said with unintended humor.

"Why don't you come down to the room?" Larry said, gesturing down the corridor. "We're having a slush party."

"What's a slush party?" Barb said, uneasily.

"First con?" Angie asked, waving the way.

"Yes?" Barbara replied. It was unlikely that she was being lured away to be axed, but she also wasn't used to being invited to a hotel room except by drunken businessmen who ignored her ring.

"Slush is the stories that are submitted to the magazine," Larry said. "It just . . . piles up. There's no way to stay ahead of it. So from time to time we bring it all to a con and invite people in to read it. That gets ninety percent, at least, thrown out. Then we can concentrate on the rest."

"That seems a bit . . . brutal," Barb said as she got to a half open door and followed Angie in. "I mean, people work hard on those stories. You just let anyone . . . toss them out?"

"Wait until you read some of them," Angie said, laughing. "Larry has a favorite he reads every con, just to give an idea how bad they can get."

There were about nine people in the room, sprawled on the beds, the floor and most of the chairs. Where there weren't people there was paper or boxes of paper. There were at least ten file boxes stacked up against the wall, every single one of them overflowing with envelopes.

"Every submission's supposed to have a self-addressed stamped envelope in it," Angie said, picking one of the envelopes out of a box at random. She slit it open with a curved opener and pulled out the folded pages within. Sure enough, there was an envelope included with the sheets of paper.

"Incredible," Angie said, grinning. "We only get about one in three that has an SASE. If there's no SASE, be pretty sure it's going to get thrown. We can't keep track otherwise."

She sat down on a partially clear area and opened up the tri-folded pages, then grimaced.

"Look," she said, handing over the pages.

Barbara slid to the floor by Angie's spot and started reading.

"'When Gunor reached the feiry wastes of Thogrun he thought that his journey was at an end. But it had hardly beginning. Acrros the feiry wastes he strode, his acks Gomail on his brawny shoulder . . .'"

Barb struggled through the tedious prose, wondering when Gunor was going to do anything of note or, dare she hope, the writer would learn to run a basic spell-checker. After two pages, Angie looked over at her.

"You're still reading that?" Angie asked.

"It seemed the thing to do," Barbara said, trying very hard not to laugh at the prose. And she was still trying to find a plot in all the killing orcs and crossing feiry, sic, wastes.

"Good God, you've got a stronger stomach than I do," Angie said, pulling the papers out of her hand. "Did it get any better?"

"Worse," Barb admitted.

Angie picked up a form, filled in a line and then tossed the sheets of paper into a box filled with similar sheets.

"This is the rejection form," Angie said, showing it to her. It had a standard "We're very sorry your story, insert name here, does not meet our needs at this time," message. Angie had already scrawled, somewhat illegibly, "The Journeys of Gunor the Great" in the space provided, which was too small so "the Great" was cramped into the space.

"Stuff it in the envelope," Angie said, fitting action to words. "Lick and toss into the out box," she said, sending the envelope skimming across the room into a box with "Kill Them All! Kill! Kill!" scrawled on it in Magic Marker. "Another tiny literary ego crushed by the evil publishing industry."

"It does seem a bit heartless," Barbara said, shaking her head.

"Do you *see* all that?" Angie asked, gesturing at the boxes. "That's the inflow of just the last three *months*. And that's just what we haven't already *read*. Wait until you get to a *really* bad one."

"That wasn't really bad?" Barb asked, her eyes wide.

"Anybody got a *really* bad one?" Angie asked, raising her voice.

"I've got the pig story," Larry called from the other side of the room, without looking up from the story he was reading.

"Not the pig story," Angie said. "That's in a category all its own."

"Try this one," a dark-haired man said, flipping some papers at her through the air. Half of them drifted off to fall on the floor as he flipped another envelope expertly through the air to hit the Kill box on the side.

Angie managed to snag the top page and grimaced.

"Look," she said, handing the page to Barbara.

The page was lined paper filled with crabbed, nearly illegible, writing. There were numerous line-outs and scratch outs with words crammed in and over the sentences in no apparent order. And despite this careful editing, more than half the words were misspelled. The word "word" was misspelled, twice. From what she could glean of the actual story . . . there wasn't one.

"Okay, that's bad," Barb said. "People actually think this stuff will get published?"

"Yep," Angie said, tossing the paper on the floor to join the drifts. "And sometimes you'll run into them at cons and they'll ask you *why* they didn't get published. Of course, as you can see, there's no way to keep up with *who* they were. But they *always* have a bad photocopy of their original story. And you have to explain that it first has to be *legible*, then it has to be *literate* and last but most certainly most important it has to actually be a good *story*. Excellent prose, interesting characters, a theme that causes people to think."

"Wouldn't a plot be nice?" Barbara asked, smiling.

"Plot is sort of optional," Angie said, frowning. "Some of the finest pieces of writing in the world don't have what would conventionally be called a plot. Theater of the absurd for an example."

"And a hook," Larry said from across the room. He tossed the papers he was reading on the floor and picked up another from a pile. "It needs a good hook."

"What's a hook?" Barb asked.

"Think of it as a topic sentence," Angie said. "A beginning

sentence, or even phrase, that makes the reader want to know what it means."

"'Before the lobster blew up we were having such a good time,'" Larry said, still not looking up.

"'I didn't like being a leaf, but it was better than the alternatives,'" the dark-haired man belly-down on the bed added.

"'It seemed that defenestration was the only solution to Ermintrude,'" one of the girls on the floor said. She was a college-aged Asian-American twisted up in a complex position that at first looked like yoga. Then Barbara remembered her own college years and recognized it as College-Study-Position Fourteen. "That's a classic, of course."

"I realized after fifteen minutes in the room that I had stepped through a looking glass without realizing it," Barb said.

"That's good," Larry replied, looking up. "I don't usually like first person, but that might work. What's it from?"

"I just made it up," Barbara said, dryly.

"Tits *and* a sense of humor," Larry said, looking down again. "Unusual combination."

"Hey!" Angie snapped.

"Well, there's a reason I let you hang around," Larry replied, equably.

"Sure, you get slave labor from my husband," Angie said. "And you like my cookies."

"I don't think I've ever called them cookies," Larry said, distantly.

"It's just doing the time," the brown-haired man on the bed said. "You stick with me. Someday they'll say, 'You remember when Angie and Eric were just lowly schlubs going to slush parties? Now look at where they've gotten . . .'"

"Bedlam," a man propped at the head of the bed said. He was big and very heavyset with a thick beard and red-brown hair. But while being overweight, he gave the impression of having a good bit of muscle. "Bellevue. Momma Patrona's House of the Seriously Mentally Infirm. God, that one was bad!" He crumpled up the manuscript, tossed it onto the floor, stuffed and skimmed, making it to the "KILL, KILL!" box despite it being across the room. "It was one of those that was so bad it was like a parody of bad. I kept thinking it was a joke and I'd get to the punchline. I couldn't believe when I got to the end and realized he was dead serious."

"Could he spell?" Larry asked, reading another manuscript.

"Yeah."

"Good, send him a letter that we want to hire him as a slush reader."

"I said it was *bad*," the man said.

"Why should we have to be put through this?" Larry said, grimacing and tossing the manuscript on the floor. "That one doesn't even deserve a rejection letter. It deserves anthrax in the envelope. Somebody hand me a bottle of foot powder. Teach him to submit that crap to me . . ."

Barbara read through a couple more of the manuscripts and found one that . . . wasn't bad. It wasn't good, but that might be taste. She supposed it was "combat science fiction" since it involved a fair bit of shooting. But she didn't think much of the tactics and the characters seemed a bit flat.

"This might be okay," she said, looking at Angie.

"Lemme see," Angie said, picking it up.

Barb went back to reading and heard an occasional snort over her shoulder.

"Pier would love this one, Larry," Angie said after a moment. "Get this, the enemy is radical greens . . ."

"Oh, God, not again," Larry said, laughing. "Are they over-industrialized despite being serious environmentalists?"

"Absolutely," Angie chuckled. "Wooden stock characters, big-titted women to be saved, not one bad guy with a clue and the prose is mostly banal at best."

"We should send it to Pier with our blessings," Eric said, looking up. "Give them all the rope they needed to hang themselves."

Barbara frowned and opened her mouth, then closed it.

"You really think that environmentalists would hyper-industrialize?" Larry asked from across the room.

Barb sensed a test question but she couldn't figure out the exact answer to give.

"I was thinking of the Soviet Union, actually," Barbara said. "It was supposed to be a worker's paradise, and it was anything but paradise. Hell is more like it. If Dante had seen it he would have written the Ninth Level differently. So, yes, I could see environmentalists acting in that fashion. Can't you?"

"No," Larry said. "Is it any good otherwise?"

"There's a plot," Angie said, shrugging. "And the grammar's okay. But the characters are pretty flat and the prose is so-so. No real style to it. I wouldn't have made it past the first page."

"Toss," Larry said. "The next thing it will be radical abortionists with an overpopulation problem."

"Like China?" Barb asked, raising an eyebrow.

"China's got its population under control," Eric said, looking up. She suddenly realized that most of the people in the room had stopped reading and were looking at her.

"They've still got a higher growth rate than Europe or America," Barbara said, ticking off items on her finger. "They have a huge imbalance in males, which will probably change that. But they're already importing brides, which will tend to redress that in the long term. They have an official one child rule that's regularly flouted by the privileged or anyone who can bribe the right officials and they have the highest rate of abortion in the world. They're radical abortionists with an overpopulation problem. That is no more unlikely than radical greens with a pollution problem, which was really what was mentioned in the story."

"Is it the population problem or the abortions that bother you?" Larry asked, frowning.

"The abortions," Barb said. "When women abort babies just because they're female, I have a problem with that. I, personally, have a problem with abortion, period. It's simply infanticide a priori."

"So you'd like to see *Roe versus Wade* reversed?" Angie said, a touch angrily.

"*Roe* was bad case law," Barbara replied, shaking her head. "Let it be legislated."

"A woman's right to her body is *inviolate*," the Asian-American girl on the floor snapped.

"So is the right of every person to live," Barb snapped right back. "Including that unborn child in the womb. It's a child. Infanticide, whether a priori as in abortion or after the fact as often happens in China is *wrong*. If you don't want the child, give it up for adoption."

"Some people can't bear children well," Angie said. "My sister—"

"If that's provable, then it is different," Barbara said, sharply. "But too often it's used as an excuse. So you're pregnant. Get over it. Have the baby and get on with your life. But you should let the *child* choose to do the *same*."

"Hey, Barb," the man on the bed said, getting to his feet. "Why don't we take a walk?"

"Probably a good idea," Barb said, coming to her feet.

"Especially since I'd never hit a lady," Larry said, nastily. "Otherwise I'd kick your ass."

"Really . . . ?" Barb said softly, then sighed. "Never mind. I'm sorry if I have caused you offense. Please excuse me."

She turned and quickly walked to the door and out.

"I haven't seen Larry that angry in a long time," the bearlike man said, following her out.

"I can't believe *I* lost my temper," Barb said, breathing in and out for calm and saying a small prayer for forgiveness.

"Larry can get under people's skin," the man admitted. "I'm Bob Dorr, by the way."

"Barb Everette," Barb said as they got on the elevator. "So what do you do, Bob?" she added, punching for the ground floor.

"I'm an illustrator," Bob replied. "General graphics and stuff. I do some of the illustration in Larry's mags."

"And I suspect you agree with him, politically," Barb said.

"Generally," Bob admitted. "Still looking for a fight? Or do I have to hold you off the ground until you calm down?"

"I think that was the thing that made me angriest," Barb replied as they exited the elevator and she looked around. "The assumption that he *could* have kicked my a . . . butt. What ever happened to equality?"

"Well," Bob said, carefully. "I think he was probably thinking that he out-weighed you by a good eighty or ninety pounds."

"I suppose that must be it," Barb said, pleasantly. "Isn't there supposed to be a martial arts demonstration tomorrow?"

"Yesss . . ." Bob said.

"I don't suppose Larry's going to be attending?" she added, sweetly.

"Why?" Bob asked.

Barbara considered the question, then lifted into the air in the Dance of the Swallow, carefully missing Bob with all five strikes, then ruffling his hair before she hit the ground. The large man had barely been able to take a defensive stance before she landed on her feet and bowed mockingly.

"Because if he *had* decided that it was okay to hit a lady, that would have been . . . interesting," Barb said, bowing again and then turning and walking away.

Chapter Twelve

"What do you *know* about Kay Goldberg?" Barbara asked Greg as they were having dinner the next morning. She'd gone back to bed after the interesting talk the previous night and she tactfully didn't mention that Janea had come in just after dawn. Or that Greg had a hickey on his neck.

Through the window of the restaurant she could still see the snow coming down. Conditions had come together to create the perfect snowfall and they were already closing roads all over Roanoke. Everyone assured her that they'd be open by Monday and they wouldn't get stuck over in the hotel. But she was glad she was inside; it was *seriously* snowing.

"Not much," Greg said, yawning and then taking a sip of coffee. "Why?"

"She knows about Special Circumstance," Barb said, as soon as Janea had taken a sip of coffee. The dancer didn't quite spit it out.

"What?" they both said, simultaneously.

"What I said," Barbara replied. "And she's got a background. At a guess, Shin Bet or Mossad."

"You're kidding," Greg said. "She's a sports writer who does some mystery. She's from Charlotte."

"She *lives* in Charlotte," Barb said. "I live in Mississippi. I'm not *from* Mississippi. Five gets you ten Goldberg's not her real name. And she's a . . . what's that term Daddy uses? Oh, she's a player. Or she was. She's going to give us a list of potential suspects sometime today. She knew I was with Janea, and you, and she knew my last *name*. I didn't give it to her, I hadn't mentioned it in public except to check in. But she knew it. What does that tell you?"

"Interesting," Greg said, getting over his shock. "Do you think she has any connection to the investigation?"

"I hope not," Barbara said. "Because I told her about it. I wouldn't have if I had the slightest thought she did. I wanted to know if she had any ideas. All she said was that she knew a lot about her fans and would give us a list of potential suspects. You probably should have talked to her directly."

"I might," Greg said, thoughtfully. "After I call the Bureau."

Not having anything else to do after breakfast, Barbara wandered back to the Dealers' Room. She wandered over to the sword dealer's booth but he was with a customer.

"I'd like to apologize for yesterday," she said to the man when the customer had wandered away with a bag full of leather stuff she wasn't willing to admit she recognized.

"It's not problem," he said, smiling. He was wearing contacts that made his eyes black except for silver irises. They were truly bizarre. "I get migraines sometimes, too. They can come on really quick. My name's Mack, by the way."

"Thanks," Barb said, smiling back. "I did feel I needed to apologize, though. I almost dropped the sword."

"Not even close," Mack said. "More like you couldn't let it go."

"It's a beautiful sword," Barbara said. "And you do very good work. Take care."

"You too, God lady," Mack said.

"Why do you say that?" Barb said, pausing as she was about to leave.

"It's nice to meet a Christian lady that's not a Bible-thumper," Mack said, smiling. "But you wear it like a skin."

"Oh," Barbara said, puzzled. "Well, thank you."

She continued around the circuit of the room and saw the brunette from the night before sitting at her book booth reading.

"Hello," Barb said. "We never really got introduced. That's a lovely blouse, by the way, it really goes well with your eyes."

"Thanks," the woman said, tilting her head to the side and smiling at Barbara. "I'm Candice."

"I enjoyed last night," Barb said, a crease appearing in her forehead. "The conversation was interesting."

"You should have stuck around," Candice said. "Folsom was really depressed when you left. You were the perfect lady for him."

"I'm married," Barbara pointed out, again.

"So is he," Candice said, frowning. "Not very happily, but . . . Anyway, his thing is he likes to find . . . how's he put it? 'The best looking, least available, woman at the con and monopolize her.' "

"I'm not the best looking woman at the con," Barb said.

"No," Candice said, "there's a redhead wandering around who's really spectacular. But she looks . . . more available. And you're probably next and you're not. And he's not by any stretch boring to be around. I was once one of the ladies he monopolized and it was an interesting night." She saw Barbara's face and sighed. "*Talking*. We stayed up all night, in a public place, *talking*."

"He certainly seems popular," Barb admitted.

"And he got that way fast," Candice said, gesturing at a bookshelf. "From nobody to best-selling with multiple books out in less than three years. The term 'phenomenon' comes to mind. He just says he made a deal with the devil."

"Deal with the devil?" Barbara asked, her eyes wide.

"It's an expression," Candice replied, shrugging. "Actually, Pier is very good with promoting new authors. And he's a good writer."

"I've got . . . things to do," Barb said. "Besides sitting out in the cold. Although . . . it was interesting."

"Folsom's very good at holding court," Candice said. "He even puts up with Baron when everybody wants to strangle him or at least ask him to get to the *point.* He even puts up with Mandy when you want to stuff a sock in her mouth."

"I met Mandy last night, too," Barbara said, pausing. "She had a lovely skirt."

"Yes, she did," Candice said, her eyes crinkling. "And you always compliment people."

"It takes nothing and makes people's lives a bit brighter," Barb said. "You can always find something to compliment in a person, even if it's their shoelaces."

"I'm not that nice," Candice admitted. "In fact, I'm not nice at all."

"Yes, you are," Barbara said, definitely. "Or, rather, you may not be *nice* but you are anything but bad or evil."

"I'm all bad," Candice said, smiling.

"You're lying, too," Barb replied. "There's not a touch of evil to you."

"You don't know me very well," Candice said, shaking her head.

"You'd be surprised," Barbara contradicted. "You've had a rough life, you've got quite a few people you'd be happy to see dead. But you've never actually tried to arrange it. And *you* didn't tell Baron to shut up or at least get to the point. Which a less nice person would have done. What happens within your mind and soul is not the definition of your personal evil."

"And you're a mind reader?" Candice asked, glaring at her.

"No," Barb said. "I'm just a very good judge of character. Aren't I?"

"I guess," Candice said, frowning. "But I'd hate for anyone to begin thinking I was *nice.* So don't spread it around. It would ruin my reputation. And Baron is . . . Baron. He's always going to be a Sad Sack. He is the consummate momma's boy. Although, at least he's gotten a job where he's not living at home all the time anymore. If you call selling water filters a job. But he's apparently making money at it; he's been able to go to more cons anyway. And being on the road gets him out from under Mom."

"He's on the road a lot?" Barbara asked, curiously.

"From what I hear," Candice said, shrugging. "He sells and installs water filters. He's from Ohio but his territory is in Virginia so he travels all over the state. Who knows, he might even cut the apron strings some day. But he's got good points. He really wants to be helpful; it's not just an act. If you need help, Baron is always right there pitching in. And a lot of the writers like him because if there's *nobody* else they recognize at the con, they can always talk to Baron. He just . . . doesn't have many social skills. Being *willing* to be social should count for something, I suppose. And I think if he didn't have fandom he'd probably hole up in a tower somewhere with a rifle."

"Do you know Sean very well?" Barb asked, filing the whole description away.

"Not much," Candice said, shrugging. "He's a former Marine. Lives in Virginia Beach and does something with the Internet. Goes to a lot of cons, especially ones with Duncan or Draxon. He'd had a live-in girlfriend for a while, but I guess they broke up."

"So do those two always hold court outside?" Barbara asked. "Duncan and Draxon, that is?"

"Pretty much," Candice replied. "There or in the Wharf Rat suite. But there aren't any smoking rooms in the hotel so they generally stay out and freeze. I couldn't hang so I left not long after you did. Especially with the snow. It's *seriously* snowing, isn't it?"

"Yes," Barb said with a sigh. "They're predicting over twenty inches just *today*. They say that it will clear by tomorrow and they can get the roads open, but right now we're stuck. You're a . . . Wharf Rat?" Barbara asked, changing the subject.

"That was a good slice of the Wharf Rats at the con," Candice said. "I suppose I am, but I don't really think of myself that way."

"And the gentleman on the ground with the notebook?" Barb asked. "The one with the minder, it looked like. It seemed like the group was . . . subtly ignoring him while including him I guess I'd say."

"Oh, that was David Krake," Candice said, laughing. "He's a big writer for Pier Books, been writing since the 1960s when, as he puts it, he escaped from the hell of being an attorney. He comes to the cons but he really doesn't like to be bothered when he's writing and he can get really . . . blunt. He writes hard-core military fiction, has for years. Former Marine, in Vietnam, so he knows what he's writing about. He's got degrees in history, ethnology and Greek. Recently, he's been trying to break into the fantasy market but his books are sort of limping along. I don't know why, they're really very good. He does a lot of research—he's known for that—and his fantasies are really based on historical characters and myth, mostly Sumerian. The last one sold well, though. Hit the *New York Times* list anyway so the big account buyers are going for it. From what I heard they more than trebled their sales on the last book, which is unusual. But it happens."

"You seem to know a lot about the people here," Barbara said, smiling.

"I go to plenty of cons. Not just ones that the Rats prefer. I won't say I know *everybody* in Southeastern fandom, but it's close."

"Selling books," Barb said, gesturing around.

"It's what I do," Candice said, smiling. "I don't work very well in offices; can't handle the politics. I've found I do better working for myself."

"There are a lot of Rats who were military," Barbara said. "Were you?"

"No," Candice replied, shrugging. "My husband is, though."

"Husband," Barb said, looking at her unberinged finger. "And you're sharing a room . . . ?"

"Plenty of people do that at cons," Candice replied. "It saves money. Don't read anything else into it. Although . . . there's other things that happen. But not with me," she added, smiling. "I've got a great husband."

Barbara nodded and looked at her watch suddenly.

"I'm going to wander," she said, smiling. "Talk later?"

"I'll look forward to it," Candice said. "Enjoy yourself."

"Hi, Sean," Barb said as she saw the Wharf Rat coming out of one of the panels.

"Hi," the young man said, smiling broadly. His gaze flicked down to her chest and then forced itself back upwards. "We met last night, right?"

"Yes," Barbara replied. "Where are you headed?"

"Nowhere right now," Sean admitted. "There's a panel in an hour I want to see on writing for art or market. I'm what I like to call an 'aspiring author' and most people call a 'wannabe.'" He said the latter with a deprecating grin and Barb had to admit that he was rather attractive if a bit young for her. Maybe she should sic Janea on him. Then again, maybe not.

"I'm sorry to hear about your break-up," Barbara said, sadly. She had subtly shifted him over to some padded benches by the door to the atrium and now sat down, waving to the seat beside her.

"I should have seen it coming," Sean admitted, sitting down and looking at the far wall. "We'd been spending less and less time together and she always wanted to know when I was going to be home. Thursday was my range night; there's an indoor range I go to and I usually went right from work to the range. But I'd forgotten to pack my guns so I went home to pick them up instead. And . . . there they were, right in our bed."

"I'm sorry," Barb said, honestly.

"I was, I thought, reasonably polite about it," Sean said, looking over at her, then down to her chest, then back at the wall. "I just nodded at them, went in the closet, got out my gun bag and went back out. So when I got home, the police were waiting for me. I explained the situation, they politely took my guns away and explained that I couldn't go back in my own apartment! I mean, it was *my* name on the *lease*! She moved out the next day and I moved back in."

"Did they give you the guns back?" Barbara asked, smiling slightly. The story had been told with a sort of blunt-instrument intensity that seemed to be natural rather than a result of the encounter. Sean was one of the most *intense* people she'd met in a very long time.

"Yep," Sean admitted. "But I had a hell of a job getting them clean; they'd been sitting uncleaned for a week."

"So what did you do then?" Barb asked.

"Went back to work," Sean said, shrugging. "I do remote installation on Internet lines. Mostly hardware work with some software troubleshooting. And the company does satellite uplink support, so I go out on those projects, too. It keeps me out of an office and mostly I'm working by myself. I don't handle office politics very well. I guess I don't really get along with most people."

"You seem to fit in here," Barbara said, her eyes narrowing.

"The Wharf Rats are sort of like an extended family," Sean said, waggling his head from side to side. "And they're mostly military oriented. They're used to . . . military types. Civilians get all excited when you just tell them what to do and expect it to get done. They used to call me General Marshall when I was working tech support. So I don't do tech support anymore. And being a field engineer pays better, anyway. Of course, it also meant I was out of town a lot. I'd guess that was one of the reasons . . . well . . ."

"Yes. Well." Barb said. "Do you mostly work in Virginia?"

"Virginia, Pennsylvania and Ohio," Sean said. "But things are looking up. I just got a promotion to shift supervisor so I'll be spending more time close to home. More office time, too, but I can handle that."

"How's the girlfriend front look?" Barbara asked, smiling.

"Well, it's looking up at the moment," Sean said, smiling at her with a slight humorous leer. "Just joking. I'm not really looking for anything serious. I thought Annette was it. Now I'm not sure I trust women. Honestly, the whole thing with Annette really has me . . . disliking most females rather intensely. So I'm keeping what few encounters I have with them . . . limited in scope." He looked over at her and shrugged. "You're an obvious exception. You seem like a very nice lady. I'd say you remind me of my mother, but my mom's *a lot* meaner. She and Dad were both Marines."

"Saying that a lady reminds you of your mom isn't a compliment, anyway," Barb pointed out acerbically.

"I didn't mean it that way!" Sean protested.

"I understand," Barbara said, laying a hand on his arm. She used the opportunity to get a quick read of him and wasn't sure what she got. He definitely had some very dark areas, but no sniff of necromancy. "Well, thanks for talking to me. I think I'll be seeing you at that panel. That's the one with K. Goldberg on it, right?"

"Yes," Sean said, standing up. "I should say thanks. This has helped in a way."

"I'm glad," Barb said, pausing. "Sean, women are as human and fallible as men. Some of them less so, some more so. Don't . . . put all women in the same category as your ex-girlfriend. In fact, don't be so quick to condemn her. Christ tells us to forgive. One of the reasons that he tells us to do so is that until we can forgive others, we cannot forgive ourselves. Until you can forgive Annette, and other women that have hurt you, it will be hard to let go of the darkness in your soul. And it's eating you up."

Sean looked at her for a moment and then nodded.

"You're a very odd lady, Barbara," Sean said, clearly puzzled.

"So I'm told."

Chapter Thirteen

The panel room had about twenty people in the audience and five members of the panel including Miz Goldberg, Folsom Duncan, Larry, the publisher from the slush party, David Krake and a redhead Barb didn't recognize. It started by the five introducing themselves and the topic of the panel which was "Art or Marketing, How to Write." The panel was moderated by the publisher she'd met last night and he opened the discussion.

"You can write for market all you want," Larry said. "But if you want to actually get published, you'd better be thinking of your writing as art or you're never going to get a single thing into print. If you just throw the words down on paper, it invariably turns out to be crap."

"Larry, you've got your head so far up your ass you can see daylight through your throat," Krake said, bluntly. "Bill Shakespeare didn't give a damn about art. All he wanted was to get paid."

That more or less set the tone of the panel and it was a pretty aggressive discussion. Goldberg more or less sat it out, only softly contributing that she thought art was important but so was getting paid and the two weren't necessarily the same. Duncan felt that being superior in art was useful and he admired those who could write artfully but he just enjoyed telling the story and worried about "style and that" as a distant last after plot and characters. The fifth panel member, the redheaded woman, was firmly on the side of art but stated her position in such a garbled manner Barbara wasn't sure she could compose a sentence much less a story. She also spent better than half her time promoting her writer's workshop.

Krake, however, wasn't hard to understand at all. He stated that anyone who thought first of "art" "might get published but only once and then get dumped into the trash bin." Oh, and they were "flaming idiots" who would spend their lives "wandering from con to con teaching writing instead of actually trying the hard work of *doing* it." The last might or might not have been pointed at the redheaded woman, but whether it was or not she looked poisonous at the comment.

Krake also had a bug up his butt about somebody named Robert who apparently wrote fantasy. Fantasy that was not, in the opinion of most of the panel members, very good. But it did, apparently, sell well, much to their chagrin. That was about the only point on which Krake and Larry the Publisher could agree. Actually, Krake, Larry and the redhead all agreed that this Robert fellow should have his fingers broken. Duncan and Goldberg were somewhat more restrained, Duncan making the point that you couldn't support market forces and then ignore them when they disagreed with your taste.

She wasn't sure what she was doing in the panel audience. She supposed that she should be observing her fellow audience members and trying to spot a suspect, but she didn't have any idea what to look for. More than half the people in the room were male, most of them with brown hair. And she couldn't tell who was a Goldberg fan and who was there to see the others. Some of the men she'd pegged as possible Goldberg fans seemed to be there to see Larry the Publisher and most of the rest seemed to be there to see the other male panelists. She finally realized that she and a couple of other females were the only ones interested in hearing Miz Goldberg's opinion.

Of the five, however, she had to admit that the one she *liked* the most was probably Duncan. When he spoke he had an aura of authority. He never seemed to cut people down, except in the most humorous way, and when he spoke people tended to fall silent. The term she was looking for was "charisma." He wasn't particularly handsome or dominating, but he had a gift for presenting things in ways that people could understand and enjoy listening to. She thought he would have made a great teacher. A few of the people present seemed to absolutely loathe him and she wasn't sure why. It wasn't what they said, the questions they asked, but how they said it. Most of the rest, those who clearly were his "fans" and others who clearly didn't know him very well, however, seemed to really enjoy hearing his thoughts.

After the panel she waited to talk to him again. He was listening to a young man talk about one of his books. Barb couldn't make heads or tails of what they were talking about and the young man . . . wasn't charismatic. He tended to stutter and repeat himself but Duncan simply nodded and seemed honestly interested in what he was saying, even smiling at a couple of very lame attempts at jokes on the part of the fan. She realized that was part of what made him so interesting; he had the ability to listen as well as talk. To really listen and pay attention to what the other person was saying, to make reasonable comments that proved he was paying attention and cared about what was being said. She'd dealt with a few people who were relatively famous and they tended to only hear their own words and thoughts. It was clear that however well known Duncan was, and he was clearly famous at least within this group, he hadn't let it go entirely to his head.

"You were very interesting on the panel," Barbara said when the young man walked away clutching his signed book.

"I've got the Irish gift of gab," Duncan said, shrugging. "It's not much more than that."

"Duncan's not an Irish name," Barb pointed out, smiling.

"Well, it's from my mother's side," Duncan replied. "You didn't say much in the panel."

"I didn't know what to say, or ask," Barbara said. "I'm sorry, I haven't read any of your books."

"I always have a book for a beautiful lady," he said, taking his computer bag off his shoulder and dipping into it. The cover of the book he handed her mostly consisted of a large-breasted blonde holding two large guns. The model didn't know how to hold a weapon, either.

"Nice cover," Barb said, dryly.

"They sell books," Duncan said, shrugging again. "The core market, as I said, is males. Sex sells. This offends the hell out of those who think that the world should be perfectly PC and males shouldn't care. That is not, however, reality."

"You didn't add 'unfortunately,'" Barbara said, flipping open the cover and glancing at the blurbs.

"That is because I am not PC," Duncan said, smiling broadly. "I like women to be women and men to be men. There *are* differences. Women who try to outdo males just to outdo males, who get all up in arms at having a door opened for them, who think males should think like women, and who get terribly upset at my covers, I think are . . . less than they *could* be. I think even less of the males who fall for their arguments."

"You don't like the modern 'urban male,'" Barb said.

"I think that telling men that they should be women leads to most of the problems we're dealing with these days," Duncan replied, arching an eyebrow. "Males respond, by and large, to arguments that feminists despise. That women should be treated as special and specially protected. That it's a male's duty to be the first line of protection and that there's a reason for 'women and children first' in a lifeboat situation. That honor and duty and loyalty are good traits and should be encouraged. Males are expendable, women are not. That may not be PC, but it's how I feel and, demonstrably, more males respond to that sort of reasoning than ones that are essentially feminine. At the same time, women should be allowed to be whoever they *are*, without either males or females telling them who they should be. If a women is a superior warrior, then let her do her thing. If she's sensitive and caring and unable to do battle, then let her do what she is called to. Ditto males. But don't say that males *should* be sensitive and caring. Most of us are lousy at it no matter how hard we try. Males tend to make lousy women. Don't create boxes and say 'This is who you must be.' Especially don't create boxes that are designed counter to the way that most men and women truly *feel*. Feminists *created* Eminem and now they're getting what they asked for, whether they realize it or not."

"Strangely enough, I agree with most of that," Barbara said, considering it carefully. "So what's this book about?"

"Magic and dragons," Duncan said, shrugging. "Actually, that series isn't going all that well. I'd thought that it would really sell, both because my other series sold so well and because the big market is high-sales fantasy. But it's just limping. I swear I'd sell my soul to get it off the ground!"

"You're a very odd person, Folsom Duncan," Barb said, frowning slightly at the expression.

"Ain't I then?" Duncan said, grinning. "Check your assumptions at the door, as Lois Bujold would say."

Barbara blinked for a moment and then sighed.

"Thank you," she said.

"For what?" Duncan asked.

"It's . . . hard to explain," she said. "I'll talk to you later."

"What's so important?" Janea asked when she met Barb in the lobby followed by Greg.

"Timson," Barbara said. "You said that he knows a lot about the occult. Right?"

"He's blond," Janea said, realizing where she was going right away.

"That's what dye is for," Barb pointed out, sharply.

"No, he's blond," Janea said, definitely. "Trust me on that one."

"Oh," Barbara said. "Damn."

"Nice try, though," Greg said. "I'm starting to agree with Janea that it's probably a LARPer."

"I'd already considered him, though," Janea admitted. "And rejected him for just that reason."

"So what do we have?" Greg asked.

"I'm looking at motive and opportunity, I guess," Barb said. "There are several of the Wharf Rats that meet the criteria for suspects. Also a couple of people around Larry Whatsisname, the magazine publisher. One being Larry. Baron and Sean both have jobs that move them around the state and both have ties to Ohio."

"The body that they found there," Janea said, nodding.

"Sean's got a real case of the bums at women at the moment," Barbara continued. "He found his live-in girlfriend in bed with another man and then she took out a restraining order on him. So he's not very happy with women right now. Baron's . . . well, he's more or less what I thought we were looking for. Not very socially apt, so having the power to compel women would probably be attractive to him. Both of them travel a good bit for their jobs. Eric and Larry both travel. Eric's married, admittedly, but I'm not sure that discounts him. And he's ambitious. Demons can tinker with earthly powers to aid in ambition. Larry . . . I just don't like. But he also fits the profile."

"There are at least six of the LARPers that fit the profile as well," Janea said. "But not Timson. And from what I've gleaned about the Wharf Rats, I'd put Sean and Baron high on the list of suspects."

"I'm interested in Duncan as well," Barb said. "He has something very strange about his . . . soul. He's like a power sink or something. If Remolus is a power absorber, then I'd expect his touch to be something like what Duncan has."

"That's . . . outside my territory," Greg said. "But don't get caught up on motivation and opportunity. Or clues. Before you know it, you'll decide that it was done by a one-legged butler in the library or something."

"I wish there was some way to go around getting DNA from all these suspects," Barbara said, then paused, looking thoughtful.

"Ain't gonna do it," Janea said, shaking her head.

"It wouldn't take all *that* long," Greg said, grinning. He had another hickey on the other side of his neck.

"Says you, Flash," Janea replied, shaking her head. "Some people take more than thirty seconds."

"Hey!"

"You don't know what I was thinking," Barb protested.

"Bet you a dollar?" Janea said. "Ain't gonna do it. What got you on Timson, anyway?"

"Somebody said to check your assumptions," Barbara said. "Timson was such a nice guy, I wondered if it was all an act."

"Oh, it's a good bit act," Janea said, fondly. "He can be a *very* bad boy if you know what I mean."

"That wasn't quite where I was going," Barb said, tartly.

"Why's it always about bad boys?" Greg said, sighing.

"I'm not sure what or who we're looking for," Janea said, seriously. "It could be one of the guys at the con that's popular and can pick up the girls. Or it might be one who seems to be a total loser on the surface and is using power to attract them."

"I guess we just keep looking," Barbara said, sighing. "This sucks."

"This is how most investigations go," Janea said, shrugging. "At least this time we know the perp is here at the con. I've done three of these investigations and never gotten so much as a sniff."

"We're doing better than I'd hoped, frankly," Greg said. "We've narrowed it down to no more than two or three dozen suspects because we *know* the necromancer is somewhere here in the hotel. That's better than the millions we started with on Friday. Just *legwork* after the con will get us to the suspect relatively quickly. It would be nice, though, if we could narrow it down more. If worse comes to absolutely worst we could call in and see about locking the whole *con* down and doing DNA tests on all the males with brown hair. The ACLU would scream bloody murder, though, and it would be all over the press. We also would have a hard time showing probable cause, come to think of it."

"Did you get in touch with the Bureau about Goldberg?" Barb asked.

"Yes, I did," Greg said. "You're correct; Goldberg is a pen name. They're trying to track down her actual identity through her employer in Charlotte but since she's not a suspect that might be hard if they get sticky. And they're a newspaper; newspapers almost always get their back up when we ask *them* for information. I also asked about back-up. But with the weather the team couldn't make it up. They're stuck in Roanoke. The Bureau's dispatching a helicopter to move them if we have to have help, though. It should be up there by sometime this afternoon."

"I hope we can close this up quietly," Janea said, looking out the window. "I was talking to the con-chair and one of the off-duty cops that's working the con says even the sheriff's department's shut down until the snow stops. The stuff is coming down faster than they can plow it."

"This is crazy," Greg said, shaking his head. "Why'd this happen *now*? This is more snow than this area gets in *three* years!"

"That's why they can't keep up," Janea said, shrugging. "This is, like, *Buffalo* snow."

"So if anything happens we're on our own?" Barbara asked, raising an eyebrow.

"Looks that way," Greg said. "If it seriously starts getting nuts we can call in the HRT from Roanoke. But they're going to be twenty minutes, maybe a half hour, away rather than five minutes. No way they can bring in a chopper in this. And even four-wheel drives are going to find it tough."

"A lot can happen in a half an hour," Barb said, shaking her head. "I hate doing this bits-and-pieces thing. I feel like I'm wrestling with fog."

"You just keep tapping away until you find your suspect," Greg said, shrugging. "There's no other way to do it."

"Well, there *is*," Janea said, thoughtfully. "But it's a bit of a risk."

"What?" Greg asked, frowning.

"We push instead of pull."

Chapter Fourteen

"Hi, Mandy," Barbara said, as she finally tracked the woman down. "Could I talk to you, privately?"

"Sure," Mandy said.

Barb led her around the corner to a stairwell and cleared her throat.

"I don't want you to think I'm a nut or something," Barbara said. "And you can't talk about this, okay?"

"Okay," Mandy said. "But it's okay if you're a nut. We're all nuts."

"Well, this is serious and very real," Barb said. "I'm not just a homemaker. I'm a consultant with the FBI. There's been a series of serial killings and they think that the killer is here at the con."

"Really?" Mandy said, her eyes wide.

"Really," Barbara replied. "You can probably guess what *kind* of consultant."

"Oh, yeah," Mandy said, totally absorbed.

"I *know* that he's here, somewhere," Barb said. "I'm just not sure who it is. But I know you're . . . sensitive. Pay careful attention to your creep-meter. We'd really like to find him before he kills again."

"Is he going to attack someone at the con?" Mandy asked.

"No, we don't think so. He seems to be picking out his victims from fen, though. So keep your eyes, all your eyes, open. And don't tell *anybody*, okay? And be careful."

"Okay," Mandy said. "You be careful, too. Like I said, guys like that like women like you and me."

"It won't come to that," Barb assured her.

"Well, I told the biggest gossip in the LARPers about it," Janea said, grinning. They'd met in the women's room to discuss their upcoming strategy. "Swearing her to secrecy, of course."

"I talked with Larry," Greg said. "He's going to have it all over the con. Which means it will make the papers. My career is toast."

"And I spoke to Mandy," Barbara said. "Which means I think I've got you both beat."

"The director is going to kill me," Greg moaned.

"Yeah, but all we have to do now is look for somebody who's running," Barb said. "This guy has always struck at weak victims and tried to hide. He's not a stand-up fighter, he's a backstabber. There's no place to hide, here."

"And it's going to be hard to run," Janea pointed out, gesturing out the window. The snow was *still* coming down, hard, and the forecast had been updated for up to *thirty* inches. "HRT's on standby, right?"

"Last I heard," Greg admitted. "Cell phone coverage is getting spotty." He reached into his computer bag and pulled out a set of short-range radios. "I brought these along just in case. I guess I'm glad I did. They're encrypted so we can talk privately."

"Great," Barbara said, unconsciously checking her piece then taking the radio. "Let's hope he . . ." She paused and grabbed at her head. "I think he just heard."

"Strong?" Janea asked. "Yes, it is, I even got a twinge of it that time."

"Angry," Barb said, her face white. "Fearful, too. But very *very* angry. He never thought anyone would get this close. He's . . . damn, it's gone."

"Cloaking," Janea said. "He's going to ground. Or running."

"I'll take the west entrances," Greg said. "Barbara, you go east. Janea, take the lobby, that will have the most people around."

"He knows who the Hunters are," Janea pointed out as she stood up. "Be careful. The hunter can become the hunted."

"Hi, Barb," Timson said as he walked down the corridor. He looked at the woman, puzzled. "You waiting for someone?"

Barbara was standing where two corridors joined near the west doors to the hotel. From her position she could see anyone approaching the doors and a bit of the parking lot. So far nobody had gone outside except a couple of hard-core smokers.

"Just watching the snow," Barb said, smiling. "I'm a bit conned out."

"It can get to you, especially at first," Timson said. "Taking some time for yourself is important. Drink, eat, sleep, game, that's the ticket."

"Where are you going?" Barbara asked, lightly.

"I've got an important meeting," Timson said, his eyes wide in mock anticipation. "An informant among the werewolves that's going to give us the location of their secret meeting. That way the Hunters can combine with the vampires and swoop down and wipe them out in one fell swoop! Bit of silliness, but it's fun if you get into it."

"I understand," Barb said, smiling. "It's no sillier than chasing a white ball around with a club and at least it can be done indoors."

"He wanted to meet at the Waffle House," Timson said, gesturing out the window. "And I told him to screw off. It's damn cold out there. Take care."

"Same to you," Barbara said, smiling as he opened the door to the stairwell.

She nodded at a couple of young guys in trench coats as they stepped out the door. But they only went as far as the portico and pulled out cigarettes and lighters with already shaking hands. She grabbed the radio when it started to beep.

"Anything?" Greg asked.

"Nothing," Barb admitted. "No feel, nobody trying to get out."

"They could have gone out by the kitchen doors," Greg admitted. "And there's a door behind the offices. But I'd think that he'd try to just nonchalantly slip out."

"I'm not sure he could get his . . ." She paused and grabbed her head. "Greg?"

"Are you okay?" Greg asked at the strained tone.

"Get Janea," Barbara gasped then summoned her power, shutting down the feeling of horror in her soul. "I think we underestimated our target: somebody's dead."

Timson was slumped against the wall of the stairwell, his eyes wide and staring at nothing.

"Oh, Freya, be kind to his soul," Janea said, looking at the boy. He had a look of utter horror on his face.

"He's changed MO," Greg said, straightening up with a frown on his face. The landing was right up by the roof, the door above locked. An out-of-the-way spot in a packed hotel, perfect for a quiet killing. "There's not a mark I can find. At the least he wasn't strangled or cut."

"No," Barb said, furious. "His soul was ripped from his body."

"Are you sure?" Greg asked.

"Very," Barbara said, shaking in anger. "It's so strong I'm surprised you can't feel it. I felt the power of the 'mancer's gear and then the death."

"I need to call in support," Greg said. "We're going to close down this con and shake it to the ground. This isn't a game anymore."

"He's hunting, now," Janea pointed out. "We can't just try to cover the entrances. We need to run him to ground and take him out."

"Why?" Barb asked. "He *could* have run even in this. At least out of the con. Why kill? And why Timson?"

"Timson's powerful," Janea said. "Well, was. He wasn't an adept, but he could have been. He had a strong soul." She suddenly looked intensively sad.

"It'll be okay, Jan," Barbara said, wrapping her arm around the woman's shoulders.

"He had a *strong* soul," Janea said, shaking her head. "One of the strongest and finest I've ever met. And to just have it . . ."

"We'll find him," Barb said, the righteous anger welling up in her again. "And we'll bring him to justice one way or another. He will face the Lord and be Judged. And there can be but one judgment for such as he."

"But you hit the nub," Greg said, looking at the dead boy. "Why has he gone to killing? Instead of running? You're the experts, you need to *think*."

"Give me a second, okay?" Janea said, wiping her eyes. "He was a friend, okay?"

"I'm not sure we've got a second," Greg pointed out. "Not if this guy is ripping souls from people's bodies, now. Not if he can kill this fast and silently. *Why* is he killing? This is *completely* outside MO."

"Power," Barbara said, suddenly. "Oh, my God."

"He's building his power," Janea said, nodding her head. "He's preparing for a battle. With us."

"That means Timson won't be the last," Barb said. "Greg, call for backup right *now*."

"I would if I could," Greg said, looking at his cell phone. "Do either of you have any signal?"

As it turned out none of the three cell phones had any signal at all.

"And I've already tried the hotel phones," Greg said. "Even the Internet connection is out."

"Well, we need to get hold of the local police, at least," Janea pointed out, gesturing at Timson. "We've got a dead body on our hands."

"I'll see what I can do," Greg said, frowning. "You two stay here, I'll go check with the management. For now, we're not treating this as a homicide. There's no indication of violence and that's just fine by me."

"This is terrible!"

The hotel manager was a tall, distinguished-looking Hindu.

Barbara had seen him around the hotel dealing with problems and he'd always risen to the occasion. Now he was wringing his hands in worry.

"This will be terrible publicity!" the man moaned. "And so horrible for the young man and his family. This is very terrible! He must have overdosed, yes? I do *not* allow drugs in my hotel! I have a well-run hotel!"

"You have a very well-run hotel, sir," Greg said, soothingly. "But we have to call the police and have them come in with this."

"You are FBI, yes?" the man asked, his face working. "Can not you handle this? Quietly perhaps?"

"It's a local jurisdictional matter," Greg said, shrugging with the lie.

"But we cannot contact the police," the manager said, his face working. "I have tried. The phone lines are out. I cannot call the 911, yes? The roads are closed with snow! And we cannot simply *leave* him here. It is very dishonorable. And if anyone else were to find him . . ."

"Jesus Christ," Greg said, shaking his head.

"Another swear, please, Agent Donahue," Barb replied. "We'll need a camera, a good one. And some plastic bags, large trash bags. And the key to this roof door."

"We *can't* disturb a crime-scene like this!" Greg said, furiously. "It has to be *meticulously* recorded. Not just dump his body in a bag and shove it out the door!"

"Oh, really?" Barbara asked. "How long do we leave him here, Agent Donahue? What do we do, post a guard? The hotel security guard left last night when the snow started to get bad. Do we get somebody from the con?" She paused and looked Greg dead in the eye, daring him to force her to go on. Because she was pretty sure unless they tracked down the necromancer, fast, this wasn't going to be the last body they discovered.

"You are with the FBI, too?" the manager asked, uncertainly.

"I'm a special consultant," Barb said then gestured at Janea. "We both are."

"Okay, okay," Greg said, blowing out. "Yeah, we'll need some big trash bags and a camera. And some time alone. Can you get that?"

"Yes, of course," the manager said, nodding. "I go now."

"And we're eventually going to need a linen cart and a bunch more bags," Janea said, gritting her teeth. "This is going to get bad, Greg."

"We need to find this perp," Greg replied. "Now."

"I'll go ask the LARPers if they knew who Timson was meeting with," Janea said, looking one last time at her former lover. "I am seriously going to go full berserker on this guy when we find him."

"And I'll go ask if anyone saw him," Barbara said. "Besides me," she added, blanching. "He walked right past me to the stairs and then went up. To meet with . . . whoever it was."

"Anyone go up the stairs before him?" Greg asked, frowning.

"No," Barb said. "He was the only person I saw use them. Whoever it was must have entered from one of the other levels. I'll go ask down there if anyone saw him or who he was meeting with."

"How do we handle this?" Janea asked. "I mean . . . do we *tell* people he's dead even?"

"Have to eventually," Greg said. "Damn, I wish we'd never tried to smoke out this perp."

"My idea," Janea said.

"Yeah," Greg said, grinning mirthlessly. "But I went along with it. As soon as I've done this crappy job cleaning him up I'll go talk to the con committee and tell them what happened. But we want to keep panic down. We'll just treat it as an unknown cause, might have been a fluke heart condition, and say there's indications there was more than one person present. We want to find out who might have been meeting with him."

"That will do," Barbara said, nodding. "I'll go down to the lower floors and check around."

"This investigation is getting seriously out of control," Greg said, shaking his head.

"No," Janea said, shaking her own. "It's simply got Special Circumstances. You don't want to see 'out of control.' "

Chapter Fifteen

There had been nobody at all in view on the third floor, directly below the landing where Timson had been found. On the second floor, however, there were several open doors and some room parties going on. Barb walked down to the first open door and poked her head through.

Despite the temperature, and the official no-smoking policy of the hotel, there was a window open and several people sitting by it filling the room with smoke. Among them was Folsom Duncan and she realized she'd found the Wharf Rat suite.

"Barb," Duncan called from the back of the room. "Come in, come in. Have a drink! Have several. There's dick all else to do!"

"You're drinking tea," Barbara pointed out, sidling into the room. She recognized several of the Wharf Rats from the rest of the con and nodded at people, exchanging greetings. Mandy and Norm weren't there, she noticed.

"I didn't say anything about alcohol," Duncan said, smiling. "Although it's around. As an alternative there are various soft drinks in the tub and for those with stronger constitutions I've broken out my stash of Indian black tea."

"You don't have any panels?" Barb asked.

"Not until tomorrow," Duncan said, shrugging. "And very few people are going to them, anyway. The weather seems to have them huddling in."

"That and the serial killer!" one of the Wharf Rats said, laughing.

"There's that," Duncan said, grinning. "Dare him to come in this room," he added with a laugh.

"I don't get the joke," Barbara said, frowning.

"Oh, you seem cool," Folsom said, smiling. "Are you bothered by weapons?"

"Not at all," Barb said, her brow creased.

"George, get the door," Folsom said, gesturing with his chin. When the Wharf Rat was standing by the door he nodded. "Wharf Rats . . . present!"

Just about everyone in the room reached behind a back, to a hip or into a purse and came up holding a weapon. And then everyone started checking and clearing them for safety. Barbara knew she was staring but it was a bit much. Especially when bags started being dragged out and the assault rifles started appearing.

"I asked if you were comfortable around weapons," Folsom said, setting an H&K SOCOM identical to the one in her purse on the table.

"I am," Barb said. "When they're in the hands of people I know are trustworthy with them."

"Everyone who just drew a weapon has a concealed carry permit," Duncan said. "In one state or another. And they all meet the minimum criteria to carry around everyone else in the room."

"They all cleared their weapons?" Barbara asked, dipping into her purse and drawing, clearing and setting down the H&K next to his.

"A lady after my own heart," Duncan replied, grinning.

"Perhaps," Barb said, picking the weapon back up, loading it and setting it back in her purse. "Could we talk for a moment, alone?"

"With you?" Duncan said, getting up. "Any time."

"Where?" Barbara asked.

"The adjoining room," Folsom said, gesturing. He led her into the room and shut the door. "You're not bothered by that, are you?" he asked, cautiously, gesturing at the door.

"I'd be more bothered if you hadn't asked," Barb admitted. "Do you know Timson?"

"Can't say the name rings a bell," Duncan said. "But I'll admit I'm lousy with names."

"He was the head of the Hunters in the LARPers," Barbara said. "He's been found dead. Overdose, apparently."

"Oh, I know who you mean," Duncan said, his eyes lighting. "He's a friend of Krake's."

"Really?" Barb said, surprised.

"He was on a panel with Krake on research in writing," Duncan said, nodding. "He and Krake had been thinking of doing a series together since Krake's specialty is Greek and Roman history and that guy . . . Timson? He's an expert in really ancient writings, all the way back to cuneiform from what Krake said."

"Well, there's not going to be a series now," Barbara pointed out. "He's most sincerely dead."

"And there's a rumor," Duncan said, his eyes narrowing, "credibly traceable to you, that there's a serial killer at the con."

"The body had no indications of violence," Barb said.

"And what would a homemaker know about that sort of thing?" Duncan asked, exasperated. "I'm sorry, the next thing you're going to tell me is that your name is Miss Marple."

"What?"

"Agatha Christie? Never mind. Look, I don't know who you are or what you're playing around with—"

"I'm a consultant with the FBI," Barbara said, throwing up her hands. "Okay? You know Greg Donahue is an FBI agent, right?"

"But he's on leave . . ." Duncan said then paused. "He's not, is he? He's actually on assignment, isn't he?" His face had gotten very blank.

"Yes, he's on assignment," Barb said, sighing. "And, yes, we spread the rumor to try to get the killer to bolt. But instead he's changing MO. Timson looks like an OD, we're . . . not sure how he was killed."

"And you're not a very good liar," Duncan said, angrily. "Somebody already tried to call out and we can't. Now you're telling me we're playing Ten Little Indians?"

"If you mean he's hunting us, yes, it looks like it," Barbara said, unhappily. "There's an HRT team on standby at the Roanoke airport. But we can't call them in. We can't even get a sheriff's car in here."

"Shit," Duncan said, standing up and pacing back and forth. "Herding cats . . ." he muttered.

"What are you talking about?" Barb asked.

"How to keep people alive," Duncan snapped. "Greg's worried about catching the perp and so are you, although from your eyes 'catching' probably isn't what you're thinking. Me, I'm trying to figure out how to cut down the casualties. And the *first* thing we need is solid police response. We need to get in contact with that HRT and get them in here. Get sheriff's deputies in here. Seal this place down, vet every single person, pull out all the suspects and find out *which* one did the killings. Which means we need to get back in contact."

"The roads are packed," she pointed out. "And it's a half mile to the nearest intersection. And there's no guarantee that there will be anything there. Trying to move through this snowstorm is suicide."

"We've got, among the Wharf Rats, a half a dozen people with serious cold-weather training and background," Duncan said, shaking his head. "This isn't a horror movie. We just get the experts in and let them run wild. And to get them in we send out a team with all the gear we can make or scrounge. If they take a few hours, if they take all night, whatever it takes. I'm thinking about what happens in the meantime."

"What if he attacks the team?" Barbara asked.

"Hah!" Duncan laughed. "Let him. None of these guys learned about hiking by taking happy little walks in the woods. They're all former military and they'll all be armed. We've got, among the Rats present, at least six former infantry, two former Special Forces and a SEAL. And before you ask, if he's *one* of them it won't matter. They will be *fully* briefed. By Agent Donahue. There's no way that he could take all of them out. Even if he's on the team. They go to a phone, pass on Greg's message and HRT gets in here if it takes calling out the National Guard with armored personnel carriers."

"Well, actually . . ." Barb said, cautiously, just as there was a furious knocking on connecting room door.

"Miz Goldberg," Duncan said, raising his eyebrows at the slight Jewish woman he saw when he opened the door.

"Where is she?" Goldberg said, striding past him and into the room. "You stupid—"

"I know," Barbara said, shaking her head. "You don't have to beat me up, I'm already doing that. All three of us are."

"Whose stupid idea was it to try to flush him?" Kay said, ignoring the oblique plea.

"I think that throwing around recriminations is a bit late," Duncan said, sitting back down in his chair after closing the door. "We need to get ourselves out of this cleft stick and *then* throw around recriminations. But, never fear, the Wharf Rat Rangers are prepared to go as far as necessary to find a phone. At which point we can call in a Hostage Rescue Team and we're all saved."

"That's what you think," Goldberg said, looking at Barb. "Are you going along with this?"

"I was just trying to figure out a way to explain," Barbara admitted, sighing.

"It won't work," Kay snapped. "If he wants to take down your team he can. The only reason he's not going straight to mass murder is either Barb or her friend."

"Excuse me?" Duncan said, frowning. "Barbara's a charming person, but . . ."

"Shut your fool mouth, youngster," Goldberg snarled, her accent clearly Hebrew. "You don't know what you're dealing with here."

"Clue me," Duncan said, seriously.

"Who are you?" Barb asked, looking directly at Goldberg.

"That's nobody's business, but . . ." Kay said, frowning.

"Barbara Everette," Duncan said, nodding in her direction and waving at Goldberg. "May I make your acquaintance of Lieutenant Colonel Hega Moshen, Israeli Defense Force and later Shin Bet. I believe your highest rank in the IDF was, in fact, major, correct, Colonel?"

"You were a *colonel* in Shin Bet?" Barb asked, surprised. She'd thought the tough little Jewish woman was probably a former sergeant or low-level Mossad agent.

"Yes," Kay said after a long pause. "I was the Shin Bet commander for Israeli Special Circumstances."

"Okay, I got all of that except that last bit," Duncan admitted, waving his hand vaguely. "Hell, I *knew* all of that except the last bit. What's Special Circumstances? Serial killings?"

"Special ones," Kay said, looking at Barbara. "She's SC," she added with a jerk of her chin at the homemaker. "American SC."

"Who was Goldberg?" Barb asked, quietly.

"Does anybody want to actually answer *my* question?" Duncan said, plaintively.

"My husband," Kay said, just as quietly. "He was our top adept."

"Ok-aaay," Duncan said, shaking his head. "I did not just hear you say that. No, tell me I didn't just hear you actually say he was an adept. Please?"

"Special Circumstances is the term used for supernatural investigations," Barbara said, sighing and still looking at the old Jewish woman. "This person isn't just a serial killer, he's a necromancer. The reason there aren't any marks on Timson's body is that he ripped his soul right out. Pull the soul out and the body stops working."

"Oh, I dunno," Duncan said, trying to catch up. "I had this manager one time . . ."

"She is not joking," Kay said, brutally. "I am not joking. If you send out a team, they would have no defense against the necromancer."

"They would if one of us went with them," Barb pointed out.

"You any good at hiking?" Duncan asked, smiling. "And if you're gone, who's going to protect *me*?"

"You'd accept me protecting you?" Barbara asked, grinning. "What was all that about women and children first?"

"I also said something about if a woman is a warrior," Duncan said, shrugging. "I'm still working on the assumption that you've both been smoking too much peyote. But I'm also not willing to trust my skin on it. I'm attached to it. Very attached."

"You would probably survive," Barb said, looking at him carefully. "You're . . . you're not protected by your faith like I am, but you've got something. I'm not all that experienced, but I can tell that you're powerful in some way."

"You're just seeing my natural sexual charisma," Duncan said, avoiding her eyes.

"What aren't you telling us?" Kay asked, sharply.

"It's stupid," Duncan said, shrugging. "I don't believe in hocus-pocus."

"Do you believe in God?" Barbara asked.

"Oh, maybe," Duncan said, shrugging again. "I'm more agnostic. But . . ."

"But?" Kay asked.

"I've had a few girlfriends, before I was married," he added, looking up at Barb. "Some of them were into witchy stuff. I didn't pay it any mind as long as they were good in bed and didn't nag too much. But one of the ones that . . . I suppose if you're not joking she might have really been strong I guess. She'd never let me be around when she was doing a rite. She said I was something like a natural power sink. She called me black silk."

"I'm not sure what that means," Barbara said, uncertainly. "I'm really new at this. But I don't think the necromancer could just rip your soul out. He might be able to kill you, but . . ." She paused and looked at him. "Can I try something?"

"You can feel free," Duncan said. "As long as it's not pulling my heart out and sending my soul to hell. I hate heat. I'll take the Ninth Level, though. All that lovely ice . . ."

"No," she said, reaching into her power base. She had found that there were two sources of power, one that was her channel and the other she supposed was just in her. She had a hard time figuring out exactly what to do, but after a moment she decided that God wasn't going to condemn her for trying a compelling charm. She'd been told how to form one in class, but never tried it because it seemed intrusive. Now she just reached out and tried to compel him to draw his weapon and set it down.

"That was an odd feeling," Duncan said, his face wrinkling. "Is it cold in here?"

"I'm not sure what I'm doing," Barb said, desperately. "Colonel, could I . . ."

"Go ahead," Kay said, nodding. "I'll be the control if you wish."

When she had tried to compel Duncan she had thrown power at him and had it simply . . . disappear. This time she just tried to compel the colonel to bend down and pick up a pen. Instead she hit something like a wall. It was strong but she knew she could overcome it if she tried.

"I could push past your resistance," Barbara said, opening her eyes.

"I could feel that," Kay said, opening her own. She looked worn. "Lord Yaweh, you're powerful. Was that coming from your channel?"

"No," Barb said, taking a deep breath. "Duncan, I don't think anyone on *earth* could compel you."

"You could," Duncan said, smiling and batting his lashes. "Just by smiling."

"I mean magically," Barbara said, sighing. "It's like punching fog."

"That's me," Duncan said, shrugging. "I guess it's because I'm never really in the present."

"I'd love to know what it actually is," Barb said. "I doubt it's that simple. But *you* could make it out and be safe from the necromancer."

"Unless the necromancer just killed him," Kay pointed out. "A bullet kills you just as dead as being soul drained."

"That would be who was faster on the draw," Duncan argued. "I'll take that chance."

"He could use power to take your gun from you," Kay said. "To make the bullets not work. To pull it apart. I've seen it, had it done to me. It's . . . annoying. Stakes just aren't my favorite weapon."

"Oh," Duncan said. "I wasn't looking forward to a long walk in the snow anyway. Heart condition, donchaknow. Too many cigars."

"You should quit," Barbara said, automatically.

"That's what my doctor keeps saying," Duncan said, shrugging. "But chicks really dig it. We're wasting time, here. We need to figure out some way to get people to cluster so we can keep an eye on them and protect them. The only problem with that is that a convention is like . . ."

"Herding cats," Barb said. "You said that before."

"And the way that you herd cats," Duncan said, smiling, "is you offer them treats where you want them to go and then shut the door. Another thing a girlfriend taught me."

Chapter Sixteen

"Yes, Miss Ruby," the manager said, waving his hands at the power outage. "The hotel is not with power. Most of the guests are with your convention. To be telling them we will open the restaurant and bar for occupancy. We have heat to heat those rooms, but all other rooms will be no heat."

"This is insane," Ruby said, tearing her hair then stopping and trying to be composed. "I'll start circulating the word, but it will take time to even get the staff up to speed. When are you opening the dining room?"

"Now," the manager said, waving his hands. "Is open! But should bring blankets, pillows. Is no maid service, none come to work today."

"I keep saying we need to move this thing to summer," Ruby muttered, darkly.

When she was gone the manager went back behind the reception desk, where angry guests were already lining up, and into his office.

"Is done," he said, shaking his head. "My cousin is cutting power to all the wings. Is only power here in the lobby and in restaurant and bar."

"Open the bar," Greg said, the shook his head. "Not *free* but open the bar. That will give them even more reason to stick around. But we need to get people centered in one area."

"Then, we hunt," Barbara said, standing up and walking out the side door.

She stopped when she was out in the snow and looked up at the sky. The snow was just barely coming down, now, but it was thick and deep in every direction, mounded up in drifts along the north sides of the buildings. They'd be lucky if they could get out of here in a week.

"What are you doing?" Janea coming through the door behind her. "It's *freezing* out here!"

"Thinking," Barb said. "Why hasn't he struck again?"

"I dunno," Janea admitted. "He might be resting after the kill, sometimes that's necessary depending upon the spell. Or he might be communicating with his demon."

"We'd feel that," Barbara pointed out. "Wouldn't we?"

"Not if he's using a circle," Janea said. "And within it, which I wouldn't do with a demon. But I don't know how he's dedicated himself. We don't even know where he found the spell to build this much power. Usually with necromancy, you lose most of the power. There's a rush that you can use, but then it fades. From that stone, he's found a way to store it."

"What's he going to use it for?" Barb asked, frowning into the distance.

"A major summoning," Janea said, shivering from more than the cold. "A really big one."

"How many souls?" Barbara asked, sadly.

"Lots," Janea said. "If it's Tiamat, lots and lots. And after that . . ."

"All hell breaks lose," Barb said, softly.

"You have to get me out of here," the man said, turning away from the image of the demon.

"You will escape, that is our bargain," the demon rasped. The sound was like the buzzing of wasps. "And you will live. If it is in my power to support you. But you must act. Now."

"There is no way I can do this and not go to prison," the man snarled, angrily. "There's *evidence*, you stupid beast!"

"It can be changed," the demon responded. "It has taken me time to research the new skills of this world. But it can be changed. Another will be made to be the killer. You will be one of the survivors. And you will be famous, which will make your sales even higher."

"Myself and my friend," the man said.

"No, only yourself," the demon snarled. "The other will be a binding. I guarantee your survival but only if your . . . friend is gone. That is a liability. End the liability."

"Agreed," the man sighed after a moment's hard thought.

"And a few will survive, besides," the demon mused. "And the one who will be chosen to go to prison in your place. The minds of the humans will be changed, computers will be changed, paper will be changed. With the power that you will gather, there is nothing that cannot be done. My Mother will return."

"Your binding holds, even upon her," the man said. "I wrote it well; being a lawyer has its uses. There is no escape. You must keep me alive and make my sales the greatest in the world. Or I am freed."

"It was agreed," the demon said. "But now is the time to act. They are gathered for the slaughter. But you must get more power. At least twenty must die before you can do battle with the White God's witch. The other is of no consequence; her goddess is weak."

"What about guns?" the man asked.

"They are of no consequence, either," the demon promised. "I have examined them as well. Simple alchemical properties, easily tampered with. But the White God's witch is strong. She is your only true enemy. All others will fall before us and then . . . My Mother will be manifest on earth!"

"Come on, folks, let's pack up the food and booze," Leo said, lifting up a case of homemade beer. "If we're going to be stuck in the restaurant we might as well have fun."

"I don't think I'm going to be able to handle being around

all those people for . . . how long?" Sadie asked, picking up a case of chips.

"We can wander out," Don said, picking up a laptop and a bottle of Glenlivet. "To smoke at least. But it's going to be cold, lass. Best bring as much cold weather gear as we can gather."

"We'll do the *S-starship Troopers* th-thing," Baron stuttered. "All p-pile up for heat."

"In your dreams, Baron," Sadie responded, sticking out her tongue.

"Go down the south hallway. When you get to the third floor, just pull the vest out of the bag. Hold it out for two minutes, then walk down the stairs and back to the room."

"Are you sure about this?"

"Yes."

"And what are *you* going to be doing?"

"Being conspicuously present."

"What are you doing here, Baron?" Barbara asked as she passed the entrance to the restaurant.

"I'm on s-staff, now," Baron said. "I'm ch-checking people in and out. Th-there's a list. You sh-should go in, m-ma'am."

"I'm sort of on staff, too," Barb said. "Anybody going out?"

"S-smokers," Baron said, gesturing down the hallway. "And s-some of the guests won't l-leave their r-rooms."

"Okay," Barbara said. "I'll go see if I can round up any strays."

"You're a s-stray, ma'am," Baron pointed out.

"Not hardly," Barb said. "Can I look at your list?"

"I suppose," Baron said, handing over the clipboard.

It had a list of all the con-goers and guests with the few "general" guests in the hotel appended to the bottom. She noticed a group of them, third floor end, that she assumed was the "Black Rose" society, whatever that was. Janea still wouldn't explain but she said they weren't the problem. And, demonstrably, they had turned up after the first twinge from the necromancer.

Most of the con-goers, guests and dealers were in the restaurant, bar and lobby area according to the list. Some of them had been ticked in and out and she recognized a few names.

"Thanks," she said, handing it back with a wide smile. "Are you going to get relieved some time?"

"Yes, m-ma'am," Baron said. "I'm only really filling in for someone."

"Well, I'm going to go try to pry people out of their rooms," Barbara said. She walked down the hallway to the outside door and looked out. Outside the door were a couple of kids who looked like gamers or LARPers, smoking, and a gaggle of Wharf Rats doing the same. She decided to brave the cold.

"Hi, Barb," Sadie said, her hands shaking as she lifted a cigarette. "S . . . cold!"

"You sound like Baron," Leo said, smiling. "It's not that cold! It was colder at the Inchon Reservoir!"

"But you weren't there, Leo," Duncan chuckled, waving a cigar. "You were barely born."

"Okay, it's colder where I go hunting," Leo said, shrugging deeper into his jacket. "What are you doing out here, Barb?"

"I'm sort of on staff," Barbara said, looking at Duncan. "I'm trying to round up strays."

"Just us out here," Duncan said, shrugging and nodding at her significantly. "And as soon as we hammer a couple of coffin nails we're going back in."

"Okay," Barb said, nodding back. She still was of two minds about whether he was on the list of suspects or not. She firmly believed he wasn't a necromancer, but that strange shield bothered her immensely. "Where's Don?"

"Dunno," Duncan said, shrugging. "I knocked on his door but he didn't answer. Probably sleeping it off. Don't worry, he won't freeze to death; too much antifreeze in his system."

"I'll check on him," she said, frowning at Duncan. He shouldn't be so flippant with what he knew. But maybe he was still thinking it was all a silly game or something.

As she walked back the hallway towards the lobby she saw David Krake talking to Baron earnestly. The former was wearing a long, heavy coat and had snow on his legs.

"Are you okay?" she asked.

"I can't find Charlotte," Krake replied, tightly. "She's not in her room or in the restaurant. She's not checked in on the list at all."

"Can I suggest that you wait in the restaurant, sir?" Barbara said, politely. "I'm one of the people designated to round up strays. I'll look for her, I really will."

"You can suggest all you'd like," Krake replied, tartly. "But I'll find her myself, thank you. She *said* she was going to be here."

Barbara looked at the list again, making some notes as he walked down the hall towards the smoking area. She also noted that Mandy, Larry and Angie were missing from the con-goers. Norm and Eric had been checked in, although both had been in and out, apparently. She hadn't felt anything from the necromancer, so it was unlikely they'd been killed. But there was *something* bothering her about the pattern.

"Janea," Barb said, walking a little bit away from the entrance and keying her radio.

"Go," Janea said.

"Go pry the Black Rose people out of their rooms, will you?" Barbara asked, politely. "And while you're up there, use the pass key to check 304. Donald Draxon is missing. See if he's sleeping it off."

"Will do," Janea said. "What are you going to be doing?"

"I'm heading over to the west wing and see if I can find a few more strays," Barb answered. "Greg?"

"Here," the FBI agent said. He'd taken up position in the manager's office. It had exits to the restaurant, the outside and the lobby so he could move in any direction to respond to trouble.

"You got that?"

"Got it," Greg said, unhappily. "Be careful."

"Of course," Barbara said, crossing into the deserted atrium. Perhaps from the rumor of a murderer running around, the con-goers really were huddling together like sheep. And something bothered her about that as well.

She entered the west wing and started to take the stairs, then stopped and pulled out her radio.

"He's here," Barb said. "Somewhere in the west wing. Janea, get those Black Rose people *out* of there. I don't care *how*."

She hit the stairs and pounded to the second floor. She could only tell he was somewhere above her and to the west.

There wasn't anyone on the second floor and she could tell he was still above her. But as she ran to the top floor the feeling . . . quit.

She burst out into the third floor corridor and looked to the end but there was nobody there. She did, however, hear the sound of the fire door closing on the far end.

She'd done that one before so she ducked back into the stairs and ran down to the second floor, darting out and looking to the far end. When nobody came out she headed down to the ground floor.

As she burst from the stairwell, she nearly ran down Duncan.

"What the hell are you doing here?" she asked, sharply. He was just coming in the door from the atrium so he clearly hadn't been on the top floor.

"I was getting another coat," Duncan said, evenly. "I had a spare in my room."

"You need to get in with the others, sir," Barbara said, definitely. "Our friend is somewhere in this wing."

"Interesting," Duncan said, looking up at the wing. "But you said that he couldn't charm me or whatever."

"I don't know that he *isn't* you," Barb said, bluntly.

"Well, I do," Duncan replied, nodding at her. "I'm just going to get my coat, then go back. I'm sure I'll be around plenty of witnesses if anyone dies."

"Damnit," she snapped, shaking her head. He went to the second-floor corridor and, with nothing else to do, she followed.

"Making sure I'm going where I said I was?" Duncan asked.

"Yes," she replied, tightly.

Duncan stopped at a room and inserted a key, waving for her to enter.

"I'll stay here," Barbara replied, suddenly not sure if she was following him or guarding him.

He emerged a moment later with a couple of flannel shirts, a pair of waterproof pants and a Gore-Tex-and-fleece jacket.

"There, you see?" he asked. "All I said I was getting. Shall we be getting back?"

"I'll follow you to the atrium," she said. "The necromancer was somewhere in this building."

When he went into the atrium she watched him cross then shook her head.

Not knowing quite what to do she walked to the far end of the first floor and looked out the exit door there. It was supposed to be locked, but it wasn't. The lock had been taped back and there was snow on the floor and footprints outside. Recent footprints, at least since the snow had stopped falling.

She stepped out into the snow, noticing that the light was failing fast, and followed the prints around the building. They appeared at first to enter the building through the back of the kitchens but on the far side of the loading dock there was another set. It looked like more than one person and she broke into a run. She could feel it in her bones, that something wicked this way comes

Chapter Seventeen

"It's done," the woman said, running up with the bag in her hand. "But you have to stop this! Nothing is worth what you've been doing."

"Thank you," the man replied, smiling at her. "And I am going to stop. Very soon. And you won't have to worry about it anymore."

"Good," she said, shaking her head. "I love you, you know."

"I know," the man said, sadly. "That's why I'm going to let you keep your soul."

She barely caught the flash of metal as the knife punched up through her diaphragm and into her heart.

"Remolus said that you must go," the man said, his face blank. "But he didn't say that I had to take your soul. This one last thing I do for you, my love."

He waited until the light had died in her eyes and then lowered her to the hotel room floor.

"Now to go kill that witch of the old gods," the man said, reaching into the bag.

"Damnit, this is serious," Janea said, shaking her head. "Put on some damned clothes and get down to the *restaurant*!"

"Oh, come on," the man said, waving a whip. "You probably know how to use one of these! Join the fun. We're keeping warm the best way, through healthy exercise."

Most of the adjoining doors in the area had been opened and the rooms were more or less filled with mostly naked people engaged in . . . healthy exercise. Janea felt it was almost a sin not to join in, but there was a time for love and a time for battle. It did look like fun, though; a few of the men were pretty good looking and a couple of the women were just spectacular. And she had to admit that if they were all dedicated to the goddess, they would be raising some serious energies. She could feel them around her, through her link, and even tap into them to an extent.

"People, listen up," she said, summoning a bit of energy and making herself . . . extremely attractive with a touch of dominance. Even the doms in the room were forced to pay attention to her. "There is a serious problem, here. Not just the heat. I'm a consultant with the FBI. We've tracked a killer to this con. He's already killed seven women and now he's killed a person at the con. The *real* reason that we're gathering everyone in the restaurant is for your own protection. Now, I need you to gather up all your warm weather clothing and *get the hell out of here*!" The last was delivered in not only her firmest voice but with a hint of the goddess behind her. It promised no nookie for life if they didn't obey.

"Well, jeeze!" the gay guy who'd been carrying the timber said, struggling in his chains. "Get these things off of me!"

Janea shook her head and stepped out into the hall, stopping at the sight of the approaching man.

"Are you still looking for . . ." she said then stopped as the man's eyes began to glow.

Barb felt the power like a bucket of vomit dropped on her head. But her channel opened up, filling her with power as she began to run.

"Janea!" she yelled, keying the mike. "Janea!"

"The Light and Holiness of Freya fills me!" Janea boomed, her arms and legs spread wide. She could feel her channel filling with power but she blanched when the power of the necromancer hit her.

"Your goddess is weak," the man rasped in a voice like wasps. His coat was drawn back to reveal a vest covered in moonstones that glowed red with power. "Remolus calls to you, come to him and your soul will be spared!"

"Death in battle is my highest calling," Janea said, reaching behind her to draw her piece. "And even necromancers die from a bullet."

But when she pulled the trigger, the hammer fell with a click. She knew it was loaded, she jacked it back in frustration anyway and fired again. Another click.

"Do you think that my lord cannot overcome earthly weapons?" the necromancer said with a laugh. He made a gesture and the weapon was ripped from her hands. "For that, however, I will take your soul."

The man reached out one hand and the stones blazed as Janea felt a terrible drawing on her. She could feel the channel filling the void but it was as if all the power was plunging into a black hole.

"Remolus is the Soul Devourer!" the man rasped. "Your power simply feeds the blackness, priestess of a weak goddess! Every bit of power you draw, simply weakens your goddess to no avail!"

Janea could feel herself getting weaker, but she also heard the members of the Black Rose piling out of the doors with screams and gasps as they saw the backlash from the magical battle in the hallway. She fell to her knees and shook her head, crawling towards the necromancer, trying to do battle to the last.

"If I die to spare one soul, then I die well," she said, panting as the blackness filled her. "My soul will rest forever in the Shin—"

Barbara burst onto the third floor and stopped, panting, then dropped to her knees.

There were two male bodies sprawled in the hallway. She didn't even have to walk up to them to know they were dead. There was the same feel in the air as when she'd found Timson. Janea was on her face further down the corridor. Barb ran to her and rolled her over, hoping against hope that she was alive.

She felt at her throat and there was a faint pulse, but Janea was barely alive. Barb opened up her channel and reached to the woman, trying to feel what was going on with her.

There had always been a feeling of great . . . wonder to Janea. A brightness that was difficult to shadow. Now there was virtually nothing, as if her soul had been almost entirely stripped. Almost, however, was different than completely. And Barbara could feel a trickle of power coming from somewhere. She suddenly realized that Janea's goddess was keeping her alive. By feeding her soul energies.

"Lord," Barb said, holding her hands over the still body on the floor. "I know that this is not a woman who would be considered of the highest by most of your worshippers. But Your Son said 'Let him who is without sin cast the first stone.' And she *is* a fellow warrior of Light. Please, Lord, give me the power to help her. I'm not sure what I'm doing here, so You may have to guide my hand as well. Blessed be Your name, amen."

She placed her hands on Janea's stomach and reached for her channel, willing power into the woman's body.

She could feel the power flow through her, not as much as when she had faced Almadu, but power nonetheless. Janea gasped and arched as if she'd been hit by a jolt of electricity and her eyes flew open as she fell back, limp.

"I saw the Shining Lands," the woman whispered, staring at the ceiling.

"Janea, who did this?" Barbara asked.

"They were so . . . beautiful," Janea replied and then her eyes closed.

Her pulse was strong but the dancer was out of it. Even a few slaps couldn't wake her. Unconscious, maybe a coma, maybe sleep. But alive, by all that was blessed.

Barbara looked at Janea and shook her head. After a moment she dragged her through the nearest open door. There were various . . . accoutrements set up in the room and a large St. Andrew's cross by one wall. She finally realized why Janea had been reticent about explaining its purpose when she saw the shackles attached to it. But it gave her an idea.

The door closed with a thump as she left. Let him get in through that. On the other hand, it was going to be a job for *anyone* to get *in*.

"What's going on?" Sadie asked as Baron came around the building.

"A b-bunch of n-naked people j-just ran into the l-lobby screaming about s-somebody fighting on th-the third floor," Baron said.

"I wonder what that was all about?" Leo said, looking through the door. "Somebody might need help . . ."

"Ah, there you are," the man said, coming around the corner behind Baron. "I was hoping someone would be out here."

"There was someone fighting on the third floor," Leo said, nodding at him. "Are you okay, sir? You look a bit . . ."

"With the power of the priestess, I only need ten more," the man said, opening up his long coat and revealing a vest of moonstones. "You will be three. Sorry about this," he added to Baron who was looking at him open mouthed. "You were always helpful. If a tad boring."

"What are you doing out here?" Barb snapped as she came out the side door. Larry, Eric and Angie were standing outside in the snow.

"Angie's smoking," Larry snapped right back. "And the rest of us are avoiding being in a restaurant that's been taken over by slope-brow, red-neck science-fiction fans."

"People are dead on the third floor of this building," Barbara growled, drawing her weapon and dropping the magazine. "Did anyone come out here?" She dropped the round out of the chamber and then dropped another one in.

"No," Eric said, looking at the gun wide-eyed. "You're not supposed to have one of those . . ."

"Shut. Up." Barb ground out. She pointed the weapon off to the side and dropped the hammer. But it just clicked. She took the other round and dropped it in, and that one fired. "Damn!"

"What was that in aid of?" Larry asked.

"Get *into* the restaurant," Barbara snapped. "Now! Or so help me God I will put a bullet in your head. If I see you wandering around, you will be terminated without prejudice. Do I make myself clear?"

"You're joking," Angie said, starting to laugh and then stopping at the look on Barb's face.

"There is a killer running around," Barb said. "I don't know who it is. It *may* be you. You are present, here, when a killing has just occurred up *there*," she added, pointing up. "Make up your own mind."

"You can't just go killing people . . ." Larry said.

"Stop me," Barbara said, pointing the weapon at his head. "One. Two . . ."

"We're going," Eric said, grabbing Larry's arm. "Come *on*."

Barb was marching them down the corridor when she felt the wave of evil sweep over her.

"Okay, it's probably not you," she said, pushing them. "In which case, you're *targets*. Now *run*!"

She passed them, despite their lumbering run, and turned towards the north side of the hotel. As before, the power appeared, spiked, and then disappeared, just as she reached the back of the hotel and burst out into the open.

Sadie, Leo and Baron were sprawled by the back door, with Duncan bent over them.

"Freeze!" she shouted, pointing the weapon at his head. She suddenly realized she'd never seen him with his jacket off. If it was lined with silk, it would mask anything he had under it.

"They're dead," he said, looking over his shoulder at her.

"I know that," she said, still keeping the .45 pointed at his head. "Pull out your piece and put it on the ground. Now."

"They're just fucking dead," Duncan repeated, softly, then turned to the side and vomited on the ground.

"I said, draw your piece and put it on the ground," Barbara repeated, sharply.

"You got it," Duncan replied, wiping his mouth, then drawing his weapon and setting it in the snow. "Who did this?"

"I'm trying to decide if it was you," Barb admitted.

"Well, decide quick," Duncan snapped, standing up slowly. "Because in a second I'm going to pick up that piece and go hunting *myself*."

"Guns don't work," Barbara said, lowering her weapon and pointing it at the ground. "Janea's bullets had been tampered with, somehow. They wouldn't fire."

"I take it you've decided I'm not the killer?" Duncan asked, turning around.

"Open your coat," Barb answered, shifting her feet into a cat stance.

"What? It's freezing!"

"Open your coat," Barbara repeated.

Duncan looked at her and shook his head but he unbuttoned the coat and pulled it wide.

"What are you looking for?" he asked.

"I'm not sure," Barb admitted, frowning.

"Can I c-close it now?" Duncan asked, teeth chattering.

"Go ahead," Barbara said. "Then turn around and spread your arms and legs."

"Oh, good, I'm going to get a pat down from a beautiful blonde," Duncan replied, but he turned.

Barbara patted him down, looking for hidden gemstones. He had a lighter and a folding knife, but his only jewelry was his wedding ring.

"What was that all about?" Duncan asked.

"The killer has to be carrying moonstones," Barb said. "Probably a lot. You don't have any. So you're probably not the killer. Now get in the restaurant. Let *me* hunt. I know what I'm doing, okay?"

"Well, I'm going to go brief the cooler Wharf Rats on what's *really* going on," Duncan said. "And get them to help me move these three. They shouldn't be just left here. Guns don't work. Okay. There will be something that will."

"Do that," Barbara said, nodding. "I have to go find this guy before he kills again."

"Oh, it's you," Larry said as the man walked up through the snow. He, Eric and Bob had come back out into the atrium when they couldn't stand the sight, or sound, of the Wharf Rats' continuing party. "One of your minions was running around babbling about someone being killed."

"My minion?" the man asked, blandly.

"The blonde, Barb I think her name is," Eric said, frowning. "She's one of your type."

"She's no minion of mine," the man said, smiling in great humor. "Quite the opposite. She's trying very hard to stop me."

"What?" Bob asked, uneasily.

"I said she's trying to stop me, you liberal moron," the man replied, unbuttoning his jacket. "She wants to stop me from raising the power to call my demon. But she's just about too late."

"Holy . . ." Larry said as the glowing gems on the vest were revealed.

"No, quite the opposite," the man said, waving a hand. The three were instantly held immobile, only their eyes moving. "Quite unholy . . ." he said as he drew the knife.

Barbara hadn't particularly cared for Larry or his crowd. But they'd died hard; the blood and pieces were splattered all over the white snow. What he'd done to Bob was bad enough and Larry was worse. Poor Eric . . . well, she was pretty sure it was Eric. The pieces looked about right.

"He's toying with me," she muttered, looking around. The snow had been trampled in the area so she had no idea which way he'd gone. With all the blood from the bodies, he should have been splashed. But there was no blood trail.

He'd been running her around in circles and she was tired

enough to just stop. Which seemed to be the thing to do, stop and think.

He'd nearly, but not quite, killed Janea. Why leave her alive? Because Barb felt him attack her and got there before he could stop to kill her? Did he not realize Janea was alive? He'd clearly taken his time with these three.

He was drawing souls. She'd felt the power flows when he'd fought Janea and if he'd simply drawn her soul it would have been over in no time. So he wasn't drawing souls so much as *power*. And Janea had had enough power that he couldn't draw it all?

Close, she felt, but not quite.

But if he could simply absorb the power of the priestess, even with a goddess behind her, then simply blasting him with power would fall right into his hands. It would *feed* him. But shooting him seemed out as well.

"*Wizards can be killed with a dagger in the back just as well as with magic.*"

She wasn't sure where she'd heard that, but it seemed like good advice.

And there was only one thing better than a dagger.

He felt full, suffused, and the power from the gems had barely been tapped.

It was time for the Great Rite. Time to kill all these worthless fen and take his rightful place.

He dared that bitch to stop him as he headed for the restaurant.

Chapter Eighteen

"It's a long way to Tipperary,
It's a long way to go.
It's a long way to Tipperary
To the sweetest girl I know!
Goodbye Piccadilly,
Farewell Leicester Square!
It's a long long way to Tipperary,
But my heart's right there."

"I think the con's better this way," Sean said, pouring another glass of beer and looking around at the group in the restaurant. "Just party the whole weekend long!"

"That's the ticket," Duncan replied, frowning. "The only bad part's the people dying."

"Speaking of which, where's Leo and Sadie?" Mandy asked.

"Sadie's probably hiding in a room somewhere," Sean replied, shrugging. "You know how she is with crowds."

"Well, David finally decided to crash the party," Norm said, waving at the entrance. The writer was unbuttoning his jacket as he entered the heated room. He had a slight smile on his face and his eyes . . .

"I think we've got problems," Duncan said, rising to his feet.

"What's the . . ." Sean replied and stopped, mute and staring as the power of the gems on David Krake's vest blazed out in the room.

The closest people to the entrance were a group of gamers and Duncan watched as they toppled over. He'd seen a few dead people in his time and they were unmistakably dead. The rest of the restaurant had gone silent as everyone seemed held by some force. He seemed to be the only one unaffected.

"I see there's another of you here," Krake said, still smiling faintly. "I take it you're one of those Special Circumstances types."

"No, just . . . odd," Duncan replied. Krake was all the way across the crowded room from him and he knew he'd never get a shot off. But there were other weapons. "I know you're going to kill me, but can I at least ask 'why?' "

"Never explain," Krake said, reaching out a hand.

"Oh, come on," Duncan snapped. "You know you want to tell *somebody*. And, since I'm going to die *anyway* . . ."

Krake appeared to consider that for a moment and then shrugged, looking for the first time slightly ashamed.

"Demons can give earthly power . . ." Krake said, then smiled thinly. "Even over book sales."

"It's that damned Robert Nile, isn't it?" Duncan said, amazed. "You did all this just to . . . what? Get better sales? Corner the fantasy market?"

"I've been in this business for thirty years!" Krake shouted, his mouth practically frothing. "And the man writes *tripe*! What's the justice in *that*? I've worked so *hard*. And he comes out of *nowhere* and sells a gazillion copies of complete crap! What's wrong with *my* books? What's wrong with people these days that they want unending series that never *go anywhere*? Nineteen pages on a *harvest*? Two hundred pages of every single step of every single character detailed? *Are people insane?*"

"So you're going to kill all these people for better sales," Duncan said, shaking his head. "I'd thought better of you, David."

"Try being near the end of your career, you upstart bastard." He reached out again and then paused, puzzled.

Duncan could feel . . . something. It was like a hand fumbling around in his chest. He stumbled forward, reaching for his knife, as the feeling grew.

"What are you?" Krake asked, puzzled.

"A warrior of God you son-of-a-bitch," Duncan replied, drawing his knife and clicking it open. "Not some demon's plaything. And I *never* liked your books! Saint Michael, Patron of Paratroopers protect us!"

Suddenly the knife flew out of his hands to clatter on the floor as Krake reached behind his back and drew out a pistol.

"Some warrior," Krake said, smugly.

The last thing Duncan saw was the muzzle flash.

Krake finished scribing the runes on the floor and stepped back.

"Remolus, come to me," he chanted. "Here is the power, here are the souls, be manifest upon this earth! *R'gom h'bameen sul!*"

He reached into Candice's chest, ripping her living heart out and holding it up as the blood cascaded down his arm.

"The way is opened, the door is opened, the walls are breached, Remolus, come to me! *R'gom R'mula! H'bamen sul!*"

He could feel the stupid FBI bitch. She was nearby but too far away to stop the rite. She'd apparently never been taught how to cloak, and her power shown brightly. But not enough power; he was filled to the brim with the power of the souls he had stolen for Remolus.

"Remolus, come to me!" he shouted, just as the arrow entered his back.

He stumbled forward onto the runes, dropping to his knees and turning as another arrow thudded into him. Kay Goldberg, flanked by the FBI agent, was standing in the door of the restaurant. Kay was just fitting another arrow into a bow. She had a distant look on her face and he realized that he could barely feel her. But he reached out his hand and drew upon his power.

"This is for Benjamin," the former Shin Bet agent said as she drove the third arrow into his face.

Barbara ran out of the Dealers' Room and down the hall to the restaurant. She had felt the power and a brief battle, the deaths and the building rite like the prickle before a thunderstorm. But something had interfered.

As she turned the corner to the restaurant, though, there was a hoarse bellow that sounded as if a billion wasps had all cried out in anger.

Kay stepped back in horror as the body on the ground began to writhe and change. The skin on the writer's face cracked and split along the line of the arrow, the bones showing through for a moment then being covered with something more like leather than skin. The body swelled, the legs bending and crackling as a mist rose that seemed to be steam swelling from within the body. The arrows blackened as if from an enormous heat, then burst into flames.

When the mist cleared, what was standing in the runes was not human.

She lifted the bow but before she could fire, it cracked in her hands.

"Thank you for opening the way for me," Remolus said, in a voice like buzzing wasps.

Kay and Greg were sprawled in the entrance to the restaurant as Barb turned the corner. She didn't have to even check to see if they were dead. Live people had heads attached to their bodies.

She skidded to a halt, though, when a wave of disorientation hit her. The "restaurant" was gone. The room seemed to shift and her sight zoomed in and out, searching for reality, as the walls faded into the distance. The floor had turned to dark stone flagging and the stone walls seemed to drip blood as distant voices cried out in pain and anger. There was a semicircular open area in the middle with a walkway raised above it about a meter on the back wall. The walkway had a stone railing that reached to about chest height, the balusters of the railing made from deformed statues that her mind recoiled from identifying.

She wasn't sure if she was in another reality or if it was some vision of the past, or, horribly, perhaps the future. Faintly, she could see through the overlaid reality the windows of the restaurant with the snow still outside. But when she reached out to the wall beside her, dark stone with worn carvings her eyes, again, refused to recognize, she could feel its solidity. It was warm and buzzing as if from a distant engine. But in the midst of all this unreality, there was one solid form.

A huge demon was on his knees on the floor, scribbling runes onto the flaggings by the simple expedient of ripping bits off of the nearest bodies and wiping them on with dripping blood. The demon had to be at least fifteen feet tall, humaniform, with skin that looked thick and tough as leather. His legs were odd, they seemed to have an extra knee, and his head was surmounted by several horns. His toes and fingers were tipped with black talons that dripped blood from his harvest. At least a dozen fen were dead and the rest seemed paralyzed.

Barb darted forward as the demon stood and turned to her.

"Fight me," the demon said, his voice a buzz. "Try to draw my power and I will suck your soul to the husk! Bring to me the power of your White God, witch of the Risen One!"

"I don't think so," Barb said, reaching behind her back. She slowly drew the Murasaki blade and took up a butterfly stance. "There's more than one way to skin a demon."

"Mortal blades cannot damage me," the demon said, his face splitting in a grin that revealed triangular sharklike teeth and long tusks.

Barb closed her eyes for just a moment and felt for the soul of the sword. Then she opened her channel and poured it into the steel. When she opened her eyes again, the sword was glowing white.

"What about now?" she asked, springing forward and slicing in a fast X motion.

The blows should have cut the demon in half but his heavy skin was like iron. They did, however, slice down his chest, leaving a broad green X on his leathery skin. The demon's ichor glowed faintly in the odd red light.

The demon bellowed and backed up, picking up one of the bodies on the floor and hurling it at her.

"The way is open!" the demon bellowed in anger. "You are in my lands, bitch! And I will use your soul to bring forth the Mother of All."

Barb rolled away from the projectile, the gamer hitting the far wall and slumping to the ground bonelessly, then ran forward to close with the demon.

Remolus leapt into the air and over the wall at the back, landing on the railing, then leapt again through the air to the far side of the room, smashing through the apparently solid wall and disappearing.

Barb followed, tripping over sprawled fen as they began to awake from their paralyzed stupor.

"Out of my way, damnit!" Barb said, kicking one of them in the head, then jumping up to the railing. It was a hell of a jump and, unlike the demon, she had to clamber up onto the walkway. The walkway, however, was also packed with fen. She ended up running down the railing, balancing like a tight-rope walker to avoid the gathered fen. As she reached the far end of the divider the screams started and got louder as Remolus reappeared through the hole he'd smashed in the wall. He was carrying a two-handed sword, a claymore, wielding it one-handed. The blade glowed black.

Barb leapt off the railing into the center of the evacuating room, landing in a crouch and taking up a guard position.

"Okay, you wanna dance, let's dance," she snarled.

"When I have killed you, I will take your soul," Remolus said, striding forward. "One of many to summon my Mother. No heaven for you, White Witch. No heaven for any in this room and Hell will be manifest on earth!"

"First you've got to kill me," Barb said, sliding forward gracefully. "I'll take my chances."

The demon hammered the sword downwards, slamming into hers and she knew she had a fight on her hands. The beast was incredibly powerful and the blows were so fast she could barely block them. Each blow struck sparks from the blade, flickering away like silver lightning. She backed across the room, her feet searching for solid purchase in the red blood on the floor, but the demon followed her just as fast or faster, raining down blow after blow. He didn't have much finesse, but with his reach and power he didn't need it.

She was being backed into a corner and she knew it. She was more than halfway across the blood-strewn main floor and if she went much farther her back would be to the raised walkway. She also couldn't do anything about it. The only good news was that the gathered fen had streamed out of the room like a herd of gazelle and the only people left in the room were herself and dead bodies. At the very least, he wasn't going to be able to gather enough power to summon Tiamat.

She needed to either circle or get up on the walkway. Neither appeared possible, however. Each time she tried to dodge to either side, she found herself blocked by the demon's long sword. And clambering up onto the walkway with him behind her . . . wasn't an option.

Suddenly the demon bellowed and turned, clawing at his shoulder which had seemingly grown an arrow.

Janea was standing in the hole he'd made, a bow in her hand, just nocking another arrow.

"Freya fill me," she whispered, pulling back on the string shakily. "Guide my eye and arm and bring to me the power of the gods!" The arrow sprang from the bow and left a trail of white light as it flew unerringly to impact on the demon's side.

It was the best opening Barb was going to get. She cut down, slicing the demon's hamstring, then up, taking off his right hand. The black blade clattered to the floor as the demon stumbled down to one knee, howling in pain and clutching at his wrist, which was spurting glowing black blood.

"In the name of the Lord Jesus Christ," Barb said, hefting the glowing sword like a batter, "I banish thee back to the Hell which birthed you!"

Remolus' head leapt from the spurting stump of his neck and rolled down the stairs. It rolled through the half-finished runes on the floor, smearing them into illegibility and only stopped when it hit the far wall.

Barbara again felt that disturbing shift in reality and dropped to her knees trying not to retch as it felt as if her insides were being twisted so they were *out*sides. She propped herself on her sword and closed her eyes, only opening them when the feeling passed. When she opened them, the room was, again, a hotel restaurant. With bodies and body parts scattered around it. The demon was still there as well, but already it had started to fall apart, turning liquid around the bones and then slumping into a putrid, stinking, mass.

She looked up at the doorway and was amazed to see Don Draxon standing in the door with one arm around Ruby and the other clutching a half empty bottle of scotch.

"Good Lord," Draxon said, looking around at the blood-spattered room and the demon deliquescing before his eyes. "Ruby, my dear, I think we should go back to warming ourselves. This looks a bit *too* warm."

But Ruby had fainted dead away.

Epilogue

"It's another fine mess you've left us to clean up," Augustus Germaine said, looking out the window.

"Hmmm," Barbara said, musingly. "The press are going to be all over it like . . . smell on poop." She didn't seem particularly worried and didn't quit what she was doing.

"Mass murderer at science fiction convention," Augustus said, shaking his head. "News at six."

"And the people who saw Remolus?" Barbara asked.

"It's amazing what people can ignore," Augustus replied, turning away from the window. "And do you *really* think that the news media is going to believe a bunch of science fiction fans who say they saw a demon? Besides, there are ways to make people . . . forget."

"I wish you'd do it for me, then," Barb said, shaking her head and still not looking up.

"If I didn't mention it, you did well," Augustus said, sitting down across from her. "You *and* Janea. I had not anticipated a full manifestation."

"Demons come, demons go," Barbara said, still not looking

up. "Do you think, with him dispelled, that any of those who died have a chance . . ."

"Heaven's inscrutable about such things," Augustus said, shrugging. "But . . . no. Whether their souls are in the service of Hell or not is unsure. But they are not going to be entering Heaven short of the Second Coming. Long may that day be forestalled."

"Lord grant that in the end of all things they may find peace," Barb replied, sighing. "I would that I'd been more able. No soul should be lost to that . . . thing. Can he . . . come back?"

"When he was banished, he lost all the power he had gained," Augustus said, thoughtfully. "The moonstone vest was shattered, so all of that power was lost as well. Pity, I'd have liked to find out what spell they used. If it was not entirely bound by evil it might come in handy. And I'd love to know where Krake found it."

"Apparently he was a pretty serious researcher," Barbara said. "But I think it might have something to do with Timson."

"Timson?" Augustus asked.

"He was the first person that Krake killed here," Barb replied, shrugging. "Janea said that he was extremely knowledgeable. And Duncan said that he'd been collaborating with Krake on research. I think, if there's anything to find, it's going to be in Timson's notes. If you can find them."

"I'll keep that in mind," Augustus said, smiling slightly. "How much longer are you going to polish that?"

"I'm not polishing it," Barbara said, running the silk cloth down the length of the Murasaki blade. "I'm sharpening it."

Barb set her bag down by the door to the garage and took a deep breath. Home.

"Mom!" Brandon yelled, charging down the hallway followed by Brook.

She hugged her two younger children and looked around for Allison. She was probably pouting in her room.

After greeting the kids she walked through the kitchen and looked in the family room. Mark was installed in front of the big-screen, watching a replay series on ESPN.

"Hello, dear," she said, smiling. "Miss me?"

"Yeah," Mark said, not looking away from the TV. "How was your conference or whatever?"

"Enlightening," Barb replied, her eyes dark with memories.

"Great. What's for supper?"

Book Three

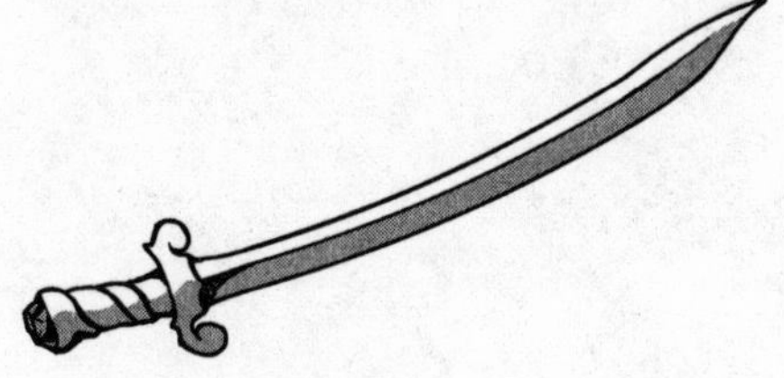

Broken Sabbath

Chapter One

"Keep your eye on the ball, Allison!" Barb screamed as her daughter swung and missed. "That was way to the outside!"

"You really get into this," Cindy Hudson said, grinning at the overwrought mother. Her own daughter had just struck out to a mild "Better luck next time, honey."

Cindy was as short and dark as her friend was tall and fair. They knew they made an odd couple but up until the last winter they had spent most of their free time together, their families even taking combined vacations. But since Barbara's trip down to the bayou and her car accident, Cindy had noticed a change in her friend. Sometimes she'd shiver as if from more than cold and get a distant look that was strange and hard. Something more than a car accident had happened on that trip but Cindy had never found it in her to ask what. She was afraid her friend had been raped, but there were simply things that nice Episcopal women, close friends though they were, didn't ask.

The two were dressed in light coats against the early spring cold and surrounded by similarly dressed parents, grandparents, friends and siblings of the players. The clothing of the group ranged from the designer labeled jackets and jeans of Barb and Cindy to oil-stained jackets labeled only with their owners' names, but on the stands the parents were one group, united in the belief that only *their* girls were in the running for the Redwater County Spring Season trophy.

"Anything you do should be done to the best of your ability," Barbara said, taking a deep breath to control her anger. "Allison *knows* better than that. She's letting the pitcher spook her."

"They're winning," Cindy said in exasperation.

"Only because Charlotte's kept the Panthers from hitting," Barb said, taking a breath again. "Don't tense up, Allison! Just watch the ball and do the job!"

The blond teenager didn't appear to notice her mother screaming at her from the stands. She waggled the softball bat then settled into position. The pitches were full-up and the pitcher chose to send a fast ball straight in over the base. Allison swung and . . . missed.

"Strike three!"

"Just what was that all about?" Coach Sherman shouted as the girls gathered in the dugout. "If Charlotte hadn't struck out most of their batters, we'd have been looking at the tail end of the season! If you girls can't do better than that I'll get a team of FIFTH graders and win! There's an additional practice scheduled for Saturday . . ."

"But, coach . . ." Sandy Adams started to protest.

"I don't want to hear about it!" the coach shouted. "I don't want to hear about dates or dances or any of the rest. Eight PM at the West Park field. Tell your parents we'll be playing late and I *don't* want them there. This is about playing ball, not making faces for your moms and dads! We are going to take the tournament this season or there will be Hell to pay! Do you girls *understand* me?"

"Wasn't the spring dance scheduled for this Saturday?" Barbara asked as her dejected daughter got in the Expedition.

"It's not *fair*," Allison complained. "I already had a date and everything. . . ."

"Your batting really *was* bad," Barb answered, tartly. "Were you thinking more about the dance than the game?"

"I don't know," Allison whined. "I just had a hard time concentrating. Mom, I don't want to play anymore. I don't like Coach Sherman. He's not like Coach Foss."

"Maybe that's good," Barbara said, finally getting out of the traffic of the parking lot and onto the one-lane access road. Despite the double line she passed a turtle-slow minivan ahead of her, whipping in and out of the lanes with the Expedition rocking on its springs. "Coach Foss was a very nice man, but he didn't have the sort of winning record of Coach Sherman. We're lucky he moved up here."

"Have you ever *talked* to Coach Sherman?" Allison asked.

"Not directly," Barb admitted. "Why?"

"He's . . . weird," Allison said, pouting. "He makes me feel creepy."

Barbara paused for a moment at that. Sexual predators came in all sorts of guises, but positions of relative power and influence, like coaches, were one that all parents had to keep an eye on. The flip side was that Allison was more than capable of using her mother's rather strong protective streak to get out of something she wasn't enjoying anymore. And since she'd steadfastly *refused* to take martial arts this year, she only had cheerleading and gym besides softball to keep her in shape.

"I'll keep that in mind," Barb said. "And I'll admit that it makes the practice this Saturday questionable. But you're going anyway. Since there are questions, you know the drill."

"Don't be alone with the adult," Allison said, sighing. "If they ask for a private meeting, insist that another girl or adult female be there. File any questionable action or statement and report it afterwards."

"And everything should be fine," Barbara said, trying not to keep the worry out of her tone. Lately she'd gotten a crash course in how unfine things could be.

~

Barb, as usual, picked up her daughter from the late practice. Allison seemed to have enjoyed it since she was smiling as she walked to the SUV.

The practice field was on the edge of Hernando State Forest on some land that the county had purchased from the state government to make a local park. Most of the county park was woodland with trails cut through it and a small lake. It was an out-of-the-way park, built in anticipation of continued growth and thus the practice field was almost always available.

"How was practice?" Barbara asked as the fourteen-year-old got in the van.

"Interesting," Allison said, distantly. "Mostly it was about mental conditioning and focus. We hardly swung a bat."

"Oh," Barb said, frowning. Mental conditioning was all well and good, but it could have been done anywhere; it didn't have to be in this out-of-the-way place.

"I was wrong about Coach Sherman, Mom," Allison said as if reading her mom's mind. "He's pretty interesting. He's got a different way of looking at things. I understand, now, why his teams won so much."

"Okay," Barbara replied, still frowning. Allison had been extremely changeable since she hit puberty, but rarely this fast. Barb had nearly had to pull her out of the house kicking and screaming. Two hours had made a pretty big change.

"Mark?" Barbara said as they were preparing for bed. Mark had spent most of the evening on the couch watching ESPN and she had the unChristian thought that her husband could do with a bit of dieting and exercise rather than munching chips in front of the games.

"Uh?" Mark replied, sitting down on the bed and pulling his shirt off to drop on the floor.

"What did you say about Coach Sherman?" Barb asked, rubbing lip gloss on to keep her lips from chapping overnight. She also hoped Mark would take the hint for a change. Lately the "magic," a nice euphemism for sex, had started to fade from the marriage. She wasn't sure if it was something she was doing or if Mark was just falling off with age. But it was simple fact that they'd slowed down from just about every night to no more than once a week.

"Allison's coach?" Mark asked, tossing the rest of his clothes, excepting underwear, on the pile. "Bob Ruckert said he'd been the big thing down around Mobile. His teams got the county championship three or four years running and even took state one time."

"So why'd he move?" Barbara asked, lying back on the pillow and arranging her hair fetchingly.

"I dunno," Mark said, crawling in bed and settling in. "Got a new job? They don't work for their coaching pay, you know."

"I guess that's it," Barb said, rolling over to look at her husband and leaning up on one elbow so her breasts created a very nice view of cleavage under her low-cut nightgown. "Mark?"

"Hmm?"

"Does this make you think of anything?" Barbara asked, raising an eyebrow.

Mark rolled over and looked at her for a moment and clearly reconsidered his plans for the rest of the night. On the other hand, Barb could see the struggle on his face.

"I guess not," Barbara said, lying back and crossing her hands on her stomach.

"Honey, you look great . . ." Mark said, rolling back over. "But I'm really tired."

"I understand," Barb said, calmly. "Good night, dear."

"Good night."

"Another Saturday night practice?" Barbara asked, incredulously.

"Coach Sherman says that there's no such thing as too much preparation," Allison said as she climbed in the SUV. The team had gotten another win, with Barb had to admit much better batting this time. "And it's not really a practice. Coach calls it a team-building exercise. We're supposed to wear walking stuff; we're going to go on a hike in the woods."

"At *night*?" Barbara asked, curiously.

"That's part of the team building," Allison said. "He said that you have to know the dark in yourself to bring out the light. So we're going on a night hike to get accustomed to looking at the dark."

"O-kay," Barb said, shaking her head. "I guess if it helps you win . . ."

Allison was not nearly as chipper when Barbara picked her up at the darkened field the next Saturday. In fact, she looked as if she had been crying.

"Are you okay?" Barb asked, worriedly.

"I'm fine," Allison said, getting in the front seat and keeping her head down.

"Team building was kind of tough?" Barbara asked, pulling out of the parking lot. The night was dark and overcast but the half moon was struggling to shine through the clouds.

"Yeah," Allison said, keeping her head down.

"So what did you do?" Barb asked.

"Nothing I want to talk about," Allison said, turning to look out the window.

"Allison, I want a straight answer," Barbara said, sharply. "Did anything *wrong* happen?"

"No, Mom!" Allison answered, looking up at her. "It was just what the coach was talking about. We just . . . went for a walk and . . . talked."

"Just walked and talked, huh?" Barb said. "So why were you crying?"

"I wasn't," Allison said, looking away again. "I just got something in my eye."

"You're a lousy liar, honey," Barbara said, softly. "You get that from me. Why were you crying?"

"Well . . ." Allison said then shrugged. "We were talking about things that bother us. It was, like, therapy, I guess. That was why I was crying. That's all, Mom, honest."

Barb started to reply and then decided it was the wrong time.

"Are you going to have another one of these 'team-building' exercises next week?"

"No," Allison said. "Next week is spring break, remember?"

"Yes, I'd remembered," Barbara said. "I was hoping that Coach Sherman had."

The season started up with a bang after spring break with two games in three days, both of which the team took. So far the Algomo Middle School Girls' Softball team had a series of straight wins and the magic of Coach Bobby Sherman seemed to be rubbing off on his new team.

The coach had scheduled two more "additional team-building" exercises that week, however, and the hours that the girls were putting in was starting to tell. By the end of the week, Allison was getting bags under her eyes from late night team-building exercises combined with her homework load, cheerleading and gym classes. Then she came home with a permission form for an "all day team-building exercise" on Saturday. The girls were to be dropped off at noon and picked up at midnight.

"This is too much," Barb said, waving the form in the air as she practically screamed over the phone to Cindy. "Is he *nuts*?"

"You're the one that's always pushing for the girls to do better," Cindy said, unhappily.

"They're *fourteen*," Barbara pointed out.

"Barb, I'm with you on this one," Cindy said. "But Coach Sherman's making these things mandatory for continuing in the team. I'm thinking of pulling Brandi, frankly. She's getting really worn down."

"So's Allison," Barbara said, bitterly. "And I'm not all that happy about a man I don't know very well spending all this time with my daughter in conditions in which parents are not welcome."

"Well, call him," Cindy said. "You'd be better at that than I am. And I'm pretty sure we're not the only ones that are getting tired of all this 'team building.'"

Chapter Two

Coach Sherman was surprisingly hard to run down. But she'd managed to contact his wife, a colorless woman on the phone, and arranged a meeting at the Hazelwood Mall Starbucks. The coach, as it turned out, worked in the Claire's Boutique in the mall, which eliminated "a better job" as the reason for the move. Unless he'd worked at a McDonald's in Mobile.

Sherman was middling height but gave the impression of size. He had broad shoulders and strong looking arms as if he'd been a serious athlete when he was younger. Over the years, though, he'd run to fat and had a large beer gut. His hair and skin were dark with a look of either Hispanic or maybe Native American in his features. He had dark eyes that were remarkably piercing, though. Barb had only ever seen him from a moderate range and hadn't realized how startling his eyes were. She could see why Allison would have dubbed him "creepy" when she first met him. He also had a small, blurred, tattoo on the web of his right thumb. Barbara couldn't quite make it out.

She suspected that some women would find him very attractive. Barb was not one of them. He came across far too much the "macho man." Barbara counted among her friends both members of special operations groups and Special Circumstances operatives who faced death from both natural and supernatural causes, often on a daily basis. This guy wasn't even in their class.

"A pleasure to meet you, Coach Sherman," Barb said, standing up from her table and shaking his hand.

"My pleasure, I'm sure," the coach replied, not even bothering to hide the fact that he was looking at her chest. She'd dressed conservatively for the meeting so there wasn't even cleavage on display. But his eyes went right to the breasts. After a long moment's perusal he looked her in the eye and winked. Then when he withdrew his hand from hers, reluctantly, he ran his thumb across the palm of her hand.

Barb had had the trick done to her before and, as always, it gave her a shiver of sexuality. She also thought it was about as low a trick as you could play on a female; the reaction was entirely involuntary and had little or nothing to do with actual attraction. It was the equivalent of a goose in her mind.

Barb realized right then that she wanted Allison off the team. Wins or no, this guy was a predator. He wasn't just flirting, he was making an overt move on her. Given that she was married and a mother of one of the girls on his team, he either had to be crazy or he thought it would help his case. Which was just as crazy.

Furthermore, he gave off the "seducer" feel. He had a bag full of tricks that probably worked on women or girls who had never been up against a seducer. Barb had been to far too many company parties, and had far too many covert and overt offers when she was selling real estate, to be even slightly interested. Teenage girls were something else.

"I wanted to talk to you about all these extra practices," Barb said, ignoring the wink and the thumb. "Some of the parents, and I'm among them, feel that the girls are getting a little worn out by all the time they're putting in. Among other things, most of the girls are involved in more than one activity. Spending all this time on softball alone is wearing them out."

"I realize that, Mrs. Everette," Sherman said, leaning forward to look her in the eye and sliding immediately into "professional coach" mode as if the original "lounge lizard" had never existed. "All I can say is that these methods *work*. My job, my *mission*, is to have a winning team. Not just this year but every year. I've honed my Focus-On-Win program and I *know* that it works. I've proven that it works. If the parents want just a regular team, win a few, lose a few, it all evens out in the end, I'm *not* your coach. If you want a team that *wins*, then they have to stick to the program. And that program is not an easy program. I put that in the information sheet when I sent it out with the girls at the beginning of the season. If Allison wants to quit the team, that's up to you and Allison. But if she wants to play, she practices when I schedule a practice. Or a team-building exercise. The mind is as ten-to-one to the body in sports. The girls have to get their minds around Focus-On-Win. To do that they have to be cleared of all the detritus that people pick up and see themselves, and their teammates, clearly. They have to know their personal strengths and weaknesses and those of their team. And they must be a *team*. Every step of their training, every practice and every team-building exercise is for the purpose of building on those points. Batting and catching come after the mind is prepared, as automatically as breathing."

He leaned back and nodded, picking up his mocha with a very straight posture as if daring Barb to debate him on his area of expertise.

"I can see that," Barb said, sipping her decaf vanilla latte. She'd decided on decaf since she was pretty sure she didn't want to lose her temper in this meeting. "Can I ask a couple of questions?"

"Sure," the coach said, warily.

"Why'd you come up here from Mobile?" Barb asked. "Mobile is a much bigger league and you were a pretty big fish. You didn't move for the job, so . . ."

"I'm ambitious," Sherman admitted. "Yes, Mobile is a bigger and more noticeable league. But the high school positions are all filled with people that, however, incompetent, are in there for life. It's very much a good-ole-boy network, no outsiders allowed. I want to be a professional softball coach and to do that you have to get into one of the colleges. *Any* college will do. To get to college you either have to know some rich alumni or you have to have been successful at coaching high school teams. *Really* successful. I looked at a lot of areas and I really liked the Sirens. This team. I want to coach them this year and then go on to coach at Algomo High School. If I can take *this* team, and the girls that are following them, through high school I *can* take state. Not just one year, but several. And if I do *that* I can get into a college spot. And the bottom line is that my methods *work*. Some people say it's about learning to play the game. Bullshit, pardon my French, ma'am, but it's about *winning*. And if you let me, your girls will *win*. And if they can't take the heat, they're not going to make it as high as I intend to take them, anyway. Up to you."

Barbara had to admit that the coach had *her* number. Barb believed in winning against any odds. If she didn't, she'd be a skeleton in a Louisiana bayou.

The flip side was that she didn't trust this guy as far as she could throw him. Of course, it was a bad analogy; he'd be surprised as hell just *how* far she could throw him.

Take a different tack.

"I can see that as well," Barbara said, nodding her head and not letting that piercing stare apparently affect her at all. "There is one small problem, though. This is . . . not the fifties. There are understandable concerns about males spending significant private time with, frankly, susceptible young girls."

"Which is why I'm *never* alone with any single girl at *any* time," Sherman replied, nodding sharply. "I have never had an allegation of sexual harassment laid against me, Mrs. Everette. Not one."

Barbara believed that about as much as she believed the rest of the spiel, but she didn't let it show on her face. On the other hand, it was possible. Especially if he was threatening enough. Vast numbers of sexual predation reports waited years until someone was willing to break the code of silence surrounding them. She hoped that Allison would come to her if anything happened. But it was better that nothing happened in the first place.

"So what you're saying, Mr. Sherman, is hang everything else," Barb said. "If we want the girls to win and win big, we have to go with your program or our girls are out of the team."

"That was in the introduction sheet," the coach said, nodding sharply, again. "If you want the girls to be *guaranteed* to win, you have to go with my program. And I *do* guarantee it."

"Nothing is guaranteed, Coach Sherman," Barbara said, softly. "Except the End of All Things. Even death is not immutable, as the Lord Jesus Christ proved in the case of both Himself and Lazarus. Taxes, admittedly, are close," she added with a slight smile.

"I hadn't realized you were . . . that staunch a Christian, Mrs. Everette," Coach Sherman said, uncomfortably.

"I don't wave a Bible, Mr. Sherman," Barb replied, quietly. "But faith in the Lord is very strong in me."

"Faith in Jesus doesn't win softball games," Sherman replied.

Barbara tried not to furrow her brow at the reply. There had been a very slight emphasis on the name "Jesus."

"Faith can work miracles, Coach Sherman," Barb said, her eyes narrowing.

"Well, on that we agree," Sherman said, obliquely. "So are you going to oppose my practices? I get the feeling that if you do, there's not going to be a team."

"I'm going to discuss it with the other parents," Barbara said, her face poker blank. "For the girls to continue at the current pace will require them to drop other activities. That's a *major* change."

"If you do, if you stay with my program, we will win," Sherman said. "If you don't want that, then make up your own minds. I *know* what wins. Despite our wins, this is a tough league. Maggie Anderson at Shipman is one of the best pitchers in her age group in the state. If we're going to win the championship, it's going to take more than faith in *Jesus*, Mrs. Everette."

"Foundation for Love and Universal Faith."

"This is Barbara Everette, could I talk to Sharice, please?"

"Hold a moment, Barb, I'll transfer you."

"Sharice, May the Lady Bless."

"Sharice, it's Barb," Barbara said, biting her lip as she weaved through traffic with the cell phone clamped to her ear.

"How are you, Barb?" Sharice asked. "Is the family well?"

"I think so," Barbara said, accelerating and cutting left in front of a semi, just missing the bumper of the car in front of her, which was slowing. She hadn't been thinking about the maneuver, she was driving in alpha state. "I need some information for something that has me worried."

"I see," Sharice said, slowly. "Barbara, I take it from the background you're on a cell phone?"

"Yes," Barb admitted.

"Perhaps you should talk to one of your friends in the area about this, dear," Sharice said. "I'm sure it's a private matter and you wouldn't want anyone with a scanner listening in."

"Oh," Barbara said, her face coloring as she cut back into the right-hand lane and then slid sideways to make the exit. "I suppose I should."

"If it's a very important matter, I'm sure someone can come talk to you right away," Sharice said.

"Not at this time," Barb said. "It might be nothing. Just a bad feeling about someone."

"I can tell you that there are no issues that the Foundation is paying attention to in your area," Sharice said, obliquely.

"What about last year in Mobile?" Barbara asked.

"Hold on a mo, dear."

Barb checked left and pulled out in a cloud of tire smoke so she wouldn't slow down the oncoming truck. By that time Sharice was back.

"I think you should probably talk to a friend, dear," Sharice said. Barbara could almost see her forehead crinkling in perplexity. "We were tracking an issue in the Mobile area last year but the local chapter didn't turn up much. If you have a bad feeling and it relates to Mobile, it might be wise to discuss it with a friend."

"Got it," Barb said, pulling in at a convenience store. "I'll do that."

"Lady bless and keep you, Barb," Sharice said.

"And may the goodness of the Lord be with you as well, my friend."

"Good day, Mr. Patek," Barbara said, picking up a packet of chewing gum and tendering a five-dollar bill.

"Good day, Mrs. Everette," the Hindu said, nodding at her. "May Vishnu light your way."

"And may the Lord be with you," Barb said as the convenience store owner slipped the note behind the five into his register.

Three of the girls left the team rather than keep up the pace but Barbara and Cindy both kept their girls there, pulling them out of gymnastics and dance, respectively.

And the team continued to win. There had been more "team-building exercises" and Barb continued to worry about Allison, who had gotten less and less communicative about the "extra practices." She was also bothered that she hadn't heard anything from the Foundation. She'd had to turn down one assignment when Mark had thrown a fit about going out of town for another week. A call she'd gotten, from Julie Lamm, indicated that the investigation had turned out to be nothing but a "normal" serial killer with delusions of grandeur. Other than that, she hadn't heard anything.

Late one Saturday, however, she had passed a stop sign near her house and seen a small Maltese cross sticker on it. She'd just dropped Allison off at a late "team-building" activity so she had more than enough time to stop by the Fast Mart.

"Good afternoon, Mr. Patek," Barb said, picking up her usual stick of gum. She didn't chew it and since she didn't like the kids chewing, either, it was given to Mark or, more often, thrown away.

"Good afternoon, Mrs. Everette," the proprietor said. "I wish you well. I have the pamphlet on the similarities between Vishnu and Christ you asked for."

"Why thank you," Barbara said, taking the folded pamphlet with a cross and a picture of Vishnu sitting on a lotus on the cover. "That is very nice of you."

"May the High Ones preserve you, Mrs. Everette," the Hindu said, making change for her.

"And may the Lord bless, Mr. Patek."

Chapter Three

Barbara stopped in the Wal-Mart parking lot, comfortably close to the front of the store, and read the information printed on the inside of the pamphlet by the interior light.

Broad rumors of a Satanist cult associated with a girls' softball team in the Mobile area were picked up by the FBI and Mobile police. Mobile police declined to investigate but local Special Circumstances personnel performed a cursory investigation. The leader was reported to be a Satanist High Priest named Robert Sherman who had struck a deal with Lower Powers for wins in softball, offering the young women of the team as acolytes and potential sacrifices, some certified to be virginal. One young woman of the team was reported missing, however no trace of her was ever found and her disappearance appeared to be unrelated to the rumored Satanist activity. There was a note left that indicated unhappiness with home-life and police treated it as a normal runaway. No trace of otherworld emanations were detected by the operatives in the area, but they were first level operatives with limited field experience.

The rumors came about after a championship softball game when some of the winning girls bragged about "making a deal with the Devil." Questioning by teachers and school psychologists revealed that Sherman had done something involving "special team building" with the girls but none of them were willing to divulge the nature of the activities.

Robert Sherman may be a person using the pseudonym of Monereaus who was involved in a low-level Satanic cult in Central Florida. Reports indicate that he has background in Santeria and has a small tattoo of an angel, indicative of Santeria and Marielitos sympathies, on the web of his right thumb. The particular tattoo is indicative of a member of the Cuban underground with a specialty in entrapping young women for immoral purposes. This leads to the suspicion that Robert Sherman is an alias. The Central Florida LeMayean cult was not noted for Special activity and appeared to be purely mundane. There are no current reports on the whereabouts or activities of Robert Sherman.

"There are, now," Barb muttered to herself, furiously. She ground her teeth and tried to control her temper. If that bastard had—

"The Lord is with me," Barbara said, quietly, controlling her breathing. "I shall not descend into the abyss of hate and anger." She used her Christian faith to control the temper that was bequeathed to her with the strawberry-blonde hair. Her mother called it "The Irish Side" but Barbara was pretty sure, after dealing with Janea, that it was more like the Viking side.

The question was what to do with the information. Technically, she should call the Foundation and report the "whereabouts and current activity" of one "Robert Sherman."

The problem was that the report specifically stated that there was no hard evidence of Special Circumstances. If they were actually working on raising a Lower Power, the emanations would be detectable. And Barb hadn't felt *anything* from Allison. Her gut told her that something very bad was happening, but that might just be a protective mother's instinct.

Well, she was a Third Level Adept . . . darnit. She should be able to conduct her own investigation. As Daddy said, it was always easier to act first and ask permission later.

She pulled out of the parking lot and headed for the out-of-the-way ballpark.

Mark and the kids had never asked about the blue and yellow bag in the back of the expedition. It was the sort of bag that was used for work-out clothes and Barbara certainly had enough activities in that area. But the bag never left the back of the Expedition for the very simple reason that Barb never knew when she might need it. She'd been caught out once. Never again.

She slowed down the Expedition as she approached the park, looking for the road she'd noticed on previous trips. It was a service and supply road for the Welcome Center that avoided the main road into the park. She didn't intend to even take it all the way to the Welcome Center for that matter.

She checked her watch as she pulled to a stop and nodded. More than enough time to do a penetration and reconnaissance before she was supposed to pick Allison up. If Mark wanted to know where she was, she'd just tell him she was having an affair. No, that was anger talking. He'd probably never notice she hadn't come home as usual.

She got out of the Expedition after turning off the interior light, and went to the back.

The black-toned digicam coverall went on over her street clothes. The digicam had crosses subtly added to it, a mod that had cost the European branch a pretty penny but that had surprised the Hell out of more than one supernatural entity. The material was also flame proof, which occasionally came in handy, and had an attached hood and mask that could be pulled up if needed. Next to the folded garment were Eagle tac-boots which zipped up the side for easy on and off by the undercover operative.

Then the body armor came out. It was useless against the supernatural, but it sure came in handy if the perp had a weapon. The particular body armor was heavier than normal, for that matter, since it included a layer of mail plated with silver, courtesy of Hjalmar.

Then the tactical armament. The .45 in attached thigh holster, short-barreled shotgun with five rounds of 00 buck up the tube, holy water mixed with silver nitrate one-shot thrower, silver-plated knife, one-shot stake thrower. The one-shots were small and tucked into the back of her vest. She didn't carry a bell, a book or a candle since nobody in Special Circumstances had ever found a use for any of the three. Last, a long "cold iron" custom knife the size of a short sword that hooked on the left side. The Murasaki blade was sitting in her bedroom closet at home. If she needed it for this mission she was going to be really sorry it was there.

"Lord bless me this night," she said, looking into the dark woods. "Bless and keep my daughter as well and give me the strength, courage and knowledge to do Your work. Amen."

With that she slipped into the underbrush like a gray phantom.

"Lord Satan, bring to us your strength!" Coach Sherman intoned.

Allison bit her lip and tried not to cry. She had a hard time figuring out how the whole team had gotten this far into nightmare. It had happened so slowly, so subtly, that she couldn't tell exactly where they'd all crossed the line. At first the "team-building exercises" had been just that. Going out on walks and sitting around fires and getting to know each other better. Coach Sherman had said that that was just the first step to being a really winning team and there didn't seem to be anything wrong with that. Then the talks had gotten deeper and stranger and the coach explained that there was only one way to be *sure* they would win. That it was secret and that they'd all have to take oaths not to talk about it.

The coach had told them that the power he was calling would make them better players, make them a better team. And it seemed to work. Without much more practice than she'd already been doing, she'd just *done* better. She could catch better, she could bat better and she could keep concentrated better. Everybody talked about it, quietly. It had to be an external power, they all knew that. And it didn't seem *wrong*. Then.

But, when Corine and Cheryl and Shelly left, they'd gotten deeper into the "mysteries." The coach had finally told them where the "power" was coming from. Now there didn't seem to be any way to turn back. She was a good Christian girl, well, okay, a *fairly* good Christian girl. She wasn't like her mother that damned saint, but she didn't fool around and she *tried* to be nice to people. And here she was trying to call in the power of the *Devil* to help them win some stupid *softball* game.

And the coach had brought a cat. She'd thought it was, like, his familiar or something. But he was going to sacrifice it. He was just going to cut the poor little kitty's throat to "raise the power."

It wasn't right. But try as she might, she just couldn't open her mouth to protest. Nobody else was, either. They'd said too many things, made too many oaths. She felt like her soul was already lost. They might as well just do it and get the power. If her soul was already lost, winning the softball game was at least *something* to show for it.

The coach was babbling in some language, maybe Latin but a lot of it sounded like Spanish or even just gibberish. He'd tied the feet of the cat together and had it pinned on a log.

She had to turn her eyes when the knife came down but she could hear the squall that was cut off in a horrible gurgle and the crunching of the knife.

"The way is opened," Coach Sherman said, raising the bloody knife to the full moon. "Let the power flow through this circle, Lord Satan, that your powers can bring us victory over our enemies!"

Barb paused at the edge of the clearing, letting her eyes adjust to the firelight without looking directly at the fire. The girls were in a semi-circle vaguely facing her. Which was problem one. Oh, not tactically, *magically*. She'd studied enough rites at this point to know that anything that Sherman was going to do using this type of rite would require a full circle. The whole team was there though, and she saw Allison's head, as well as others, turn aside as the knife came down.

She could see what was happening but what she couldn't do was feel a thing. And that was problem two. There was a miasma over the whole group, but she'd come to realize that was more on the lines of empathy through her channel than anything. There wasn't a *touch* of power. Nothing. This guy had just killed a poor little black cat for *nothing*.

She froze as the coach raised the bloody knife and then said something to the girls. Some of them shook their head but a few came forward hesitantly. When he dipped his finger in the blood, though, she had had enough.

"This stops right now," she muttered, striding into the red firelight.

Allison's eyes flew wide as a ghostly figure just seemed to *appear* in front of them. The person, a woman from the voice, was clad from head to foot in some sort of camouflage that just seemed to blend her into the background. It was hard to even look at and she felt her eyes start to water.

"In the Name of the Lord Jesus Christ this farce will end *now*!" the woman said, striding determinedly up to the "altar."

"You have no power here!" Coach Sherman said, but there was a quaver in his voice.

"That is what you think, you impostor," the woman said. "You don't know the first thing about power! There *is* no power here. You're no more a High Priest than I am the Virgin Mary. This isn't a rite, this is just some idiot butchering poor defenseless animals!"

The girls started to back away from the fire but Allison stood rooted. She could swear she knew that voice. . . .

"What do you know about power, Christian," Coach Sherman spat. "Your God is *weak*! All you do is sing hymns and—"

"Weak?" the figure hissed. "I have fought demons from Hell manifest upon this Earth, you *poser*. I've defeated monsters that would freeze the blood in your *veins*, you loathsome imbecile. And I'm not about to let you use your pretty stare and seducer ways to twist these girls!"

Allison could swear there was a blue glow forming around the woman as she stepped to the altar and picked up the still dripping cat.

"Lord," the woman said, dropping her head and holding the cat in front of her, "this is as much a battle for the souls of these innocents as any that I have performed for you in the past. I ask You, Lord, for the power you have given me in battle. Fill me, this night, Lord, that these children can see the light and the beauty of God and His only begotten Son, the Lord Jesus Christ. Let the Holy Spirit fill me, Lord, as it has filled me in battle against Almadu and Remolus."

There was no question about it, now. The woman, her *mother*? was surrounded by a blue-white glow that was beginning to wash out the light from the fire. Allison turned her head away as the glow became too bright to look at.

Barb cradled the cat to her chest, unsure even of what she wanted. She just knew that she had to show these girls, and Allison especially, that God was stronger than any machinations of the Enemy. She could feel the power flowing through her and it seemed that she could feel every vein and sinew in her body straining in the rush of power to do *something*. She could also feel the cat, not as a light weight, but as a live thing that . . . could *be* again.

Something seemed to ask a question in her mind, an important question. She wasn't sure of even the nature of the question, just that it was terribly important. She was being asked to give up something, something vital. She was asked for a sacrifice. But in this place, with the example of the Lord and Savior, she could do no more than acquiesce.

She felt every part of the cat now as something reached through her and knit flesh and veins, closed the gaping wound and even cleaned the blood from the fur. Then she felt more as life seemed to flow from her veins into those of the cat. Last there was a terrible wrenching, as if something had been pulled out of her heart, her head, her whole body, a bit of her very essence, the central core of her soul, and flowed out of her and into the creature in her arms.

She opened her eyes and looked across the tree stump at the "High Priest" as the recently dead cat in her arms first sat up, then mewed quietly, then climbed up onto her shoulder.

And she watched as Coach Sherman fainted.

Epilogue

Barb looked at the note in her hand and nodded.

Barbara,

The time has come to resume God's work. A ticket has been prepared for you to Chicago. Delta Flight 386 from Jackson to Chicago on Thursday. You must be there, E Nomine.

Augustus

She got out of the Expedition and let Lazarus climb up onto her shoulder, then walked into the house.

Allison was washing the dishes and Brandon was sweeping the kitchen floor as she walked through. She'd never spoken to Allison of the night in the woods nor did she intend to any time soon. And while her face had been covered, her voice was impossible to disguise. Then there was Lazarus.

For whatever reason, the teenager no longer complained about going to church, or even Sunday school. And did her chores with remarkable speed and efficiency. She was even learning to control her temper and manage the younger kids.

She was, in other words, trying to be as much like her mother as possible.

Which told Barb all she had to know about that night in the woods.

Mark was parked in front of the TV watching Fox and she sat down, letting Lazarus slip into her lap.

"I hate that cat," Mark said, glancing over at her and then back at the TV.

"Nonetheless," Barbara said, smiling faintly, "he is here to stay."

"He's spooky," Mark said, not looking at the black cat calmly watching him from her lap. "I don't think it's right for us to have a spooky black cat in the house. The neighbors think it's funny. And he's always following you around or hanging on you. He even *acts* like you. It makes you look like a witch."

"Mark, I have to go out of town," Barb said, ignoring the ongoing argument.

"Not that again," Mark said, angrily, as he turned away from the TV. "It was a complete disaster when you left the last time."

"Mark, this is the work of the Lord," Barbara said, quietly but firmly. "I'm going to be leaving on Thursday. I'll explain to Allison what has to be done in my absence. But I must go."

"This religion thing is getting out of hand," Mark snapped. "I go to church, too, you know, but I remember my responsibility to my family! You can't just go off at a whim. I swear, Barb, sometimes . . ."

She paused and waited for what the "sometimes" would be, but when it was clear he was finished, she simply nodded.

"I'd better go pack," she said, standing up.

"That's it?" Mark said, surprised. "I said I didn't want you to go!"

"God does," Barbara replied quietly. "You may be the lord and master of this house. But I am, first and foremost, a Servant of God."